# The
# Graveyard
# Apartment

Also by Mariko Koike

*The Cat in the Coffin*
*A Cappella*

Also Translated by Deborah Boliver Boehm

*The Cat in the Coffin*, by Mariko Koike
*The Changeling*, by Kenzaburo Oe
*Death by Water*, by Kenzaburo Oe
*The Tattoo Murder Case*, by Akimitsu Takagi

# The Graveyard Apartment

## MARIKO KOIKE

Translated from the Japanese
by Deborah Boliver Boehm

THOMAS DUNNE BOOKS
ST. MARTIN'S PRESS ✠ NEW YORK

This is a work of fiction. All of the characters, organizations, and events portrayed in this novel are either products of the author's imagination or are used fictitiously.

THOMAS DUNNE BOOKS.
An imprint of St. Martin's Press.

www.thomasdunnebooks.com
www.stmartins.com

Designed by Anna Gorovoy

Library of Congress Cataloging-in-Publication Data

Names: Koike, Mariko, 1952– author. | Boehm, Deborah Boliver, translator.
Title: The graveyard apartment : a novel / Mariko Koike ; translated from the Japanese by Deborah Boliver Boehm.
Other titles: Bochi o miorosu ie. English
Description: First U.S. edition. | New York : Thomas Dunne Books, 2016. | "First published in Japan under the title Bochi o miorosu ie by Kadokawa Shoten Publishing Co., Ltd." (Tokyo, 1993)—Verso title page.
Identifiers: LCCN 2016007862| ISBN 9781250060549 (hardback) | ISBN 9781466865822 (e-book)
Subjects: LCSH: Young families—Fiction. | Apartment houses—Fiction. | Basements—Fiction. | BISAC: FICTION / Horror. | GSAFD: Horror tales. | Suspense fiction.
Classification: LCC PL855.O3525 B6313 2016 | DDC 895.63/5—dc23
LC record available at https://lccn.loc.gov/2016007862

Our books may be purchased in bulk for promotional, educational, or business use. Please contact your local bookseller or the Macmillan Corporate and Premium Sales Department at 1-800-221-7945, extension 5442, or by e-mail at MacmillanSpecialMarkets@macmillan.com.

First published in Japan under the title *Bochi o miorosu ie* by Kadokawa Shoten Publishing Co., Ltd.

First U.S. Edition: October 2016

10  9  8  7  6  5  4  3  2  1

# The Graveyard Apartment

# BRAND-NEW LUXURY
## APARTMENTS FOR SALE

- All units boast sunny southern exposure.
- Quiet, peaceful, and private.
- Resident managers on the premises, 24-7.
- Convenient access to shopping and public transportation.
- Enjoy a lush greenbelt view, right in the middle of the city!
- All apartments priced to sell at ¥35,000,000.

## PROPERTY DESCRIPTION

- Name: Central Plaza Mansion.
- Location: 4 Takaino, "K" Ward, Tokyo.
- Construction: Reinforced concrete; eight floors, plus basement.
- Total number of units: 14.
- Floor plan: 2LDK.
- Total area: 900 square feet (approximate).
- Balcony area: 100 square feet (approximate).
- Date of construction: August 1986.
- Monthly maintenance fee: ¥18,200.
- One elevator serves all units.
- Basement features a designated storage compartment for each unit.
- On-site parking.
- Developer: The Green Corporation.

# 1

March 10, 1987

When they got up that first morning, the little white finch was dead. The bottom of the cage was covered with a thick layer of loose feathers, and it looked as if there had been a violent struggle before the bird finally gave up the ghost.

"I wonder if it was just his time to go," Teppei Kano said softly. "How old was he, anyway?"

"He was only four years old," replied Teppei's wife, Misao. "We bought him right after Tamao was born, remember?"

"Oh, right. That seems like an abnormally short life, even for a bird. Maybe he was sick or something."

"Or he might have hit his head during the move and gotten injured somehow, maybe when the cage was jostled. I think that's more likely."

Misao opened the door of the metal cage and gently placed the dead bird in the palm of her hand. The tiny body was already cold. When Misao held it up to her nose, she caught a faint whiff of dried grass—the same earthy scent the little finch had given off when he was alive. Hot tears filled her eyes.

Making an effort not to cry, Misao stroked the stiffening corpse with her forefinger. "Poor little Pyoko," she murmured. "You were so cute."

"He really was," Teppei agreed.

The family's mixed-breed dog, Cookie, trotted up and laid her front paw on Misao's knee. The dog's nose twitched convulsively as she sniffed the air.

"Your friend Pyoko went and died," Misao said. Choking back another sob, she held out the bird's lifeless body, now cradled in both her hands, until it was nearly touching Cookie's muzzle. The dog inhaled deeply, taking in the dead bird's aroma, then wagged her tail and looked up at Misao with sorrowful eyes.

"We'll bury him later, outside," Teppei said, putting his hand on Misao's shoulder. "It's kind of ironic that our new location is already coming in handy. At least when we need a graveyard, there's one right in front of our building."

"Oh, don't say things like that! Anyway, I thought we agreed not to talk about the cemetery." Misao was feeling distinctly depressed about the fact that a living creature they'd been caring for had died so soon after their move to a new place. *What on earth happened overnight?* she wondered. As recently as yesterday the little bird had been in fine shape, chirping merrily away like an avatar of good cheer, both while he was riding in the back of the moving truck along with Cookie and after his cage had been installed in the living room. And yet now . . .

"Mama?" Misao's reverie was shattered by the sound of her daughter's voice coming from the child-size bedroom—which they called, aspirationally, the nursery—down the hall. Tamao always went to sleep docilely enough, but as soon as she woke up in the morning she would call out for her mother in a whimpering voice that sounded, to Misao's ears, like an abandoned puppy.

Handing the little bird's corpse to Teppei, Misao responded in a perfectly normal, everyday tone, "Good morning, sleepyhead! Time to get up!"

A few seconds later Tamao's face peeked around the corner of the door to the living room. It was a beguiling little face, with her father's large, bright eyes and her mother's sharply chiseled features, framed by soft, slightly wavy black hair. Every time Misao saw her daughter she thought, *She looks as if she could turn into an angel on the spot, if you just attached a pair of wings to her back.*

"Sweetie, come here for a minute, okay?" Misao said in a subdued voice, beckoning with one outstretched hand.

Tamao's big brown eyes flicked quickly to the birdcage by the window, then back to her mother. "Where's Pyoko?" she asked.

"He's right here," Teppei said quietly, holding out his cupped hands.

Tamao's bare feet slapped on the floor as she nimbly threaded her way among the jumble of packing boxes to join her father. Teppei opened his hands and showed Tamao the tiny, motionless bird. Tamao took a quick peek, then looked up at her father. "Is he sick?" she asked anxiously.

Teppei shook his head, while Misao explained, "Listen, sweetie, I'm really sorry, but Pyoko's dead. He's in heaven now."

Tamao stared at her parents for a long moment. She looked utterly stupefied, and her thin chest was heaving under her Snoopy-patterned pajamas. Then, very timidly, she stretched out a plump pink finger and began to caress the dead bird. "Poor little thing," she said.

"Later today we'll all go outside together and dig a grave," Misao told Tamao. "We'll make it extra-specially nice, because Pyoko was such a good friend of yours."

Tamao was a delicate, sensitive child. As Misao watched helplessly, tears welled up in her daughter's eyes and rolled down her rosy cheeks. "Poor Pyoko," Tamao moaned. "Poor little Pyoko."

Misao nodded, fighting back the urge to burst into empathetic tears. "Yes," she said, "it's very sad that Pyoko's gone. That's why we have to make a really nice grave for him."

*How on earth did this happen?* Misao wondered again, with a growing sense of uneasiness. It really looked as though the entire cage had been attacked and mauled by a cat, and the water dish was filled with the bird's minuscule feathers, possibly shed (Misao theorized) in a life-or-death battle. Could a rat have gotten into the cage during the night? But surely there wouldn't be rodents running around in a sparkling new apartment building like the Central Plaza Mansion.

"It's really strange, though, isn't it?" Misao said, cocking her head and attempting to dispel the melancholy atmosphere in the room by changing the focus from loss to cause.

"Definitely," Teppei agreed. "It occurred to me that Cookie might have been trying to play with Pyoko and things just got out of hand. But the cage was latched, so that explanation doesn't hold water."

"Besides, Cookie would never do something like that!" Tamao declared indignantly, roughly wiping away her tears with both hands. "Cookie's a very nice dog, and she and Pyoko were really good friends."

"You're right, of course," Misao said in a soothing tone. "Cookie would never do anything to hurt Pyoko, but it's just so mystifying. I mean, what could have happened? What do you think, Tamao?"

"I have no idea," Tamao said, shaking her head.

"We were all sleeping like a pile of logs last night, so we wouldn't have heard anything," Teppei said, as he carefully wrapped the bird's remains in an old newspaper, then laid the bundle on a nearby packing box. "Hey, maybe it was a giant monster cockroach, almost as big as Tamao. *Grrrr!*"

Tamao's eyes were still brimming with tears, but now they crinkled around the edges and she began to giggle. There was something a bit forced about her laughter, but she was clearly doing her best to play along with her father.

"Could there really be cockroaches on the eighth floor of a new building? And wouldn't March be a little early for them to show up, in any case? If this apartment has cockroaches, even if they're just the normal size, I'm going to move out right now!" Misao said playfully.

Scooping Tamao into his arms, Teppei said, "Did you hear that? Your silly mom got totally hysterical at the very mention of a bug. Who's afraid of the big bad cockroach? Not I!" he chanted in a comical singsong.

Tamao laughed outright at this, and Cookie began capering manically around the room, apparently sensing the change in mood. Misao was relieved to see that things seemed to be returning to normal. Briskly, she picked up the empty birdcage and took it out to the balcony. After sending Tamao off to wash her hands, she set about brewing a pot of coffee.

The spacious, south-facing living room was flooded with morning light. *Okay,* Misao told herself, *it was a terrible shock to find that Pyoko had died in the night, but now it's time to put aside our feelings of sadness and confusion, and get to work.*

The to-do list for the day was as long as Misao's arm. For starters, she needed to clean and organize the kitchen; go out and buy enough groceries to keep them going for the next couple of days while they were settling in; and air all the quilts and other bedding, which had no doubt picked up some dust during the move. She could put Teppei to work hooking up the electrical appliances and pushing the furniture into place, but she would still need to give the toilet, washroom, and bathroom a thorough scrubbing, and arrange both bedrooms for comfort and convenience. There were so many stacks of cardboard boxes waiting to be unpacked that just looking at them made her feel slightly ill.

Still, compared with the rather dark, cramped rental apartment they had lived in until yesterday, their new home seemed like a vacation condo at some glamorous seaside resort. The eight-story building had only fourteen units, not counting the husband-and-wife caretakers' quarters on the ground floor. There were two units per floor, and while the floor plans of those units were mirror images of each other, the placement of the balconies differed a bit from apartment to apartment, so the building's facade had an interesting irregularity when viewed from outside.

The entry hall opened into a spacious, airy living room with a sunny southern exposure, which abutted a separate kitchen. Ranged along a corridor were a toilet cubicle, a washroom, and a separate bathroom with a tub lined up along one side; next came the two Western-style bedrooms, each with a single window and both facing north. The master bedroom was about half again as large as the nursery, and thanks to numerous built-in cupboards there was no shortage of storage space.

Heading south on foot from Japan Rail's Takaino Station, it took only seven or eight minutes to reach the Central Plaza Mansion, and another railway stop—the privately operated South Takaino Station—was just a few blocks farther away. From Takaino Station the train took just under twenty minutes to reach the center of Tokyo, and Teppei's daily commute to the advertising agency where he worked was a straight shot, with no need to change trains along the way. As for St. Mary's, the kindergarten where they were planning to enroll Tamao, it was a ten-minute walk from the apartment. Looking ahead a couple of years, the district's public elementary school was even closer; it wouldn't take more than eight or nine minutes to walk there, even for a child.

A convenient shopping area and a large, privately owned hospital were situated nearby, just steps away from the north exit of Takaino Station. Best of all, the apartment building didn't have any bothersome rules against keeping pets indoors, so there was no need to worry about Cookie.

*It's pretty close to perfect,* Misao thought. What more could anyone want? Two LDK (real-estate shorthand for two bedrooms, living room, dining area, and kitchen); nearly a thousand square feet, including the balcony; a building that was only eight months old; full-time resident managers, right on the premises. For a family in search of a wholesome, peaceful life, it was really quite ideal. Not bothering with a tablecloth, Misao laid out two coffee cups on the bare dining table, along with Tamao's mug, which was adorned with a picture of a cartoon bear. When she happened to glance toward the balcony, a fleeting wave of misgivings about the location washed over her. Shaking it off, she made a conscious effort to focus on the positives. Beyond the sliding-glass doors, the verdant-smelling March air was whipping around, and there were no buildings nearby to obstruct her field of vision. If only the sublime greenery belonged to a park, and not a graveyard . . .

Misao gave her head a quick, purposeful toss, as if to banish such futile thoughts, then laughed out loud. There she went again, fretting about minor drawbacks and useless hypotheticals. As if she had time to waste on that kind of nonsense! *Cut it out,* she told herself sternly.

The percolating coffee began to fill the room with a delicious aroma. Misao grabbed a frying pan that had just been unpacked a few moments earlier and gave it a quick rinse under the tap. She heated the pan on the stove and added a splash of cooking oil. When the oil began to sizzle, she dropped in three of the eggs she had brought from their previous place—painstakingly packed to make sure they wouldn't get broken in transit.

As she worked, Misao couldn't keep her eyes from wandering to the living-room windows. The nearly perfect apartment was partially surrounded, from the south to the west side, by a vast graveyard that belonged to an ancient Buddhist temple. To the north were some uninhabited houses, long since fallen into ruin and engulfed in weeds, while on the east side there was a patch of vacant land. Beyond that empty field the smokestack of a crematorium was clearly visible, and from time to time the tall, cylindrical brick chimney would belch out a billow of thick black smoke. Depending on which way the wind was blowing, it wasn't inconceivable that some of that mortal smoke might waft in through the apartment's open windows from time to time.

"We really lucked out, finding this place," Teppei said when they came to look at the Central Plaza Mansion for the first time. "If it weren't for the proximity to a graveyard, there's no way the price would ever be so low nowadays. I mean, think about it. Do you really believe that a large luxury apartment like this in the Tokyo metropolitan area would be priced so low if the surroundings were different?"

"And look, there's a crematorium practically next door!" Misao said with mock enthusiasm. "That'll be handy for the next step, when the time comes. Talk about a stroke of luck!" Upon hearing this, the agent who was showing the property launched into a spiel that was clearly designed to be persuasive, explaining that sophisticated people in Europe simply thought of graveyards as another type of public park, with no negative connotations whatsoever.

"Yes, I see your point," Misao said, her voice dripping with sarcasm as she gazed at the view from the balcony. "If only the ground beneath the graveyard weren't full of the decomposing bones of human beings, it would be exactly like a botanical garden."

Misao had absolutely no desire to live in a place like this. However low the price, however marvelous the accommodations, however sunny the exposure, however close to the center of the city the apartment might be, her initial gut feeling was still: *Uh-uh. Never. No way. Surely,* she thought, *nobody in their right mind would intentionally invest in a property surrounded on three sides by a cemetery, a temple where funerals were held, and a busy crematorium.*

Yet at the same time, from the very first viewing of the apartment—indeed, from the instant she looked out at the graveyard and thought, *No way*—the truth was that Misao was being inescapably pulled in the opposite direction by the stark numerical realities. She had given up her freelance illustration work when

Tamao was born, and that had taken a severe toll on the family's finances. As for Teppei's salary, the advertising business was in an industry-wide slump, and there was no chance of his getting a raise any time soon.

But still, at their current rental—a dilapidated, sun-deprived apartment where even in the midsummer heat, the laundry Misao hung on the north-facing balcony took forever to dry—they were essentially pouring money down the drain every month. Fortunately, they had managed to hang on to some of their savings, and Misao got the feeling that if they were going to use that money for a down payment on a suitable apartment, it was probably now or never.

As Teppei pointed out at every opportunity, you could look all over Tokyo and not find a single comparable unit at this price: only thirty-five million yen for a great deal of space. When you factored in the convenience for commuting, shopping, schools, and so on, it wouldn't be unusual to pay sixty million yen or, more likely, seventy million yen for an apartment of similar size, or smaller. So on the one hand there was the disadvantage of having to look out at a graveyard and a crematorium smokestack, while on the other hand you were getting a very attractive living space for something close to half price. *I need to look on the bright side here,* Misao thought. *I mean, if you need to live within commuting distance of central Tokyo, finding an affordable, family-size home that offers perfection inside and out is the proverbial impossible dream, with no chance of ever coming true. This apartment is gorgeous inside, at least, and (if you don't think too much about the view) the location really couldn't be more convenient.*

As for resale, Misao knew the unconventional setting might make it more difficult to find a buyer, but she couldn't imagine that they would want to move out and find another place until sometime in the extremely distant future, and there was no point in thinking that far ahead. She had every expectation that the three of them (four, with Cookie) would enjoy living at the Central Plaza Mansion so much that they wouldn't need to think about selling for many years to come. The dank little rental apartment where they had been living until yesterday was tainted by some exceptionally unpleasant memories, and it was a wonderfully liberating feeling to be making a new beginning here.

"Mama?" Tamao said quizzically, poking her head through the kitchen door. Misao had been absently spreading a piece of toast with butter, and she jolted back to reality with such a start that she dropped the pat on the floor.

"I can make Cookie's breakfast," Tamao announced.

"Really? You're sure?"

"Yep! I'm sure!"

"Well, that would be a big help. You don't need to add any water, though."

The moment Tamao took the box of dog food out of the cupboard and rattled it, Cookie came galloping up with her tail wagging at maximum velocity. She wasn't a purebred dog by any means, but her round black eyes and tawny coat were a clear legacy of the Shiba Inu branch of her family tree.

*Oh, that's right,* Misao thought, staying positive. *This area is an ideal place to walk a dog, too. And even if Cookie barks a bit from time to time, we won't need to worry because there's nobody living next door.*

They had bought unit 801; the other apartment on the eighth floor, 802, was still empty. Of course, there was a good chance that someone would move in eventually, but as long as their future neighbor wasn't a curmudgeon with an extreme dislike of dogs, it should still be all right, assuming Cookie didn't suddenly start howling loudly at all hours.

The big front window stood open, and the breeze wafting into the apartment caused the newly purchased white lace curtains to undulate softly. The air smelled like springtime. Although it was only nine a.m., the warm rays of the morning sun had already flooded the entire left side of the living room with light.

"After we finish breakfast, we'll have a funeral for Pyoko," Misao told Tamao. "Then you can tidy up your room and put all your clothes and books and toys where they belong. All right?"

"How are we going to make a funeral for Pyoko?"

"Well, first we'll dig a grave outside and put a cross next to it, with 'Here Lies Pyoko' written on it. Then we'll all say a prayer: 'Please let Pyoko be happy in heaven,' or something like that."

"That's all?"

"Is there something else you'd like to do?"

"No, it's just—don't we need to make one of those long, skinny sticks, like the one I've seen you and Papa praying over some-times?"

*Oh dear. Not this,* Misao thought, averting her eyes. "You're talking about a memorial tablet," she said. "No, Pyoko doesn't need to have one of those."

"Why not?"

"Because those are only for people. Pyoko was a bird, so we don't need to make one for him."

"Huh," Tamao said doubtfully, watching as Cookie plunged her snout into the dog food dish and began wolfing down the dry kibble.

Misao hadn't yet talked to Teppei about where to set up their small, portable Buddhist family altar. Last night she had stuck it in the closet of the master bedroom, as a temporary measure, but they couldn't very well leave it there forever. After all, the altar needed to be somewhere out in the open, where the spirit of a cer-tain deceased person could bask in the refreshing breeze that wafted through the new apartment.

Teppei was continually teasing Misao about her old-fashioned insistence on observing traditional rituals regarding people who were no longer among the living. In this case, the person in ques-tion was Teppei's first wife, but that didn't stop him from giving Misao a hard time. It wasn't because he was heartless or unfeeling; he just happened to be the kind of tough-minded, strong-willed positive thinker who always found a rational explanation for everything, and refused to be haunted by painful memories or might-have-beens.

The event that changed everything had taken place seven years ago, during the summer when Misao and Teppei were twenty-five and twenty-eight, respectively. They had taken a secret weekend trip to a resort on the Izu Peninsula, where they had spent two blissful days (and nights) swimming in the hotel pool, enjoying poolside barbecues, and later, in bed, making love again and again. Teppei returned to his house in Tokyo late Sunday evening and found his wife, Reiko, standing silently in the unlit entry hall, waiting to welcome him home—or so he thought.

"What's going on?" he asked casually as he slipped out of his shoes. "Why are you just waiting here in the dark?" When Reiko didn't reply, Teppei groped around for the wall switch and turned on the overhead light.

His wife, he saw then, wasn't standing on the landing, at all. She had hung herself from a crossbeam by a silk kimono cord, and the architectural element holding her upright was the ceiling, not the floor.

Reiko had left behind a suicide note, addressed to Teppei. In it, she wrote that she harbored no ill feelings whatsoever toward him or the woman he was having an affair with. She was just tired. Life no longer offered her anything to enjoy, and all she wanted was to go to sleep, forever. *Good-bye*, she concluded. *Please be happy*.

Even now, Misao still knew every line of that brief letter by heart, and she could have recited it word for word. *Life no longer offers me anything to enjoy . . .*

Before Reiko's suicide, Misao was just a carefree young woman who had never given any serious thought to the nuances—or the ultimate stakes—of romantic relationships. She hadn't had the slightest intention of engaging Reiko in a territorial tug-of-war, or of trying to coerce Teppei into getting a divorce. She would have been lying if she'd said she wasn't bothered by the fact that Teppei was married, but their mutual attraction (stoked by workplace pro-pinquity) had simply been impossible to resist.

Misao and Teppei had met at the advertising agency where they were both employed, and after Reiko died their coworkers began to say nasty things about the two of them, quite openly. Misao deci-ded that the only remedy was for her to quit her job, so she re-signed and became a freelance illustrator.

At the time she had every intention of breaking things off with Teppei as well, but somehow they went on seeing each other. Eve-ning after evening the two of them would huddle together in Misao's tiny apartment and spend endless hours rehashing every detail of Reiko's death. They knew it wasn't healthy to keep going over the same things, but they also understood that while their psychic wounds would never heal if they kept reopening them again and again, retreating into silent denial would have been even less ben-eficial. There was no way to whitewash the harsh fact that their selfish, illicit actions had driven another human being to end her own life, and Misao and Teppei felt compelled to continue talking until they were able to accept that terrible truth, and forgive them-selves, and move on. They were, in effect, equal co-conspirators who shared the burden of guilt, and neither of them wanted to take the easy path of pretending that nothing had happened, or that it hadn't been their fault.

And so they talked, and talked, and talked about the suicide of Teppei's wife, to the point where they were sick and tired of the sound of their own voices, but instead of driving them to break up and go their separate ways, that painful process brought them closer. And then, finally, after all those long, dark nights, Misao had a major epiphany. She realized she and Teppei were meant to be together, for the long haul—marriage, children, the whole nine yards—and that was when she committed fully to their relation-ship, in her heart.

Misao had just turned twenty-seven when she discovered she was pregnant. At that point Teppei was still living in the house he had shared with Reiko, but he moved out and came to live with Misao in her small, sunless apartment, bringing Reiko's memorial tablet with him. They got married in a low-key civil ceremony, and the following year Tamao was born. And then . . .

"Hey, what's for breakfast? I'm starving!" Teppei strode into the kitchen, wiping his damp hands on a towel. "I just finished putting up our nameplate next to the front door. Turns out, that's hungry work!"

"I'm afraid there's only coffee and toast and fried eggs," Misao said.

"That sounds perfect. Wait, it looks like Cookie went ahead and ate before the rest of the family."

"I made Cookie's breakfast, all by myself!" Tamao announced proudly.

Teppei smiled at her. "What a good girl!" he said.

"Well, you know, I'm Cookie's mother, so it's my job," Tamao explained.

"You don't say." Teppei's grin grew broader. "Then I guess that means Mama and I are Cookie's grandparents?"

"That's right." Tamao's expression was still completely serious.

Teppei slid his arm around Misao's waist. "Hey, Grandma," he said slyly.

Misao laughed. "Are there really any grandmothers who look as good as this?" she asked with mock arrogance. "I mean, I don't have a single wrinkle yet, and my bottom isn't even a little bit saggy."

"Oh, *this* bottom? Hang on, let me check," Teppei said. The hand that had been encircling Misao's waist inched slowly down, tickling her playfully through the cloth of the jeans she was wearing, until it came to rest on her rear end.

"Stop it, you! You're going to make me spill the coffee!"

"Now that you mention it, it's our first day in a new place and you haven't even kissed me good morning yet," Teppei whispered in Misao's ear.

"That isn't going to happen," Misao said primly.

"Wow, you're a regular ice queen."

"I don't know what I'm going to do with you." Misao sighed. "Okay, go ahead, knock yourself out," she added with feigned weariness, turning to face Teppei with her lips extended in a comically exaggerated way.

Tamao was watching with great interest. "Me, too!" she clamored.

Teppei swept his daughter into his arms. Holding her tightly, he twirled her around and around, planting noisy kisses all over her face. Tamao responded with a torrent of high-pitched giggles and shrieks of delight.

# 2

Ever since they moved in, four days earlier, there had been an un-
broken string of flawless blue-sky days. Before that, all the way
through the end of February, cloudiness had been the daily norm
in Tokyo, and a cold, damp wind laced with rain and sleet had
blown almost around the clock. The current change in weather was
so radical that it felt as though winter had turned to spring the moment the Kano family arrived at the Central Plaza Mansion.

In the flower gardens that bordered the immense graveyard, the
buds of aromatic daphne seemed to be bursting open moment by
moment, releasing their sweet fragrance into the balmy air. It probably wouldn't be long before the tulips and violets began to bloom,
as well. On the other side of the flower garden, some long-dead
temple gardener had planted a variety of cherry trees. By the time
people started coming to visit their ancestors' graves during the
week of Buddhist ceremonies centered on the spring equinox,
the cherry trees, too, would most likely be sprouting some leaves. The
graveyard was so old that many of the wooden grave markers—long,

narrow planks adorned with calligraphic characters in Japanese or Sanskrit—were on the verge of toppling over, and most of the gravestones had been darkened by smoke and age. From a distance, as just one element of the larger vista (which included trees, hedges, flowering plants, vacant lots, narrow lanes, and a few scattered clusters of abandoned-looking buildings), those gloomy tombstones could almost be seen as nothing more disquieting than a handful of pebbles strewn across the landscape. At least, that's what Misao kept telling herself. Every time she gazed at the view from her eighth-floor balcony, she would repeat, over and over, "This really isn't so bad."

An ancient cemetery, right in the middle of the city. It was just as the man from the real estate agency had said in his obviously rehearsed pitch: "This area is no longer merely a place where the dead find their final resting place. Instead, it is being transformed into a haven where the living can relax and enjoy themselves." *Whatever you say*, Misao had thought sourly.

The graveyard was directly in front of the apartment, with only a narrow driveway between them. If Misao stood on the balcony, craned her neck, and peered off to the left, she could see the Buddhist temple with its lustrous black-tiled roof, and the tall, spooky-looking smokestack of the nearby crematorium soaring into the sky. When the trees were bare, it was hard to ignore the fact that the apartment looked out on a cemetery and a perpetually active cremation facility, but when summer rolled around and all the trees were lushly leafed out, surely it would be possible to forget about that unsettling proximity.

There was so much to look forward to. First, the exquisite canopy of cherry blossoms in early spring. Then in summertime, the entire green belt would be thronged with thousands of cicadas, singing their exuberant songs all day long. When summer turned to autumn, there would be the spectacular display of fall colors: crimson, russet, orange, gold. And so it would go from beauty to beauty, as the scenery morphed through its seasonal changes. It occurred to Misao (who was a city girl, born and raised) that she had never before lived in a place where it was possible to experience the natural wonders of each of the four seasons so directly. *No, it really isn't so bad here, at all . . .* that was how she needed to feel about her new home, and the more often she repeated the "not so bad" mantra, the closer she came to believing it.

On the day she finally finished unpacking and nearly everything had been put away in its proper place, Misao took Tamao over to St. Mary's Kindergarten and filled out the necessary forms for enrollment in the two-tiered school's junior class. She and Teppei had engaged in lengthy discussions about the pros and cons of this move, and they had ended up agreeing that it was a necessary step. In order to minimize any possible ill effects from Tamao's being an only child, the sooner she became accustomed to functioning in a group the better it would be for everyone.

In addition, Misao was planning to start easing back into work beginning in April. While in theory an illustrator who also happened to be a mother should have been able to do her work at home, the reality was that there was a seemingly infinite number of ways in which having a young child in the house all the time could undermine that rosy scenario. If Misao could only have the morning hours to herself, she could devote that entire stretch of time to working. She knew she couldn't expect to generate very much income, but (needless to say) a little was better than nothing at all. That was the best plan for the time being, she thought: to live frugally and continue to look for freelance assignments to bring in a bit of extra money. It was unrealistic to wish for a situation that was perfect in every way. Self-indulgence always came with a hefty price tag. Just as it had seven years ago . . .

St. Mary's Kindergarten was tucked away in a residential district on the other side of the highway in front of Manseiji, the temple attached to the graveyard. There was no school bus, so whenever Misao and Tamao made the trip back and forth they would have to cross the busy highway. Every day, Misao would need to walk Tamao to kindergarten in the morning, then walk back over to pick her up at the end of the session. There were no other options.

After the admissions procedure had been completed, Misao paid her respects, first to the young teacher of the kindergarten's junior class, and then to the head of the school—an imposing older woman whose gnarly-looking skin and hefty build made Misao think of a rhinoceros. Then she and Tamao headed off to a nearby clothing store to buy the required uniform.

There was a shopping district around the station's south exit, but compared to the lively, thriving area outside the north exit, it had the forlorn aspect of a ghost town. A weather-beaten signboard wishfully proclaimed the district the "South Exit Ginza," and the eaves of the shops were strung with cheap-looking plastic cherry blossoms and paper lanterns. All the stores looked so shabby that it would have been no surprise if they had gone out of business the next day, and the overall effect was relentlessly bleak.

"Official Uniforms for St. Mary's Kindergarten" read a hand-painted sign outside one of the stores. When Misao and Tamao walked in, an elderly couple emerged from the back of the shop. In a corner, dressed in a dark blue uniform, stood one of those rudimentary mannequins you see in country stores, looking rather like an anatomical model from a science lab. The uniform's design couldn't be called chic by any means, but it wasn't unsightly, either; it was just a run-of-the-mill school uniform.

"Oh, what a little cutie," the female shopkeeper gushed, patting Tamao's head while she beamed down at the child. Misao smiled in return.

"The hats used to be blue, but they're yellow now," the woman chattered on, putting one on Tamao's head. "Oh, look, it's a perfect fit. Some of the mothers don't care for these hats because they look like helmets, but the hard hats really are the best. When you think about the accident that happened on the highway, it makes you realize that safety is more important than style."

"There was an accident on the highway?" Misao asked nervously.

"You didn't hear about it? Yes, one of the younger children from St. Mary's Kindergarten was hit by a car."

"Well, we just moved here recently, so . . ." Misao said.

"Oh, I didn't realize that," the woman said. Her kindly face reddened slightly, as though she had said something inappropriate. "It was the year before last, in the fall. A little boy was hit by a car right in front of the temple—you know, Manseiji? Apparently his mother glanced away for a split second and for some reason he decided to try to cross the street by himself. It was really tragic."

"Why don't you give it a rest," the male proprietor chided. "There's really no need to tell that kind of story to someone who's new to the area."

"You're right, dear. I'm sorry," his wife said contritely, and her gentle-featured face flushed an even deeper rose.

"So, um . . . is that child all right now?" Misao asked hesitantly.

"No, he died instantly," the man said with a morose expression.

"And ever since then, the hats for that school have been yellow instead of blue," his wife added. "You know, to make them easier to see."

Tamao had been standing in stoic silence during this conversation, obediently raising and lowering her arms while the shopkeepers took her measurements. The older woman looked at Misao and brightly changed the subject. "So what part of our neighborhood are you living in?"

"We just moved into the Central Plaza Mansion," Misao replied. "You know, the building on the other side of the cemetery?"

"Ah," the woman said, nodding. She caught her husband's eye and they exchanged a quick glance that struck Misao as suspiciously close to a wink.

While the man was jotting down the measurements for Tamao's skirt in a notebook, he said, "That site was a vacant lot for the longest time. Of course, the land belonged to the temple. Now that somebody went and built a fancy apartment complex there, it's really turned into a showplace." Misao smiled politely.

"Well, I think that about does it," the female proprietor said, wiping her hands on her soiled apron in what appeared to be a habitual gesture. Misao paid in advance for the uniform, and after having been given a pick-up date, she and Tamao left the shop.

Wandering along the shopping street, they passed a dusty-looking fruit shop that was advertising a special sale on strawberries. The fruit didn't look especially fresh, and Misao wasn't tempted to buy any. Holding Tamao's hand tightly, she turned around and headed for home.

As they were walking through the quiet streets, Tamao suddenly looked up at her mother and said in an oddly enervated tone, "Mama? Do I really have to go to kindergarten, no matter what?"

"You don't want to?"

Tamao didn't reply.

"Did you dislike the uniform?" Misao probed.

"No, that's not it . . ."

"You're bound to make new friends in kindergarten, and I promise you'll have lots of fun—much more fun than if you just stayed home and played by yourself all day."

"But I already have friends."

"Really? Who?"

"Cookie and Pyoko."

Misao smiled. "Really? Pyoko, too?"

"Uh-huh. I was just playing with him yesterday."

"Oh, I get it. You had a dream about Pyoko."

"No, it wasn't a dream. Pyoko came to visit me at night, while I was still awake. He came flying into my room, full of life. And the thing is, he just went on talking and talking. I can understand some bird language now, so I knew what he was saying."

"Wow, that's really something," Misao said, barely managing to maintain a neutral tone. "So, um, what was Pyoko talking about?"

"He was telling me about the place where he's living now. He says it's a really dark and dangerous place, and I should never go there because once somebody goes in, it's almost impossible to get out again. But Pyoko is very clever, and he knows how to escape sometimes. That's how he can visit me. Oh, and Mama? He says that place is full of bad monsters with big, scary faces. And he told me that when those monsters speak, a big wind starts to blow and everyone gets sucked into a giant hole."

Misao sighed. It was supposed to be healthy to let a child's imagination run wild, but Tamao had a tendency to carry make-believe to extremes. Maybe the way they'd been raising her was overly indulgent, and this kind of far-fetched flight of fancy was the result. Or perhaps she and Teppei, as a couple, had unconsciously been transmitting their own somber feelings and residual regrets about the past, and over time that ambient gloominess had percolated down to Tamao, bit by bit, and had influenced her behavior.

"Pyoko is looking down from heaven and watching over you," Misao said gently, as if she were reading aloud from a children's book. "He'll be checking to see that you go to kindergarten and make lots and lots of wonderful new friends, the way you're supposed to. Also, he wants to make sure you stay safe and don't catch a cold or anything like that. That's why—"

"Yes, but he really did come to my room," Tamao interrupted. "He was perched right next to the bed. And he really did talk to me, a whole bunch."

"I know, but that was just a dream."

"No, I keep telling you, it wasn't a dream," Tamao said impatiently. "It was real. Pyoko perched on the headboard of my bed for a while, and then he flew around the room, and a few times he landed on Pooh-Bear's head." Pooh-Bear was Tamao's favorite stuffed animal: a fuzzy white teddy bear.

"I see. Of course, that's probably what happened," Misao said, trying to keep the distress out of her voice.

"I wonder if he'll come again tonight," Tamao mused.

"Hmm, I wonder," Misao said uncomfortably.

Tamao continued prattling on about the dead bird, but while Misao made a show of listening intently, her thoughts were elsewhere. Was it maybe a bit too soon to be sending Tamao off to kindergarten? It was troubling to hear her daughter talking about something she had dreamed, or imagined when she was half asleep, as though it were empirical reality. Rather than abruptly plunging Tamao into a group situation, maybe it would be more appropriate to find some playmates of the same age or thereabouts, and let them run around outdoors and come home covered in mud. *Baby steps*, Misao thought.

No question about it, having Pyoko die mere hours after their move to a new house had been traumatic for Tamao. Misao suddenly remembered that the birdcage (encased in a plastic bag) was still out on the balcony, where she had hastily stashed it the first day. She really ought to put the cage somewhere out of sight, sooner rather than later. And to minimize the chances of Tamao's having any more of those disquieting dreams, she should probably put an end to her current custom of giving Tamao bedtime snacks of cookies or chocolate. No sweets after dinner, and an absolute minimum of liquids: that should be the policy from now on. Those indulgences were probably the reason behind Tamao's monthly lapses into bedwetting, which soaked through the sheets and the quilted pad underneath, as well.

As Misao and Tamao approached the narrow street leading to the Central Plaza Mansion, which wound past Manseiji and skirted the adjacent graveyard, they saw a petite, winsome-faced young woman standing by the side of the road. Her hair was stylishly cut in shingled layers, and she wore black leggings and a long black cardigan with shoulder pads. A small girl was squatting nearby, drawing pictures on the asphalt with colored chalk.

*Maybe they live in our building,* Misao thought. She gave a slight nod and was about to pass by when the woman addressed her.

"Excuse me, but are you the folks who just moved in, by any chance?"

"That's right," Misao replied.

"Ah, just as I thought," the woman said, with a smile that struck Misao as open and friendly, with a touch of mischief. They traded the customary bows.

"It's nice to meet you," the woman said. "I'm Eiko Inoue. We live in apartment 402."

At a glance, Eiko Inoue struck Misao as the kind of woman who had been raised by conscientious parents, had married in the usual way, and then had popped out a couple of kids, as expected. Wherever she went, a woman like that would find it easy to make friends, and she would never stop to wonder whether her own essential loneliness might be the driving force behind her compulsive sociability. *She just looks like that type, somehow,* Misao mused. She made an effort to smile back as amicably as she could.

"I'm Misao Kano. I'm sorry I haven't been down to say hello before this, but I've been busy registering my daughter for kindergarten and so on."

"Oh, really?" Eiko Inoue's eyes grew wide. "Will your daughter be enrolling at St. Mary's?"

When Misao nodded, the woman's attitude became even friendlier. "Kaori!" she called out to her own daughter. "Aren't you going to say hello to our new neighbor? This nice little girl is going to be in your class at kindergarten."

"Hello," Kaori said reticently, squinting at Tamao. Kaori's eyes wore an open, unguarded expression, just like her mother's.

"What's your name, dear?" Eiko asked, turning to Tamao.

Tamao introduced herself, but her shy smile was directed toward Kaori. Her face was alight with curiosity, and she seemed to have forgotten all about the dead bird.

"What a little doll," Eiko said. "Does she have any brothers or sisters at home?"

"No, she's an only child," Misao replied. "Maybe that's why we've been, um, having some problems."

"One child is the way to go," Eiko laughed. "At least for the parents! When you have two or three kids running around the house all day, before you know it they've turned you into a worn-out old lady."

Misao chuckled at this, and Eiko went on, "Seriously, though, I'm very happy to meet you." Her body language seemed to suggest that she would have liked to go over and give Misao a hug, on the spot. "We moved here at the end of last year, so it's been a little over four months, and I still haven't gotten to know anyone. My older child, Tsutomu, is in the senior kindergarten class, and he's made quite a few friends there. I haven't really socialized with any of the mothers, though, so I'm really pleased to run into you like this!"

Misao didn't entirely understand why Eiko was so overjoyed about their encounter, but she didn't find her new acquaintance's ebullience off-putting at all. She figured it was only natural that someone who moved to a new place would feel an initial sense of isolation and loneliness, and would long for a kindred spirit to talk to.

After the two little girls had wandered off to play, Eiko continued to dominate the conversation, which suited Misao fine. "We used to live in Omori," Eiko said. "I made quite a few friends there, mostly through the kids, and some of my friends from college used to drop by often, as well. But now, ever since we moved here? Nothing. Zippo. Zilch. I'm not sure, but I think it might be because this area seems okay during the day, and then when night falls, it starts to feel kind of creepy. My husband isn't normally frightened of anything, but even he was saying that as soon as he steps into this alley in front of the temple, he gets a bad feeling. I mean, you'd think someone could install one measly streetlamp, at least, to light the way. Anyway, I'm almost certain that's why nobody feels comfortable coming to visit me here after dark. Oh, I'm sorry. I shouldn't be talking this way to someone who's only just moved in . . ."

Eiko's comments were clearly candid rather than spiteful, so Misao just laughed and said, "That's okay—no need to apologize. We were aware of all those things from the beginning, before we decided to move here."

Eiko looked relieved. "Well, on the bright side," she said, flashing Misao a grateful smile, "living next to a graveyard does have some advantages. It's quiet, and there's oodles of greenery around us. If it weren't for the cemetery, this area would probably be completely built up by now, with wall-to-wall high rises and unaffordable prices. Oh, by the way, have you been finding everything you need? Since I've already been here awhile I know this area pretty well now, and I'd be glad to share my discoveries, such as they are."

"Thank you. That would be great!" Misao said.

Eiko then proceeded to divulge the inside scoop about the neighborhood. One bakery had special sales on bread every Monday; another bakery specialized in reduced-calorie cakes; a certain dentist was supposed to have an excellent reputation; and so on. At one point in the litany of recommendations Eiko stopped for a moment to scold her daughter, who had been about to touch her mouth with hands that were covered in chalk dust.

Misao thanked Eiko for the useful information, then added, "I hope you'll drop by our place for a nice, leisurely cup of tea sometime soon," and Eiko issued a reciprocal invitation. Misao thought she and Eiko were probably around the same age, and having an amicable acquaintance in the building could only be a good thing—not least because of the obvious benefits for the children.

As the women approached the building's front entrance, herding their small daughters ahead of them, Eiko turned to Misao and said in a mock whisper, "You know, people are saying that the units in this building haven't been selling too well. When we moved in there were only seven occupied units, including the resident managers' quarters, but your family finally brings the number up to eight. Though now that I think about it, one of the apartments is only being used as a company office, so we're really still stuck at seven. It gives the building kind of a desolate feeling, having so many empty apartments, and I'm hoping lots of people will start moving in from now on."

Thanks to the loquacious real estate agent who had handled

their purchase, Misao already knew that only about half of the fourteen units were occupied, and she didn't find the low sales figures surprising. Living in an apartment building that looked out on a graveyard was never going to be everyone's cup of tea. Some people simply wouldn't be able to convince themselves that the quiet, the space, the greenery, and the appealing price point were adequate compensation for living next door to a crumbling old cemetery.

"I guess any building would feel a bit lonely, graveyard or no graveyard, if it had so few residents," Misao mused.

Eiko gave an emphatic nod. "Yes, I think you're right," she agreed. "But especially for someone like me who would rather be where the action is, there are times when all the quiet just gets to be too much to bear. I swear, sometimes at night it feels as if we're living on a stage set. My husband's always teasing me about being the kind of person who expects life to be an endless party. He says I'd feel more at home crammed into a two-room apartment in some noisy high rise in downtown Tokyo, and I can't honestly say he's wrong about that."

When Eiko and Misao opened the glass door that led to the building's lobby, Kaori ran ahead, then turned and beckoned to Tamao to hurry up. The two little girls seemed to have hit it off from the moment they met, Misao thought. That was a huge relief.

Timidly, Tamao reached out and took Kaori's proffered hand, then looked up at her mother with an expression of bashfulness tinged with doubt. As the group moved slowly through the lobby, Eiko seemed to be paying close attention to the nascent friendship that appeared to be developing between the two girls.

Suddenly she wheeled to face Misao, as if something important had just occurred to her. "Oh!" she said. "I assume you know about the storage facilities in the basement?"

"Yes, I do."

"It's really super convenient. You can stash all your extra stuff down there, and then forget about it."

"I know." Misao nodded. The agent had mentioned that each apartment in the building was allotted a designated storage locker in the basement.

Eiko went on, "We've already put quite a few things in our storage unit: some chairs we never use anymore, and Tsutomu's old tricycle, and so on. Have you gone down to check it out?"

"No, not yet," Misao said, shaking her head. There were definitely some things that either didn't fit or weren't needed in their new apartment, but she had been too busy to explore the basement.

"Well, then, why don't we pop down now. I'll give you the grand tour," Eiko suggested, pressing the elevator's down button as she spoke.

As they were waiting, Eiko said, "Is it just me, or is the design of this building kind of weird? I mean, they went to the trouble of building a basement, but they didn't bother to include a staircase? The only way to get there is by taking the elevator. I mean, what if there was a power failure or the elevator broke down—how would someone who happened to be in the basement get back upstairs? They'd be stranded down there. Really, it makes no sense."

While Eiko was grumbling about the building's illogical construction, the elevator arrived. After they were all inside, she reached into the pocket of her cardigan and pulled out a red leather key holder.

"Oh, you need a key?" Misao asked.

"Yes, every storage unit has its own padlock and key. It's easy to get them; you just fill out an application and submit it to the resident manager. Though even if nobody bothered with a lock, I doubt whether any self-respecting burglar would touch most of the junk that's stored down there," Eiko said with a laugh.

The elevator coasted to a stop, and the moment the doors opened Tamao and Kaori charged out into the basement, whooping with excitement.

"Careful! Don't fall down!" Eiko called after them. The large open space was shrouded in twilight, with the only illumination coming from a single exit sign above their heads. "Hang on a sec, the light switch is right here," Eiko said. She touched the wall next to the elevator and the area was immediately flooded with ultra-bright light of the sort used on tennis courts at night.

The walls were unfinished concrete and the ceiling was obscured by a welter of exposed pipes, but there wasn't a single speck of dust on the gray cement floor. The cavernous basement was empty except for a couple of rows of cheap-looking storage compartments that had been painted white. Stenciled on each of the lockers was the number of the corresponding apartment.

The scene reminded Misao of a photograph she had seen in some old magazine a long time ago, of the communal shower room in a ruined building. The photo had been taken in the basement of a Western-style structure that had once served as a dormitory for single women. The paint was peeling off the walls, and the door to the shower room hung limply from a single broken hinge. The nozzles dangling in a row from the ceiling were oddly curved, like the beaks of a flock of eagles. All the scummy layers of soap and grime that landed on the tile when those legions of long-ago women washed themselves off had accumulated to the point where it looked as though someone had spread a layer of snow-white loam over the floor of the showers.

"I do believe you'll find the extra storage space surprisingly useful," Eiko said, impishly adopting the elevated manner of a real estate agent trying to convince a potential buyer. "As for the lockers themselves, I admit that they aren't quite as stylish as one might wish, but they serve the purpose well enough. Hey, look at this!" Eiko exclaimed, abruptly reverting to her normal tone of voice. "You know I mentioned there's a company that has its offices on the second floor? Well, they distribute health food, and they've apparently overflowed their storage unit and are storing their unsold inventory right out in the open here. Doesn't that strike you as kind of shameless?"

Eiko gestured at the cardboard boxes lined up along one wall. Each bore a printed label that read "Health Japan, LLC."

"What kind of health food is it?" Misao asked.

"Apparently they're some kind of high-calorie protein bars that were originally developed for the space program," Eiko explained. "A salesman for that company actually came to our door and tried to persuade me to buy some. I was like, *Seriously?* So I said to the guy, 'You should know this is an exercise in futility, trying to peddle high-calorie bars to a woman who's on a perpetual diet.' Honestly, I don't know a single person who would dream of even looking at a weight-gain bar. Do such people even exist nowadays?" Eiko burst into incredulous laughter.

Kaori was standing nearby, scratching idly at the rusty fender of a derelict bicycle that someone had propped against one of the unused lockers. Turning to glare at her daughter, Eiko snapped, "Kaori, stop it! You know better than that!" As her exasperated voice bounced off the walls, the amplified echo made it sound almost like a roar.

Eiko went over to the storage locker that bore the number of her apartment, 402, and stuck her key in the padlock. The sliding door opened easily. Inside, a bare lightbulb hung from the ceiling, and on the floor was a motley tangle of worn-out chairs, reusable plastic beer crates, and an old tricycle.

"I've heard that if you go to Europe you'll find facilities like this in nearly every apartment building. I guess this basement is proof that they're catching on here, as well," Eiko said as she slid the door closed again.

Misao felt a sudden, frigid draft swirling around her ankles, and she shuddered involuntarily. *How can it be windy?* she thought, looking around. She had a sudden feeling that the concrete walls were closing in on her.

"Mama?" Tamao came up and stuck her hand into her mother's. "Can we go home now?"

"Yes, let's do that," Misao said quickly. "Let's go home." Once again, she felt the icy breeze caressing her feet and legs. Misao called out to Eiko, and the four of them trooped off to the elevator.

The Inoues got off at the fourth floor in a flurry of farewells. Just as Misao and Tamao disembarked and were standing in front of the door of their eighth-floor apartment, the telephone inside began to ring. Hastily, Misao jammed the key into the door, dashed down the hallway, and flew over to pick up the phone in the living room. But when she lifted the receiver to her ear, the line went dead.

"Oh dear, they hung up," Misao said. "It might have been a call about Mama's work. I hope they'll phone again."

Tamao was busy playing with Cookie, and didn't exhibit the slightest interest in her mother's missed call.

As Misao was replacing the receiver in its cradle, her eyes were drawn to the pale pink memo pad next to the telephone. There was a small white bird feather resting lightly on top of it. Misao picked up the feather between two fingers and held it in the air, level with her eyes. On closer inspection, she noticed that the white shaded into gray at the very tip. She remembered that while Pyoko, the little Java finch, was still alive, she had come across feathers exactly like this one every time she tidied the birdcage. But how did it come to be here, after all this time?

Still holding the feather, Misao let her gaze wander out to the balcony. The birdcage was still there, right where she'd left it. Maybe there had been an overlooked feather on the bottom of the cage after she'd given it a final cleaning, and the wind had carried that single feather into the living room? No, the cage was tightly wrapped in a plastic trash bag, and secured with a twisty tie. Even if they had somehow neglected to close the sliding-glass doors all the way and an incredibly strong wind had been blowing during the night when everyone was asleep, it was still hard to imagine a scenario in which one stray feather could have been extracted from the bag-enclosed cage and carried into the apartment.

"Um, Tamao?" Misao called out.

Tamao stopped cavorting with Cookie and looked over at her

mother. "What, Mama?" she asked, with an expression of perfect innocence on her face.

"Look what I found," Misao said.

Tamao cocked her head and came running over, waving a plump arm in the air. "Oh!" she said happily, as she took the feather from her mother's hand. "That's Pyoko's! So I guess Pyoko was flying around in this room, too, Mama!"

Misao didn't reply. Scowling grimly, she snatched the feather from Tamao's grasp and tossed it into the kitchen wastebasket.

# 3

"My old lady's in a rotten mood," said Teppei's younger brother, Tatsuji. He had returned from the hostess bar's pay phone looking like someone whose mind is miles away: present in body, but definitely not in spirit. "It's because I went out drinking last night, too, and came home late again."

Tatsuji had only been married for about a year. The woman he chose as a life partner had been the belle of the university tennis club they both belonged to. Maybe it was because he had pursued her with single-minded persistence until she finally agreed to marry him, but he seemed to be perpetually in the doghouse at home.

"In that case, maybe we should call it a night," Teppei said, glancing at his wristwatch. Ten o'clock. It had been months since he and his younger brother had gotten together like this, and after they'd shared their respective bits of news there didn't seem to be anything left to talk about. Tatsuji worked for a giant food conglomerate, while Teppei had been on the creative side of the advertising business for many years, so their jobs didn't really provide much common ground. Beyond that, though, Teppei simply couldn't enjoy hanging out with someone who was constantly fretting about staying on his wife's good side, and he was also fed up with the inevitable repercussions. Every time he saw Tatsuji's wife, she would say something snide like, "Oh, I hear you've been leading my poor husband astray again."

Try as he might, Teppei found his sister-in-law almost impossible to like. He didn't even like to say her name: Naomi. As the saying went, even a hungry mosquito wouldn't want to get too close to her.

Naomi was the only daughter of a university professor, and while she was undeniably pretty, she clearly believed that the entire universe revolved around her. She had been a model daughter and an outstanding student, constantly striving to meet her parents' rigorous expectations, and as a result there were no youthful follies, dark secrets, or flaws of any sort in her past. Perhaps, Teppei mused, that parentally enforced perfection might be the reason Naomi had turned out to be so insensitive, self-centered, superficial, and judgmental.

"Oh, no, you aren't leaving us already?" wailed the hostess sitting next to Teppei, when she noticed him tucking his cigarettes into a pocket of his sports jacket. "Please, stay a little longer. The night's still young!"

"I'd like to, but this guy's wife keeps him on a very short leash," Teppei said. "She likes to be treated like a fairy princess, or maybe a queen, and if I don't make sure he gets home on time he might end up sleeping on the couch."

Tatsuji shot his older brother a warning look. "Don't say that kind of thing," he snarled, curling his upper lip. His combative words hung awkwardly in the air.

Although Tatsuji was already past thirty, there were still times when his face looked exactly as it had when he was a child of four or five. One day during their boyhood, when Teppei was about to head off with his elementary-school buddies to explore the gravel pit at a nearby excavation site, Tatsuji tried to tag along uninvited. Teppei sneered, "Go home, little baby," and his followers broke into a cruel chant of "Little baby, little baby!" Teppei felt an overwhelming urge to ride the intoxicating wave of power born of being both an older brother and the leader of his class, and he crossed the line from mischief into maliciousness.

"Okay, little baby, if you don't go home I'm going to tell everyone that our mother is still suckling you late at night," he taunted. "What do you say to that?" This outrageous accusation got Teppei's fellow rascals even more worked up, and they cheered him on, cackling like mean-spirited fiends.

Tatsuji had just stood there, biting his lip. His eyes were blurred with unshed tears, but he somehow managed to keep from crying. "You're a stupid-head!" he yelled at Teppei. "I hate you!" He glared daggers at his brother, and his little face was so contorted with misery that he seemed to be carrying the weight of the world on his shoulders.

Teppei had started to feel slightly sorry for Tatsuji, but he didn't apologize or offer any comfort. Truth be told, he took a certain perverse pleasure in tormenting his baby brother. Even now, Teppei still remembered the complicated expression on Tatsuji's face: wounded petulance mixed with outright hostility, along with an unyielding determination to go on an adventure with the bigger boys, despite their unkindness. It was the face of an innocent, trusting, foolishly hopeful kid, and even today Teppei occasionally caught a glimpse of that vulnerable, childlike face peeking out from behind Tatsuji's sophisticated adult facade.

"Do you really have to rush off?" the hostess asked again. Teppei had noticed that her makeup had started to flake as the night wore on, gradually revealing the dark circles under her eyes. Maybe she had liver disease.

"Well, I guess we can hang out for another half hour or so," Tatsuji said, in a grudging tone, as if he wasn't eager to stay but didn't want to be perceived as a wet blanket, or a henpecked husband.

Teppei laughed. "Don't force it on my account," he said. "I'm worried about what might happen when you get home."

"Like I said, it isn't a problem," Tatsuji said impatiently. "It's not as if I'm having an affair or something. She just needs to get used to the fact that I may have to stay out late from time to time."

There was something almost comically defensive about the way Tatsuji delivered this speech, but Teppei just nodded and said, "That's the spirit!" with a perfectly straight face.

The small club they'd gone to was in Yotsuya, not far from that district's main shopping and amusement area. There were three hostesses, and when the place had ten customers, there was no room for anyone else to crowd in. On this night, though, it was barely a third full. Indeed, the only other customer apart from Teppei's party of two was a boisterous, high-spirited man with a rapidly receding hairline who was flirting nonstop with two of the hostesses while he drank his way through a bottle of cognac with lip-smacking gusto.

The bar was set up for karaoke, but hardly anyone ever got up to sing. In Teppei's past experience, most of the patrons looked perpetually baffled, as if they weren't quite sure what had made them think that coming to this place might be enjoyable. After sitting around sipping watered-down whiskey and trading stale jokes with the hostesses, all of whom were attempting to pass for at least ten years younger than their actual ages, they would usually wander out and head for home, or for a more interesting bar.

Teppei had made his way to this club any number of times since he was first brought here by some coworkers, but when he stopped to ask himself what the appeal was, he was unable to come up with an answer. It was just an easy place to sit and have a drink or two, lost in reverie. If you felt like getting up and singing a song, you could do that, and then you could take your leave and make it an early night. Teppei had thought more than once that spending that kind of uneventful, laid-back evening was curiously well suited to his temperament.

"Won't you give us a song? How about it?" the hostess asked Teppei with a false air of urgency, as if the background music had already begun to play. "This may be your last chance, because the guest over there is probably going to get up and treat us to his famous medley any minute now."

"What sort of medley?" Teppei asked warily.

"War ballads, most likely," said the hostess, with a dismissive shrug.

"Why don't you sing something, Tats?" Teppei suggested. "I really don't want to be subjected to a medley of depressing war ballads."

"I'm not really in the mood tonight," Tatsuji said. "You should get up and sing, though, for sure." Just then the kimono-clad hostess returned with a list of songs organized in the Japanese way, by vowels: *a, i, u, e, o.*

*Okay, fine,* Teppei thought. *I'll sing one song, and then we'll go home.* From time to time when he was out drinking, he would suddenly find himself wondering what he was doing in that place. He would be overcome by a sensation of detachment, as though he were an untethered balloon floating through the air, and he would start to feel exceedingly restless and displaced. That's what was happening to him tonight.

Now, as always, it wasn't because he was tired or tipsy. He just felt a soul-deep craving to find a place where he was truly, entirely at home. It gave him a hollow, empty feeling to think that maybe there was no such place, and never would be—not even in the bosom of his family, whom he loved with all his heart. There were times when the almost cosmic feelings of emptiness and loneliness seemed to threaten to suck him into an existential whirlpool. At moments like that, he would usually crack a joke to hide his true emotions.

As Teppei leafed idly through the list of songs, his eye came to rest on one title: "The Foghorn Is Calling Me." It was an old song, circa 1960, made famous by the late actor and singer Keiichiro

Akagi. Teppei had learned the lyrics by osmosis when he was a boy, because a certain university student in the neighborhood used to go around incessantly crooning that song.

"I'll sing this one," Teppei said, and when Tatsuji saw the selection he chuckled derisively. "You're really showing your age, old man," he teased. "Is that blast from the past the kind of thing you like to sing these days?"

"This'll be the first time I've done it as karaoke," Teppei said, ignoring the jibe. "Though I must admit that I've been known to sing it in my bathtub on occasion."

"I doubt whether Misao . . ." Tatsuji began, then quickly stopped and bit his lip before correcting himself. "I mean, I doubt if Sis even knows that song."

"You're right," Teppei said. "She's from the generation that grew up with Western pop songs."

Teppei was acutely aware that Tatsuji found it difficult, unnatural even, to call his current sister-in-law "Sis" in the customary way. The only person Tatsuji had ever been able to address easily as "Sis" was Reiko.

While Teppei didn't appreciate his brother's attitude, he understood it. He had been married to Reiko for only a fraction of the number of years he'd now spent with Misao, but everything he and Reiko did as a couple had been impeccably conventional and proper: the wedding, the reception, the honeymoon, the respectful visits to each other's parents. His early relationship with Misao, by contrast, had been characterized by furtiveness, secrecy, and lies.

Tatsuji had been very attached to Reiko. No, maybe "attached" wasn't the right word. It would be more accurate to say that he admired and looked up to her. Reiko was the old-fashioned type of woman who radiates an aura of quiet, deferential serenity, and Tatsuji had frequently remarked that she seemed to have stepped out of an early novel by Natsume Soseki. He seemed to see Reiko as the embodiment of the womanly ideal, so Teppei was mystified when his younger brother fell in love with Naomi, who didn't resemble the docile, sedate Reiko in any discernible way.

No one who knew Reiko was likely to perceive her as an independent modern woman with a firm grip on the pragmatic realities of life. She had a way of smiling vaguely when other people were talking, and the faraway look in her eyes gave the impression she was off in a private world of her own. She never seemed to react strongly to anything, either way, and her passive equanimity could make other people feel uncomfortable. In retrospect, Teppei thought his first wife might have been one of those women who somehow manages to live her life without ever learning how to communicate effectively. Whether intentionally or inadvertently, Reiko had failed to acquire the basic tools of self-expression, and perhaps that was why she had reacted to Teppei's betrayal with such an extreme gesture.

Just as Teppei had pushed Tatsuji around when they were children, and had spoken to his brother in a deliberately heartless, hurtful way, at some point in his first marriage he began to address the emotionally buttoned-up Reiko in a way that was unkind, if not downright sadistic. Then he fell in love with Misao, and the more deeply they became involved the more repelled he was by the way Reiko clung to her usual placidly graceful demeanor, with no visible changes in her behavior even after she realized what was going on.

Teppei's negative feelings toward Reiko continued up until (and through) the instant in the entryway when he realized that she had committed suicide. His first thought when he saw her hanging from the ceiling was, *Oh, great, now I'm going to have to spend the rest of my life feeling guilty about the way I treated this pathetic woman.* Of course, he was in shock, but at that moment he felt more resentment than sorrow, by far.

In the immediate aftermath of Reiko's death, everyone around Teppei was amazed by how cool and calm he was. Strangely, he was never suddenly overwhelmed by feelings of remorse, nor did he ever think, *I'm entirely to blame for everything.* He kept expecting that guilty-conscience revelation to strike at any moment, but meanwhile he and Misao continued to see each other. Time passed and now, seven years later, entire days went by when Reiko's tragic death didn't cross his mind at all.

Although Misao did have a demure side, she was far more modern than Reiko: perpetually cheerful and exceptionally adept at expressing her feelings, which tended to run very deep. But Teppei was aware that while he saw Misao as an unusually genuine and cosmopolitan woman, she probably appeared quite ordinary and unremarkable to Tatsuji. In addition, Tatsuji clearly still saw his brother's current wife as a woman who had, in effect, murdered Reiko, and no one knew better than Teppei that his brother had taken a deep dislike to Misao from the beginning. It was also obvious that all these years later, Tatsuji still hadn't begun to forgive Teppei.

"Earth to Tepp—you're up! Here's the mic," the hostess said perkily, handing Teppei the portable microphone. The recorded instrumental introduction to the song began to play. Looking away in a blatant display of indifference, Tatsuji lit a cigarette.

Without leaving his seat, Teppei began to sing, keeping his eyes on the page of lyrics on the table in front of him. The balding man abruptly stopped his raucous repartee with the hostesses and fixed his eyes on Teppei. He had a fat, ruddy, oily-looking face—the face, Teppei thought, of someone who might drop dead any moment from a heart attack or a cerebral aneurysm. The man took a big gulp of cognac, then stuck a cigar in his mouth and lit it. He was the type of man who always gave an impression of crudeness and vulgarity, no matter what he was doing. Only the eyes seemed alive in that overstuffed face, glittering ferociously like those of some wild beast monitoring its prey.

Tatsuji, sitting next to Teppei in the padded booth, made an ostentatious show of glancing at his watch. *You little brat*, Teppei thought, but he went on singing without missing a beat. *You think I wouldn't rather be on the way home, too?* It occurred to him, not for the first time, that going out drinking with his resentful younger brother really wasn't enjoyable at all.

The balding man said something to the hostess, then went back to staring at Teppei. The man's fleshy lips wore a knowing smirk, but there was no laughter in his eyes. Teppei's already minimal desire to sing had now evaporated completely, and when he reached the end of the second verse he placed the microphone on the table.

"Wait, what about the third verse?" the hostess asked.

"That's okay, I'm done," Teppei said with a doleful smile. "That song is just too old, and I got sick of singing it about halfway through. Hey, Tats, I don't know about you, but I'm going to hit the road."

"Hang on, I'll just be a minute," Tatsuji said as he stood up and headed toward the restroom. The abandoned karaoke track continued playing until it reached the end of the song. The bald man and the three hostesses applauded halfheartedly.

In the instant before the karaoke machine reverted to background-music mode, a rare silence enveloped the room. Then the shiny-pated man, without removing the cigar from between his teeth, said to no one in particular: "Oddly enough, everyone who sings that song seems to end up dead."

"You shouldn't say such wicked things!" one of the hostesses admonished the man in a low voice—moved, perhaps, by consideration for Teppei's feelings. The stranger's gaze seemed to be fixed on something in the far distance, but after a long beat he turned to catch Teppei's eye and muttered, "Seriously, I've personally known three people who died not too long after singing that song."

Teppei made no response. Every club or bar seemed to have one or two characters like this man, and the best tactic was to ignore them. Just then Tatsuji returned, and the two brothers left the bar together.

"Hey," Teppei said with a laugh as they walked toward the station, "it looks like I'm doomed. That old geezer was saying that everyone who sings the foghorn song ends up dying soon after, as a direct result."

"Really?" Tatsuji's eyes widened in surprise. "That's hard to believe. Maybe he was thinking about Keiichiro Akagi, who died young in an accident on a movie set?"

"I don't know, but when I get home I'm going to ask Misao to scatter some salt on the doorstep, just to be safe," Teppei quipped.

"Huh," Tatsuji snorted. "To me, you always seem like the type of man who wouldn't die even if someone killed you, as the saying goes. I'm sure you'd be immune to a silly curse like that, if such a thing existed." On the surface Tatsuji's words sounded like a compliment, but Teppei thought he detected a needling subtext.

At the station, as they were about to head off to their respective train platforms, Tatsuji said, "One of these days Naomi and I need to stop by and bring you a housewarming gift. It's been too long since I've seen Tamao and, um, Sis."

"It has been a while," Teppei said. "Please feel free to drop by anytime."

"Thanks. We'll do that soon, for sure. Evenings are probably out, though, since Naomi isn't big on graveyards after dark."

Teppei felt like suggesting that spending a night locked inside a cemetery might improve Naomi's attitude, but he managed to suppress that impulse.

Instead, he bid his brother a hasty good-bye, and they went their separate ways.

# 4

When Misao got up that morning and gazed out from the balcony, she saw that the usually deserted graveyard was teeming with families. With all the people running around, it almost looked like one of those hedge mazes sometimes seen at botanical gardens or amusement parks. Children were playing among the rows of neatly laid-out gravestones, and seen from the eighth floor, the legions of long, narrow wooden grave markers simply looked like decorative posts.

It was the day of the vernal equinox, also known as the spring solstice—the official end of winter. The air was pleasantly warm; there was no wind to speak of, and not a cloud in sight. It was perfect weather for a picnic.

No doubt the weather reporter on the midday news would say something formulaic, along the lines of "Today is the first day of spring. The Tokyo area will be blessed with clear and cloudless skies, and city dwellers will no doubt be setting out in droves to pay their respects at memorial parks within the city limits and in the outlying countryside, as well."

*The verbiage never changes,* Misao thought. The terms that the newscasters used for describing fine weather on holidays seemed to be set in stone. Really, she couldn't remember a single time when she had heard one of them use any phrasing other than the predictable "blessed with clear and cloudless skies" or "city dwellers setting out in droves." The TV announcers were inordinately fond of expressions like "frolic among the gravestones," as well. In fairness, though, that was exactly what the people outside Misao's window appeared to be doing at that very moment.

Just as Misao finished hanging the week's accumulated laundry out on the sunny, south-facing balcony to dry, Tamao and Teppei returned from taking Cookie for a walk.

"I only ran a few laps, but look at me—I'm covered with sweat," Teppei said, swiping at the perspiration that gleamed on his forehead. "It's really warm out there. Not just that, but you know the little road in front of the temple? There are so many people coming in from outside that it looks like rush hour on the train platform. We saw lots of folks laying out their lunches on the grass at the entrance to the graveyard, too."

"I guess visiting your ancestors' graves on the first day of spring is the next best thing to a picnic in the park," Misao said. She filled a dish with water for Cookie, then set it on the floor. The dog's pink tongue splashed water in every direction as she began lapping eagerly from the bowl.

Tamao showed her mother a fistful of dandelions that she had picked along the way. The buds were still tightly closed.

"Mama, do you think these dandelions will bloom if I put them in water?"

"They might," Misao said. "It's certainly worth a try."

"Oh goody. I'll go stick them in a cup."

As she watched her little daughter flying toward the kitchen sink, Misao spoke to Teppei with consciously feigned casualness. "Speaking of visiting graves, do you have any thoughts about how we should spend the day?"

"You're talking about Reiko's grave, right?" Teppei asked as he blotted his sweaty neck with a towel.

Misao was relieved to hear her husband address the subject so directly. Taking a cue from his decisive manner, she said lightly, "Well, it has been quite a while," as if she were talking about nothing more fraught than, say, visiting the last resting place of her own grandmother—who had died ages ago, when Misao was only two or three years old. "I remember you were busier than usual at work during the autumn solstice, so we didn't pay a visit then."

"Well, then, shall we go today? Hey, what if we brought lunch? We could join all the picnicking hordes. No, what's the word they use on TV—'droves'?"

"Joining the droves sounds good to me," Misao said with a grin, and Teppei, too, seemed pleased that the decision had been so easily made.

*This is a perfect plan,* Misao thought, still smiling with satisfaction. *If we just keep doing normal things, we'll eventually be able to put the past behind us completely and move ahead with our lives, one step at a time . . .*

Misao and Teppei were acquainted with a couple who had lost their precious three-year-old son when he wandered into the street and was run over by a three-wheeled trash truck. The bereaved parents had lived in a realm of perpetual grief—a literal vale of tears—and to an outside observer they appeared to be in very real danger of dying themselves, from unbearable sadness. The father was so devastated that he wasn't able to bring himself to do any work, while the mother spent every day obsessively praying at the family's Buddhist memorial altar from morning to night. Every month on the anniversary of their son's death, the couple would make a pilgrimage to his grave. This continued until they had another child. After that, their visits to the graveyard dwindled rapidly, until they reached the bare minimum: once a year. In Misao's experience it was almost universally true that with the passage of time, the living feel ever more distant from people who have died. Surely the same thing would happen eventually with Reiko.

"By the way, the occupants of 201 seem to be moving out," Teppei said offhandedly as he romped around the living room with Cookie.

"Really?" Misao was standing in front of the refrigerator, peering at the shelves in search of something she could turn into cold dishes suitable for a picnic. "Some company was using 201 as a business office, right?"

"That's right," Teppei said. "There was a moving truck out in front of the building just now."

"I'll bet there were lots of cardboard boxes—you know, the unsold inventory from the health food products they were peddling."

"Oh right. Yes, there were tons of boxes. Maybe that company went bankrupt because they couldn't sell their products."

"I doubt that. They're probably just moving to a better location. I mean, this place isn't exactly . . ."

This place isn't exactly *what*? Realizing that she wasn't sure how to complete that sentence, Misao quickly closed her mouth. After a moment's reflection she went on, disingenuously, "This location isn't exactly convenient, being a bit outside the city center and so on. I mean, a retail business wouldn't really get any walk-in traffic here." She suddenly remembered the piles of cardboard boxes stored in the basement. Maybe they weren't excess inventory in the normal sense but, rather, had simply been abandoned when the company found a predictably limited market for extra-fattening protein bars and lost interest in trying to sell them. Misao hadn't gone back to the basement since her first visit with Eiko, so she didn't know whether the boxes were still there.

Tamao returned with the dandelions in a cup of water, which she placed near the balcony. "Look, Mama, if I put them here they'll bloom soon, right?"

"Yes, they should, because that spot gets lots of sun."

"So if flowers will bloom here, what about a tree? Would it bear fruit?"

"Sure, I guess that would be a possibility."

"Okay, then, could we grow bananas here by the window?"

"No, I'm afraid it wouldn't work for bananas. They need a warmer climate than this."

"Aw, darn. If we could grow our own bananas here, Pyoko would be really happy. He's always saying that he wants to eat a banana."

*Oh, no, not the dead bird again,* Misao thought impatiently. She shot a significant glance in Teppei's direction, but he appeared to be absorbed in perusing the TV listings in the newspaper. After a moment, he looked up. "Pyoko was a funny little bird, wasn't he?" he said. "I mean, liking bananas so much and all. Hey, how about this? We could pay a visit to Pyoko's grave today, as well, and we can take him a banana."

"Yes! Yes! Let's do that," Tamao enthused, clapping her hands.

When Tamao first mentioned that the dead bird was coming back to life and visiting her in the nursery late at night, Misao had worried that her daughter might be suffering from some kind of mental disturbance. She shared her concern with Teppei, but he dismissed it out of hand, saying, "Come on, it's just a harmless little fantasy. I think it's cute."

Then he launched into one of his outlandish stand-up-comedy riffs: "Look, here's an idea. These days they have medical insurance for pets, and we've been doing the ad campaigns for one of those companies. So maybe we should have invested in an afterlife insurance policy for Pyoko! It could also cover the survivors, in case they need therapy after having nightmares or seeing ghostly apparitions. And the copy could be something like, *We'll watch over you and your beloved pets, even after they're dead.* What do you think? Genius, right?"

Teppei took a dynamic, laissez-faire approach to child-rearing, and Misao often thought that her husband's easygoing attitude made it necessary for her to pay extra attention to the nitty-gritty details.

Having to be the pragmatic one occasionally made her uneasy, and at times she even wondered whether the fact that she wasn't working outside the home might be causing her to fixate on minor matters. She remembered something one of her female friends had said, years before: that when you quit your job and start staying home all day, little things that wouldn't have fazed you in the past begin to bother you, a lot. Maybe her friend had been right. Perhaps she had too much time on her hands, and it had turned her into a chronic worrywart.

Misao thought about the "Who, What, When, Where" game she had delighted in playing when she was a young child. The participants cut paper into small pieces, then wrote a phrase that fell into one of the W categories on each slip. The scraps of paper were then sorted into face-down stacks, and players would pluck one from each category, in order. This often resulted in boringly anodyne sentences—for example, "My friend sneezed last week at school"—but the real fun began when the sequence of phrases, while still grammatically coherent, conjured an outlandish or even outré situation. Misao still recalled one particularly naughty combination: "My teacher was sweeping up a pile of excrement yesterday at the department store."

Remembering the hilarity that had ensued, Misao thought wistfully about how free and imaginative her young mind had been. Maybe filtering her present concerns through the lens of that childish game would help her to laugh off her worries, and let them go. *Tamao was chatting up a storm with a dead bird yesterday in the nursery.* Or how about this: *My hedonistic self-indulgence drove Reiko to hang herself from the rafters seven years ago, in her own entryway, while Teppei and I were enjoying an adulterous romantic getaway.*

Misao shrugged her shoulders as if to dislodge the invisible demons perched there, then forced herself to return to the present. Opening a cold bottle of Calpis, she filled three glasses with the tartly sweet, milky-looking soft drink.

Out in the living room, Teppei turned on the television. Two brassy-voiced women, both speaking in affectedly high-class tones, were discussing an education issue on a daytime talk show.

Cookie padded up to Teppei and sat down expectantly next to the sofa. The animated buzz of people reveling in a day of recreation drifted in through the open doors to the balcony. As she was carrying the cold drinks from the kitchen, Misao glanced at the TV screen and noticed something odd.

The majority of the screen was taken up by the two women, who were both in late middle age. The face of one was covered with fine wrinkles and crowned with what was almost certainly a wig, styled in a jaunty bob. The other woman sported a pair of oversized eyeglasses with lavender frames. Misao had never seen either of them before, but she deduced that they were probably professors at some university.

The talking head with the purple glasses was intoning, "That's why it's important to implement appropriate countermeasures in the home," when a shadow appeared in one corner of the screen. It was a dark, dense shadow, unmistakably shaped like a human being. The shadowy figure seemed to be fidgeting restlessly, in a way wholly unrelated to the action on camera.

Misao went up to the TV set and rubbed the dark patch with one finger. The friction of flesh on glass made a squeaking sound, and she felt a swift jolt of static electricity. She snatched her finger away, and once again examined the screen intently. "It isn't dirt," she said after a moment.

"What isn't dirt?" Teppei asked.

"There seems to be something on the screen. See here? The black spot."

Teppei joined Misao in front of the TV screen. After staring for a minute or two, he said, "You're right. I see it. Maybe something blew out in the cathode ray tube or something." He picked up the remote control and began to cycle through the channels. The humanoid shadow wasn't visible on any other stations, but when

Teppei returned to the original channel, it immediately appeared again. "There must be some kind of static or interference," he declared confidently.

"Hmm, I wonder," Misao said. "Maybe try flicking through the other channels again?"

On Channel One, there was a cooking show. Channel Three was showing a health program that focused on the role of diet in diabetes, while Channel Six had a rerun of a popular singing show. Channel Eight was running an old period drama; Channel Ten featured an art education program; and finally, way over on Channel Twelve, a noisy anime series was in progress. There were no shadows apart from the one on the original station: an image with a featureless face like a silhouette cut out of black paper and a body that suggested a stage actor dressed in black tights and gesturing in an overstated way.

"It doesn't seem to be mechanical," Misao said. "I mean, it's only on this one station." Teppei turned off the television. When the screen went dark, the strange shadow vanished, as well.

"Nah, it must have just been some kind of interference," he said. He switched the TV set on again. The shadow was still there in a corner of the screen, and now it began executing a curious series of calisthenic movements: placing both hands on its knees, then raising its arms to the heavens, and finally bringing its hands down to cradle its head.

Tamao had been watching the TV screen intently the entire time, and now she spoke in a voice that barely rose above a whisper. "It's just like Pyoko said," she breathed.

"Huh?" Misao was disconcerted. "What about Pyoko?"

Tamao cast a quick glance at her mother and then, as if confessing a guilty secret, she said nervously, "It's just like what Pyoko was saying. He told me the other place is full of people like that. They don't have any faces, and their bodies are completely dark and shadowy . . ."

Misao could feel the color draining from her face. She was

seized by an urge to reprimand her daughter for spouting such drivel, and she had to bite her lip to keep the angry words from tumbling out. For an instant, she seemed to see the single white feather she'd found lying next to the telephone floating languidly past her eyes.

An awkward silence filled the air. Teppei switched the TV off again and said, "Okay, no more talk about that. Everyone here is acting a little bit crazy. It's just some interference: nothing more, nothing less. All right? Can we agree on that? Some wires just got crossed somewhere. Lately lots of tall apartment blocks have been going up not too far from here, so it isn't surprising that the broadcast signals would run into some interference from time to time. That's all it was. The picture will be back to normal before you know it."

"But . . ." Misao began, pushing back a lock of hair that had fallen into her eyes. "You have to admit it was kind of strange."

"Hey, anything can happen when you live in an overcrowded city like Tokyo," Teppei said. "The other day one of the guys at work was saying that late one night when he was listening to music on his stereo, a man's voice suddenly came out of the speakers. It turned out that my friend's sound system had picked up a short-wave radio broadcast from a truck that was driving past his house, but he said that he really thought he was losing his mind until he figured out where the disembodied voice was coming from."

"No, I know," Misao said. "You often hear stories about crossed signals or electromagnetic interference and so on. It's just that in this case, I—"

"It was just a temporary glitch," Teppei interrupted. "Shall we try turning it on again, as a test?" Sure enough, when he pointed the remote control at the TV set and hit the on button, there was no sign of the shadow. "There, you see?" he said triumphantly. "Vanished without a trace."

Tamao was stroking Cookie's head, but her eyes were glued to the TV screen. "It went away," she observed.

"That's right," Misao said. "It's gone." Feeling relieved, she went over to where her daughter was standing and took Tamao's two small hands in her own.

"Listen, sweetie," she said quietly. "Could you please tell me exactly what Pyoko was saying to you?"

"It was about all the, um, people," Tamao said. "He just said there were lots and lots of people with no faces, and shadowy bodies. They live in a dark place, and there are bad monsters watching over them, or something."

"I see. And?"

"That's all."

"And those shadowy people, or whatever they are—do you think they look like the dark shape that we saw on the TV screen just now?"

"Uh-huh. Just like that."

"How can you be sure they look like that? Have you ever seen them?"

"No, not really, but . . ."

"But what? Somehow, I'm getting the feeling you *have* seen them."

"Hey, that's enough," Teppei interjected. "It's clearly something from Tamao's dream world, so there's no point in cross-examining her. Would you please just drop it?"

"But—" Misao protested.

"You know, I actually had a similar experience myself, when I was five or six," Teppei said reflectively, lighting up a cigarette. "I was absolutely convinced that there were monsters living in the ceiling. I'm not kidding."

"What kind of monsters were they?" Tamao asked.

"The soft, mushy, icky kind, like amoebas," Teppei replied.

"Uh-mee-ba? What's that?" Tamao cocked her head.

"An amoeba is a kind of living organism that looks a little bit like a drop of pancake syrup. It doesn't have arms, or legs, or a face." Teppei held up his index finger, as if asking for everyone's full attention. "This is how it was," he said with mock solemnity, looking first at Tamao, then Misao. "At night, I used to imagine that while I was sleeping that mushy monster would slowly spread over the ceiling like a giant puddle, and then it would creep down and tickle my face. Here's the thing. In the old days, ceilings were very thin and flimsy, and you could see the grain of the wooden beams through them. So if you stared at the ceiling for long enough, those patterns alone would be enough to give you the willies. Right? For me, it was very easy to imagine that a hideous, grimy blob of a monster might come oozing out of the ceiling. It was such a disturbing thought that every night I had to burrow under the futon, with the quilt covering my head, before I could fall asleep. I tried talking to my mother about the ceiling monsters, but of course she just laughed. I was scared of plenty of other things when I was little, too. For instance, hangers!"

"Hangers?" Tamao sounded puzzled.

"Yes, you know: the long clothes hangers they use for kimonos. There are different kinds, but the ones at my house were bamboo poles, about as long as your arm, with a hook at the top. Anyway, when I used to get up during the night and see one of those hangers in a corner of the hallway, it would frighten me half to death. See, I believed the hangers could move on their own. And I was convinced that very late at night they would get down off the wall and chase after children like me, trying to hit them on the head!"

"You've got to be kidding," Misao said with a chuckle.

"No, it's completely true. Like sometimes a kid gets up in the middle of the night to use the bathroom, right? That's when I would see the hangers in the hall and be certain they were going to come to life. They seemed to have a kind of unearthly glow, too. I would be so petrified that I could only make it to the john if I covered my eyes and ran past the hangers as fast as my legs would carry me."

"And did the hangers run after you, Papa?" Tamao asked with a perfectly straight face. Laughing, Teppei shook his head.

"No, they never chased me, not even once," he said. "But that didn't stop me from thinking they were going to, every time."

Misao had a terrible premonition that from now on Tamao was going to be adding stories about being pursued by demonic clothes hangers to her current repertoire of tales about the chatty bird who returned from the dead on a regular basis, so she said emphatically, "When Papa thought the hangers might come chasing after him, that was all in his imagination. A hanger is just a hanger. There's no way one of them could even move, much less chase anyone. Do you understand, Tamao?"

"Yes, I do," Tamao said, bobbing her head.

"The truth is, I was a huge scaredy-cat when I was a kid," Teppei said, turning to Misao. "People who have very active imaginations tend to be easily frightened. If you let your imagination run wild all over the place, you can end up becoming immersed in a realm of make-believe. There are some hazards to a fantasy-driven approach to life, of course, but it can also be very entertaining—if you don't mind the occasional nightmare! I think that's why I turned out to be such a superbly creative copywriter, if I do say so myself. I've noticed that the people who didn't grow up with a rich fantasy life never seem to be very good at my line of work, no matter how hard they try."

"No, I totally get it," Misao laughed, fondly draping an arm around her husband's shoulders. "That was a very persuasive speech. You're so good at that sort of explanation—I really think you could go on educational television and give lectures. Seriously, you're a natural!"

Teppei smiled and gave Misao's hand an affectionate tap. "Well," he said as he got up from the sofa, "shall we get to work on the picnic prep? I'd like to hit the road while the sun's still high, so we can get back by early evening."

Tamao's face was alight with curiosity. "Picnic? Where are we going?"

"We're going to pay a visit to a grave, and then we'll eat some rice balls in a nearby meadow," Teppei said.

"Whose grave?" Tamao asked.

Without the slightest hesitation, Teppei replied smoothly, "It's a friend of Papa's—someone I used to be close to a long, long time ago."

As he spoke, he caught Misao's eye and gave her a conspiratorial wink. Misao nodded. When her gaze wandered back to the television set a moment later, she saw that the shadow seemed to have reappeared in one corner of the screen, even though the set was turned off. She closed her eyes and told herself, *It's just interference.* She really was worried about Tamao, though, with her crazy stories about conversing with the dead bird. She wondered again whether Tamao's delicate nervous system had somehow been affected by the move and the subsequent death of her pet.

"All righty, then," Misao said brightly. "I guess I'd better go and make the rice balls now." As she headed into the kitchen, she heard Cookie growling. Looking back, Misao saw the dog hunkered down in front of the blank television screen, arching her back like an angry cat.

"Cookie?" Misao called. The dog turned and glanced at her, then let out a single brief yelp and went back to staring at the TV screen as if hypnotized.

"Cookie, come here right now," Misao ordered. Her tone sounded harsher than she intended, and Cookie responded by slinking into the kitchen with her tail wagging weakly and a penitent expression on her face.

Misao knelt down and took Cookie in her arms. "It's all right, girl," she whispered into the velvety ears. "Everything's okay. Everything has to be okay."

# 5

*An afternoon in early spring. A busy thoroughfare in the Ginza district of Tokyo. The sudden, frantic honking of a car horn, followed by the screeching of brakes.*

Jolted abruptly back to awareness, Misao looked around and was startled to realize that she had very nearly stepped into the path of a moving car. If she stretched out her hand, she could have touched the hood of the dark blue minivan that had barely managed to skid to a stop in front of her. The driver of the car was glaring angrily at her through the windshield, his features distorted by fury and indignation.

Glancing up, Misao saw that the pedestrian-crossing light was red. She could hear people behind her murmuring things like "What was she thinking?" and "Whoa, that was close." Her heart was pounding a mile a minute, and her armpits were drenched in sweat. The driver stuck his head out of the side window and shouted, "You stupid idiot!" Misao stared at the ground in embarrassment, unconsciously running her tongue over her parched lips.

It wasn't that she had been lost in thought or fretting about something in particular. No, her mind had simply gone blank. In that nearly fatal instant she wasn't thinking about anything, and although her eyes were open, she wasn't seeing anything, either. She felt as though she'd been sleepwalking, or hypnotized, or in a trance of some sort.

*What just happened?* Misao took a deep breath. True, she hadn't been to the Ginza in ages, but had she really turned into a country bumpkin in the interim, lacking even the most rudimentary urban-survival skills?

When the light turned green, Misao waited until everyone else had surged ahead, then started across the broad boulevard. Two young men who looked like university students glanced back at her from amid the pack of pedestrians and began to snicker. Misao gave them a dirty look. The odd thing, she thought, was that they didn't seem to be reacting to her absentminded behavior; rather, she got the distinct feeling that they were laughing openly at her appearance.

Was there something funny about the way she looked? Once that thought took root in her mind, Misao became consumed by an obsessive desire to figure out what the young men had found so amusing. Maybe she had torn a hole in the back of her jacket along the way.

There was a large department store on the other side of the street, just a few feet from the end of the crosswalk. Misao went through the revolving door and rode the escalator to the ladies' room on the second floor. Inside, a quartet of middle-aged women was monopolizing the mirrors. When Misao walked in, every gaze slid to the door and gave her the once-over. The look in those eyes was undisguisedly appraising and judgmental. Ignoring the women, Misao sauntered over to the only open patch of mirror and looked at her reflection.

She was wearing a black-and-white glen plaid jacket over a pair of fitted black slacks that hugged the curves of her derrière. The back of the jacket was intact, with nary a rip in sight. Her glossy black shoulder-length hair fell in soft waves around her face, and while she could see two or three white hairs, as usual, they were barely noticeable. A partially visible pair of gold earrings gleamed behind the curtain of hair. The anti-aging cream she had been using faithfully every night must have been doing its job, because there were no crow's feet around her eyes. As far as Misao could see, there was nothing unusual or ludicrous about her appearance whatsoever. That was a distinct relief. Maybe the students had just been reacting to her spacey behavior, after all.

The headline of an ad for a woman's magazine she had seen somewhere—"Thirty-two is the peak of womanhood"—drifted across her mind. As it happened, Misao was thirty-two years old, and she would certainly have liked to think of herself as a woman in full bloom. "Start preparing for your later years, strengthen your relationships with mates and friends, try to become your best and most fulfilled self, then add just a dash of love," the copy had gushed. "That's the recipe to make you shine. And now just for you, a woman in her beautiful prime, there's a new magazine!"

*All the women's magazines are basically the same,* Misao thought. *Leaf through any one of them and you'll see that they're either encouraging their readers to pursue an impossibly elevated ideal that bears no resemblance to everyday reality, or else tossing out sensationalistic scraps of other people's trials, tribulations, and triumphs—which, again, have very little in common with most readers' own daily lives.*

Taking her makeup pouch out of her handbag, Misao dabbed on a quick coat of blush. The middle-aged women were still primping in front of the mirrors, and she glanced at them out of the corner of her eye. They appeared to be on their way home from a movie matinee. A couple of them were holding rolled-up pamphlets, and the print was so large that Misao was able to deduce right away that they had been to see a well-known romantic melodrama, which was currently ruling the box office.

"Shall we go have tea somewhere, before we call it a day?" one of the women asked, and her companions all responded in the affirmative. Laughing in a way that sounded shrill and artificial to Misao's ears, the giddy foursome trooped out of the restroom.

When Misao looked down at her wristwatch, she saw that it was three o'clock. She had gone to the Ginza office of a business acquaintance to talk about a possible illustration assignment, but they had gotten to chatting over a cup of coffee and the time had flown by. Misao had left Tamao with Eiko Inoue, promising to return no later than half past three, so if she didn't want to be late she would need to catch the next available train.

The meeting had gone smoothly. The editor Misao met with had been unfazed by the five-year gap in Misao's résumé, and it was encouraging to see that this past connection was likely to yield some freelance commissions. To start, Misao had been asked to provide an illustration for a monthly visual design magazine targeted at women.

If she could just generate a steady stream of small-scale assignments like that, she should easily be able to meet the deadlines, even with her weekdays broken up by having to escort Tamao to and from kindergarten. And now that the preliminary discussions were out of the way, it didn't sound as if she would need to go to the Ginza more than a couple of times a month. In truth, though, Misao would have welcomed an excuse to go into town more often than that. After all, someone who spends her time cooped up at home can end up forgetting the most basic life skills—for example, how to negotiate a big-city crosswalk without nearly getting run over!

Misao passed a telephone booth, and stopped. She thought briefly of giving Teppei a call to let him know she was in the neighborhood, since his agency's main office was in the Ginza area, but then it occurred to her that if he had stepped away from his desk and one of his colleagues were to answer the phone, that could be awkward. After what happened with Reiko, Misao didn't feel that she would ever again be able to face (or talk to) anyone at the office where she, too, had worked.

She decided to ring Eiko Inoue instead. When Eiko lifted the receiver, Misao could hear the euphoric voices of Tamao and Kaori in the background, along with that of a slightly older male child: Kaori's older brother, Tsutomu.

"The kids are having a great time," Eiko said. "Until a while ago they were running around outside and riding the trike in the basement, but now they're playing trains all over our apartment. How's it going on your end?"

"I'm afraid I may be a little bit late," Misao said. "I'm just about to leave the Ginza now." Then she added, with studied casualness, "So, I guess you were down in the basement, too, with the kids?"

"No, I stayed up here to do some vacuuming. Why do you ask?"

"Oh, um, no special reason. I just wondered. Well, I'm going to head for home now. I'll be grateful if you could look after Tamao for a little while longer."

After hanging up, Misao was overcome by a feeling of deep uneasiness verging on displeasure. Eiko Inoue was very loose and easygoing, and her laid-back attitude was an undeniable part of her charm, but to let small children play unattended in a basement—and a basement with no egress apart from an elevator, to boot—while the adult in charge was upstairs? Misao found that kind of behavior impossible to understand.

*That dreadful basement,* she thought anxiously as she walked rapidly toward the train station. *I mean, you never know what could happen. It's the kind of place where a pervert could sneak in from outside and then lie in wait, hidden in the shadows. And to let little kids run around down there, without supervision! There's no way to sugarcoat it: Eiko's approach is simply too careless and relaxed for my taste. And I'm just so creeped out by those absurdly large white storage lockers, lined up so neatly in rows down there. They remind me of something, but I can't quite put my finger on it. Oh, wait, now I know: they look like giant coffins!*

Misao gave an involuntary shiver. For some reason it hadn't struck her until now, but there was something distinctly coffinlike about the storage lockers. Not coffins for human beings; they were much too big for that. No, those lockers looked like containers that had been specially designed to house the remains of some kind of strange, monstrous creatures.

Not long after they moved in, Teppei had gone down to explore the basement. He returned full of praise for the convenience of the storage lockers, but Misao had flatly refused to make use of them, even then. When Teppei asked for an explanation of her negative feelings about the basement, she had found it difficult to express in words.

"Well, for example, what if Tamao somehow ended up playing alone in the basement and there was a power outage?" she'd said after a pause. "It would be pitch-black, and the elevators wouldn't be running, so our daughter would be stuck down there all alone. And who's to say that a child molester might not wander in the front door and find his way to the basement? It's just the kind of place where psychopaths like to lurk, waiting to prey on little girls, and there's no guarantee that someone like that wouldn't just stroll in from outside, take the elevator down to the basement, and wait for his chance. I know that's kind of far-fetched, but stranger things have happened," she concluded lamely.

"Wow," Teppei had laughed. "If you're going to take your fantasies to that level, you may as well start living in fear of all the calamitous things that could happen every day when I go to work. I mean, the possibilities are endless: train wrecks, heart attacks, hit-and-run accidents, earthquakes, high-rise fires . . . and, of course, you never know when some random lunatic might just run up to me on the street and stab me in the back, for no reason!"

In the end, Misao allowed Teppei to have the last word, and she agreed (albeit with undisguised reluctance) that they could utilize the storage locker assigned to their unit: 801. Teppei immediately began hauling things down to the basement—mostly old magazines that might theoretically come in handy someday and empty beer bottles, which could just as well have been tossed in the trash. "This is great," he exulted. "It's unbelievably convenient!" He and Misao each had a key to the locker, but while Teppei made frequent trips to the basement, Misao never joined him unless it was absolutely necessary, and she never went down alone.

When people talk about not getting along, they're usually referring to interpersonal relationships, but as far as Misao was concerned, she and the basement were terminally incompatible. *Maybe there's such a thing as not hitting it off with an inanimate object,* she thought, trying to analyze her reaction. If she was honest with herself, there was no "maybe" about it. She simply hated the basement, for reasons she couldn't explain.

•

Misao got off the train at Takaino Station. After stopping at a nearby supermarket to pick up a few ingredients for the quick, easy dinner she had planned, she walked back to the Central Plaza Mansion. Standing in the hallway in front of the Inoues' unit, 402, she was pleased to hear the sound of children at play inside the apartment. Even as she was breathing a sigh of relief, Misao realized the absurdity of her fantasies, and she very nearly laughed out loud.

*There must be something wrong with me,* she thought. *I mean, seeing those standard-issue storage units as coffins for monsters?!* It was just an ordinary basement, filled with ordinary storage lockers. Children had the ability to enjoy playing in all kinds of places—in a storehouse, inside a car, even in some fetid drainage ditch with mosquito larvae floating around—so it was only natural that they would be drawn to the wide-open spaces of the basement.

Misao rang the bell, and a minute later Eiko opened the door. The entire apartment was filled with the aroma of ripe bananas. The three children came running, and a huge smile spread across Tamao's face, which was flushed pink from all the activity and excitement. "Mama!" she cried. "You're back!"

"Yes, and I'm really glad to be home," Misao said, still hesitating on the doorstep. "Have you been behaving yourself?"

"Yes, I've been very good. And Kaori's mom made us banana juice!"

"Oh, what a treat!"

"Also, you know what? Kaori was saying that . . ."

As Tamao prattled on, Eiko—who was standing just behind her—beckoned to Misao. "Won't you come in for a few minutes?" she asked. "One of the resident managers stopped by a while ago, and we're having ourselves a tea party."

When Misao peeked inside, she saw the female half of the building's team of caretakers. Mitsue Tabata was sitting at the dining table, her lips working furiously in an apparent effort to finish chewing the food in her mouth as quickly as possible before she had to speak.

The Tabatas didn't have any children, and Mitsue paid frequent visits to the Inoues' apartment on a variety of pretexts, perhaps because she had too much time on her hands. Or maybe she had simply taken a shine to Eiko's contagiously ebullient personality.

When Misao walked into the apartment, Mitsue Tabata stood up, hastily wiping her mouth with a napkin. "Well, well, isn't this nice," she said, inclining her head in the requisite bow. The resident manager was probably in her late fifties, but she looked at least ten years older. Her face struck Misao as rather extraordinary: large and squarish, with oversized eyes and a nose and mouth to match. Misao sensed something a trifle malicious about the expression in those big eyes, but it was easy to imagine that when she was younger, people might have flattered this person by telling her that she bore a slight resemblance to the famous French actress Simone Signoret. *Well, maybe*, Misao thought uncharitably. *But only if that gorgeous actress was playing the role of a woman who was transformed into a wicked witch, in some long-forgotten horror movie.*

"So you were out working, Mrs. Kano? That's really admirable," Mitsue Tabata said in an affable tone.

Misao nodded. Tamao was clinging to her, and Misao reached down and gave her daughter's hand a gentle pat.

"So how did your big meeting go?" Eiko asked, as she poured out a cup of coffee for Misao and refilled the other two cups, as well.

"It went fine," Misao said, sliding into a chair. "It looks as if assignments should be coming in on a fairly regular basis, starting next month."

"That's great, isn't it?" Eiko enthused. "It almost makes me feel like doing something, too, although when push comes to shove I'm just a lot of talk and no action. For my type of personality, it's a better fit to run around the house all day yelling at the children, or sit and daydream over glamorous photos in magazines. I guess that's just the way I am."

Eiko sat down at the table, next to Misao, and her face assumed the gleefully conspiratorial expression that precedes a machine-gun blast of gossip. "Hey, did you hear the news? Mrs. Tabata was telling me before you came, but anyway, it looks like this building's going to be turning into a ghost town over the next couple of months."

"A ghost town?" Misao paused with her cup in midair.

"Well, more or less. I mean, for starters, the people in 201 moved out the other day, right? And apparently our neighbor in 401 is going to be leaving in April. This is the real shocker, though: in May, *three* tenants are moving out. Hang on a tick. Which apartments were they again, Mrs. T.?"

"That would be Ms. Harashima in 502, and the Yoshinos in 602, and the Yadas in 701," Mitsue Tabata replied, and her facial expression—avid, yet slightly sheepish—seemed to say, *Look, I can't help it if I hear all the juicy gossip about the residents of this building, and get a kick out of sharing it.* "Ms. Harashima is a hostess at a bar in Shinjuku," she went on, obviously enjoying the attention, "and Mr. and Mrs. Yoshino are both high school teachers. The Yadas are two sisters who live together. They both work as aerobics instructors, and—"

"That's right, those three apartments," Eiko interrupted decisively, as if to wrest the conversational baton from Mitsue's grasp. "So if you add the office in 201, which has already been vacated, and 401, which will be empty in April, the bottom line is that by May, five apartments will be vacant, in addition to the ones that were unoccupied when we moved in. Yikes."

"I forgot to mention that the man in 401 is called Mr. Shoji," Mitsue said. "He does something with yoga and Indian philosophy— what do they call it, meditation? Apparently he's an expert on that sort of thing, and he owns an institute where they offer yoga classes and so on."

When Mitsue stopped talking, Eiko immediately hopped back onto her own train of thought. "So anyway, do you see what that means, bottom line?" she asked dramatically, looking at Misao. "By the end of May the only occupied apartments will be ours and yours—and, of course, the ground-floor unit where the Tabatas live."

"But why would everyone leave en masse like that?" Misao asked.

Eiko lowered her voice, even though Tamao and the other children were now playing in another room and there was no danger of being overheard.

"From what I've heard, every single one of them had a problem with the setting," she said. "I mean, look, this building is more or less surrounded by a graveyard and a crematorium and a temple where funerals are held, right? It's, like, wall-to-wall reminders of death. Why would anyone choose to live in a place like this, long-term, if they had other options?"

"But then why even move here in the first place, if they were just going to turn around and leave after a few months?"

"That's a good question," Mitsue said. "It isn't so surprising with the people who are just renting from month to month, but even the residents who bought their units only a short while ago seem to be wanting to get out as quickly as possible. I guess they're thinking it would be easier to find buyers while the building is still nice and new."

"I see," Misao said, trying to digest the news. She was happy to hear that the Inoues, at least, were planning to stick around, but that didn't keep her from feeling uneasy at the thought of living in a building that wouldn't even be half full. For one thing, without the safety of numbers the remaining residents could be more vulnerable to burglary, and accidents, and so on.

"Good lord, what have we gotten ourselves into?" she said out loud. "At this rate, when we do decide to sell, we won't just be unable to make a profit, we could even end up losing money. Buying a unit in this building is starting to look like a huge mistake."

"Oh, don't worry, before too long a new batch of people will start to move in, and the building will come to life again," Mitsue said reassuringly, as she took a sip of coffee and blinked her exceptionally large eyes. "After all is said and done, this location really is incredibly convenient. Right now this building is kind of a well-kept secret, that's all. As for the surroundings, they're really quite lovely if you can just overlook the graveyard. You may not have heard about this, but somebody was telling me the other day that at one point there was actually a plan to build an underground shopping area between Takaino Station and South Takaino Station— you know, the little station that serves the private railway line?"

Eiko opened her eyes in surprise. "Really? That's news to me. So, what's the scoop?"

"Well, these days the area around the north exit of Takaino Station is a thriving shopping area, but apparently there was a time, many years ago, when the south side of the district was where the action was, and it was even livelier than the north side is now. Add to that the fact that it isn't a very long walk from the main Japan Rail station to South Takaino Station, and some municipal developers evidently decided it would make sense to create an underground road lined with shops to connect the two stations. From what I heard, they figured an underground shopping mall would attract customers from farther downtown, as well, although that could have been wishful thinking."

"Huh." Eiko sounded amazed. "What time frame are we talking about?"

"Well, this is just what my husband heard from the lady proprietor of a bar near the station that's been there forever, but I gathered it was sometime in the 1960s. Maybe 1964 or thereabouts? I'm not sure. Anyhow, they got as far as starting the underground excavation, and then the project was shut down."

"Why? What happened?" Misao asked. Instead of replying, Mitsue burst into mirthless laughter, as if to disguise the fact that she really didn't know very many details.

"I'm just guessing now," Mitsue admitted, "but maybe the loan they got wasn't enough to cover the expenses? Or else maybe the merchants down at the north end were unhappy about the prospect of competition and made such a big fuss that the project was abandoned?"

"So they went to all the trouble of digging an underground hole up to some point between the two stations, and then they filled it back in when the project fell through?" Eiko inquired.

"I'm not too clear about that," Mitsue replied. "It wouldn't be safe to leave a big gaping hole like that, so I imagine it would have been filled in."

"It's a shame it didn't work out," Misao said. "If they had been able to build that underground shopping mall, the land value around here would have shot up, and maybe the temple would have been forced to move the graveyard to another location."

"That's a good point," Mitsue nodded. "Yes, if things had gone differently, this entire area could have been unbelievably prosperous right about now."

"But instead we get to live near an abandoned underground shopping street," Eiko remarked to Misao, twisting her features into an exaggeratedly jocular expression. "There's nobody around except us, and of course there are no underground shops. All that's left is a phantom road to nowhere . . . I mean, if that road really does exist, it could be interesting. You know, like those stories you hear about the sewer system in New York City, where people flush baby alligators down the toilet, and then those creatures somehow survive and grow up to be enormous, and they're all running around under the city streets? I mean, maybe something could be living in that big underground hole! Hey, Tsutomu?" Eiko raised her voice and called out to her son, who was playing nearby. "What was the name of that TV program we were watching the other night? You know, the one where a giant crocodile was chasing people all over the place, like Godzilla or a dinosaur or something?"

"The show was called *Alligator*," Tsutomu said complacently. "That's another name for crocodile, of course. You really didn't know that, Mama?"

"Of course I did," Eiko said. Then she added, laughing, "This kid cracks me up. He's at the stage where his idea of fun is trying to make his mother look like a fool."

Eiko's phrase, "phantom road to nowhere," stayed with Misao, fermenting deep inside her mind like some kind of fetid psychic sediment. Whether or not the urban legends about reptiles running amok belowground were true, the mere idea that the remnants of a subterranean hole might still be in place near this building seemed utterly absurd. At the same time, there was something surreally amusing about the image of a busy shopping area beneath the temple and the cemetery, where merchants would hang their "AMAZING BARGAINS!" banners from a ceiling that was only separated by a thin layer of wood and plaster from the decaying bones of human beings.

After making desultory chitchat, Misao said her good-byes and left the Inoues' apartment with Tamao in tow. Mitsue Tabata was all smiles as she saw them off, but she showed no signs of being ready to leave herself.

Misao and Tamao were in the elevator, going up, when Tamao suddenly exclaimed, "Oh, no!"

"What's wrong?"

"I left something behind! I took off my cardigan, and then I forgot to put it back on again."

"Where did you leave it? At Kaori's house?"

"Uh-uh. In the basement."

"No worries," Misao said. "I'll go down and get it later." She suppressed the words she really wanted to say: *I wish you wouldn't play down there too often . . . or at all.* As Teppei had pointed out more than once, constantly nagging Tamao or giving her too many rules to follow was not the way to go. You had to let children get a few scrapes and bruises, and deal with some unpleasant experiences; that was a natural part of growing up. It was their duty as parents to try to avoid burdening their daughter with a long list of taboos derived from their own fears and concerns.

After settling Tamao on the sofa with a snack and a pile of picture books, Misao returned to the elevator and went down to the basement alone. The children had apparently forgotten to hit the off switch when they left, because the entire space was ablaze with light.

The first thing Misao saw, standing out in the open, was a lone tricycle—Tsutomu's, no doubt—that appeared to have been cast aside. In front of the storage compartment marked "402" there was a stack of newspapers tied up with string, probably put there by Eiko.

Tamao's cardigan—yellow cotton, with a rabbit embroidered on one tiny pocket—lay in a heap next to the bundle of newspapers. As Misao bent down to pick it up, she heard a faint rustling sound from somewhere nearby.

Startled, she straightened up and looked around. All she saw were the innumerable exposed pipes that crisscrossed the ceiling; the neat rows of large, square, white-painted storage compartments; and the mountainous pile of cardboard cartons left behind by the departed occupants of unit 201.

"Hello? Is someone there?" After blurting out those words,

Misao felt a cold shiver of fear for the first time. *I should have kept quiet,* she thought. Hastily, she grabbed Tamao's cardigan, balled it up, and wedged it tightly under one arm. She felt a sudden, unnaturally frigid gust of wind nipping around her ankles. It wasn't the kind of draft you might expect to feel in a basement—that is, a breeze that originated outdoors, where the landscape was still bathed in warm late-afternoon sunlight, then floated through the treetops with their branches heavy with buds, and somehow found its way into the building. This current of air was considerably colder, and it carried a faintly unpleasant odor, too.

Something rustled again, not far away, and Misao felt chilled to the very core of her being. "Must be a mouse," she said, deliberately speaking in a strong, clear voice. She began walking down the row of storage lockers, making her footsteps as noisy as possible and peering inside each locker as she passed. Even if the noises had been made by a mouse, that creature was hardly likely to respond with "Yes! I'm a mouse!" But still . . .

Once again, Misao spoke aloud. "That really isn't acceptable," she said. "I mean, a new building like this shouldn't have a rodent problem already."

There didn't appear to be anything amiss in or around any of the storage compartments, and there was no sign of a mouse, or a cat, or even a spider. Misao had the distinct sensation that the breeze had grown stronger, and she stopped in her tracks. It wasn't so much that the wind had picked up speed in a natural way; rather, it felt as if the ambient air itself was somehow being engulfed or devoured by the chilly draft.

Misao heard a familiar *ga-tonk* sound. Someone on a floor above must have called the elevator back up from the basement.

She looked carefully around her once more, then continued toward the exit. *I'm just being silly,* she thought. *Nothing has happened, so why am I panicking? I mean, come on, even little kids feel safe playing down here.*

When she got to the elevator, the indicator light above the doors showed that it was stopped on the fourth floor. Mitsue Tabata must be on her way home. But after a few minutes, during which the elevator remained on the fourth floor, Misao realized that Mitsue was probably still chatting with Eiko in the hallway while one of them held the elevator doors open.

After a moment, from very far away, there came the sound of liquid—water, perhaps?—falling steadily onto the ground. It was like the inexorable dripping you might hear in some dank underground cavern filled with limestone stalagmites and stalactites.

Misao turned to look behind her, then peered up at the ceiling with its convoluted network of pipes. Perhaps one of them had sprung a leak, or maybe someone had stashed a container of liquid in a storage compartment and it had spilled.

The chilly draft was climbing now, insinuating its way from Misao's ankles up to the small of her back, and she got the uncanny feeling that it had deliberately chosen to wrap itself around her. For a brief instant, she found herself regretting the fact that she was an adult. *If I were a child,* she thought, *it would be perfectly all right for me to let out a long, loud scream right now.*

At long last, the elevator began to move: 3 . . . 2 . . . 1 . . .

Misao opened her mouth with the intention of singing something, to pass the time and dispel her nervousness. However, her mind had suddenly gone blank, just as it had earlier that day in the Ginza, so she settled for humming a wordless tune.

On the elevator panel, "B1" finally lit up and the door slowly slid open. There was something inside the elevator, but for an instant Misao couldn't tell who or what it was, and she let out a small involuntary shriek.

"Oh, Mrs. Kano!" Mitsue Tabata sounded cheery and relaxed. "I didn't know you were down here."

Misao forced her face into a reasonable facsimile of a smile, then said, "Sorry, I was just surprised. I didn't expect anyone to be on the elevator."

"Were you doing something with your storage locker?"

"What? Oh, no, Tamao just left something down here, that's all."

She held out the yellow cardigan, and Mitsue peered at it, beaming. "What darling embroidery," she said. "Did you do that yourself?"

"Oh, gosh, no. Not at all. I bought this at a store . . ." Trailing off, Misao made an effort to summon up another pleasant smile.

Mitsue pointed in the direction of the storage lockers. "I just decided to put on my chef's hat and make some pickled vegetables today, from scratch," she said. "I came down here to get my pickling stone, to put on top. My husband adores *tsukemono*, but even so, he's always teasing me and calling me 'Auntie Pickle.' Of course, he has no idea how much work goes into making the pickled veggies he loves so much."

Misao conjured up yet another polite smile, then stepped into the elevator. For some reason, the innocuous sound of Mitsue's slip-on sandals slapping on the bare floor as she walked away into the basement echoed in Misao's ears for a very long time.

# 6

After Teppei got off the train at Takaino Station, he brushed past a noisy group of people on the platform, evidently on their way home from an evening of celebrating the cherry blossoms. There were five or six men and three women, and they were laughing and squealing and generally raising a ruckus. One of the women, who was obviously several sheets to the wind, appeared to be on the verge of vomiting at any moment. Even so, her pale face wore a broad grin as she stumbled along, drunkenly clutching the arm of one of the young men.

There was a small but renowned grove of cherry trees near South Takaino Station, and Teppei guessed that the rowdy group had gone there for a picnic dinner (featuring copious quantities of alcohol), and then had walked or taken a taxi to Takaino Station. Teppei had recently been invited to a couple of blossom-viewing parties by his colleagues at the advertising agency, but he had begged off because he was swamped with work. Also, there were plenty of cherry trees in bloom near his apartment building, and if he wanted to see them all he had to do was to step out onto the balcony. The trees dotted around the cemetery were at their glorious peak right now, and the abundant greenery created a lush backdrop for the fluffy pink-petaled domes.

Teppei's younger brother, Tatsuji, had dropped by three days earlier with his wife, Naomi, and she'd gone into extravagant rhapsodies over the cherry blossoms. "Oh my god, what an absolutely exquisite view," she sighed, as if she had momentarily forgotten that the beautifully blooming trees were surrounded by tombstones, burial mounds, and grave markers.

*Ha*, Teppei had thought. *If that woman had come to visit us during the bleak, gray winter and saw the view then—nothing but legions of dark, dingy gravestones, with the leafless tree branches lancing the air like crooked needles—she would probably have said something like, "Oh my god, what a dreary view. Why, you half expect a vampire to jump out at any moment!"*

As a housewarming gift, Tatsuji and Naomi had brought a set of linens: a white lace tablecloth, with napkins to match. The cloth was a perfect fit for the dining table, and Misao was delighted.

Teppei strongly believed that his wife's intelligence and tact were the main reasons she was able to maintain a reasonably amicable relationship with her sister-in-law. He often thought that to get along with someone like Naomi you had to be either very clever or else a natural-born coward like Tatsuji. *Oh well*, he thought. *She isn't my problem, so I'm not going to lose sleep over it.*

After passing through the station gate, the majority of people who had gotten off the train with Teppei headed for the north exit and scattered into the night. Even though it was past midnight, the streets around the exit were still garishly aglow with the neon lights of pubs, ramen joints, specialty restaurants, convenience stores, and pachinko parlors. Sidewalk vendors of octopus fritters and *oden* had set up their carts just beyond the train station and were loudly touting their wares, trying to lure the passing inebriates into stopping for a snack on their wobbly way home.

The less popular south exit, by contrast, was quiet, and the rows of small shops had all been shuttered for the night. Only a couple of coffee shops remained open, with their electrified Coca-Cola signs casting a dim, rosy radiance over the nearly deserted street.

Teppei emerged from the south exit into the mild spring night. After pausing briefly to let the sweet, balmy air wash over him, he lit a cigarette and continued on his way. A single taxicab pulled up directly in front of him, and the rear passenger door flew open. A second later a female emerged from the backseat of the cab with such force that it almost appeared as though she'd been hurled from an ejector seat.

The woman was dressed in a blossom-pink kimono, and no sooner had she tumbled out onto the street than she angrily began to kick the side of the taxi with one dainty foot shod in a white wedge-heeled zori. "Get out of here, you jerk!" she shouted. "I never want to see you again!"

The taxi driver stuck his head through the open window and shouted, "You evil wench!" Looking as if he might leap out at any moment, he snarled, "You think you can ride for free and run off without paying?"

Wrenching open a small clutch purse, the woman pulled out some paper currency and tossed it through the window of the cab. "Here you go, you money-grubbing bastard. Are you happy now?"

"Crazy slut," the taxi driver growled, baring his teeth. Opening his door, he came flying out onto the pavement, clutching the woman's money.

It looked as if things were about to get interesting, so Teppei decided to stop and watch the spectacle unfold. His lit cigarette dangled from his mouth, momentarily forgotten. A small crowd of passersby began to gather, forming a spontaneous ring around the combatants.

The woman seemed to draw energy from the growing audience, because she gave a disdainful snort of laughter and said haughtily, "Oh, are you really going to hit a woman now? Stupid jerk!"

The enraged driver glanced around at the onlookers, then let out a loud groan of frustration that sounded more wolflike than human. He was a rather plump man of fifty or so. Apparently he had spilled something oily on his brown slacks at some point, because a yellowish stain on one leg of his trousers was gleaming in the street-light.

"If you want to play it that way, be my guest," the woman taunted. "It would give me great pleasure to call the cops on you." Glaring at the driver, she reached back to tidy the drooping bun at the nape of her neck, then resolutely patted her bangs into place, as if she were a modern-day gladiator preparing for battle. A ripple of titillated laughter ran through the crowd of onlookers.

The cabbie clenched both hands into fists and shook them angrily at the woman. "Damn you!" he roared, wadding up the yen notes the woman had given him and tossing them onto the road. "I don't want your filthy money. Just get the hell out of my sight, you disgusting piece of trash! I should never have stopped for the likes of you."

Fuming, the man marched back to his taxi. He started up the engine with a roar and angrily stomped on the gas pedal. After lurching first back, then forward, the cab took off at top speed, tires screeching on the pavement.

The crowd of rubberneckers dispersed, chuckling among themselves. Grumbling loudly, the woman squatted to pick up the money that was lying on the street. After carefully smoothing out the bills, she stuck them into the lapel of her pink kimono. Teppei, who had been nonchalantly watching the proceedings (while pretending not to), began to walk away. From behind him he heard the woman mutter, to no one in particular, "Bastard!"

As Teppei was entering the deserted shopping arcade, which was bathed in the wintry light of mercury vapor streetlamps, he became aware of the woman's footsteps behind him. At first the cadence of her shoes striking the pavement gave an impression of anger and restlessness, but she must have been gradually calming down, because after a few moments it just sounded like someone trotting along with small, measured steps.

"Hey! You!" the woman called out. There were no other pedestrians in the vicinity, so Teppei slowed his pace and glanced over his shoulder. The woman was galloping toward him with arms akimbo, flapping the wide sleeves of her kimono like a giant bird. When he saw the disjointed way she was running, Teppei realized for the first time how very drunk she was.

As the woman drew closer to where Teppei stood waiting for her to catch up, she began to pant in a loud, theatrical manner. "Oh my god, I'm dying," she wheezed. "I don't exercise enough, so I get out of breath right away. Anyway, hi there! Don't you live in the Central Plaza Mansion?"

"Yes, I do, but . . ." Teppei looked intently at the woman. The truculent expression she had worn during her confrontation with the cab driver had vanished, and in repose her rather sallow face appeared almost eerily sleek and expressionless, as though she had spent a great deal of money on expensive wrinkle creams and anti-aging procedures.

The artificial smoothness of the woman's skin made her age hard to judge, but Teppei thought she might have been about as old as Misao. No, on second glance, she was probably a few years older—maybe even pushing forty.

"Oh, thank goodness." The woman smiled, crinkling her eyes the way a cat does when it yawns. "I noticed you in the crowd, and I knew right away that I'd seen you around the building."

"You live there, too?"

"Yes," the woman said, bobbing her head up and down like a child as she tried to catch her breath. "I'm Ms. Harashima, from apartment 502. Pleased to make your acquaintance." Perhaps she intended to give an elegant formal bow, but because she was so intoxicated her head seemed to loll aimlessly around on its stem like that of a broken doll.

Teppei wondered whether he needed to reciprocate by intro-
ducing himself. After a moment's thought, he decided to remain
silent. He remembered Misao's mentioning that the hostess who
lived on the fifth floor would be moving out in May, so really, what
was the point of pursuing her acquaintance?

"I'm sorry to impose on you," the woman said, "but would it be
all right if we went the rest of the way together? I'm afraid to walk
around this area by myself at night. To be honest, I'm not really a
big fan of graveyards."

"Sure, no problem," Teppei said with a smile. He couldn't believe that a woman who had been prepared to engage in a knock-
down, drag-out fight with a taxi driver in the middle of the street
would be intimidated by a mere cemetery.

"Oh, thank you so much." The woman sighed. "I always take a
cab right up to the entrance to the building, but tonight that stupid
shithead . . ." She spat out the words with undisguised rancor, then
gave an embarrassed laugh and said in a considerably milder tone,
"I mean, I just happened to get into a bit of a tiff with that unspeak-
able ass of a taxi driver."

"Yes, what was going on back there, anyway?"

"Oh, it was just one of those things. I guess the driver was trying
to flirt, or be funny, or something, but anyway he asked how much
I would charge to add him to my 'list of customers,' as he put it.
That really teed me off, so I gave him a piece of my mind. I don't
remember what I said, but right after that he pulled up in front of
the station and told me to get out."

"You showed a lot of spunk, standing up for yourself. It was
really kind of awesome."

"Well, I'm afraid I let my anger get the better of me, but I guess
I came out ahead in the end. I mean, I got a free cab ride out of it,
at least as far as the station. Luckily, I was able to find a handsome
bodyguard to escort me the rest of the way." As the woman staggered along she hooked one arm through Teppei's, and his nostrils

were assailed by an almost unbearably intense aroma of hard liquor mixed with perfume.

"Actually, I've had a pretty disastrous night, all around," the woman went on. "For starters, I got into an argument with someone at the club. Not with a client, with my boss. She isn't even the owner, she's just what they call a 'hired mama,' but she acts like she's the queen of the world. She really is the worst. She's arrogant and overbearing, and—this is something you see a lot in my line of work—she doesn't care about anything except money. She never goes anywhere without her pocket calculator, and she's constantly docking my pay for the most trivial things. And she isn't just greedy. On top of everything else she's a total tightwad, too . . ."

The woman blathered on, badmouthing the "hired mama," and as her agitation increased she clung ever more tightly to Teppei's arm.

"So anyway," she concluded, "that's why I ended up coming home so early tonight. I usually don't get back until two or three in the morning. Oh, sorry, I've been making this all about me. What kind of work do you do? And what in the world made you decide to move into an apartment building that's more or less in the middle of a graveyard?"

"I work in advertising," Teppei said. "And as for why we moved into the building, it's because the price was right."

"I hear you," the woman said. "It's amazingly cheap, that place. What happened in my case is that I got to be, shall we say, friendly with a certain customer at the club, and he bought me a unit there. Well, it would probably be more accurate to say that he bought a unit for himself, as an investment, but anyway, he's letting me live there rent-free, for now."

"How long have you been in the building?"

"I moved in last year, not too long after construction was finished," the woman said. She hiccupped delicately, then went on: "So, I guess it's been six months and a bit? But I'm moving out in May."

"Yes, I gathered that."

"Wait, how did you know?"

"My wife heard about it from one of the resident managers."

"Oh, that gossipy old hag? She's such a pain in the neck. Whenever I run into her, on Sundays or whenever, she always corners me and starts bombarding me with personal questions."

As Teppei and his companion emerged from the shopping arcade, the Central Plaza Mansion was visible in the distance. Casually yet firmly, Teppei extricated his arm from the woman's grasp. They turned onto the narrow road that ran past the temple, where the outstretched branches of the blooming cherry trees sprinkled the path with a constant shower of petals. The unlighted alleyway was so dark and so quiet that they could almost hear each gossamer petal hitting the ground.

"Look, I don't like to be negative," the woman said, "but you folks really ought to . . ." She paused to stifle another hiccup, then continued, "You really ought to move out, too. You have a child, right?"

"Yes, we do," Teppei replied, although "have a child" struck him as a radical understatement. Tamao was a miracle: the priceless jewel he and Misao had created in an attempt to forget the past and get their lives back on track.

"Well, in that case, it's even more important for you to sell up and get out of that place, the sooner the better. I don't mean to spook you, but . . ."

"Wait, why should we move? Because one of the resident managers is a little bit obnoxious?"

"Don't be silly. That has nothing to do with it." The woman licked her lips, then wrapped both arms around her torso and gave herself a hug. "Look, the thing is, the building we live in simply isn't a good place. I don't mean to toot my own horn, but I happen to have a special sensitivity to the spirit world, and that building just gives me a really creepy feeling."

Teppei laughed. "What, did you see a ghost or something? Or maybe some poltergeists dropped by from the graveyard next door?

No, wait, maybe it's more like something from a science-fiction movie. You know, little green aliens from outer space?"

The woman didn't laugh, or even smile. Her face wore an expression of extreme solemnity, although the aura of gravitas was undermined by her ongoing case of the hiccups, which she seemed unable to control. "I'm not saying that I've actually *seen* anything," she said. "It's just that I never feel comfortable in that building, and I haven't been able to settle in. What do they call it—bad vibes? Anyway, that's the way I feel there, all the time. It's hard to explain, but I can never really relax, and my nerves seem to be constantly on edge. Lately those feelings have been getting stronger, and sometimes late at night when I'm alone in the apartment, watching TV or just lying in bed, I get so frightened that I can hardly stand it. You probably think I'm foolish, or insane, but it's completely true. I've never talked to anyone about this, until now. It would be hard to explain without sounding like a crazy person, and they probably wouldn't believe me, in any case."

*She probably had a fight with her patron, and he's tossing her out on her ear,* Teppei thought cynically. Up ahead of them, on the left side of the road, a cluster of wooden grave markers came into sight, gleaming in the moonlight. Once again, Teppei laughed out loud. The things the woman had been saying were utterly outlandish, of course, but it still seemed like rather poor taste to introduce such topics while they were walking alongside a graveyard late at night.

"I imagine we'll be staying for a while," he said. "I mean, sure, if we could save up and move to a better location in the near future, that would be nice. You know, someplace that didn't have a graveyard or a crematorium next door?"

"The sooner the better," the woman said. "Seriously, I mean it. Do you know why I'm so soused right now? It's not because of what went down at work. No, I do this every night. Do you understand what I'm saying? If I were sober, there's no way in hell I could drag myself back to this awful place."

The apartment building, with its glass-walled entry, was now in sight, and Teppei's eyes were irresistibly drawn to the eighth floor. Evidently Misao was still up, because a line of gilded light was seeping out along the entire length of the balcony. In Teppei's mind, that warm glow evoked an image of their new apartment, safe and cozy and filled with the wholesome aroma of sunlight.

A few minutes later, as they stood in front of the elevator, the woman looked up at Teppei with a sour expression on her face. "Oh, one more thing," she said, "I refuse to go down into that nasty basement, ever. Do you use it at all?"

"Well, we've been using it to store a few things, but . . ."

"Wow, really? You must be completely fearless. Color me impressed."

The elevator arrived and they both got in. As she was pressing the button marked "5," the woman said, "There's something weird about that basement." A demure hiccup escaped while she was speaking, and she reflexively clapped one hand over her mouth.

"What do you mean, 'weird'?" Teppei asked.

"Like I said, it's very hard to explain. It's just—I felt it the first time I went down there. Something isn't right."

"Rats? Mice? Spiders?" Teppei said playfully.

"No, don't be silly. It isn't anything *alive*."

"Oh, then it must be goblins. Or maybe zombies?"

"I know you're joking but honestly, you could be right. I really don't have a clue what's down there, and I hope I never find out. All I know for sure is that it's something seriously scary. In this creepy-ass building, that horrible hellhole is the creepiest place of all."

The elevator stopped at the fifth floor and the door opened. "This is the point where I would normally invite you in for a nightcap," the woman said, twisting her head to look back at Teppei as she stepped out into the corridor. "But I guess there's no point in even trying with someone like you who has a wife right here in the building. Thank you very much for everything tonight. You really saved my life."

Teppei raised his hand and gave a small wave. "Good night," he said politely. "I enjoyed our conversation."

He worried for a fleeting moment that the woman might interpret that benign remark as veiled sarcasm, but it seemed unlikely that she would even remember their encounter when she woke up the next morning. The elevator doors closed and the lift continued its ascent.

*She was just a babbling drunk, and all those things she said about the building were nothing more than tasteless jokes,* Teppei told himself. There was no way he was going to share the hostess's kooky theories with his wife; they would only fuel Misao's already strong dislike of the basement and might cause needless alarm. Yet at the same time, even though Ms. Harashima's powers of rational thought had clearly been derailed by alcohol to the point where nearly everything she said was an unhinged fantasy, Teppei couldn't say that he would never consider moving out. But to turn around and sell the apartment right away, when they had barely gotten settled? That would be a complete waste of money, time, and effort.

The elevator stopped at the eighth floor, and the doors slid open. *We've settled in a bright, comfortable space,* Teppei thought as he stepped out. *Things are different now. We're no longer the same people we used to be.*

Suddenly, an old memory popped into his mind. When he was at university, two of his classmates had lucked into an astonishingly low-priced apartment rental. The pair—a close friend of Teppei's and the woman he was living with—knew going in that the previous occupant had committed suicide in the unit, but they were both magnificently rational by nature. So when they discovered that the cupboards were still full of the deceased tenant's tableware, they simply went ahead and used those plates and cups and dishes themselves.

Teppei had visited the couple in that apartment any number of times, and it always struck him as a clean, cheerful, well-lighted place. His friends lived there in perfect harmony, and shortly after graduation they got married.

*That's just the way it is,* Teppei thought, as the memories filled him with feelings of nostalgic tenderness. *We used to get together and play mahjong in that so-called problem apartment, where the previous tenant had hung himself because of unrequited love. No one ever thought about the fact that someone had committed suicide there. We were all too busy having fun, and figuring out how to pay our bills, and obsessing over our own love affairs. We didn't have time to worry about some sad stranger who was dead and gone.*

*Yes,* he told himself, *that's how it is. Fear begets fear, and regret breeds more regret. Once you invite those emotions in, they will flourish in your damaged heart, like a kind of sickness, and you'll start to feel perpetually dissatisfied with your situation, while your life force ebbs away and your mind becomes permanently warped. No regrets, no fear, no guilt, hard work, and a relentlessly positive attitude: That's the recipe for a happy life.*

Arriving at his own front door, Teppei rang the bell. He could hear the musical chime resounding inside, and a moment later the interphone clicked on and Misao's voice said, "Yes?"

"It's me."

There was the sound of a dead bolt clicking open and a security chain being removed, and then Misao's face appeared in the open doorway. She looked as though she might have been asleep. "Welcome home," she said.

Smiling, Teppei stepped over the threshold into the apartment. It smelled like sunshine, and ease. As they built their life there together, day by day, that comfortable, homey aroma was permeating the walls and the ceiling.

"It's really warm out tonight, isn't it?" Misao remarked, looking at Teppei across the dining table, which was strewn with papers and art supplies for her illustration work. "I'll bet we could even open the windows, and it still wouldn't be cold at all." She walked over to the glass door that led to the balcony, and grasped the handle.

Silently, Teppei crept up behind Misao and put his arms around her waist. Misao squealed in surprise, then began to laugh. "What's gotten into you all of a sudden?" she asked.

Teppei nibbled gently at the nape of her neck. "I am Count Dracula, and I have come to make you mine," he intoned in a guttural, melodramatic tone.

Still giggling, Misao extricated one arm from Teppei's embrace. "Hang on a sec," she said. "Just let me open the door first." After fiddling with the handle for a few seconds, she clicked her tongue in irritation. "It won't budge," she said. "I wonder what's wrong."

With both arms still wrapped around his wife from behind, Teppei let out a mock-vampiric snarl—"*Garrrh*"—then continued in his normal voice, "Maybe it just froze in the mesmerizing presence of Count Dracula."

"Please stop fooling around," Misao said, suddenly serious. "I'm not kidding. The door really won't open."

Abruptly, Teppei released Misao and stepped forward. Grabbing the handle with both hands, he pulled as hard as he could. The glass door made a creaking sound and began to move jerkily along the rail. "It's probably just shoddy construction." Teppei sighed. "I'll put some wax on the rails tomorrow."

Exchanging a glance, Teppei and Misao shrugged their shoulders. Then, as though nothing unusual had happened, they stepped out onto the balcony and took a deep breath of the fresh, blossom-scented night air.

# 7

It was early afternoon: time for the junior kindergarten class to go home. As Tamao ran out through the gate, Misao, who was waiting outside, noticed right away that the top of her daughter's head was covered with sand. Tamao's soft, wavy hair was liberally sprinkled with grains of sand all the way down to the curly ends, as well.

Tamao didn't offer a word of explanation, but she seemed to be laughing louder than usual and skipping around with excessive energy. From time to time, when she thought her mother wasn't looking, she would surreptitiously try to brush some of the sand out of her hair.

*Welcome to the group dynamic,* Misao thought with a silent, rueful chuckle. *It looks as if the hazing has already begun.*

No doubt about it: Tamao had been on the receiving end of some mean-spirited teasing. Misao was impressed to see that there were no traces of tears on Tamao's face. *My strong, brave daughter,* she thought proudly.

Misao made no attempt to extract an explanation from Tamao

on the way home. She had decided right away that it would be best to simply wait until Tamao was ready to share what had happened, of her own volition.

After they got home, Tamao began to gobble her lunch—spaghetti doused with ketchup, and a salad of lettuce and tomatoes—with evident relish, but halfway through she suddenly put down her fork and burst out crying in a way that suggested she had been struggling to hold back the tears for a long time. A livid mixture of ketchup mixed with saliva dribbled from her little mouth.

"What's wrong, sweetie? Come on, tell Mama all about it," Misao coaxed.

"Somebody threw sand on me." Tamao sobbed through great gusts of tears. "I was playing in the sandbox, and one of the big boys came along and threw sand on me. And on Kaori, too."

"Was the boy one of the kids from the senior kindergarten class?"

"Uh-huh."

"But why did he only throw sand on you and Kaori?"

"I don't know. He just kept saying 'Graveyard apartment kids, graveyard apartment kids,' and throwing tons of sand all over us."

"Graveyard apartment?"

"Uh-huh. Mama, what does 'graveyard apartment' mean?"

*It's clearly a reference to the fact that someone put an apartment building smack-dab in the middle of a graveyard,* Misao thought, with a sudden rush of anger. The parents of the older boy must have come up with that derogatory phrase; she was certain of that. She could imagine them gossiping around the neighborhood: "Have you seen that new building, right next to the graveyard? I wouldn't be *caught dead* living in a place like that. Ha, ha."

"It's just because we live in a building that's near a cemetery. That's why someone decided to give it that silly kind of nickname," Misao said in a carefully flat, unemotional tone. *There are some really poor excuses for parents out there,* she thought. *The day will come when they'll be needing a graveyard themselves, and it's*

*simply unconscionable that they would teach their small children
to believe a cemetery is something to be discriminated against,
or feared.*

"Our house—this building—is next to a graveyard, right? Most
likely, the boy who was teasing you and Kaori is afraid of graves. I
think what he really wanted to say was that you girls are very brave to
be able to live in a place that seems so scary to him, but he couldn't
put that into words and so he just ended up throwing sand at you
instead. It isn't worth crying about, though. If it happens again, you
should just tell him, 'We aren't afraid of graveyards, at all!'"

"But he threw sand on us!" Tamao said, wiping her tears away
with one hand. "And then Kaori threw a rock at him, and all three
of us got scolded by the teacher."

Misao let out an involuntary chortle, then said soberly, "Listen
to me, Tamao. You need to be tough enough to deal with that kind
of thing. Okay?"

"I hate it," Tamao said, blowing her nose into the tissue her
mother had offered her.

"Hate what?"

"Living near a graveyard."

"Oh, because you were teased about it?"

"Unh-unh. I was already thinking that I hate this place, from
before."

"You're saying you don't like our new home?"

Tamao stopped to think for a moment, then raised her big,
round eyes to her mother and asked, "Do you like it here, Mama?"

"Hmm," Misao said, picking up a fork and beginning to poke at
a piece of tomato Tamao had left on her salad plate. "You know
what? I really *do* like it here. It's quiet, and all the greenery is very
pretty. And when the cherry blossoms are in bloom, we don't have
to make a special flower-viewing trip. Don't you think it's kind of
special that we can just look out our own windows and see lots of
cherry blossoms, without having to ride on a train? Cookie enjoys
living here, for sure, and it's a great place for taking walks."

"That's very true," Tamao acknowledged in a startlingly grown-up manner, nodding her head sagely. "To tell you the truth, I like it here, too. It's much more fun than the place we used to live." She smiled faintly and got up from the dining table. Cookie came flying in from the other room and began eagerly licking the remnants of ketchup and tears from Tamao's fingers.

It was about an hour later when Eiko Inoue turned up with Kaori at her side. The moment Misao opened the door, Eiko stormed in. "Did you hear?" she demanded. "Did Tamao tell you about the sand-throwing incident?" Her face was contorted into an expression of outraged dismay.

"Yes, I did." Misao nodded casually, as if it were no big thing. "I'm really proud of Kaori and Tamao. It sounds like they stood up to a big bully and gave as good as they got."

"Yes, I got that impression, too, but . . ." Eiko flared her tiny nostrils. "I mean, it's just so mean—calling our children 'graveyard apartment kids'! Have you ever heard anything more insulting? I asked Tsutomu about it, and he told me that the boy who was throwing sand spends a lot of time with his grandmother, and she's the one who takes him back and forth to school. Apparently the family has been living in this area for generations. Anyway, it's clear to me that the grandmother is the one who's been running around saying nasty things about our building."

*When all is said and done, it's really just a playground tiff,* Misao thought wearily as Eiko continued her indignant tirade. The bigger the fuss the adults made over the "sand-throwing incident," the more distressing it would be for everyone involved, especially the children. In Misao's opinion, the best way to deal with this sort of thing was just to shrug it off and let it go.

Out in the hallway, there was the *ga-tonk* sound of the elevator stopping on the eighth floor. A moment later, Tsutomu came bouncing through the door of the Kanos' apartment. In one hand he carried the cap gun that was his current favorite toy.

"Did you go off and leave our apartment unlocked again?" Eiko asked in an accusatory tone, glaring at her son. Ignoring the question, Tsutomu smiled self-consciously and mumbled, "I just came to visit Tamao and her mom."

"What are you talking about? Why don't you go play outside? Tamao's mom is busy right now."

"No, it's all right," Misao said. In fact, it wasn't all right at all; she was on deadline and urgently needed to get back to work, but she felt obliged to make a show of being hospitable toward her child's playmates.

"Auntie?" Kaori said, turning to Misao. "Is it okay if we play with Tamao?"

"Yes, that would be lovely," Misao responded.

Eiko looked at her children and said in a tone that brooked no argument, "Okay, but you kids need to go play outdoors. You can't be running around underfoot at somebody else's house."

"Mama, can we take Cookie with us?" Tamao asked.

"Sure, but don't let her off the leash," Misao said. "And while you're playing outside, be sure to tie Cookie up somewhere safe."

"Okay, we'll do that."

The three children trooped off to the elevator, with Cookie frisking at their heels. As the doors closed they waved good-bye to their mothers, who had come out into the hallway to see them off.

"I'm sorry my children are always such a nuisance," Eiko said. "I mean, here I am, too, intruding on your working time, but the thing is, that incident today is making me kind of crazy. I'm so angry I feel like my blood is literally boiling, and I honestly wouldn't be surprised if steam started coming out of my ears. I'd like to see that boy's grandmother and give her a piece of my mind."

"Well, what we've been teaching Tamao is that if you're bullied, you need to respond aggressively. My husband is a big proponent of giving as good as you get. I'm not so sure about that, but I guess it's better than running home in tears every time someone teases you, right?" Misao said with a nervous laugh.

"Now that you mention it, our girls did hold their own," Eiko said with a proud smile. "But anyway," she went on, "because of that incident, lunchtime at our house was a total disaster. Kaori kept squawking nonstop about the mean boy, and Tsutomu was being Mr. Know-It-All, trying to explain what happened even though he really didn't have a clue."

"And I'm guessing you were probably too upset to eat anything yourself?"

"Yes, but now that the children have gone off on their own, I'm going to sit down and have a nice, leisurely cup of coffee. I suppose you need to work?"

"Yes, I'm afraid I do. I need to get this project out the door by the day after tomorrow, and I haven't made a lick of progress," Misao lamented.

"Oh, too bad. I was hoping you could take a break and join me, but I guess we'll have to do it another time. I went out and bought some extra-special coffee beans—they run about two thousand yen for one bag! It's a blend of Blue Mountain and another type . . . I forget the name. Anyway, those beans make the most delicious coffee, and I really want you to try a cup. I'll come up and get you one of these days, when you aren't so busy."

"Thank you! I'd love that."

When Eiko pushed the elevator's call button, Misao noticed that the light above "B1" was illuminated. Surely the kids hadn't gone down to the basement?

Eiko said, "Good luck with your deadline," then added, "When the magazine with your illustration comes out, I'm going to buy a copy!"

"Oh, no, please don't. I'd be embarrassed for you to see it," Misao said automatically, but her eyes were fixed on the indicator panel. "I mean, my illustration won't be anything major, so . . ."

Eiko smiled and waved, then disappeared behind the elevator's closing doors. Left alone, Misao stood in the hallway for a long moment. She was seized by a desire to call the elevator back to the eighth floor and ride it down to the basement, just to check, but she managed to restrain herself. There was no reason to feel uneasy just because "B1" happened to be alight. It wasn't necessarily the children who had taken the elevator down there; it could have been one of the caretakers, or a resident. And so what if it *was* the children? What was the harm in letting them run around in the basement once in a while? When you thought about all the city kids who went out and played on big, busy streets, the basement seemed relatively safe. And besides, they had a clever, sturdy dog along to protect them.

Misao went back into the apartment and locked the door behind her. While she was clearing the dishes off the dining room table, the glass condiment bottle slipped out of her hands and fell to the floor. Ketchup splashed out of the open bottle and flew in all directions, and a puddle of crimson spread over the carpet, surrounded by what looked like drops of blood. Misao grabbed a tissue and began to rub the stains as hard as she could, but the red splotches remained stubbornly vivid. Exasperated, she fetched some all-purpose liquid cleaner from the kitchen and sprinkled it on the spots from above. Then she began to scrub the carpet with a rag, so vigorously that she feared she might end up scouring it all the way down to the pad. Gradually, the bright red stains faded to a pale rose, but the carpet was standing up in stiff bristles and the affected patch looked as though it might never return to its original pristine state.

*This must be what it's like to try to get blood out of a rug,* Misao thought as she positioned a chair on top of the stain, to hide it from view.

Half an hour later, Misao was finally settling back down to work when the telephone rang. No sooner had she picked up the receiver than she heard Eiko on the other end. Her neighbor's voice was very close to a scream.

"Misao? Something happened to Tamao! You have to go there, right away!"

"What? Go where?" Misao felt the floor spinning unsteadily

beneath her, and her heart was beating in her throat. "What—what happened?" she stammered. "Is Tamao okay?"

"You need to go to the basement, right now. From what I can gather, Tamao was injured somehow. Tsutomu's up here with me now, but he won't stop crying and I haven't been able to get all the details. Kaori's still down there, too."

"I'm going right now." Misao slammed down the receiver and flew out the front door. The elevator was on the fourth floor, where it had evidently remained after having brought Tsutomu up from the basement. Misao hit the call button again and again, but the elevator showed no signs of moving, and she concluded that Eiko must be in the process of boarding.

"Come on, hurry up!" Misao urged. She waited impatiently for what felt like a very long time, but the elevator remained on the fourth floor.

Then, abruptly, she remembered the emergency staircase. Why hadn't she thought of that before? The doors to the interior stairwell on each floor only opened from the inside; otherwise, you needed a key. Misao unlocked the door with trembling fingers, then darted into the stairwell.

She didn't even want to think about how long it would take to get to the basement from the eighth floor; she just plunged headlong down the stairs. About halfway there, one of her sandals fell off, but she didn't stop to retrieve it. As she ran, she chanted, "Don't fall down, don't fall down," over and over, like a mantra. If she took a tumble and sprained her ankle, or worse, what would become of Tamao?

Misao was approaching the first-floor landing when she suddenly remembered that, for reasons known only to the builders, the emergency stairs didn't go all the way to the basement. The only way to get there was via the elevator.

Panting, Misao emerged into the lobby. There wasn't a soul in sight, and the indicator light above the elevator was still stuck on "4." Perhaps it was out of order—but why now, of all times?

Making both hands into fists, Misao pounded loudly on the door to the caretakers' apartment. After a moment Sueo Tabata opened the door a crack and peeked out. He was holding a skewer of rice dumplings dripping with soy sauce in one hand, and had obviously been about to take a bite.

"The elevator isn't working!" Misao shouted, then added, "Call an ambulance, please! I need help!" She was almost out of her mind with worry. Continuing to jabber hysterically, not even knowing what she was saying, she grabbed Sueo's arm and pulled him out into the lobby.

"What's going on?" Sueo's wife, Mitsue, called as she came running from the interior of the apartment.

"It's Tamao," Misao said frantically. "She's trapped in the basement, and they're saying she's been injured or something!"

The Tabatas scurried to the elevator, both shouting incoherently. They took turns punching the button, but the indicator light remained stuck on the fourth floor. "What kind of building is this?" Mitsue wailed. "Why do the stairs end on the first floor instead of going all the way to the basement?"

"Go call the ambulance!" Sueo barked. Mitsue ran back into their apartment in a dither. At that moment there was the sound of footsteps, and Eiko and Tsutomu came tumbling out of the door to the emergency stairs. When Eiko caught sight of Misao she yelled through lips that were visibly quivering: "We couldn't get the elevator to move—it's still stuck up on the fourth floor! It stopped working right after Tsutomu rode up to tell me about Tamao!"

Seeing someone who seemed to be even more wildly distressed than she was helped Misao return to her own senses, to some degree. Taking Tsutomu's hand, she said in the calmest tone she could muster, "Please try to think, okay? Where did Tamao get hurt?"

"On her leg," Tsutomu replied. He was clearly frightened, and there were tears in the corners of his eyes. "Something cut her leg."

"What do you mean 'something'?" Eiko bellowed.

"I don't know what it was," Tsutomu said defensively. His face flushed scarlet as he glared at his mother. "There wasn't anything sharp around, but Tamao got a cut on her leg."

"And then what happened? Was Tamao crying?" Misao asked. *If he says she wasn't crying, I don't know what I'll do,* she thought. *Crying would at least mean that she was conscious, and not too badly injured.*

Tsutomu nodded.

"So she was crying?" Misao pressed, desperate for details.

Tsutomu nodded again, then burst into noisy tears. He clearly felt he was being unjustly rebuked by the grown-ups despite the fact that he was only the messenger and hadn't even witnessed the accident.

Sueo Tabata was hammering on the elevator button with one fist. The mechanism made a clacking noise at every blow, but there was no other response. "This is hopeless," Sueo said hoarsely. "We need to call the repair place right away, and ask them to send somebody."

"What? We don't have time for that!" Eiko exploded. "There's an injured child lying in the basement, and we need to get to her as quickly as possible. My Kaori is stranded down there, too."

*Please, please, please,* Misao prayed silently, placing one hand on her heaving chest. *Just keep Tamao alive until we get there.*

"This is a mess. This is a such a horrible mess," Eiko muttered over and over as she wandered helplessly around the lobby, wringing her hands.

"Well, anyhow, okay," Sueo said vaguely, then went into his apartment to phone the elevator service center.

A few minutes later a middle-aged man with a goodly amount of facial hair entered the lobby through the big glass door. Noticing the general uproar, he asked, "Is something the matter?" in a quiet, reserved manner.

Mitsue rushed up to him and said in a shrill voice, "Oh, Mr. Shoji! Apparently there's a child down in the basement who's been injured somehow, and we can't get the elevator to move at all."

The new arrival—Mr. Shoji—was carrying a large manila envelope. He set it down on the floor and approached the elevator. After
pressing the up and down buttons, to no avail, he placed one ear
against the metal door and closed his eyes.

"Can you tell what's wrong?" Misao asked the new arrival. She
knew he wasn't an elevator technician, but while she was skeptical
about a layperson's ability to get the machinery running again,
something about the man's body language kindled a small flame
of hope in her turbulent mind. He was startlingly serene, and his
quietly confident aura seemed to make the people around him feel
calmer, as well.

"This may sound odd," Mr. Shoji said quietly, "but I'm getting
the sense that it isn't a mechanical malfunction, at all."

"Well, then, what is it?" Eiko demanded, shouting again. "What
caused the breakdown? Oh, never mind that—just hurry up and
do something!"

"Please don't make such a fuss," Mr. Shoji said. "It should start
running again any minute now. I just need you to pipe down while
I see what I can do."

Everyone who was gathered around exchanged meaningful
glances. *What's with this guy, anyway?* their eyes seemed to be
saying. *Is he off his rocker, or what? But he somehow seems to
know what he's doing, so maybe . . .*

Mr. Shoji stood stiffly at attention in front of the elevator. Lightly
placing both hands on the door, he closed his eyes again and began
to repeat some incomprehensible syllables under his breath. The
chant wasn't a Buddhist sutra, and it wasn't in a foreign language
that any of the listeners recognized, either. No one in the group
had ever heard such sounds before.

Mr. Shoji was in mid-chant when Eiko broke the silence, shrieking, "What do you think you're playing at? There's no time to be
wasting on this kind of New Age nonsense!"

"Shush!" Mr. Shoji hissed, without raising his voice. Eiko closed
her mouth, and a moment later something astonishing happened.

From far away they heard the familiar *ga-tonk*, and then the elevator began to descend from the fourth floor: 4 . . . 3 . . . 2 . . .

Eiko, Tsutomu, and the Tabatas began to whoop and holler, while Misao breathed an audible sigh of relief. In the far distance an ambulance's siren could be heard—faintly at first, then gradually louder.

Mr. Shoji, his face suddenly haggard with exhaustion, picked up the envelope he had left on the floor and walked toward the stairwell. He was the only one who didn't pile in when the elevator came to a stop on the first floor.

The moment the elevator doors opened on the basement level, Misao charged out. The sound of a child crying—no, the sound of two different children crying—was echoing off the walls. Cookie's rapidly wagging tail was visible in the shadow of the storage closet farthest from the elevator.

Kaori must have heard the approaching footsteps because she came hurtling out of the darkness, calling, "Mama! Mama!" Eiko swept Kaori into her arms and held her tightly.

Cookie peeked out from the shadows with eyes that were oddly still and expressionless, but seemed to have a glint of madness, too. The dog shot a glance in Misao's direction, then went back to staring at whatever had been mesmerizing her before the crowd arrived.

"Tamao! Are you okay?" Misao found Tamao sitting up in the shadows next to the storage locker. Her face was shockingly pale, and from time to time a weak, whimpering sob escaped from her mouth. It was the same way she cried whenever Teppei got angry and scolded her, but in this case she was in genuine physical pain. One of her legs was covered with blood from the knee down.

Eiko and Mitsue both let out small screams. Misao was shaking all over as she squatted down and hugged Tamao, then looked more closely at the wound. Tamao's right knee was split open, and blood was spurting out in a steady stream. It looked as if she had fallen down in a puddle of blood.

"The ambulance is here!" Sueo Tabata announced from the other side of the room. "Come on, she's right over there."

Three emergency medical technicians wearing white uniforms and surgical masks loped across the basement, carrying a stretcher. One of them did a quick examination of Tamao's wound, then turned to Misao and said, "This injury isn't as serious as it looks, so there's no need to worry. Your daughter should be fine."

"But there's so much blood," Misao said.

"As I said, there's nothing to worry about," the EMT reiterated, through his white mask. "How on earth did she get this cut on her knee, though?"

Misao shook her head. "I have no idea," she said.

The ambulance attendants scooped up Tamao's little body—which, to Misao's dismay, looked like one of those broken dolls you sometimes see discarded in a public trash can—and deposited her gently on the stretcher. Misao suddenly felt weak and woozy, and Eiko had the presence of mind to reach out and prop her up. "I'll go with you to the hospital," Eiko said.

"Thanks, but there's no need," Misao replied. "We'll be fine by ourselves."

Misao was following close behind the stretcher that bore her injured daughter when something made her pause and look over her shoulder. She could see the back of Cookie's head, and she noticed that the dog's attention was focused on a spot on the back wall, near where Tamao had collapsed.

It struck Misao as peculiar that a sociable dog like Cookie would be oblivious to all the noise and activity in the basement, but apparently there was something even more interesting beyond that wall. Maybe a mouse, or a cat? Misao shrugged, then turned and ran to the elevator.

# 8

Teppei was absentmindedly watching Misao administer (or rather, attempt to administer) Tamao's after-dinner dose of medicine, but he was thinking about his daughter's injury.

As the ambulance attendant had predicted, the wound wasn't as serious as the volume of blood might have suggested. The chief of medicine at the nearby surgical hospital to which Tamao was transported had carefully stitched up the cut and prescribed the appropriate medications, while declaring confidently that it wouldn't be necessary for the patient to remain at the hospital overnight. Nevertheless, Tamao was clearly in a great deal of pain. She cried nonstop through the entire process, and her parents were greatly relieved when her normal, healthy color returned the following day.

The doctor told Teppei and Misao that there was no need to worry about infection, and assured them that as long as they gave Tamao the prescribed meds on schedule, fed her nutritious meals, and made sure the affected leg was kept immobile, she should recover completely in ten days or so. After this healing period Tamao would be ready to go back to kindergarten, and any scarring should be minimal. In fact, as Tamao grew, the scar on her knee might very well disappear entirely.

So there was really nothing to fret about—at least, not where Tamao was concerned. However . . .

"Ooh, yuck!" Tamao said. Misao had been trying to force the foul-tasting liquid medicine down her daughter's throat, and when Tamao involuntarily swallowed it, tears sprang to her eyes and she stuck out her tongue in disgust.

"Unfortunately, there's no such thing as medicine that tastes like candy," Misao said with a strained expression. That wasn't true, of course, but Tamao accepted her mother's white lie at face value. "If you don't take this medicine like a good girl, germs could get into your cut and it might get infected. Then it wouldn't get better, and it would start to hurt again, too. We don't want that to happen, do we?"

"What kind of germs?" Tamao asked.

"Germs that would make the cut on your leg feel sore and painful. Then the bacteria—the germs—might spread through the rest of your body, and you could end up running a fever and having a really bad tummyache, among other things."

"Would I not be able to walk, then?"

"That's certainly a possibility. Wouldn't that be awful? That's why you need to be patient right now, and keep taking your medicine."

"I just want to play," Tamao moaned.

"I know, and you can play as much as you want just as soon as you get better. You'll be able to start going to kindergarten every day, too."

"But the medicine tastes yucky, and I hate the way it feels in my mouth."

"I know, sweetie. You only have to hang in there a while longer."

Tamao was sitting on the living room couch, nervously jiggling her uninjured left leg up and down. "Damn it to hell!" she blurted out.

Misao grimaced. "Who taught you that? Where did you hear it?"

"Oh, Tsutomu says it all the time: 'Damn it to hell.' Kaori says it, too."

Misao shrugged and looked at Teppei with an expression that was meant to convey, A *little help here, please?* But Teppei's thoughts were elsewhere, and he didn't meet her eyes.

There was something he just couldn't wrap his mind around. Three days earlier, when he got the phone call saying that Tamao had been injured, he had immediately left the office and rushed to the private surgical hospital where she was being treated. As soon as he arrived at the examination room, Misao went to a nearby restroom to try to wash the worst of the blood out of the clothes Tamao had been wearing.

Teppei had thought of a number of questions on his way to the hospital. "Is it safe to assume that my daughter's cut was caused by a foreign object?" he asked the doctor right away. "Maybe there was something sharp in one of the storage lockers, and it somehow came into contact with her leg?"

"Strictly speaking, I can't really endorse that theory, Mr. Kano," the handsome doctor responded, with a faintly smug smile. He didn't appear to be much older than forty, and the professional gravitas conferred by his white coat was the only thing that kept him from looking like a libidinous lounge lizard.

"What do you mean by that?" Teppei asked.

The doctor turned his face, with its remarkably rosy, lustrous cheeks, toward Teppei. "If we consider the circumstances, there are a few things that might have caused a laceration this deep," he said briskly. "It would have had to be something very sharp—for example, an old kitchen knife, or a sharp-edged piece of stainless steel. However, even if a static object like that had chanced to graze the skin, it wouldn't have caused this type of gaping wound."

Reluctantly, Teppei raised a troubling question: "Do you suppose the children might have gotten into a fight, among themselves?" If that turned out to be the explanation, dealing with the Inoue family could become very awkward in the future.

The doctor just smiled again and said, "No, that doesn't appear to be what happened. Your wife was asking the same thing, though."

"Then what *did* happen?"

"Well, it's an unusual case, but this is what I'm thinking right now," the doctor began slowly, reflectively rubbing the back of his neck. "It might be what we call a weasel slash: that is, a flesh wound caused by contact with some type of sharp object propelled through the air by a sudden gust of wind. The scientific term for the phenomenon is 'atmospheric vacuum,' and it occurs fairly often in the mountains when people are out skiing or hiking or whatever."

"'Weasel slash'? So you're saying that something can just come along and slice someone's leg open for no reason, out of the blue?"

"No, I didn't say 'for no reason.' As you know, around this time of year, in early spring, it isn't unusual for a sudden burst of wind—weasel wind, if you will—to crop up in a matter of minutes, almost like a miniature tornado. That gust can pick up a rock or a jagged piece of wood, and if someone's extremities chance to be in the path of the sharp-edged flying object, that person might conceivably get slashed and sustain a wound like this. The fact is, something of the sort happened to my older sister, many years ago. Her leg—or rather her ankle, to be precise—was sliced open in the blink of an eye. It was really something to see."

"You don't say," Teppei mumbled. "So I guess we just have to look at this injury as a freak accident, and chalk it up to being in the wrong place at the wrong time?"

The doctor looked thoughtful. "The only hole in the theory I mentioned is that the kind of wind that could cause a weasel slash doesn't usually develop indoors in a closed space. Are you absolutely certain your daughter was inside the entire time?"

"From what I heard, she and her friends were playing down in the basement of our building."

"Even so, I'm very nearly positive that the injury must have hap-pened outdoors. It's possible your daughter didn't notice it at the time. Then, after the children went inside to play in the basement, the cut began to bleed profusely, and that's when she finally real-ized she was injured. That makes sense to me."

"But wouldn't someone notice such a deep cut right away?"

"Not necessarily," the doctor said. His supercilious smile seemed to say, *Don't worry, you aren't the first ignorant parent I've had to explain this to.* "Children have an extraordinary ability to keep on playing obliviously through pain or fever," he went on. "You'd be amazed. I once had a patient, a five-year-old boy, who fell off the slide at a playground and broke a bone in his leg. It was a clean fracture, but he picked himself up and continued to run around on the damaged limb for the next few minutes, as if nothing was wrong."

Teppei wasn't satisfied with the doctor's answers to his ques-tions, by any means, but a moment later Misao came back into the exam room, so he didn't pursue the conversation.

After he and Misao had taken Tamao home in a taxi and put her to bed, Teppei decided to take a look around the basement. Evi-dently someone else had already been down there—probably one or both of the caretakers, although it could have been Eiko Inoue—because the entire floor had been mopped, and no traces of Tamao's blood remained. Teppei might not have been able to locate the site of the accident (or of its aftermath, if you subscribed to the doctor's delayed-reaction theory) if Misao hadn't spoken of finding their daughter next to an unused storage locker at the rear of the basement. That gave Teppei an idea of where to look, and when he noticed some extra-large puddles of mop water in the im-mediate area, he was certain he'd found the place. He stood there for a long moment, gazing around.

All the storage compartments were padlocked, and there was no way to open them without a key. Teppei tried running his hand along the outside edges of the closest storage locker. If someone was racing around the basement and accidentally crashed into one of the lockers, that person might conceivably sustain an injury that broke the skin. However, it was still difficult to imagine a scenario in which a small child collided headfirst with a locker and only sustained a cut on one knee.

Teppei went over to his own storage compartment, unlocked it, and carried one of the old chairs to the back of the basement. He clambered up onto the seat and surveyed the area, but the only thing atop the tidy rows of storage lockers was several months' worth of dust. Teppei didn't see anything that could have made a scratch on a human being, much less opened up a flesh wound.

From his elevated vantage point, he did spy Tsutomu Inoue's ancient tricycle. It was lying on its side in one of the corridors between the lockers, and Teppei got down off the chair and went over to examine it. There wasn't a single bit of bent or broken-off metal on the tricycle, and he couldn't find any dried blood, either. *So I guess it wasn't the attack of the killer tricycle,* he thought self-mockingly. *But what else could it have been?*

Sharp objects, sharp objects: maybe something like a worn-out straight razor that someone had carelessly tossed out, or a pocket-knife, or a kitchen utensil? Teppei didn't find anything of the sort. Apart from the furniture and other items locked away in the storage compartments, the only things lying around the basement were a few bundles of old newspapers and a pile of cardboard boxes containing some kind of dubious "health food," left behind when the corporate occupants of 201 moved out. Evidently no one had ever bothered to come back for those boxes.

It occurred to Teppei that a shard of glass might have been lurking unnoticed on the floor, but he made a complete circuit of the basement with his eyes peeled and didn't see a speck of glass. There was no sign that any of the fluorescent overhead lights had been cracked or broken, and all the serpentine pipes on the ceiling appeared to be intact, as well.

In the end, Teppei concluded that it was probably just as the doctor had surmised. The children had been running around outdoors and, by chance, Tamao had been in the path of a sudden, coruscating surge of wind laden with sharp pebbles (or something), but she didn't notice the so-called weasel slash on her knee until after she and her friends had gone to play in the basement.

Later, Teppei and Misao were able to piece together what had happened by cross-referencing Tamao's version of events with the accounts of Tsutomu and Kaori, who had also been on hand. At the time of the accident—or at least, at the point when Tamao collapsed near the back wall—the three children had been playing by themselves in different parts of the basement.

Tsutomu had been roaring around on his old tricycle, while Kaori was leading Cookie on the leash, pretending they were out for a walk. As for Tamao, she was using Tsutomu's plastic toy pistol to knock on the doors of the storage lockers, one by one, in an impromptu variation on the popular Japanese game of "Knock-Knock Tag," in which children march around calling out, "Hello, is anybody home?" the way adults do when they pay unannounced visits.

Since they were all engaged in solitary pursuits, nobody was watching Tamao when she sustained the injury—or, in keeping with the doctor's theory, when she finally realized she was bleeding. The odd thing was that the injured party herself kept insisting that she had no idea what caused the cut on her knee, or when the accident took place. According to Tamao, she was playing at the back of the basement when she suddenly felt cold all over. She happened to glance down and saw blood gushing out of her knee. The wound hadn't yet begun to hurt, so the pain must have kicked in a couple of minutes later.

As Tamao stood there, completely befuddled, Cookie bounded up to the wall with a great burst of energy. Kaori was flustered because the leash had just been ripped out of her hands, and she came running after the dog. Cookie proceeded to go berserk, growling and barking and jumping around as if she'd taken leave of her senses.

Tsutomu arrived on the scene a minute later. He and Kaori were both so unnerved by the dog's bizarre behavior that, in his words, "We thought maybe Cookie was sick or crazy or something." The Inoue children had been actively afraid that the dog might attack them, so in his role as a protective big brother, Tsutomu put his arms around Kaori and held her close. After a minute Tsutomu looked around to make sure Tamao was safe, and that was when he noticed her sitting on the floor nearby, covered with blood and wearing a dazed expression.

Tamao must have begun to feel the pain right about then, because she started to bawl at the top of her lungs. Galvanized into action, Tsutomu ran over to the elevator, hopped on, and rushed upstairs to tell his mother.

In his quest for the truth, Teppei had also questioned Eiko Inoue and both the Tabatas, but they'd been unable to cast any light on the mystery of what had caused Tamao's injury. Tamao herself remembered almost nothing, and there was no one else to talk to.

Teppei didn't think there was any chance that the children were lying when they claimed to have been in the basement the entire time. If they had been playing outdoors, there would have been no reason to conceal that information, but they were all adamant about the fact that they hadn't set foot outside on that particular afternoon.

*There's something weird about this building.* Teppei kept remembering his unsettling conversation with the bar hostess who lived on the fifth floor, on that balmy cherry-blossom night when they'd walked home from the station together. Although he didn't recall her exact words, he knew she had said something like, "I can't understand why anyone would want to use that horrible basement. You couldn't pay me to go down there. I don't mean to spook you, but you really ought to sell your apartment and move away from here as soon as you can . . ."

*That was just the booze talking*, Teppei assured himself as he returned his attention to the newspaper he had been holding during this lengthy reverie. *Why am I even thinking about such things?*

He firmly believed that everything in life could be explained away as happenstance. Tamao's accident was simply a freakish confluence of unusual coincidences. True, the doctor did say it was unlikely that a weasel wind could develop indoors, but if that wasn't what happened, then what did? Did the air itself somehow become sentient and three-dimensional, and slice Tamao's knee to ribbons with malicious intent? That was absurd, of course. No, there had to be a reasonable scientific explanation. Maybe some kind of atmospheric aberration, like a chance convection of incoming air, had created a powerful vortex. The air in the basement was always still and stagnant, so some other air must have flowed in from outside and created that curious phenomenon, just for a few minutes. Yes, that must be how it went down . . .

Misao, meanwhile, seemed to have bought into the doctor's explanation that the injury was caused by a sudden, shard-laden wind that had kicked up out of nowhere. Or rather, she was making a concerted effort to believe the "weasel slash" theory. As for Teppei, he had no desire to beat that particular dead horse anymore. The important thing was that Tamao was safe; there was no need to obsess about what had caused her injury. It was just one of those things where no matter how long and hard you thought about it, you would never be able to reach a satisfactory conclusion.

"Honey?" Misao said as she emerged from the kitchen, and Teppei lowered his newspaper in response. Tamao was still sitting on the sofa with her leg propped up, watching a cartoon on TV. Keeping a maternal eye on Tamao, Misao walked over to where Teppei was sitting.

"Listen," she said quietly, "don't you think we ought to drop in on Mr. Shoji, to say thanks and let him know how Tamao is doing?" Her tone sounded slightly on edge or, at best, businesslike. Either way, Teppei thought it was probably just because she was tired.

"Do you really think that's necessary?" he asked. "Besides, he's probably moved away by now."

"No, he's definitely still around. I was on the balcony this afternoon and I saw him going out. I haven't run into him since the day of the accident, and it's been bothering me that we haven't at least gone down to pay our respects."

"'Pay our respects'? What could we possibly say to him? I mean, are you proposing that we drop in and say something like, 'Thank you very much for magically getting the elevator to move the other day'? You can't be serious. That would be like bowing down to some divine being with supernatural powers."

"You can laugh, but it really did seem like magic at the time. Eiko said the same thing. Mr. Shoji laid both his hands on the elevator doors and chanted something, and a few seconds later the elevator started to move. I wish you could have been there. I swear, everyone was speechless with astonishment."

"It was just coincidence," Teppei said shortly. He was starting to get a bit annoyed. What was it with everybody these days (though if he was honest he had to include himself, as well), thinking and talking about weird supernatural stuff all the time? They were like a gaggle of elementary school students sitting around the campfire on an overnight field trip, squealing with terror over spurious tales of ghosts and monsters. "It was coincidence," he said again. "The elevator had some kind of temporary electrical glitch, and it just happened to straighten itself out at that exact moment."

"Hmm. I wonder."

"There's nothing to wonder about. I'm telling you, that's what happened. Apparently your Mr. Shoji is just some kind of tiresome meditation teacher or something, trying to cash in on the human appetite for pseudo-spiritual baloney. He probably sized up the situation and saw it as a chance to impress some potential customers by showing off his so-called skills. I mean, a lot of people seem to be susceptible to that kind of con artist these days. And then before long he starts bragging about seeing apparitions and communicating with spirits beyond the grave. Charlatans like that are only ever interested in the 'other side': which is to say, in something that exists only in people's wishful imaginations. In reality, the dead are just that—dead—and it's simple consideration toward those who have passed on to accept that fact. All that matters is the here, and the now, and the people who are still alive."

"I know, I know," Misao said. Her words carried a complex undertone: gentle, but also subtly reproving. "I understand what you're trying to say, I really do. We've both come this far believing that this is all there is, and what matters is the here and now. That . . . thing that happened a long time ago . . ."

Teppei nodded quietly, then took a long, deep breath as if in preparation for what he had to say next. "As long as you understand where I'm coming from, that's all I need," he said gently. "You know me—I'm a rationalist at heart, and I'm simply not willing to acknowledge the possibility that a supernatural realm might exist. It's just absurd to imagine that there's a crowd of dead people and their ilk milling around on some other plane. I mean, let's face it: life is complicated enough when you only have to deal with the living."

Nodding in agreement, Misao rubbed abstractedly at a spot on the dining table. "Quite aside from that, on a human level, I still think it would be rude to just let Mr. Shoji move away without saying a word of thanks," she persisted. "I mean, we dragged him into our emergency situation the other day, and he did his best to help out."

"So you intend to go down there and pay your respects, after all?"

"Yes, but can we please go together and pay *our* respects? I really feel as though that's the least we can do." Misao turned to face Teppei. Holding his gaze with her own, she said candidly, "Look, someone may or may not have made the elevator move by meditation, or the power of his mind. Or maybe it was pure coincidence, as you say. Whatever happened, it has nothing to do with Reiko, or the afterlife, or anything like that. Isn't that right?"

Teppei pondered for a moment, then broke into a grin. "Yes," he said, reaching out to take Misao's hand in his. "You're absolutely right, as usual."

Misao chuckled, but her smile was strained, and her laughter sounded oddly brittle.

# 9

Teppei and Misao left their daughter on the couch, drowsily watching television, and went down to the fourth floor to call on Mr. Shoji. When they rang the bell, he opened the door and greeted them in a friendly, relaxed way.

Standing on the doorstep, Misao inclined her head in a slight bow and said formally, "Thanks to you, everything turned out well the other day. Our daughter is doing fine now, and her injury is healing right on schedule. We just wanted to stop by to express our gratitude, and to apologize for any inconvenience or worry we might have caused."

From the depths of the apartment, the faint aroma of incense floated down the interior corridor and drifted through the open door. Mr. Shoji blinked once or twice, and his rosy-fleshed mouth twitched behind his whiskers in a spasmodic way, like some restless mollusk. "I'm very glad to hear that the injury wasn't anything too serious," he said at last. "And it puts my mind at ease to hear that I was able to render assistance, however small." Some crumbs from a cookie or cracker had evidently become lodged in the man's bristly mustache, but he still managed to project an aura of quiet dignity as he bobbed his head up and down in a congenial manner.

Teppei thought he sensed an undertone of arrogance about the way the man delivered those ostensibly humble words. Standing silently next to Misao on the doorstep, he stared long and hard at Mr. Shoji, whom he was meeting for the first time.

Misao, meanwhile, was thinking: *I can just imagine what my husband is going to say when we get home. Probably something like, "That guy seems to think he's some kind of miracle-working guru. I wouldn't be surprised to see him in one of those late-night infomercials on TV, peddling his psychic wares and spewing gibberish about how he saved a child's life with his magical super-powers."*

The truth was, Misao's own thoughts were running along those lines, as well. She was finding it difficult to believe that the man standing in front of them now was the same impressive person who had worked his magic on the stalled elevator the other day. Maybe it was because she had been half insane with worry about Tamao. At any rate, that afternoon in the lobby, this same man had struck Misao as saintlike, or even godly. No, check that; it would probably be more accurate to say that he had seemed like the kind of super-naturally powerful being you read about in mythology and folk tales. But the person who stood in front of them now just appeared to be a drab, unexceptional middle-aged man with crumbs in his mustache.

Misao felt a wave of disappointment as she realized that her initial impression of Mr. Shoji as a man who possessed some special occult power might have been miles off the mark. Perhaps he was just an ordinary person with extreme delusions of grandeur, happily taking credit for every uncanny coincidence that came along. Or maybe he was a run-of-the-mill swindler, one of those self-styled psychics who is the modern equivalent of a snake-oil salesman, conning people into buying overpriced gold pendants depicting some lower-echelon bodhisattva. Suppose they asked him what really happened that day with the elevator, and he tried to sell them a cheesy talisman in lieu of a straight answer? That would be too much to bear.

After both sides had run through the customary pleasantries, there didn't seem to be anything left to say. Misao caught Teppei's eye, then murmured politely, "Well, I guess we'd better be running along now."

As she and Teppei were stepping away from the doorway, Mr. Shoji said hesitantly, "Um . . . I know it may be out of line for me to ask a question like this, but I was wondering whether you might have found out what caused your daughter's injury."

Apparently sensing that Misao was about to reply, Teppei jumped in ahead of her. "Well, the doctor was saying that it looked to him as though a weasel wind had materialized somehow, out of the blue," he said.

"Oh, is that so?" said Mr. Shoji, opening his deep-set black eyes wide in surprise. "That seems rather remarkable. I mean, I'm familiar with the phenomenon of weasel winds, of course, but you wouldn't expect a sudden gust to kick up in a windowless basement, of all places."

"No, apparently it really isn't that unusual," Teppei said, but his certainty sounded suspiciously like bravado. "If the basement in this building was never properly sealed, there could be drafts when air comes in from outside, and at one of those entry points I guess the breeze must have developed into a vortex. That sort of thing can occur indoors, especially now in early spring, when the wind is blowing nearly every day. It really isn't strange at all. At any rate, on the day in question, an extra-strong gust of wind must have come up, and one thing just led to another."

"You'd hate to think this building was so poorly constructed that something like that could occur indoors, though," Mr. Shoji persisted. "Not to mention the fact that the basement is underground, and has no windows."

"Well, I looked around later that day and didn't find a single thing that could have caused such an injury, so we may never know what really went on down there, or outside, or wherever. At this point I think we just need to write it off as 'wrong place, wrong time,' and let it go," Teppei said with an air of finality.

"That place is dangerous." Mr. Shoji uttered those words in a voice so quiet it was almost a whisper, and Teppei shot him a sharp look. "The basement is dangerous," the older man repeated, "and that's why it would really be better if you didn't allow your child to play in that space, ever again."

"What do you mean, 'dangerous'?" Teppei asked in a tone that straddled the line between curiosity and scorn.

"No, I mean . . . I just wanted to let you know. Simply put, that basement is a place where—how shall I say this?—where evil entities congregate."

"'Evil entities'?" Teppei echoed with a bitter, incredulous laugh. "You mean like monsters? Are there ghosts and goblins down there, too?"

"No, no, nothing as simple as that," Mr. Shoji said brusquely. "Even I was surprised, and I'm not a stranger to the dark side myself, by any means. I've encountered malevolent vibrations all over the world, but this is the first time I've ever felt such a strong concentration of evil energy in one place."

Sneaking a glance at Misao, Teppei laughed weakly. "I do believe we're in the presence of someone with really extraordinary powers of imagination," he said in a sardonic tone. "Maybe this is one of the side effects of living in a place that looks out on a graveyard and a temple and a crematorium: you start to have trouble telling the difference between fantasy and reality."

Mr. Shoji didn't reply. He just shrugged his shoulders and stared intently at Teppei, who got the disconcerting sense that the man was silently exhorting him to do whatever he could to protect his adorable little daughter, at all costs.

"I'll be moving out the day after tomorrow," Mr. Shoji said, "but if I had my druthers I wouldn't spend another night in this place. It wasn't too bad when I first moved in; the level of paranormal activity in the basement hadn't yet become a major cause for concern, and the building itself was comfortable and quiet. However, things have really gotten out of hand since then. I'm just completely worn-out by the constant onslaught of negative energy."

*This certainly isn't your usual doorstep conversation,* Misao thought. She'd been thrown for a loop by Mr. Shoji's remarks, but she made an effort to summon up a gracious smile. The older man glanced at her, and his weary expression seemed to soften somewhat.

"Surely *you* must understand, Mrs. Kano. When the elevator suddenly stopped working that day, at the precise time your daughter was injured, it wasn't a coincidence, at all. It was . . . well, I really don't know how to even begin to explain this to people who don't work in this field, but at the risk of oversimplifying, I'll just say that it was a deliberately aggressive act by a certain type of . . . um, noncorporeal entities."

Teppei burst out laughing, in a way that barely avoided being rude. "I must say, your explanation doesn't really work for me," he scoffed. "Are you some kind of expert on 'paranormal activity,' to use your term?"

"No," Mr. Shoji replied in a calm, measured tone. "I'm just a humble teacher and practitioner of meditation. I spent the better part of my twenties in India, you see. I studied yoga there for many years, and I was able to master certain meditation techniques and other skills. When I returned to Japan I opened a yoga studio here in Tokyo, and I still teach classes there every day."

"So you're saying that you were somehow able to get the elevator to move just by meditating over it?"

"No, but I am able to use a meditative state to channel chi— you know, positive energy—through my hands. It's what we call a parapsychological effect. Actually, the technical term in this case would be psychotronics, though it's probably easier to think of it as a kind of channeling or redirecting of energy."

As he said this, Mr. Shoji held up both hands, palms facing out. In contrast with his weathered, whiskery face, his hands were surprisingly soft and smooth. Then he continued, "Through the energy I generate with my hands, I'm able to absorb chi from the cosmos, or the universe, if you prefer. By the same token, I can channel or redirect that cosmic energy outward. The only catch is, when I use my skills to deal with the spirit world I very quickly become exhausted. It depends on the situation, but there have been times when I became ill as a result of one of those sessions. To be perfectly frank, I, too . . ." He paused, and lowered his eyes in evident embarrassment. "That day, after I had gotten the elevator moving again, I was so drained that I fell into a complete funk, almost like a trance state. I'm nearly back to normal now, though."

*Uh oh*, Misao thought. *Was that their cue to say, "We're terribly sorry you had to go through that on our account"?* The stress seemed to have caused her saliva to dry up, and instead of apologizing she posed a question: "What I don't understand is, why do things like that seem to happen in this building?"

"I really don't have a clear handle on that myself," Mr. Shoji responded. "I'm not a fortune-teller or a spiritualistic medium or anything like that. I've just acquired certain abilities over the years, through long training and experience, and I seem to have developed a sensitivity to this type of thing. This building is a perilous place; that's all there is to it. At this point, it would really be better if you didn't use the basement at all. Ideally, I would like to give all the remaining residents of this building the same warning, but they would probably think I was delusional, so I've decided to keep my opinions to myself."

Mr. Shoji smiled and looked first at Misao, then at Teppei. "Could I interest you in a cup of coffee, or perhaps some chai?" he asked. "If you're so inclined, there's a great deal more that I could tell you."

Before Misao had time to respond, Teppei shook his head emphatically and said, "Thank you, but we left our child alone in the apartment, so we need to be getting back now."

"Oh, I see. I'm sorry to hear that." Mr. Shoji gave Misao a look of deep compassion. "If anything else should come up—well, I'd like to say that I would be pleased to be of assistance again, but I won't be here for much longer, and it's unlikely that we'll meet again after I move away. In any case, I wish you and your family every happiness from now on."

Then, to the surprise of the two people standing on the doorstep, the door to unit 401 closed softly in their faces before they had a chance to say good-bye.

Inside the elevator, Teppei snickered, "Holy cow, what a con man."

"Really? That's what you came away with?"

"Why, are you saying you disagree? Because the answer to the question 'Is that man a total quack, or not?' could end up having a drastic effect on our bank balance going forward. If you agree that he's a phony, then we can continue as we are right now. But if you think he's for real, that could lead to financial disaster."

"What are you talking about?"

"Just that if you bought into that charlatan's spiel, I guarantee it will just be a matter of time before you decide that we ought to sell our apartment here and move to a different building, based on all the alarmist drivel he was spouting. Just to be clear, I want no part of that scenario."

"So it doesn't bother you at all?"

"What's that?"

"You know, the things he said about this building."

"You mean the fact that the elevator malfunctioned at an inopportune moment, and apparently there was a weasel wind in the basement, one time?"

"Well, yes, but also there was that strange shadow on the TV screen, and the little bird died right after we moved in."

"Come on, get a grip," Teppei said, pulling a droll face. "I think you've been watching too many horror movies again!" He laughed, but there was something awkward and unnatural about his tone, as if he were making a conscious effort to keep things light.

For a moment, Misao debated whether to tell Teppei about the creepy feeling she got every time she ventured into the basement, or the chilly, unnaturally invasive wind that always seemed to be swirling around. She couldn't imagine that such a conversation would end up going particularly well, so she decided to keep those matters to herself. She had a premonition that if she even attempted to discuss her misgivings about the building with Teppei, their relationship might be damaged in a way that could never be undone.

•

The ward office wasn't too far north of Takaino Station, and it only took Misao fifteen minutes to get there on foot. The official headquarters of "K" Ward fronted the highway, while the library occupied a nondescript three-story building tucked away at the rear. Even so, the incessant noise of fast-moving traffic was clearly audible in every room of the library, so it wasn't exactly an optimal environment for quiet reading or complex research.

When Misao explained to the poker-faced, white-haired man at the reception desk that she was hoping to be able to look at some materials pertaining to the district's history and public administration, he held up three fingers and mumbled almost inaudibly, "Third floor." There was no one else within earshot, but evidently the man thought it would be inappropriate to use a normal tone of voice in a library, under any circumstances.

Upstairs, there were a few people scattered around the room devoted to public administration records. An age-yellowed card reading "Archives for 'K' Ward" was affixed to a large bookcase in one corner of the room, but the shelves were sparsely filled. There were three pamphlets labeled "Government Public Opinion Survey Regarding 'K' Ward," along with a row of books (all crammed with maps and numerical charts) bearing titles such as *Regional Emergency Preparedness Plan for Natural Disasters* and *The Current State of Environmental Pollution in "K" Ward*. Also in the mix was a slim volume of personal essays by some long-dead writer titled *Our Town: Now and Then*, and a number of thick clothbound books, all tersely labeled " 'K' Ward History."

Misao's opening move was to select a booklet with the alarmingly long title *Background Research and Progress Report on the Proposed Development Plan for an Underground Shopping Arcade at Takaino Station* and carry it over to one of the reading desks. The publication date was March 1963, and the pages, like the card on the bookcase, had acquired a jaundiced tinge over the years. On the first page, the following sentence appeared: "This written report, which was prepared by the Center for Regional Development under a mandate from the Tokyo Metropolitan Headquarters, encompasses (a) the results of background research and feasibility studies regarding the redevelopment of the Takaino district; and (b) an account of the subsequent actions that have been implemented." The pamphlet went on to provide an itemized list of the basic policies covering the redevelopment of the Takaino area.

1. A plan is in place, commencing in 1964, to erect municipally managed high-rise apartments in an area extending roughly one kilometer south from Takaino Station, on a site comprising approximately fifteen acres. The land is presently occupied by Manseiji, a Buddhist temple, and an adjacent cemetery. A concomitant plan, currently under consideration, proposes the construction of an underground shopping area that would also extend in a southerly direction from Takaino Station. This addition would aim to (a) accommodate the

anticipated population growth; and (b) revitalize the economy of the area.

2. The underground shopping area would originate on the belowground level of Takaino Station (operated by Japan Rail), and would terminate, variously, at the basements of each of the high-rise apartments.

3. The primary goal is to attain a harmonious consolidation of this underground shopping arcade with the shopping streets already in existence in the neighborhoods around the station, without in any way undermining the atmosphere or market share of the latter. Additionally, the new shopping development would actively seek to attract the patronage of people who live near other stops along the same train line.

4. Needless to say, safety and security would be prime considerations. This project would provide numerous car parks as well as terminals with boarding areas for various bus lines, designed to separate pedestrians from vehicular traffic. In addition, all the latest safety systems would be put in place to handle fire, earthquakes, and other natural disasters.

Misao went back and reread the first item on the numbered list. So the land currently occupied by Manseiji—the temple itself and the adjoining cemetery—had once been officially targeted as a site for high-rise apartment blocks, operated by the city?

If the temple and graveyard had been transplanted to another location and high-density housing had been built on that land, there would surely have been a significant increase in the area's population. If a typical building had fourteen floors, with approximately seven units on each floor, that would work out to close to a hundred households. Factoring in extended families, it would be reasonable to assume an average of four people per household. So if there were ten apartment buildings, that would mean the wholesale addition of approximately four thousand new residents to the neighborhood. Such a sizable influx would inevitably cause the existing shopping areas around the station to become far busier than usual, if not inconveniently overcrowded, so the reasoning behind the proposed creation of an underground shopping mall or arcade definitely made sense.

Misao continued leafing through the pamphlet. Several pages were devoted to demographic aspects of the Takaino area, such as consumer spending habits and longevity of residence. Next came specifications for the underground arcade, including the number of shops and the amount of retail space allotted to each one. There were even diagrams showing the physical layout of the subterranean shopping mall, plotted out in minute detail.

The proposed underground shopping area was long rather than deep, and its layout was quite compact. If that mall had been built, the facing rows of stores would probably have projected a distinctly low-key, homey atmosphere. It would have been the kind of place where the residents of the local apartment towers could do their shopping dressed in casual clothes and plastic shower sandals, or stroll out on a Sunday afternoon to enjoy a late brunch with the entire family in tow. Twice a month, there would have been "megadiscount" sales, and the specialty food stores were to have had "charismatic barkers" out front, to lure customers. There would have been clothing shops offering what the brochure described as "tasteful, stylish fashions—for a song!" The lineup would also feature an assortment of family-friendly pubs, restaurants, and snack bars, where parents could feel comfortable about bringing their children along. Judging from the plans, the mall would have been a safe, cozy, convenient place to shop and spend some leisure time. However, those plans never became a reality. Why?

Leaving the pamphlet open on the desk, Misao stood up and once again went over to browse the bookshelves. There were any number of other publications on the topic of the redevelopment of

"K" Ward, but at a glance they all seemed to contain the same basic information.

In one corner of the bookcase, she noticed a stack of forsaken-looking old scrapbooks bound in heavy brown paper and bundled together with string. The books were covered with a thick layer of dust. When Misao extracted one scrapbook from the pile and pried it open, the metal staples that held the pages together made a reluctant creaking sound.

Inside was a large assortment of full-color PR releases, specially issued pamphlets, and other publications related to the underground mall project, all dating from the late 1950s through 1965 or so. The bound pages were arranged in chronological order, and as Misao flipped through them one by one she came upon a thin, flimsy booklet bearing the headline "Let's Make Them Relocate the Manseiji Graveyard ASAP, Without Further Delay!" In addition, there were detailed maps of the temple and the graveyard, along with densely written text.

Manseiji, with its adjoining graveyard, located in "K" Ward, owns and occupies a space to the north and south of Takaino Station, comprising a total area of approximately fifteen acres. At present, the Tokyo metropolitan government has drawn up plans to develop this centrally located area into high-rise apartments, along with a complementary underground shopping arcade to serve the area's burgeoning population.

In order to facilitate those plans, the municipal government has requested that both Manseiji (the temple itself) and the adjacent graveyard be relocated. A search is currently under way for a suitable alternative site. The candidates at present include (1) an existing graveyard in the Kodaira area, on the outskirts of Tokyo, which has ample room for expansion; and (2) an extensive plot of empty land with terrain that includes both hills and forests, located in the suburbs of the city of Musashino, in Saitama Prefecture. There are other possibilities, as well.

However, the representatives of Manseiji continue to insist that because the history of the graveyard in its current location dates back to the Taisho Era [July 1912 through December 1926]—a period when interment (ground burial), as opposed to the currently popular cremation, was the prevailing custom—moving so many skeletal remains to another location would be an impossibly difficult task. For this and numerous other reasons, the temple refuses to accept the city's proposal, and as a result a redevelopment plan that would benefit the area has reached an impasse. That is where matters stand at the present time.

For their part, the city's representatives have given careful consideration to the temple's highly detailed conditions and demands, and have stressed their commitment to making the process of moving the remains as respectful, efficient, and faultless as possible. Therefore, there seems to be no reason to expect that the surviving family members would experience any significant degree of inconvenience.

We deeply regret that our visionary plan for creating a new, improved township in the area has been stalled due to logistical complications. We will not abandon this vision, and it is our hope that the current residents of the area will help us neutralize the opposition to the relocation of the cemetery, so that we can all work together to make this forward-looking development a reality.

The next publication was titled *The Committee for a Grass-Roots Protest Movement Against the Relocation of Manseiji*. At a guess, that "committee" probably consisted of a small group of people—relatives of some of the graveyard's occupants, perhaps?—looking for a way to make their voices heard.

Misao moseyed back to her desk, where she sat down and spent the next few moments lost in thought. She couldn't begin to explain why she had become so preoccupied—if not obsessed—with the matter of the underground shopping arcade. The facts had become clear: A couple of decades ago, planning was under way for the building of a cluster of publicly managed apartment towers in tandem with the construction of an underground shopping mall, but that two-pronged plan was opposed by the temple-and-graveyard coalition because it would have required the relocation of a large number of graves containing uncremated human remains. In a nutshell, the city wanted to buy some land and the temple declined to sell, and that was the end of it. There was nothing remarkable about the outcome; in the annals of urban planning, tales of abortive developments were a dime a dozen. This was just another of those close-but-no-cigar stories.

So why did the details of the narrative bother Misao so much? More specifically, what had motivated her to make the trek to this out-of-the-way place to research the matter of the underground shopping area—which she had only heard someone mention once, in passing?

Misao glanced at her wristwatch. It was eleven a.m. She had another thirty minutes or so before she would need to head out to fetch Tamao from kindergarten. This was Tamao's first day back at school since the accident, and Misao couldn't help worrying. She hoped Tamao wouldn't fall down on the playground and reopen the wound.

Outside, the sky had begun to cloud over, while a lusterless, sleepy-looking cherry tree seemed to be trying to stretch its misshapen branches past the reading room's third-floor window. Misao now had that room completely to herself. Two young men who appeared to be university students had been aimlessly milling around, but they had either left the building or gone to another section. Misao could feel a slight headache coming on.

The bottom line of her research was that the ambitious construction project had ultimately been abandoned. The subterranean shopping arcade and the apartment towers were never built, and the neighborhood around the train station's south exit had gradually fallen into its current state of seedy disrepair. What remained? Nothing but a handful of modest shops and a gigantic graveyard.

"Ground burial." That term popped into Misao's head as she was remembering a sentence she had read about the temple's reasons for refusing to sell the land, whose wording (she thought) seemed to teeter on the edge of insolence. Snarky tone aside, she hadn't realized that the Manseiji graveyard had been in use since the Taisho Era, when interment was more common than cremation.

So when she gazed at the view from her balcony, some of the graves she saw every day contained the remains of human beings who had died a long time ago and been buried as corpses, instead of being cremated. The thought made her skin crawl. If the temple had decided to go ahead and try to move all the buried skeletal remains to another location, how on earth would they have gone about transporting them? Sixty or seventy years would have passed since the initial interments, so surely the wooden coffins would have decayed to the point where they would immediately crumble into dust upon being exposed to the air.

Misao got up from her chair and carried the pamphlet she'd been perusing back to the bookcase. After reshelving it, she once again ran her eyes over the materials on the shelves, but she didn't see any later accounts of what had become of the underground construction project when the redevelopment plans hit a terminal snag.

She wondered what Teppei would say if he knew she had made a special trip to the ward library to delve into a matter like this. Would he laugh indulgently? Or would he say something like, "Why don't you just give all this nonsense a rest," with no attempt to hide his disapproval? Probably the latter. Ever since Tamao's accident, Teppei had appeared to be waging an internal battle against a legion of personal demons—a struggle he couldn't (or didn't choose to) talk about.

Misao's headache was becoming more severe by the minute. *I need to take some aspirin as soon as I get home,* she thought.

When she reached the first floor of the library she saw the white-haired man sitting idly at the reception desk, staring into space. Propelled by a sudden impulse, Misao approached the desk and said, "Um, excuse me?"

The man turned his head to glance at her, but he didn't say a word.

"This is probably going to seem like a strange question," Misao began.

"Huh?" The man seemed startled.

"I'm sorry, are you by any chance familiar with this part of the city?"

The man shot her an indignant look, then mumbled, "Well, I've been working here for the past thirty-two years, so I ought to be."

"Oh, that's great!" Misao said happily, beaming at the man. "The truth is, I'm trying to get some perspective on the history of this area, and there's one thing that isn't clear to me."

"What would that be?" If the man was intrigued by the question, he didn't show it. Wearing a bored expression, he turned away from Misao and once again stared straight ahead.

"Quite some time ago, there was a plan to build an underground shopping arcade beneath Takaino Station. Did you know about that?"

"Oh, that. Yes, I do know about that plan. It was back in the sixties."

"I gather there was some difficulty with relocating the graves from the Manseiji cemetery, and that's why the plan never came to fruition?"

"Yes, that's right. It just fizzled out in the end, even though the developers had already gone to the trouble of digging a hole. That was a major waste of time and money."

"A hole?" Misao asked with mounting excitement. "So the excavation work had already been done when the project was abandoned?"

"Well, I'm not sure, but that's the impression I got. Apparently the developers got into a big dispute with the temple, and in the end the whole thing just blew up in their faces. I don't know what they were thinking, but I guess at some point the developers must have been feeling optimistic, so they said, 'Hey, let's go ahead and spend a small fortune digging out this underground road, just in case our plan works out.' I gather they had high hopes of building some big apartment complexes in the neighborhood, too. Before they could do any of that, of course, they had to reach an agreement with the temple about buying the land, but even when it started looking like that wasn't going to work out, they continued with the excavation." The previously stolid man seemed to have become almost manic. His voice had risen in both pitch and volume, to the point where it seemed to be echoing faintly off the walls.

"It was really an exercise in futility," he went on. "I mean, to go ahead and dig a hole before everything was signed, sealed, and delivered? That makes no sense at all. There used to be a signboard for the construction company at the building site. I remember seeing it every day, and then it suddenly disappeared. It really was an incredible waste, doing all that work for nothing."

"Are there records of that excavation in the archives here?"

"Hmm," the man said thoughtfully. "I couldn't say for sure, but I have a feeling there aren't—at least not here. Like the proverb says: 'If something stinks, you'd better put a lid on it.' That's the go-to formula in government, too, of course. If a project has a negative outcome, they prefer not to publicize it too much. Why are you so interested in this, anyway? Are you planning to write an article or a book or something?"

"No, no, nothing like that," Misao protested, shaking her head.

The man shot her a warning look that reminded her of a parent trying to caution a headstrong child against doing something rash, then crossed his arms over his chest. "The thing is, it isn't exactly a pleasant topic, so people tend to avoid looking into it too deeply," he said. "I guess most folks would rather let sleeping dogs lie."

"No, as I said, I have no intention of writing about this," Misao protested. "I just got interested because I live nearby, and a neighbor was talking about the development. So do you happen to know what became of the hole, in the end?"

"You really are an inquisitive one," the man said with a laugh that showed his unnaturally white front teeth. Misao recognized them immediately as dentures. "Hey, after all, we aren't mole people, right? The hole would have been useless, so I imagine they must have filled it in after the project went belly up."

"Of course, that must be it," Misao said. She laughed, too. "Thank you for your help. I'm sorry to have taken up so much of your time," she added, with a minimal bow.

The receptionist responded by bobbing his own head ever so slightly, and Misao left the building.

As she was walking back to the station, she suddenly remembered the phrase Eiko had used—"phantom road to nowhere"—and a small shiver ran down her spine.

# 10

May 6, 1987

It was the Wednesday after the annual Golden Week holiday. Sitting at her pinewood work desk, Misao looked out the window and yawned. The air in the living room was hot and sultry. Outside, the sky looked as though rain might begin to fall at any minute. It wasn't yet three in the afternoon, but the day had turned so dark and gloomy that Misao found herself craving light.

Over the long weekend the Kano family had gone to a department store to buy a new sports jacket for Teppei, then stopped off in the trendy, upscale Aoyama district to grab a bite at an Italian bistro on the way home. Aside from that outing they hadn't really done anything special, and midway through the holiday Teppei had been called away for two days to work on a TV commercial being filmed on location for one of the agency's new accounts.

During his absence, Misao's mother came up to Tokyo from the family home in Izu City for an overnight stay, which (in Misao's opinion) had ruined what would otherwise have been a pleasant couple of days. Her mother's last visit had been more than a year earlier, so she had never been to the new apartment. When she saw the graveyard in front of the building her eyebrows shot up, but she refrained from commenting.

That had always been her mother's style, Misao thought. Sometimes—though by no means always—her mother would manage to stop herself just as she was on the verge of saying something vicious, biting back the nasty words before they could slither from her mouth like a passel of hissing snakes.

Several years earlier Misao had finally confessed to her parents that Teppei's first wife committed suicide, and her mother's savage tongue-lashing still reverberated deep in Misao's psyche. As her mother spewed forth that torrent of venom, all blame and shame and animosity, Misao really did feel as if she were being flogged by a live whip of sharp-fanged, poisonous snakes.

"I'm ashamed to have brought a daughter like you into the world," her mother had ranted. "I've never said this out loud before, but for as long as I can remember you've been a sordid, sleazy kind of girl. You never were any good. I'll bet you seduced that man while he was still married. Oh, yes, I know all about your tricks. You really are a disgusting child. You'll be going to hell, that's for sure. Maybe that dead woman—what was her name, Reiko?—will put a fatal curse on you from beyond the grave. That's exactly what you deserve."

Misao's father had never been one to hold back when it came to nagging or criticizing his daughter, but on that painful occasion he didn't say a thing. Seven years had passed since then, and during that time her father had never once gotten in touch with Misao, much less stopped by to see her.

Misao's mother started bad-mouthing the absent Teppei (albeit in a roundabout way) soon after she arrived. Then she adopted a purring, wheedling tone and said, "You know, if it was just you and Tamao, you would be more than welcome to come home for a visit, any time at all."

Misao refused to get angry, because she knew that was the reaction her mother was hoping to provoke. If Misao took the bait, it would only egg her mother on. When she thought about how messy and awful it would be to endure another barrage of hateful words, she decided that no matter how much unwarranted abuse her mother might heap on her, she would remain silent and ignore the invective.

Back in the present, Misao gave her head a good shake to clear away the cobwebs of memory, then returned her attention to the work on her desk. She didn't have time to worry about her mother's cruelty or her father's ongoing stubbornness (although it hurt her deeply that so many years later he was still withholding forgiveness). She had too many other things to deal with right now.

Her current assignment was an illustration for the self-promotional magazine of a cosmetics company. It was going to be a double-truck spread under the title "Urban Poetry," and Misao had been asked to draw a picture, using a palette of pastel colors, that would evoke a sense of the city.

The poem itself had been contributed by one of the magazine's readers. Misao had been given an advance copy, and now she read it over once again.

*Longing to smell the aroma of earth,*
*Yearning to hear the chirping of birds,*
*Here I dwell atop this tower of concrete.*
*And even though there's no soil to smell,*
*And no birdsong to hear,*
*At least I have the sun.*
*I have the evening.*
*And I have you.*

The poem's author was a twenty-nine-year-old mother of one, and it wasn't clear whether the "you" in the last line was meant to be her child, or her husband, or someone else entirely. Was the poem well done, or not? Misao hesitated to judge it one way or the other, but the verse struck her as somewhat facile: designed, she imagined, to appeal to the sensibilities of women who were still very young. Nonetheless, Misao had an instinctive understanding of where the author was coming from, and what she was trying to convey.

*And I have you . . .* The last line, in particular, resonated with Misao because it reminded her of the deep sense of camaraderie she and Teppei had felt when they finally started to move on from Reiko's death, more closely bound together than ever.

Misao hadn't told Teppei yet about the fruits of her research at the ward library. Maybe one of these days, in the not too distant future, they would end up being able to laugh about all these absurdities. When she thought about it that way, her mood lightened a bit.

The thing was, she knew without a doubt that if she were to say she wanted to put this apartment on the market right away and start looking for another place, Teppei would be flabbergasted, and irate. Really, she told herself, the only major drawback was the basement. If she didn't like going down there, she could just choose not to use the storage locker. The danger with flights of fancy was that they could easily get out of hand and lead to delusional thinking. When you started believing in the existence of things that weren't really there, that was a sign that your imagination was working overtime.

The telephone rang. It was Eiko. "Yoo-hoo!" she said playfully.

It had only been a few hours since the two women had run into each other on their way to pick up the children from kindergarten. As they walked together, Eiko had shared an animated account of the long weekend she and her family had spent at the home of her older sister in Chiba; they had all gone to Tokyo Disneyland, where, in Eiko's words, they spent "oodles of money." Misao was surprised to hear from her neighbor again so soon.

"Is everything okay?" Eiko asked now, with a nervous giggle. It was an odd question, and Misao sensed something jittery and un-balanced beneath the laughter, as though Eiko might be about to explode at any moment.

"Everything's fine," Misao said warily. "What's going on with you?"

Eiko laughed again and said, "Oh, nothing much," then let out a histrionic sigh. "Honestly, though, I'm starting to think I might be losing my mind."

"What do you mean? What's going on?"

"I'm sorry for the interruption—I know you're probably trying to work."

"It's no problem at all." Misao would have said the same thing to whoever was on the other end of the line, but the truth was that she actively welcomed the interruption. "I've actually been floundering around trying to figure out what kind of imagery would work best for my illustration, and I was just about to take a break anyway," she added.

"Then would it be okay if I stopped by for a minute? Kaori and Tsutomu are at a friend's house this afternoon. Is Tamao around?"

"I put her down for a nap a while ago. Since the injury, she's been sleeping a lot more than she used to."

"Okay, great. See you in a bit!" Eiko said in a rush, ending the call in a way that struck Misao as uncharacteristically abrupt.

Misao barely had time to pour two cups of coffee before Eiko appeared at the door, ashen-faced and agitated. She was dressed in a light gray sweatshirt with matching jodhpur-style pants, and her makeup was more minimal than usual. Misao reckoned that was why her skin appeared so pale.

"Oh, just seeing your face makes me feel better," Eiko exclaimed with a dry, artificial laugh. She sounded a bit like a sick child try-ing to feign high-spirited good health to reassure (or deceive) her mother.

"What happened?" Misao asked.

"It's really nothing," Eiko replied. "I must be getting senile before my time or something, 'cause my ears seem to be playing tricks on me."

"Your ears?"

Eiko picked up the cup of coffee that Misao had set in front of her and took a big gulp. Only after swallowing did she seem to realize how hot it was, and she made a humorous show of clawing at her throat.

"What do you mean, your ears are playing tricks on you?" Misao repeated.

"It's just that I heard something weird. I really do feel like I'm losing my grip on reality. Okay, so I went down to the basement, right? I think it was about half an hour ago. Tsutomu had dragged his tricycle up to the apartment, and I went to stick it back in our storage locker. I swear, that kid never puts anything away after he's finished using it. It's probably my fault for not disciplining him enough. So anyway, I hoisted the trike onto my shoulder and lugged it down to the basement. And then . . ."

Eiko's mien turned suddenly sober. She plunked her coffee cup down with so much force that it rattled in the saucer, then looked at Misao with her face contorted into an expression that could have been the prelude to laughter or tears. Misao had been about to take a sip from her own cup, but now she put it down and waited without saying a word.

"There were voices talking on the other side of the wall," Eiko stated in a flat, uninflected monotone. After a moment's silence she burst into laughter, then said sheepishly, "I'm probably just being stupid about this. Don't you think I'm being foolish? I mean, there's no way I could have heard that for real, right?"

Misao rubbed her lip thoughtfully. "When you say 'on the other side of the wall,' what do you mean, exactly?"

"Look, like I said, I'm sure my ears were just playing tricks on me. As for the place, I think it was right around the spot where Tamao collapsed that day, after she was injured. I just got this weird feeling that I could hear voices whispering and muttering behind the wall. I didn't get any sense of what they were saying, but it sounded like a lot of people, all talking at once. I started to shiver, and I thought my hair was going to stand on end. There was something really ghastly about those voices. I mean, like, beyond dreadful."

"How so?"

"It's kind of hard to explain. It was as if they were talking among themselves, and their voices were making a kind of rustling sound. You know how when you go to the movies, people will be chatting in hushed whispers before the show starts? It was sort of like that. I'm sure it was just the wind, or else maybe there were some people in the elevator lobby on the first floor, and they were all talking to each other."

*The wind? People in the elevator lobby?* Misao thought incredulously. "And you think these sounds were coming from the other side of the back wall?" she asked in the calmest tone she could muster.

"Yes, but . . . Oh dear, I hate this. Please don't look so serious, Misao! I'm telling you, I just imagined it. I need you to assure me it was all in my head—that's why I came up here." Eiko laughed and put both hands on her cheeks, and Misao noticed that some of the natural color seemed to have returned to her friend's face.

"Even if it was just my imagination, it really gave me the creeps at the time," Eiko went on. "I was just cowering there, unable to move a muscle. I couldn't make a sound, either. I wonder why I reacted that way? I mean, it was just some voices. I really am silly sometimes."

Ever since Tamao's accident, Eiko had declared the basement off limits for Tsutomu and Kaori. She gave no specific reason for forbidding her children to play down there, but the new policy seemed to be an implicit expression of the way everyone was feeling about the basement these days.

Unconsciously, Misao rubbed her arms, which were suddenly

covered in gooseflesh. "And you're sure about what you heard?" she asked.

"Yes, absolutely. Even if my ears were deceiving me about the source or the tone, the one thing I'm sure about is that I did hear voices. I was just trying to fool myself into thinking it was the wind earlier."

"That really is spooky," Misao said slowly.

"You can say that again." Eiko looked down at the table. "To tell the truth, I was so scared I couldn't move—like literally paralyzed with fear. And even after I was safely back in the apartment, that feeling wouldn't go away. Ugh, this is such a gray day. Would it be okay to turn on some lights?"

Before Misao had time to reply, Eiko jumped up and went over to the wall switch. The room was immediately flooded with a soft yet vibrant golden light; it illuminated every corner and even cast its glow on a shiny covered picture book of Tamao's that had fallen under the sofa.

Wearing a relieved expression, Eiko returned to her seat at the table and took a noisy slurp of coffee. "Anyway, I was completely freaked out, and I was so antsy after I got home that I finally just had to give you a call. I need to be running along soon, though—I have to go pick up my kids. It looks like it might be going to rain, too. But really, what do you think I heard down there?"

"Hmm, I wonder," Misao mused, gripping her cup with both hands. Her fingers had grown unnaturally cold, and no matter how tightly she gripped the warm cup she couldn't seem to get their temperature back to normal. She noticed a slight fissure in the rim of the bone china cup. *It's cracked, it's cracked*, she repeated over and over, inside her head. Should she go out one of these days and splurge on a coffee set made from Imari porcelain or something like that? She could imagine Teppei saying, "Hey, we don't have that kind of money to throw around," but when you are trying to create a pleasant, tidy home, every little detail contributes to the overall impression of loveliness, right down to the everyday tableware.

Misao knew she was making a conscious effort to focus on safe domestic details in order to prevent herself from blurting out her wild hypothesis to Eiko. Namely: *What if the underground hole that was prematurely excavated, decades ago, ran directly under the graveyard and ended up dead-ending (so to speak) at the basement of this apartment building?*

Misao remembered what the receptionist at the ward library had said the other day, as a joke: "After all, we aren't mole people, right?" Yes, surely that useless tunnel would have been filled in after the project went bust.

But what if the underground hole never had been refilled? Wasn't it possible that the disappointed developers could have hastily paved over the mouth of the excavation instead, leaving a tunnel-like segment that ran under the cemetery and continued all the way up to the external wall of this building's basement?

Mr. Shoji had moved away, but some of the things he'd said were still resonating in Misao's head: troubling things, like describing the basement as a gathering place for evil entities. She didn't remember his exact words—something like, "I'm no stranger to the dark side, but I've never felt that kind of evil energy before." Could there be a connection between that unwholesome energy and the part of the underground road or tunnel that might have been left unfilled beneath the graveyard?

"So, um, what's going through your mind right now?" Eiko asked uneasily.

Misao shook her head and said, "Nothing special. I was just thinking how happy I would be if I never had to set foot in that basement again. I don't even want to use the storage locker anymore."

Eiko nodded. "I know what you mean. I swear, after today I'm never going down there again. No, seriously, I'm not kidding. 'Spooky' doesn't even begin to describe it," she declared, looking Misao full in the face. "Really, I wonder whether that basement was the scene of a murder or a suicide or something."

The way Eiko spoke those words was uncharacteristically solemn, and Misao felt a sudden prickling of goose bumps at the base of her neck.

Eiko evidently had a similar reaction to her own words, because she wrapped both arms around her torso and moaned, "Oh, now I went and said something awful. But even so, you do hear stories about that kind of thing quite often, don't you? Like when they're putting up a new building and they come across human remains. Of course, it isn't uncommon to find old bones during the excavation stage, before they even start construction, but I've also read news stories about people who sneak onto a site right after a building is completed and kill themselves there, for reasons unknown. Naturally, the project's sales agent would never mention such things, so who's to say something like that didn't happen here, too? That would explain a lot."

The lace curtain covering the big plate-glass window billowed slightly. The wind was kicking up, and a light rain had begun to fall. Misao stood up, walked over to the radio, and turned it on. It seemed as though every time she decided to listen to the radio there was some obnoxious "personality" yammering breathlessly at maximum volume, and this day was no different.

"Hey, lady over there, won't you tell us your name?" the annoying man was bleating. "No? Okay, be that way. Geez, Miss Thing, I see you've slathered on that gaudy red lipstick again today. You look like you've been chewing betel nut or something. Come on, 'fess up. Is your hubby really the only man in your life? Sure, right. Don't make me laugh. Anyhoo, little lady, here's the thing. It's time for a quick quiz. Okay? We're running short on time, so I'm just going to shoot you a question, point-blank. If you get the answer right on the first try, you'll win ten thousand yen. If you get it on the second try, you'll win five thousand yen. And if you don't manage to guess the answer at all, then you'll get the booby prize: a big fat kiss from little old me."

The sounds of laughter from the studio audience echoed around

the room. Eiko let out a giggle. "I swear, that guy says the most idi-
otic things. And what's the deal with talking in that racy, suggestive
way in the middle of the afternoon, when children could be listening? Who does that, anyway?"

"I know," Misao agreed. "He carries on like this all day, from ten
in the morning till four in the afternoon. It's usually unbearable but
today, for some reason, I'm in the mood for his kind of foolishness."

Misao went into the kitchen to heat up the remaining coffee.
Cookie was lying on the floor, gnawing on a rubber toy in the shape
of a bone. She wagged her tail and gave a friendly yelp of greeting.

"Aww, what a good girl, behaving herself so nicely. Tamao's still
asleep, you know," Misao crooned, bending down to scratch behind
the dog's ears.

"I wonder whether we should get a dog, too," Eiko mused, peering into the kitchen. "Actually, I think I might rather have a lion.
Maybe that way I wouldn't feel so frightened all the time."

Misao took a deep breath as she turned on the gas under the
coffeepot.

"You know what? I think you just need to try to forget about
what you heard today, and move on," she said. "I mean, both our
families bought units in this building with the intention of living
here for quite a while, right?"

The gas flame burst into bloom, vigorous and brilliantly blue.
Misao's eye lit on a can of potato chips and she thought of putting
them out in a basket, then decided that neither she nor Eiko was
likely to touch them. Instead—despite the fact that she rarely
smoked—she plucked a couple of cigarettes from a pack of Teppei's
that was lying on the counter. By that time the coffee was bubbling
again, and Misao carried the carafe and the cigarettes out to the
dining table. Silently, Eiko took one of the proffered smokes and
the two women lit their cigarettes.

"I'm starting to think that buying an apartment here might have
been a huge mistake," Eiko said, blowing out a long plume of
smoke. "Maybe it would have been better just to lease one of the

units. That way, we would have been able to move out, like all the other tenants who've left already."

"Are you saying that you want to move out?"

"I don't know. I'm not sure." Eiko let out a tired-sounding laugh. "I'm just not good at dealing with this kind of thing." Misao didn't need to ask for clarification of what Eiko meant by "this kind of thing." She knew only too well.

Just then the door to the nursery creaked open and Tamao called out, "Mama?"

It was raining harder now. Misao got up and closed the sliding door that opened onto the balcony. She glanced quickly at the graveyard and felt an unreasoning wave of revulsion at the way the rainy mist was rapidly engulfing the graves, obscuring them from sight. As Misao turned away from the window, Tamao came barreling down the hall with her face still swollen from sleep, and leaped into her mother's waiting arms.

# 11

Early one evening, Teppei and Tamao were on their way back from taking Cookie out for a run when they encountered Sueo Tabata, who was in the building's lobby polishing the elevator's brushed-metal doors. The nearby entrance to the caretakers' apartment stood open and Sueo's wife, Mitsue, was visible through the lacy door curtain, pacing back and forth in the kitchen.

"Oh, you've been out for a walk?" Sueo asked in a friendly way.

Teppei smiled and said, "You know how it is—when you have a dog, you can never take a day off from exercising." As he spoke, he bent down and gave Cookie's head a rough pat. Cookie looked up at her master with the eager, invigorated face she always wore after an outing.

Mitsue Tabata slipped into her sandals and emerged into the lobby. Her body language struck Teppei as brisk and resolute, and it was immediately clear that she had come out with a specific aim in mind.

"Hasn't this been a lovely Sunday?" Mitsue began, wiping her

damp hands on a blue apron that was already covered with a con-
stellation of grease spots. "Tamao, dear, did you go somewhere
with your papa in this nice weather?"

"Yep, we went *waaaay* over there," Tamao replied, childishly
stretching out the vowel in "way" as she pointed toward the front
door. She was thirsty after the long walk, and she just wanted to go
home as soon as possible and drink some Calpis—her favorite
beverage—so her response was more perfunctory than usual.

Mitsue smiled down at Tamao in a way that seemed to make
her large-featured face collapse inward on itself. Then she turned
her attention to her husband and Teppei, looking from one to the
other in a transparent attempt to gauge the expressions on their faces.
When Teppei pressed the call button, Mitsue finally spoke up.
"Um . . . er . . . ," she stammered in a tentative manner.

"Yes?" Teppei turned to look at her.

"No, it's just—I mean, it's something really silly and unimport-
ant," Mitsue said, showing her teeth in a forced smile.

"What is it?"

"Um, well, it's just that it seemed like something out of the ordinary might have been going on in the basement last night, and
we . . ."

*Oh, not the damned basement again*, Teppei thought, but he
held his tongue. Mitsue shot a glance at her husband, as if seeking
affirmation. Then, having apparently received the go-ahead signal,
she launched into her story.

"Anyhow, late last night, maybe around two a.m., I was awakened by sounds coming from the basement. First there was a kind
of scraping noise, like somebody whittling away at something, and
then I heard some loud crashes that sounded like objects being
tossed around. I thought a burglar might have gotten in, so I woke
up my husband. Isn't that right, dear?" Mitsue looked at Sueo with
a pleading expression, as if asking for backup.

"Yes, that's right. It was an infernal racket," Sueo said. "We
couldn't figure out what was going on, but there were unmistakable

banging or thudding sounds coming from down in the basement. I'm telling you, I was shocked. 'It's a burglar,' I said. 'We'd better call the police right away!' I was about to dial the number when my better half here stopped me. 'Don't jump to conclusions,' she said. 'It could just be one of the tenants tidying up their storage locker.' So instead of calling the police, I went down to the basement to take a look around."

By that point, Teppei knew, Mr. and Mrs. Yoshino had already moved out, as had the Yada sisters. Mr. Shoji, too, was long gone. Besides the caretakers, the only remaining residents were the Kanos, the Inoues, and the hostess, Ms. Harashima: four households in all. Ms. Harashima's moving date was rapidly approaching, and since she worked late every night it wasn't inconceivable that she might have been down in the basement in the wee hours, obliviously making noise while she got her possessions in order.

*Except for one thing*, Teppei thought. *That woman swore to me that she had no intention of ever setting foot in the basement again, for any reason, so it seems highly unlikely that she would have ventured down there alone in the dead of night. Besides, she stopped using her storage locker ages ago, so what would she have been doing there, at any hour?*

"So anyhow, I went down to look around," Sueo repeated with a flustered expression on his face. "And there was nobody there! I thought a cat or some other animal might have gotten in, but there was no sign of life at all."

"Huh," Teppei said, shifting Cookie's leash from one hand to the other. "So where do you suppose the noise was coming from?"

"I have no idea," Mitsue said, shaking her head. "But there were definitely noises coming from downstairs, loud enough to wake us from a sound sleep on the floor above. It wasn't mishearing on our parts, or imagination, or anything like that."

"What could it have been?" As Teppei stood there, looking baffled, he surprised himself by remembering something he had never expected to think about again: the conversation with Mr. Shoji,

several weeks earlier. What had that con man said about the basement? Some nonsense about its being a gathering place for evil
entities, or spirits. *Hogwash*, Teppei thought.

When Misao told Teppei about Eiko's uncanny experience the
other day—hearing, or thinking she heard, people conversing on
the other side of the wall—he had been on the verge of shouting,
"Okay, that's it. I've had enough. I'm declaring a permanent morato-
rium on talking about anything having to do with that stupid basement, starting now." It was the first time since their wedding day
that he had come close to raising his voice at Misao, for any reason.

Misao was clearly terrified of the basement, and she hadn't ventured down there even once since Tamao's accident. She had a
knack for being able to think things through in a rational manner,
and she was also remarkably adept at exercising self-control; those
faculties just seemed to come naturally to her. Even when Reiko
committed suicide, Misao had managed to move beyond that dev-
astating event in an admirable and even heroic way. Indeed, there
was a part of Teppei that believed Misao's support was the primary
reason he had been able to make it this far. It simply wasn't like her
to get all worked up over something as inoffensive as a basement;
it was as though she had fallen under the influence of one of those
supernatural-mystery TV dramas, and was getting absurdly over-
wrought about nothing. Teppei tried to be patient, but he was
finding his wife's obsession with the basement increasingly hard to
tolerate.

*Here I am*, he thought, *day after day, being jostled by other
passengers on the rush-hour train morning and night so I can do
battle at my workplace, which is a vortex of viciousness overlaid
with a toxic mix of cynicism, sarcasm, and false pride. I spend my
days writing copy that's basically trying to sell vinegar as wine (or,
as the old Chinese saying goes, to pass dogmeat off as mutton), and
I am fully complicit in concealing the squalor that lies beneath the
corporate mask, because I need to bring home the bacon every
week. With everything I have to deal with out in the real world,*

*does Misao really think I'm going to join her in believing a crock of occult mumbo-jumbo, and hold her hand while we both quake in our boots for fear of the big, bad basement? Not likely!*

Sueo's voice brought Teppei back to reality. "The thing is, there's something we wanted to ask you," the older man said, lowering his voice and inching closer. "We were wondering whether you might be willing to go down to the basement with us—preferably tonight, or whenever it's convenient—to do a little reconnaissance."

"Reconnaissance?" Teppei was still a bit disoriented from his internal rant.

Mitsue let out a booming laugh. "My husband here is too timid to go down there again by himself, or even with me," she explained. "He's just a big old scaredy-cat. So I was telling him he ought to ask Mr. Kano or Mr. Inoue to go with us, but he didn't feel comfortable about asking either of you."

Teppei frowned. "What would you be looking for?"

"Well, that's the thing. I don't really have anything particular in mind," Sueo admitted, scratching his bumpy, balding scalp in a way that made his few remaining hairs sway slightly, as if stirred by a gentle breeze. "It's just that your daughter got injured there, and it's troubling to think that we might have overlooked something dangerous around the edges of the basement or wherever."

"Okay, fine. I'll go with you," Teppei said without enthusiasm. "Sure, let's check it out. My wife and Mrs. Inoue spend entirely too much time griping about the basement, and I've actually been thinking recently that it might be a good idea to go down and prove once and for all that there's nothing to be afraid of. I mean, the fact is, we've made a sizable investment in this place, with the down payment and our mortgage and everything, so I'd really like to put an end to all the fuss about the basement right now."

"My sentiments exactly." Mitsue smiled.

After a brief discussion, it was agreed that Teppei would stop by the caretakers' apartment later that evening, at his convenience, and the two groups went their separate ways.

In the elevator Tamao said, "You're going down to the basement, Papa?"

"That's right," Teppei replied.

Tamao was silent for a long moment, gazing up at her father's face. Finally, she let out an exaggerated sigh and murmured, "Mama isn't going to be too happy about that."

"Nah, she won't mind." Teppei laughed. "Your papa's super strong, you know. If there are any monsters down there, he'll chase them away, for sure."

"You really think there are monsters?"

"No, of course I don't. I was only joking. There's no such thing as monsters in real life, anyway; they only exist in stories. The noises last night probably came from a great big mouse, or maybe from a homeless man who found a way to get into the basement and slept there overnight because he didn't have money for a hotel, or something like that. I'm sure there's a simple explanation for the noises the Tabatas heard last night."

"Um, what kind of person is the homeless man?"

"He's a very nice person, I promise," Teppei said, taking Tamao's hand. "Not like a monster, at all, so there's really nothing to worry about."

•

When Teppei announced that he and the resident managers were planning to go down to the basement on a so-called reconnaissance mission, Misao stared at him with eyes that had suddenly lost their customary sparkle.

"Are you serious?" she asked.

"Why, you don't want me to go?"

"I just don't see the need for reconnoitering, or whatever you want to call it. I mean, both Eiko and I have already decided not to use the storage lockers anymore. If you include the caretakers, there are only four occupied units in the building now. That's four out of fourteen, so if we have extra things that won't fit in the cupboards we can just stack them up in the exterior hallways, instead of putting them in the basement."

"That's all very well, but we're talking about apples and oranges here," Teppei said in a placating tone. "If we can locate the source of the noises, which will probably turn out to be the same thing that's been giving you and Eiko such a bad feeling, then from now on we can just shrug it off and be like, 'Oh, right, it's just *that thing* again.' Because I guarantee that the explanation is ultimately going to turn out to be something harmless, like a family of noisy mice."

"I hope you're right," Misao said glumly.

"Of course I'm right. Anyway, that's why we're going down to take a look around. It's really not a big deal."

Misao remained visibly unconvinced. "That place isn't safe," she said.

"You know, it isn't like you to swallow the superstitious nonsense that old Mr. Snake Oil Salesman—you know, that Shoji guy—was dishing out."

"But even you can sense that there's something peculiar about that space, right? I know, I can read between the lines."

"Who, me?" Teppei let out a staccato bark of laughter, but only because that seemed like the proper response. "Hey, when I was at university, we used to go to summer camp every year, and any time they had a contest to test our courage or nerve, I always won. Nobody else had a chance. So, no. To me, the basement just seems like a perfectly normal space."

Tamao was watching television in the living room. It was a new program, a cartoon featuring a bear cub that was pale pink, like a baby pig. Every time the bear said something, Tamao would roll around on the couch, laughing as if it was the funniest thing she had ever heard.

Misao let out a long, sibilant sigh and began to fiddle with a small glass jar of black pepper that was sitting on the dining table. She often engaged in this sort of displacement activity when she felt the need to say something difficult or awkward.

"What if I were to suggest that we put this place on the market and start looking for another apartment?" she asked. "Would you be angry?"

"Yes, I would be *very* angry," Teppei said without hesitation.

"That's what I thought."

"Look, could you please give it a rest? I mean, just for the sake of argument, suppose there really are some restless ghosts or spirits in the basement, popping up and raising a ruckus and then vanishing again. Well, what does that have to do with us? We're human beings who are alive right now, in the real world. If they want to pick a fight, there's no chance a group of puny specters could win against us. Don't you see? We're too busy living to worry about people who are already dead; that's all there is to it. I've managed to make it this far by believing that when people die, they're gone forever, and I'm certainly not going to start believing in ghosts at this point."

Misao fixed Teppei with a frosty stare. "Let me get this straight," she said slowly. "You're saying you don't have time to bother with the dead?"

"That's right."

"What a heartless thing to say. That's just too cold for words."

"What? How so?" Teppei stared at his wife in perplexity.

"I'm talking about Reiko," Misao said, her voice quavering as she scratched at the label of the black-pepper jar with one fingernail. "There's just no way . . . I mean, how could you say something like that about her?"

"No, you completely misunderstood," Teppei said gently. "That isn't what I was getting at, not at all. I wasn't even thinking about . . . that person."

"That's good, because I would have been very disappointed in you."

"I'm sorry, I didn't mean to upset you. I was speaking in general terms, and I just didn't phrase it very well, that's all. We've had this conversation before, so I assumed you'd understand what I meant."

They both fell silent for a while. From her perch on the living room couch, Tamao was watching her parents intently.

*What the hell is going on?* Teppei thought. *Misao's nerves really seem to be on edge these days. It's getting downright ridiculous. I mean, overreacting to a simple misunderstanding, and making a constant fuss over a totally ordinary basement? It all comes down to one thing: our unwise decision to buy a unit in an apartment building next to a graveyard.*

Teppei had an uncomfortable sense that the conversation had changed abruptly from what seemed to be an abstract discussion of the supernatural into something far more personal, and volatile, but he decided to keep that thought to himself. With luck, by the time he returned, Misao would have forgotten about this minor hitch in their usually harmonious communication.

"Well, then," he said, affecting a brisk, cheerful tone. "I'm going to take off now. I'll conduct a thorough investigation of the basement, just to put your mind at rest. I don't suppose you feel like coming along?"

"Are you joking? No way!" Misao said emphatically, chewing her lip. "To be honest, I'd be happier if you didn't go, either."

Teppei looked into Misao's eyes for a long moment. "I'll be fine," he said. "I promise, this whole expedition is going to turn out to be much ado about absolutely nothing."

Misao took a deep breath, then exhaled audibly. "Yes, of course, you're right," she said.

"Listen," Teppei said earnestly. "I'm afraid I didn't do a very good job of expressing myself earlier, but I was just trying to say that what's important to me right now is us: our family."

"Of course, I know, and I feel the same way." Misao smiled wanly.

Playfully tousling his wife's hair, Teppei teased, "Seriously, Mrs. Kano, you really do need to pull yourself together."

When Teppei arrived at the door of the caretakers' apartment he found Sueo Tabata waiting for him, freshly dressed in a pristine white polo shirt. Mitsue hastily shed her grease-spotted apron and followed them into the lobby with undisguised excitement, brandishing a jumbo flashlight in one hand.

Teppei wondered silently whether it was really necessary to make such a production out of a humdrum errand, but he didn't say anything. He pressed the button for the elevator and then, in a subtle attempt to emphasize the routine nature of what they were doing, he struck up a nonchalant conversation about professional baseball with Sueo.

In the game Teppei had been watching out of the corner of his eye during dinner, the leadoff batter for the Giants had hit a home run on the first pitch. When he mentioned that to Sueo, the older man broke into a delighted grin. Evidently he was a Giants fan.

"I'm really sorry about this," Mitsue said as they boarded the elevator. "I gather you were in the middle of watching a game?"

"No, it's fine. Anyway, at our house Tamao usually gets to choose the channel, and she wanted to watch something else."

When they got to the basement, Sueo turned on the overhead lights. Maybe it was because the weather had warmed up outside, or perhaps the air was just stagnant because hardly anyone ever came down here anymore, but the atmosphere seemed unusually close and stuffy—almost to the point where it was difficult to take a proper breath.

The storage lockers stood in neat, orderly rows. Tsutomu's tricycle wasn't occupying its usual place in front of the Inoues' locker, but apart from that detail the basement looked just the way it always had. There was nothing abnormal, nothing different, nothing out of place.

The cardboard boxes of high-calorie protein bars were still piled in one corner, where they had been all along. Teppei and the Tabatas carefully examined each of the cartons, but there wasn't a single bit of evidence to indicate that rodents had been nibbling at the cardboard.

"Everything looks spick-and-span, doesn't it?" Sueo said. "I mean, now that we're here, nothing seems to be amiss."

"The cleaning is completely up to date, too," Mitsue declared proudly. "I've been coming down alone once a week, without fail. Well, I usually just run the vacuum over the floor, but I always make sure to do a thorough job, including the corners. Needless to say, I would never dream of neglecting my duties."

Teppei had heard about Mitsue's tendency toward self-aggrandizement, and now he understood what Misao and Eiko had been referring to.

*The only thing that matters is the here and now,* Teppei told himself as he glanced around. Even if certain things occurred that seemed at the time to defy logic and common sense (like the indoor weasel wind, for example), an impeccably rational explanation would eventually emerge—an explanation that simply happened to involve some obscure scientific principle that hadn't immediately sprung to anyone's mind. Once you started jumping to subjective conclusions, matters could get out of hand very quickly. Nothing good ever came of that approach, and it often led to chaos, confusion, and a destabilized mental state. On that score at least, Mitsue, with her regular trips down to the basement to vacuum the floor as part of her caretaker duties, seemed to be taking a commendably reasonable, down-to-earth approach to the place, and that was as it should be. In Teppei's opinion, rational and objective was the only way to go.

After a quick huddle, the three explorers decided to divide the basement into three approximately equal parts. Sueo took the front section, which included the elevator; Mitsue claimed the central area; and Teppei set off to examine the periphery.

Teppei's assignment included the spot where Tamao had sustained her mysterious injury. He began by peeking behind every single one of the unused storage lockers, where he found nothing more sinister than the usual colonies of fluffy dust bunnies. At one point something glossy caught his eye, but when he looked closely it turned out to be just a flake of paint.

The floor, the ceiling, the tops of storage compartments: Teppei walked slowly around, executing the same meticulously attentive type of survey he had performed just after Tamao's accident. Methodically, he opened each of the unused storage lockers and peered inside, but they were all empty and—contrary to the dramatic outcome he suspected Misao and Eiko might have been hoping for—he didn't catch a single glimpse of a strange, scary monster from realms unknown.

"How's it going over there?" he called out to Mitsue.

She was apparently experiencing some pain in her lower back, because she pounded on the base of her spine with both fists as she replied, "I haven't found anything at all."

Sueo was standing in front of the elevator, admiring the metal door. "This really is a splendid building," he declared in a loud voice. "The construction is sturdy, and everything looks nice and new, inside and out."

Teppei jammed his hands into the front pockets of his jeans and began to whistle quietly: "Can't Take My Eyes Off of You." He had no idea why that particular song had suddenly popped into his head. When he was in college, Frankie Valli's rendition had often been played at the clubs he frequented. Then, years later, he and Misao had gone to see an American film called *The Deer Hunter*, and that same song was part of the soundtrack. On the way home from the movie theater, he and Misao had quietly crooned the chorus as they strolled through the Shibuya district of Tokyo.

*I doubt if I ever sang a song that way with Reiko, even once,* Teppei mused. Reiko had disliked any kind of noisy, high-spirited behavior. She couldn't stand unexpected developments, or excessive liveliness, or the kind of momentary vicissitudes that can boost people's moods, causing them to feel (and express) a sudden rush of joy or elation.

Teppei sauntered up to the back wall, where Eiko claimed to have heard a vague hubbub of human voices, and placed one ear against the concrete surface. He thought he detected a faint rustling on the other side of the wall, but he assumed it was just the sound of his longish hair brushing against the concrete. Next, he tried knocking on the wall with his bare knuckles. From the other side, there came a muffled sound, almost like an echo. *The concrete must be thinner here, or perhaps the builders used hollow blocks,* he thought.

He examined the wall carefully, keeping his eyes peeled for any sign of irregularities. There wasn't a single fissure, and the coat of paint that had been used to finish the concrete was as flawless as the day it was applied.

"Okay," he said to himself, sotto voce. "I am now officially sick and tired of this whole damn thing. I've had it up to here with all the talk about the big, bad basement. I mean, we're all adults, and then some. What the hell are we doing anyway, poking around down here? This is downright embarrassing—I mean, there's no way I could ever tell anyone about this little expedition."

Turning around, Teppei said in a louder voice, "Okay, there's nothing here whatsoever."

"Nothing here, either," Mitsue and Sueo called back, almost in unison.

"I'm going to tell my wife that she needs to start putting things in our storage locker again," Teppei announced. "It's wasteful to have a facility like this and not make use of it."

"So I guess the noises we heard last night must have been coming from outside the building," Sueo speculated, tilting his head to one side. "I don't know—maybe there's something about the construction that turns this place into a sort of conduit for noises from outside? You know, like an echo chamber?"

"That must be it." Teppei nodded in agreement. "I mean, the fact that we haven't found anything out of the ordinary would seem to support your theory, as well. Oh, Mrs. Tabata? I was just wondering whether you ever got any kind of strange or, I don't know, unnerving feeling when you were down here alone."

"No, not really." Mitsue smiled, automatically putting one hand up to cover her mouth while she spoke. "Even if I had, I wouldn't have been afraid. For me, real-world dangers like burglary, or fire, or getting an 'insufficient funds' notice from my bank—*that's* the kind of thing that scares me!"

Chuckling at her quip, the three of them assembled in front of the elevator. As he touched the call button, Sueo told Teppei that he hoped they would both get home in time to see the remainder of the baseball game.

"We have radically different tastes when it comes to watching TV," Mitsue said, with a wry glance at her husband. "This guy here is all about baseball, and pro wrestling, and sumo, while I love dramas—you know, like those recent thrillers with women in all the lead roles? That series was really something . . ."

As Mitsue rambled on, Teppei's eyes were fixed on the elevator panel. *That's odd*, he thought. The elevator was taking an inordinately long time to respond. The door hadn't opened, and the indicator light remained stuck on "1," which meant the elevator had returned to the first floor after they got out.

The call button was already illuminated, but Teppei stuck out an index finger and pressed it again, to be safe. Still, the elevator door remained closed. Mitsue interrupted her monologue about the women's suspense dramas and said, "Huh? What's going on? Why isn't it opening?"

Sueo stretched out one arm and jabbed repeatedly at the call button, with escalating force. The elevator door remained stubbornly closed, almost as if it were making fun of them, and there was no movement on the indicator panel.

Teppei felt a sudden draft on the back of his neck: damp, penetrating, and freezing cold. He turned and glanced at the rows of storage lockers. Just then, the overhead lights began to flicker.

A moment later they went off completely, and the entire space was enveloped in darkness. An afterimage of light in the form of orange filaments lingered deep inside Teppei's eyes; it was the kind of optical effect you might experience if you walked into a dark beach house after having been out in the brilliant sunshine at the seashore.

"What the—?" Sueo shrieked in a panic-stricken tone. Teppei, too, was seized by an almost overwhelming desire to scream, but he managed to suppress it. A large vein began to throb at the base of his throat.

"I wonder if it's a power outage?" Mitsue said shrilly. She fumbled frantically with her large flashlight until she located the power button, then turned it on. "Even the emergency lights have gone out."

"This isn't good. This isn't good at all," Sueo chanted over and over. He snatched the flashlight from his wife's hand and bounced the arc of light haphazardly around the immediate vicinity. The wintry wind had grown noticeably stronger, and it seemed to be actively trying to burrow under Teppei's loosely tucked T-shirt.

"Did you get a notice about any power outages scheduled for tonight, as part of regular maintenance or something?" he asked in an exaggeratedly calm, relaxed manner, surprising himself with his acting ability.

"No, I didn't hear about anything like that," Sueo replied.

"This can't be a power outage," Mitsue pointed out. "I mean, look, the elevator light is on."

Sure enough, she was right. They had all been so busy reacting to the blackout that they hadn't noticed that "B1" was now alight on the panel above the elevator. However, the door remained stubbornly closed. Sueo seemed to have taken leave of his senses, and he pounded futilely on the call button with such excessive force that it seemed likely to shatter under the assault.

"Well, drat," Mitsue said. "I wonder if the elevator's on the fritz again." She spoke in an easygoing manner, which had the perverse effect of making Teppei feel even more alarmed. Meanwhile, the wind seemed to be gaining strength. Even though the weather outside was warm enough to make a person sweat during a brief jog, the temperature inside the basement had dropped so precipitously that Teppei felt as if his entire body were covered with goose bumps: every inch of his skin, and inside his head, too. It was cold on cold, like eating a shaved-ice cone in a snowstorm.

"What should we do?" Teppei said, to no one in particular. "This is really getting weird."

"Help us, please!" Sueo shouted. His voice reverberated throughout the basement, creating an otherworldly echo. "Somebody, help!"

"It's gotten really cold down here," Mitsue whined, rubbing her bare arms. "What's going on, anyway?"

"The wind must be blowing in from someplace," Teppei replied. "You know, through a crack or something." He turned to look behind him. He had a distinct sense that something was stirring in the dark corners of the basement, where the beam from the flashlight didn't reach. An instant later he thought he saw a brief, sudden burst of unnaturally bright light, and he got the feeling that the moving thing (whatever it might be) was trying to intimidate or even actively threaten them. But no, surely that was just his imagination running wild.

Rousing his unnerved self to action, Teppei carefully surveyed the area around him. "Is there an emergency call box, or any other way to get in touch with the outside world when the elevator breaks down?" he asked calmly.

Sueo was visibly trembling and could only shake his head, so Mitsue answered in his stead. "No, there isn't," she said. "That's just one of this building's many design flaws. I've always thought it was odd, though."

Teppei was wearing slip-on sandals without socks, and the chilly wind twined around his bare ankles and crept up his legs in a way that felt oddly aggressive and clingy. He bent down and swatted vigorously at his ankles with both hands, as though brushing away a cloud of mosquitoes. He was finding it increasingly difficult to breathe, and when he tried to suck in a deep, restorative lungful of air, that simple action caused his chest to quiver uncontrollably.

"I don't understand what's going on," Sueo said in a plaintive, high-pitched voice. He began to hammer on the closed door of the elevator with both fists. "After Tamao's accident we had the elevator serviced, so there's no way it could have broken down again so soon!"

"What if all three of us shouted together at the top of our lungs?" Mitsue suggested. "Somebody might hear us upstairs."

"Somebody? Who?" Sueo thundered, his eyes ablaze with frustration. "Do you really think anyone will be able to hear us all the way up on the fourth floor, where the Inoues are?"

"You don't have to yell at me!" Mitsue snapped. The lazy, circular beam of the flashlight—bright at the center, more diffuse at the edges—cast surreal shadows on their faces, making them look like a trio of grotesque goblins.

Teppei placed both hands on the elevator. There was a small crack where the two halves of the door met, and he thought he might try sticking one finger into that opening and wiggling it back and forth, in the hopes of prying the doors open. However, the crack was so narrow that he couldn't even maneuver his pinky finger into a position where it would have any leverage.

"It's so cold," Sueo whispered. In fact, "cold" didn't begin to describe the unearthly chill that had descended on the basement. Teppei could actually hear his own teeth chattering.

*There has to be a rational explanation,* he thought in desperation. *I mean, things like this simply don't happen in the real world . . . do they?*

"Help us, please!" Sueo's voice was a plaintive squeak. Mitsue just stood there, stock-still and silent, almost as if she had lost the ability to speak.

Teppei stuck his arm into the beam of the flashlight and peered at his wristwatch. It was nearly half past eight. Less than half an hour had passed since they had come down to the basement. It was much too soon for Misao to start wondering why he was so late in returning home. When she did reach that point, she would go out into the hallway and push the button for the elevator, and when there was no response she would realize it was out of order—or else she might intuit that something else was going on, something that boggled the mind and flew in the face of reason. Either way, surely she would rally the troops (that is, the Inoues) and they would call someone outside the building, asking for assistance. But that sequence of events wouldn't commence for at least another fifteen minutes, at the earliest. In the meantime, they were on their own down here.

"I know why the wind has kicked up all of a sudden," Mitsue said softly. "It's because of that underground road they dug. I'm sure of it."

"What underground road?" Teppei asked incredulously.

"Oh, you haven't heard? Apparently at one time there was a plan to build an underground shopping mall that was supposed to stretch from Takaino Station to right around here."

Teppei had a sudden urge to shout, "What the hell does that have to do with what we're dealing with now?" He managed to suppress that outburst and only said, "You don't say." He placed both hands on the elevator door, hoping to feel a sense of movement, but the mechanism was as inert as ever.

Half to herself, Mitsue said, "It's kind of a sickening thought—I mean, the idea that there could be an old, abandoned tunnel passing under the graveyard and leading right up to this building."

Teppei wasn't listening. The velocity of the already powerful wind had ramped up another notch, almost to the point where you could call it a gale, and he could feel it lifting his hair. Mitsue stopped muttering to herself and latched onto her husband's arm.

Not long after that, the noises began. They were macabre, disturbing, and distinctly unpleasant. The unsettling cacophony included the whistling of a high wind, which seemed to be traveling along the electrical cables on the ceiling; a sort of discordant screech, as if an unmusical child were fooling around with a violin and bow, randomly scraping at the strings; a squishy slapping, as of a throng of giant reptiles thrashing around in the murky mire of a swamp; and the stealthy murmuration of an immense number of voices, whispering secretly among themselves. Teppei was standing perfectly still, his mouth hanging open in disbelief. His T-shirt was now completely untucked from the waistband of his jeans, and the icy wind lifted it into the air, exposing his slightly flabby midriff.

"Stop it! Somebody help us, please!" Sueo cried. He and Mitsue were clinging tightly to each other, and without letting go they plopped down onto the floor and sat there, looking stunned. The wind stole under the gathered skirt Mitsue was wearing, causing it to billow so high that her baby-blue granny panties were plainly visible.

The adrenalized stress was making Teppei feel lightheaded. He couldn't believe that he was still able to remain upright, with his feet on solid ground, and it occurred to him that this must be what people meant when they talked about losing it. Psychologically, he was already at the end of his tether.

*I think I owe Misao an apology,* he thought. *It's starting to look like she was right about the basement all along. This is definitely not a normal place.*

Mitsue had been clutching the flashlight, which had somehow found its way from Sueo's hands back into hers, but now she let it fall to the floor with a clatter. Teppei felt weak at the knees, and he realized that he was physically unable to move. In the darkness, something was squirming and wriggling. This was no hallucination born of fear; some amorphous, hazy, unimaginably huge *entity* was moving toward them, slowly and inexorably.

"*Gaah!* No!" Mitsue shrieked, while Sueo could only gasp in terror.

A sudden flurry of ice-cold wind whipped noisily around them, making Teppei feel as though he had suddenly lost his hearing. Some rough force seemed to be trying to knock him off his feet; he staggered around for a moment, then collapsed onto the floor. He felt someone or something striking him repeatedly on the head, and then the world went black.

# 12

An hour had passed since Teppei set out on his reconnaissance mission. Misao felt upset after he left, so she had busied herself with tidying up the dinner dishes before settling in front of the television with Tamao to watch a home drama about the troubled relationship between a young wife and her shrewish mother-in-law. At the same time, doubling down on her determination to improve her mood, she was leafing through an enticingly illustrated article titled "Three-Minute Recipes," in a cooking magazine. The voice of the ingenue playing the part of the new bride began to grate on Misao's ears, and she turned down the volume.

Tamao had been happily playing with her teddy bear, but now her eyelids began to droop. When she got drowsy, Tamao had an unconscious habit of vigorously rubbing her ears. Tonight she had already kneaded one ear to the point where it was visibly inflamed.

Misao gave her daughter a light tap on the bottom and said, "I know you're sleepy, but you need to wait till Papa comes back, okay? You always take a bath with Papa on Sunday night, isn't that right?"

"Do I really have to take a bath?"

"You worked up a sweat today, didn't you? You'll sleep better if you take a bath before you go to bed."

"I don't want to. I'm already super sleepy."

Misao looked at the clock on the wall. *How long are those three planning to stay down in the basement, anyway?* she wondered. *Does this extended stay mean they found something?* Even so, it would have been nice if Teppei had taken a minute to run back upstairs and give her an update.

Craning her neck to peek into the hallway, Misao caught a glimpse of Cookie lying asleep on the floor with both forelegs stretched out in front. When Misao turned back to look at Tamao, her eyes were drawn to the TV screen. It was filled with an extreme close-up of the face of the actress playing the young wife, but the image was wavering and shimmering, almost as if it were being projected on the ripply surface of a body of water. In addition, the screen was streaked with a veritable blizzard of diagonal lines.

Misao jumped up from the sofa and changed the channel. The picture looked the same on every station: quivery and obscured by slanting lines. "That's funny," she said. "Tamao, something's wrong with the TV."

Tamao showed a brief flicker of interest, then immediately went back to sleepily massaging her ears. Misao tried fiddling with the picture adjustment button. Just like the other time when there had been some kind of electronic interference, the image on the screen continued to waver and sway.

Misao felt an unpleasant sense of foreboding. Ignoring Tamao, who was becoming increasingly fretful, she went into the kitchen. Lifting the receiver of the telephone on the counter, she punched in the Tabatas' number. It rang and rang, but no one picked up.

Misao's forehead broke out in prickly beads of sweat. The basement was basically an open space, and it wasn't all that large, so how could it possibly take this long for three people to conduct an inspection?

When she checked on Tamao, she saw that her little daughter had already begun to doze off, right where she was. Misao grabbed a large cushion and stuck it gently under Tamao's head. Then she went to the nursery and fetched a light terrycloth coverlet to drape over the sleeping child. Tamao's face still wore a resentful expression, but her breathing was already deep and regular. Clearly, she was sound asleep.

A moment later, when Misao headed toward the front door, Cookie got up and followed her. "No, you can't come," Misao said, shooing the dog away. "Stay. Stay, okay?" Cookie slunk off in disappointment as Misao locked the door behind her and stepped into the outside corridor.

The light on the panel above the elevator showed that it was still on "B1": the basement level. With one shaky forefinger, Misao pressed the call button. Normally, she would have heard the usual *ga-tonk* as the elevator began to move, but now? Nothing. Not a sound, and no sign of movement.

"Oh, no, this can't be happening again," Misao said aloud. She could almost feel the color draining from her face. On the day when Tamao was injured while playing in the basement, the elevator had refused to budge. Maybe the three explorers were holding the door open at the basement level, for some reason. But why? What possible reason could they have for doing that?

Misao hurried over to the entrance to the emergency staircase, unlocked the door, and sprinted down the stairs. *It's just like that other time,* she thought. The air in the stairwell was lukewarm, and when she took a deep breath she could feel its tepid stickiness spreading through her lungs.

As soon as she reached the ground floor, Misao checked the elevator panel. "B1" was still lit up, and there was no indication that the car had moved at all. As she hit the call button over and over, to no avail, Misao's mouth filled with saliva that seemed, in her stressed-out state, to have the metallic taste of blood. She walked over to the caretakers' apartment and rang the doorbell. Nobody appeared. She tried twisting the doorknob, but the door was locked.

Weak-kneed, shaken, and fighting back tears, Misao went back to the emergency staircase and galloped upstairs. She was panting like a thirsty dog, and she could have sworn she heard her knee-caps knocking together. Her heart was pounding so violently that she felt it might explode.

When Misao got back to her own apartment, she found Tamao still fast asleep on the sofa, breathing softly through her mouth. The television's picture quality had deteriorated to the point where it was nearly impossible to make out the images on the screen.

Misao switched off the TV and plunged toward the telephone, in a desperate motion that was more like falling forward than running. She surprised herself by remembering Eiko's phone number right away.

"Hello?" Eiko answered on the first ring, in a voice filled with eagerness. It was almost as if she had been waiting for Misao to call. "Um, listen," Eiko said after Misao identified herself, "has your TV been acting strange?"

"Yes, very strange," Misao replied. "The picture's all wavy and blurry."

"I know, right? Same here. It's really weird. There doesn't seem to be anything wrong with the set itself, though."

"I'm actually calling about something else," Misao said. "My husband went to the basement with the Tabatas, and he hasn't come home. They said they were going to take a look around, but it's been more than an hour since he left. I started to get worried, so I thought I'd pop down and check on them, but the elevator's stuck on the basement level and I can't get it to move."

"Really?" Eiko's voice rose in concern. "That's just like what happened the day Tamao was injured! Are you sure it won't move?"

At that point Eiko apparently passed the receiver to her husband. "Mrs. Kano? Is something wrong?" he asked hesitantly.

"I don't know," Misao replied. "The elevator seems to be stuck on the basement level. It's been more than an hour since my husband went down there, and he still hasn't come back."

"Hang on a minute," Mr. Inoue said, and there was a clattering thump as he put the receiver down. Misao could hear the familiar sound of the couple's rambunctious children running around in the background.

After a few moments, Eiko's husband returned. "You're right—the elevator's out of order again," he said. "I couldn't get it to move at all."

"What should we do?" As she spoke, Misao could feel hot tears welling up in her eyes. Her vision blurred, and her throat felt constricted from the effort of holding back the sobs that kept trying to escape.

"Do you have the number for the elevator maintenance company?" Mr. Inoue asked.

"No, I don't. I think the Tabatas are the only ones who have it."

"In that case, maybe we should call the police. Or would it be better to phone the fire department? I really don't know what to do. What a mess!"

Mr. Inoue evidently handed the phone to his wife, because Eiko spoke next. "Listen, Misao," she said urgently, "why don't you just come down to our place, to start with? I'll be waiting by the emergency door, so you can take the stairs. Oh, what about Tamao?"

"She's sound asleep."

"Well, in that case, it's probably best not to disturb her. Just be sure to lock your apartment door behind you, okay? I'm leaving right now, so . . ."

"On my way," Misao said. Grabbing the key ring, she flew out the door. The elevator was just as she had left it: stalled on the basement level.

She charged headlong down the emergency staircase, and as she approached the fourth-floor landing, she saw the door opening inward. Eiko was standing in the doorway, her face unnaturally pale. Mr. Inoue was beside her, a long drink of water next to his diminutive wife. As Misao entered the hallway Tsutomu dashed up, calling "Auntie!" and took hold of her hand.

"I think calling the police is the best plan," Eiko said. "Even if we could figure out how to contact the maintenance company, they probably wouldn't be answering the phone. I mean, today's Sunday, right?"

"The thing is, we don't know for sure that anything has happened to them. They may be perfectly fine down there," Misao said, but she shivered involuntarily as she spoke.

Mr. Inoue gave his head an emphatic shake. "That's probably true, but the fact remains that we need to do something," he said. "If we just sit around worrying, the elevator could remain out of order for the rest of the evening, and that would be inconvenient for the tenant on the fifth floor who works the night shift and comes home late."

"This is no time to be talking about a minor inconvenience to someone we hardly know," Eiko said grumpily. "We need to focus on making sure that Teppei and the Tabatas are safe."

Just then Kaori wandered out of the Inoues' apartment and looked around uneasily. Misao took a deep breath and tried to muster a reassuring smile. Tsutomu, meanwhile, was banging on the call button, over and over. "It's broken for sure, Mama," he announced.

"Yes, I know," Eiko said shortly, making it clear that Tsutomu's attempt to be helpful was more of a nuisance. She laid a sympathetic hand on Misao's arm.

Eiko's husband pressed one ear against the elevator door. When his father died, Mr. Inoue had immediately taken over the family factory, which his dad had owned and operated for decades. Misao knew that he and Teppei weren't too far apart in age, but Mr. Inoue always struck her as quite a bit older. She thought that might be because his male-pattern baldness was already well under way, especially toward the back of his head. Misao had only met Eiko's husband on a couple of occasions before tonight, and this was the first time she had ever gotten a good look at him from behind.

*I'll have to tell Teppei about this later,* she thought. She would say something like, "Mr. Inoue seems to be losing his hair, and he looks a lot older than you in other ways, too." She could imagine Teppei's comical, mock-boastful response: "Hey, I'm still in the prime of manhood, you know. Looking at other men will just make you realize what a spectacular specimen of youthful masculinity I really am."

*Please let him be okay,* Misao prayed. *I'd give anything to be able to have that kind of bantering conversation again. Yes, if Teppei does come home safely, there are so many things I want to say to him. And so many important things we need to talk about, together.*

Mr. Inoue looked at his wife with eyes made hollow by alarm. "If someone were shouting for help in the basement, don't you think we'd be able to hear it up here, through the elevator shaft?" he asked.

Eiko responded impatiently, "Look, let's just phone somebody. I don't care if it's the police or the fire department; anybody will do. Oh, I hate this so much. I've had it up to here with living in this atrocious place!" She put both hands to her flaming cheeks. "And the TV going haywire again has some connection with this bizarre building, too—I'm sure of that. I swear, this place is cursed. No, seriously, it seems to be under some kind of spell, or possessed by evil spirits!"

"Stop it," Mr. Inoue said quietly. "That kind of talk isn't appropriate at a time like this, especially in front of the boy."

From inside the Inoues' apartment came the sound of pattering feet, and Kaori scampered out into the hallway again, calling, "Mama, Mama!"

"What is it?" Eiko asked, calmer now.

"The TV is fixed! The picture isn't jumping around anymore."

As Kaori was making that announcement, Tsutomu suddenly said, "Hey!" in a loud, excited voice. Far below, in the bowels of the building, they heard a faint *ga-tonk* sound. "It's moving!" Tsutomu squealed. "The elevator is moving!"

The lights on the indicator panel were on the move, as well: from B1, to 1, to 2 . . .

"Oh, thank goodness," Misao breathed, reaching out to clasp Eiko's hands. A relieved smile played around Mr. Inoue's lips. They all stood there in silence, listening to the creak of the elevator as it drew closer.

"It was probably just a loose connection or a crossed wire or something. That's the most likely explanation," Mr. Inoue said, but it was obvious from the expression on his face that he didn't believe a word he was saying. No one even bothered to make a pretense of nodding in agreement.

The numeral 4 lit up, and the elevator doors slowly swished open.

Eiko ordered Tsutomu and Kaori to go back into the apartment and lock the door from the inside. Tsutomu balked, shouting, "No way. I'm going with you!" At that, Eiko lost patience and bodily shoved him into the apartment from behind. Tsutomu's angry parting words—"I hate you, Mama! You're an idiot!"—reverberated through the corridor.

Misao and Eiko got into the elevator, with Mr. Inoue bringing up the rear. Someone touched the "B1" button. The doors closed and the mechanism made its unvarying *ga-tonk* sound as the car began to descend: 3 . . . 2 . . . 1 . . . B1. Vibrating slightly, the elevator came to a halt in the basement and the doors slid open with a smooth, fluid motion.

The fluorescent lights were bright overhead, and the first thing the newcomers saw was the two caretakers slumped on the ground with their eyes bugging out and horrified expressions on their slack-jawed faces. There was a large puddle of liquid beneath Mitsue Tabata's skirt, which seemed to suggest that she had lost control of her bladder.

Misao came flying out of the elevator and immediately spotted Teppei lying in an unconscious heap a short distance from the Tabatas. She rushed to his side, grabbed his shoulders, and began to shake him as hard as she could.

"I'll go up and phone for an ambulance," Mr. Inoue shouted.

"No, wait," Misao called back. "Could you please just stay there for a minute?" If he went upstairs to call an ambulance, leaving them stranded in this hellhole . . . *I'd rather die,* she thought.

Teppei opened his eyes a crack. He took a deep breath, the way people do when they've been abruptly awakened from a deep sleep, and muttered some incoherent syllables under his breath. He gazed blankly at Misao for a moment. Finally he let out a strangled cry, and sat up.

"What's the matter with you?" Misao said anxiously. "Look, it's me!"

Teppei stared at her with big, round, vacant eyes, then blinked a few times. After a long moment he finally seemed to recognize his wife. Profound relief washed over his face, and he pulled Misao into a tight embrace. "I'm cold," he whispered. "It's so incredibly cold down here."

"It's okay. You're safe now," Misao said. She was trembling all over.

The Inoues were busy helping the wobbly Tabatas to their feet and supporting them as they made their slow, silent way toward the elevator. Nobody said a word, but even though no questions were raised and no answers given, it was already clear that none of the people who were in the basement at that moment had the slightest doubt that something very ominous—and undeniably supernatural—had just occurred.

"We'd better get a move on," Mr. Inoue said with quiet authority. Eiko, who was helping Mitsue along with one arm looped around the older woman's waist, looked back at the Kanos and shouted, "Come on, hurry up!" in a tone that bordered on the hysterical.

Teppei nodded and got to his feet, staggering a bit. Misao took his arm and then, summoning every last drop of courage, she looked back at the row of storage compartments. The lockers were lined up in neat rows, the same as always. However, there was something different about the wall at the rear of the room, beyond the last of the lockers—the same place where Tamao had been injured and where Eiko had heard voices. On that far wall Misao could see something that definitely hadn't been there before: a large black splotch or stain. She exhaled, and her breath hovered in front of her like a ghostly cloud. The air around her feet and legs was so bone-chillingly cold that she could barely remain standing.

Misao bundled Teppei into the elevator and pushed the button for the eighth floor. The door closed, and the occupants heard the familiar sound effects as the mechanism shifted into gear. Just as Misao's emotions seemed to be returning to normal, she was seized by a sudden urge to vomit. She clapped one hand over her mouth and managed, just barely, to gulp back the wave of bitter bile that rose from the depths of her esophagus and flooded into her throat.

# 13

Around noon, Misao was dithering in front of the elevator, trying to decide whether to take it down to the fourth floor. Finally, she gritted her teeth and pressed the call button. Lately she'd had to make a major effort to psych herself up to get into the elevator every time she needed to go somewhere.

In the weeks since that night in the middle of May, Sueo Tabata, in his capacity as the building's caretaker, had brought in an elevator maintenance crew not only once or twice but three times. On each visit the experts had made a complete examination of the elevator's working parts, but they hadn't been able to find anything that could have caused the stoppages.

Next, Sueo had summoned a local locksmith to remove the automatic locking mechanisms on the emergency staircase doors on every floor of the building. Once this was done, the doors could be easily opened from either the inside or the outside. While this might have appeared to be an invitation to burglars, the building's few remaining residents—the Inoues, the Kanos, and the Tabatas themselves—all agreed that it was more important to have immediate access to the emergency stairs without needing to carry a key.

*Really*, they were all thinking, *suppose a prowler did somehow manage to sneak in through the lobby, then used the emergency staircase to reach the higher floors? Honestly, at this point, who cares?* They had far bigger problems to deal with, and they were past worrying about hypothetical real-world threats.

After their terrifying experience in the basement back in May, Teppei and the Tabatas were especially reluctant to use the elevator. "Suppose we get in and press the button for the lobby, and instead it goes all the way to the basement?" Teppei would say. "Or what if it suddenly stopped moving, and we were stuck? What would we do then?" However, since the Kanos lived eight flights up, it would have been exceedingly impractical to stop using the elevator entirely.

The elevator arrived on the eighth floor. Warily, Misao got in and gave the button marked "4" a forceful push. The doors closed, and she heard the usual *ga-tonk*. Squeezing her eyes shut, she said a silent prayer. A few seconds later the elevator came to a halt, and the doors slid open with a rush of air. When Misao opened her eyes she saw the hallway of the fourth floor, looking safe and familiar.

With a feeling of relief, she stepped out of the elevator. The front door of the Inoues' apartment was standing open, and there was a pile of cardboard packing boxes in the entryway. Misao gave the doorbell a cursory ring, out of politeness, then poked her head through the open door. The first thing she saw was Eiko, standing in the living room holding a telephone.

"That's right," Eiko was saying into the receiver, "Central Plaza Mansion, apartment 402. I called in an order for four portions of cold soba more than an hour ago. What? Really? Well, I hope he gets here soon. We're moving today, and we're on a tight schedule."

As she was hanging up the phone, Eiko spotted Misao at the

door and made a beckoning gesture. "Come in, come in!" she called, smiling broadly.

Eiko's husband was in the process of detaching a hanging light fixture from the living room ceiling. "Yes, please come in!" he echoed.

"I just wanted to drop by and see how you were getting along," Misao said as she entered the chaotic room.

"Well, I think we're nearly there," Eiko said. "I ended up just kind of randomly tossing stuff into boxes, but I did at least take the time to pack the breakables carefully. We aren't going far, so it should be okay."

"When is the truck coming?"

"I think it should be here before too long. I'm just hoping we'll have time to finish eating the noodles we ordered." Eiko glanced at her wristwatch, then stared abstractedly into the distance for a long moment. The sky outside the windows was covered with clouds, and now that the overhead light fixture had been taken down, the living room seemed dark and gloomy.

The Inoues had put their apartment on the market the week after the incident in the basement, back in mid-May. Eiko had apparently talked about nothing else for days on end, but it wasn't as if her husband required much (if any) persuasion. Indeed, it turned out that even before that night he had begun thinking it might be better to move away sooner rather than later.

Since it went without saying that they wouldn't be able to find a buyer on such short notice, Eiko had spoken with her parents, who lived in Itabashi, and they had agreed to rent the Inoues a prefabricated two-bedroom house that had been installed in one corner of their property some years before. The structure had originally been built to serve as a studio where Eiko's mother could teach the neighborhood brides and housewives the complicated art of dressing in kimono, but the older woman's health had deteriorated to the point where the prefab house was hardly used anymore. Even though this move meant making the transition from a deluxe, spacious apartment to a much smaller cottage, none of the Inoues—not Eiko, not her husband, not the children—had the slightest objection to that change in lifestyle.

"It's really just a temporary measure, a place to camp out for a while," Eiko explained when she came to tell Misao the news. "We'll stay there long enough to catch our breath and get our bearings, and then we'll start looking for something more suitable, long-term. It would be ideal if we could sell this place first, but I'm not holding my breath about that."

Of course, everyone knew what had galvanized Eiko into taking action so quickly. After the events in the basement, she seemed to have been transformed into a different person. Overnight, her relatively mild objections to the apartment building had turned into full-blown antipathy. She even started spending the better part of the daytime hours away from home—far more time than could reasonably be explained by the need to do moving-related errands.

*After everything that's happened here, Eiko can't even relax and feel secure in her own apartment,* Misao thought. Of course, she and Teppei were feeling the same way, but . . .

Initially, Teppei hadn't talked to Misao at all about what he experienced in the basement on the night of May 17. Misao could think of several possible reasons for his silence. It could have been thoughtful altruism, born of concern that knowing the harrowing details would make her feel afraid. Or it might have been embarrassment about having the stubbornly rational attitude he'd clung to until now regarding the basement—and the realm of paranormal phenomena in general—proved wrong. Also, in a more general sense, when someone is subjected to a traumatic experience, that person's unwillingness to discuss the event in question is likely to be in direct proportion to their degree of shock.

*Teppei definitely saw something in the basement the other night,* Misao thought. *And it seems clear that whatever he saw, it was not of this world.*

The first time Teppei spoke about his ordeal was five days afterward. "It was so cold," he said abruptly. "I literally felt like I was going to freeze to death. And the wind—the wind seemed to be alive, somehow." Then he went on to talk about some formless, numberless *something* that had seemed to be wriggling and squirming in the darkness. He could only describe the entity (or entities) by the vague word "something," but there was no doubt in his mind that he had heard a vast rustling, as of a great many *somethings* moving in the unseeable blackness. Those ominous sounds were accompanied by an extreme escalation of the already unnatural chilliness in the basement, and a moment later Teppei began to feel lightheaded.

"And then . . . and then I guess I just passed out," he stammered.

That was when Misao finally shared everything she had learned on her research trip to the ward library, and gave voice to the suspicions she had been harboring privately. Teppei didn't immediately embrace her theory about the subterranean road, but he didn't dismiss it out of hand, either.

"I still don't understand what happened," Teppei said over and over again during the weeks following his misadventure in the basement. "I can't even begin to wrap my mind around it. I mean, what in the world was going on down there? What were they trying to do to us? And who, or what, are *they*?"

The doorbell of the Inoues' apartment chimed, followed by a cheery greeting: "Hello! Anybody home? I'm from the soba shop—sorry I kept you waiting!" Clutching two thousand-yen bills in his little hand, Tsutomu raced to the front door.

"I wish I'd thought to order some noodles for you, too," Eiko told Misao as she trotted by, a few steps behind Tsutomu. "The thing is, we didn't have time to eat breakfast, so I wasn't thinking too clearly when I made the call."

"Please, don't give it another thought," Misao said with a smile.

Eiko, meanwhile, had joined Tsutomu at the door to their apartment, with her husband close behind. "You're awfully late, you know," she groused, glaring at the uniformed deliveryman. "We've been waiting for ages."

"I'm really sorry," the young man replied as he handed the take-out orders to Mr. Inoue. "The thing is, the front door of the building was closed when I got here, and it took quite a while to get the caretaker to open it."

"Closed?" Eiko echoed in surprise. "In the middle of the day?"

"That's right," said the deliveryman. He pocketed Tsutomu's eagerly proffered payment and smiled at the little boy in a friendly way.

"You mean it was locked?" Eiko sounded incredulous.

"I don't know whether it was locked or what, but it wouldn't open. I kept banging on the glass and after a while the caretaker must have heard me, because he came out and opened the door from the inside. I'm sorry, but I need to get back to work now. Please just put the empty dishes in the hall outside your apartment, and I'll pick them up later today. Thank you very much!"

After the deliveryman had taken his leave, the family trooped back into the living room. Mr. Inoue wore a troubled frown as he distributed the bamboo plates. Everyone had ordered *zaru* soba: a heap of cold buckwheat noodles topped with strips of seaweed, accompanied by a soy-based dipping sauce and tiny pyramids of wasabi and finely grated daikon radish for each diner to stir into the sauce, to taste.

"Whatever the Tabatas may have suffered through the other night, this is going too far," Eiko complained. "I mean, locking the front entrance during the day? That's unheard of. And today, of all days, when they know very well that we're moving out. What if the truck had shown up while the door was locked? That would have been a major hassle."

"Poor old Mr. Tabata has really been on edge since that night," Misao said. "He probably just inadvertently turned the lock or something."

"Still, that's no excuse. I mean, what were the postal carrier and the newspaper person supposed to do when they couldn't get into the lobby?"

While Misao watched, the Inoues began to slurp up their cold noodles in the traditional manner—that is, as noisily as possible. Without air conditioning, the living room was suffocatingly warm and humid.

Looking out beyond the balcony, Misao said, "Speaking of the mail and the newspaper, it looks as if it'll just be us and the Tabatas from now on. We're really going to be lonely here without all of you. I can't believe it's come to this: an entire apartment building with only two occupied units."

"But what about you?" Eiko began, quietly laying down her chopsticks and turning to look at Misao. "Have you been giving it any thought?"

"It? Oh, you mean moving?"

"Of course. What else?"

Misao lowered her eyes. "As a matter of fact, we have been thinking about that," she said. "Quite seriously, too." She found it hard to believe that she was having a conversation like this barely three months after moving into the building. Three months ago she and her family had arrived here so full of hope and anticipation, and now . . .

Mr. Inoue looked at Misao with a sympathetic expression. "Finding a place to move to isn't that easy, especially when most of your capital's tied up," he said. "We were lucky to have family in the city, with extra space."

"Well, Teppei and I agreed early on that we would never even think about moving in with either of our parents, so that isn't an option for us," Misao said.

Eiko used the palm of her hand to wipe away a trickle of sauce that was running down her chin. "Well, for us, I mean . . . this time last year we were making do in a tiny rental apartment no larger than an eel's bed, scrimping and saving so we could buy a place of our own, and for what? To have it turn out like this? I mean, it would almost be funny if it weren't so tragic."

"I'm sure this apartment will sell before too long." Misao spoke the requisite words in a determinedly upbeat tone, but she could tell that both Eiko and her husband were struggling to remain optimistic. Kaori, meanwhile, was beaming fondly at Misao. Smiling back, Misao said, "Tamao and I will definitely come to visit, Kaori. We'll stop by one day soon, I promise."

Kaori bobbed her head in an exaggerated manner, as children do. "There won't be any spooky things at our new house," she declared in an extra-loud voice. "That's why we're moving, to get away from all the scary stuff."

"Yes, of course it is," Misao responded automatically.

Eiko and her husband just went on inhaling their noodles, without saying a word. Large drops of rain began to pelt the balcony's sliding doors, leaving dark splotches on the glass.

When Misao remarked, "Hey, it's raining again!" Eiko furrowed her brow and muttered sarcastically, "Oh, perfect. That's just what we need." Then she added in a normal tone, "I hope the truck will get here on time, at least." At that, Misao took her leave, promising to return later to see the Inoues off.

It was Saturday and Teppei had the day off from work for once, so Misao had sent him to pick Tamao up after school. St. Mary's Kindergarten had only a half-day session on Saturdays, and father and daughter returned around 12:30. Tamao was wearing a lightweight pink vinyl raincoat with a hood that kept her dry when the sudden downpour began, but Teppei had left the house without an umbrella, so he was soaked to the skin from head to foot.

"Papa ran all the way home," Tamao reported enthusiastically as they shed their soggy shoes in the entryway. "I mean, *all* the way. He ran from my school to our house, carrying me on his back. It was amazing!"

"Since when did you turn into such a superhero, honey?" Misao teased. "Was it when you noticed you were getting a little paunchy around the middle?"

"A mere woman can never know the pleasure of running through a June rainstorm, carrying a rather large child," Teppei retorted with a laugh as he darted past her on his way to the bathroom. "I really feel sorry for you."

Misao couldn't help feeling that her husband's show of light-heartedness was just a facade.

Teppei turned around in the hallway and said, "Oh, by the way, the Inoues' moving truck showed up. They were loading the boxes and furniture as fast as they could, but I could tell the rain was making things difficult for them. Eiko was grumbling nonstop, of course."

"I told them we'd go down later to see them off," Misao said. "So please hurry up—you need to take a shower and change into some dry clothes."

"Aye, aye, Captain." Teppei gave an ironic salute as he disappeared into the bathroom. After a moment the sound of the shower's vigorous stream was joined by his strong tenor voice, singing some old tune.

Tamao had left her wet raincoat in a heap on the floor, and Misao said sternly, "You know you're supposed to put your coat away, sweetie. Stick it on a hanger and we'll leave it out on the balcony until it dries. Otherwise the water will get all over the living room."

"Woa-kay," Tamao said, responding with an obscure colloquialism. It wasn't something either of her parents would ever say, and Misao wondered fleetingly where her daughter had picked it up. Probably at school, or perhaps from watching TV.

As Tamao was jamming her pink slicker onto a cream-colored plastic coat hanger decorated with a picture of a rabbit's face, Cookie approached and nudged the child's hand with her snout, clearly wanting to play. Giggling with delight, Tamao stroked Cookie's fur affectionately while she murmured, "Aw, such a good little girl."

Suddenly, it all struck Misao as impossibly artificial. *Everything Teppei and I do these days—no, really, everything the four of us do, including Tamao and even Cookie—somehow feels as if we're all acting in a play*, she thought. *A theater-of-the-absurd play about the daily routine of an utterly ordinary family living in a beautiful, sunny apartment, without a care or worry in the world. Just an average family, living in a perfectly normal building, playing their parts to the hilt. Except that something isn't quite right about this idyllic tableau . . .*

Misao went into the kitchen and began whipping up a batch of Chinese-style fried rice, using some cooked white rice and vegetables left over from the previous night's dinner. Soon a light, pleasant sizzling sound rose from the wok, along with a delicious aroma. As she stirred the ingredients with deliberately histrionic hand movements, like a stage actress portraying a housewife, Misao reached out and switched on the radio they kept on the kitchen counter. A young woman's voice was delivering an updated traffic report.

"On Metropolitan Expressway Route Four, near the Shinano-machi area, there is a two-kilometer stretch of slow-moving traffic because of routine congestion. Metropolitan Loop Line Number Eight, in the vicinity of Roka Park, is experiencing extreme gridlock as the result of a rollover accident involving a truck. The Metro Expressway Route One has been severely congested due to an accident during the morning hours, but as of midday all the lanes are open again and traffic flow has returned to normal."

When Misao thought about the traffic accidents, and the clogged roads, and the cranky drivers trying to get from point A to point B out there in the world, it felt very strange to her. The things that had happened in the basement of this bright new apartment building had just been too unfathomably alien, as if that underground room were part of some eerie parallel universe.

The three Kanos sat down to a late lunch, during which they carried on a conversation that struck Misao as almost theatrically boisterous. The rain outside the windows was pelting down harder than ever.

It was around two o'clock when the entire Inoue family showed up at their door to say good-bye. "These are for Tamao," Kaori and Tsutomu chorused, holding out their parting gifts: a lollipop wrapped in polka-dot paper, a handful of multicolored marbles, and a small plastic action figure of a cyborg.

"Can you stay for a cup of tea?" Misao asked, but Eiko shook her head regretfully. "We're already running late," she said, "and my folks are getting impatient. They keep calling and asking when we'll be arriving."

It occurred to Misao that this might be the last time she ever saw Eiko's smiling face in her doorway, and she was suddenly overcome by a feeling of profound loneliness. It wasn't as though their friendship had a long history. They were just a couple of neighbors who had hit it off, and now one of them was moving away; that was all. Misao felt as if she had turned into a weak, pathetic person, to be taking Eiko's departure so hard. *It's probably because my nerves are basically fried,* she thought. Too many weird things had happened lately, and the parade of distressing events had taken a toll on her mental state.

Teppei looked at Eiko and her husband and said, "We're really going to miss you," in a way that came across as sincere rather than emptily formulaic. Then he added in a more jocular tone, "I mean, who am I going to run my ad copy past to find out if it works or not, now that the perfect family is moving away?"

It was a rather meager attempt at a joke, but everyone chuckled nonetheless.

The entire Inoue clan, along with Teppei, Misao, and Tamao, crowded into the elevator, filling the air with animated conversation. Even Cookie was allowed to join the party, to the dog's tail-wagging surprise. The mood was buoyant, but all the adults were making a conscious effort to avoid looking at the indicator panel. No one wanted to see (or even think about) the "B1" button.

When the group disembarked on the ground floor, Mitsue and Sueo Tabata emerged from the caretakers' apartment to join them. Being surrounded by such a large group of people was more excitement than Cookie could handle, and her loud, staccato barks filled the lobby.

After the Tabatas and Inoues had voiced the usual expressions of reciprocal gratitude and farewell, Sueo patted Kaori and Tsutomu on their heads and handed them each a piece of candy wrapped up in old-fashioned handmade Japanese paper. No one made any mention of the basement.

Beyond the glass entrance door, the graveyard fence was clearly visible through the mist. The Inoues' car, a gray Honda Civic, was parked in front of the building, off to one side. The rain was still pelting down.

"It's just now hitting me that this is really good-bye, and I'm starting to get all soppy and sentimental," Eiko said, looking at Misao. "Please take good care of yourselves, okay? And do come and visit us sometime very soon."

"Of course we will," Misao said. As she was speaking, she and Tamao both put their hands on the glass door. The entrance, usually a neutral zone, now seemed to be transmitting a tangle of heavy, dismal, depressing feelings directly into the palm of Misao's hand.

"Well, then, shall we be on our way?" Mr. Inoue said in a firm voice. Misao gave the glass door a push.

The door didn't budge.

"Huh," Eiko said, turning to look at the Tabatas. "Did you lock the door again? The guy from the noodle shop was saying that—"

Mitsue Tabata cut Eiko off in midsentence. "No," she said. "We didn't lock it, then or now."

Until that moment, everyone in the group had been wearing a congenial expression, but now the smiles froze on their faces. Sueo rushed up and gave the glass door a forceful shove. "What's going on?" he demanded.

Teppei was speechless. Silently, he stretched out one hand and jiggled the metal handle, but the door didn't move.

"What . . . ?" Eiko's lips were trembling. "What's the problem here, anyway?"

"Oh no. It's beginning again," Sueo whispered, almost inaudibly. He looked at the thunderstruck faces around him, one by one. Misao felt a shudder travel down her backbone.

Cookie, meanwhile, was behaving very oddly indeed. She had been frolicking agreeably around the lobby, wearing what appeared to be the canine equivalent of a human smile. Now she stopped abruptly, with a ferocious glint in her eyes. Tamao had been holding the dog's leash, but as her own fear took over she loosened her grip and Cookie ran free.

"Open up! Open the damn door!" Eiko shouted, pounding on the door with both hands. Her damp palms left a faint afterprint on the glass.

Kaori was on the verge of tears. "I'm scared, Mama," she whimpered.

Misao put her arms around Kaori and pulled her close. The men all stood rooted to the spot, like a cluster of statues. Teppei was visibly shaken, but after a moment he made a supreme effort to appear unperturbed. "Is this door the only way in or out?" he asked.

"Ye-yes, that's correct," Sueo stammered.

"No, that isn't correct at all!" Mitsue contradicted, her eyes gleaming wildly. "Our apartment's on the first floor, so someone should be able to get out through one of the windows."

"Oh, of course, you're right," Sueo said in a relieved tone.

Mr. Inoue, who was holding Tsutomu's hand, said, "Well, I guess that's our only option, then. I'll squeeze out through a window and come back around to the door."

"Oh no, what's happening *now*?" Eiko pointed an unsteady forefinger at the door, and everyone turned to look. Misao was shocked at the incomprehensible sight that met her eyes, but she managed to keep from crying out.

On the surface of the glass door, a large quantity of ghostly white handprints had appeared. They looked as if they were being made by rubber stamps. While the little group in the lobby watched, aghast, the handprints rapidly multiplied before their disbelieving eyes.

*Slap, slap, slap* . . . The sound of damp flesh meeting glass reverberated through the lobby with every new handprint.

Mitsue let out a shrill cry. The children began to sob. Cookie seemed to have been transformed into a rabid beast, barking her head off, with fangs bared and flecks of white foam flying out of her mouth.

The scenario unfolding before them was, unmistakably, not of this world.

Misao recoiled, then bent down to comfort Tamao and Kaori with a hug. Sueo Tabata collapsed in a wilted heap on the floor near the entrance, breathing heavily and clutching the left side of his chest while his wife hovered over him in concern.

On closer inspection, the handprints weren't identical. Some were large; some were small; some had the fingers spread wide apart, while on others the digits were close together. All the prints were white, but it wasn't the white of house paint or of milk. It was a more ephemeral kind of whiteness, almost like the effect you sometimes see when children slap their sticky hands all over the front windshield of a car, and then the sun shines through those marks: a gummy, translucent white.

An agonized shriek escaped from Misao's mouth, followed by another. The small screams kept on coming, welling up in the back of her throat and forcing their way out into the air, for what seemed to her like a very long time.

Almost unconsciously, Teppei enfolded Misao in an embrace, then grabbed his daughter's arms and pulled her into the hug, as well. Tamao hadn't stopped crying since the handprints first appeared, and now she was wheezing and gasping like someone in the throes of an asthma attack. To make matters worse, she had started hiccupping uncontrollably, as well.

No one had any sense of how much time had passed, but at some point the handprints stopped appearing, then began to fade away. Through the gaps among the remaining prints, the fence that surrounded the graveyard came dimly into view. The rain had been falling all along, and the cemetery was shrouded in haze.

Eiko's teeth were chattering noisily, and Cookie was still out of control. With a huge leap, the dog hurled herself against the glass door, banging her nose so hard that she let out a yelp of pain. It was painful to watch, too.

*Slap, slap, slap . . .* Strangely and illogically, the same adhesive smacking sound was heard (albeit not so loudly) every time a handprint vanished from the window, as well.

Misao closed her eyes. *Leave us alone,* she screamed silently, from the depths of her heart. *Please. These people are supposed to leave here today, and before too long we'll be moving away, too. Why is that so upsetting for you?*

Wait—who was she pleading with, anyway? Misao didn't know the answer to that question. Wave after wave of chills ran down her spine, and it felt as though someone had applied an extra-large ice pack to her back.

When she opened her eyes again, all the handprints were gone and the glass door had completely returned to normal. Mr. Inoue yelled something inarticulate and flew toward the entrance. The door opened easily, but he had pushed it so hard that his forward momentum carried him all the way outside, and he nearly fell down in the driveway.

"Quickly!" he shouted. "Let's get out of here, while we can!"

Eiko appeared to have regained her faculties, and she grabbed her children's hands and dragged them along behind her. A lukewarm wind mixed with rain was blowing through the open door. Cookie bolted outside and sped away as fast as her legs could carry her.

"Cookie!" Tamao wailed between sobs. "Where are you going?"

Mr. Inoue got into the Civic and started the engine while Eiko and their two children ran up. After Eiko had strapped Kaori and Tsutomu into the backseat, she turned around and gazed at her friends and neighbors with a gutted expression. She seemed to be barely holding back a flood of tears. "I'm so sorry," Eiko said, and the desperate look in her eyes was like a silent scream.

"Well, then, we'll be off now," Eiko called over her shoulder as she climbed into the car. The sound of the rain grew louder and more violent. Misao was still staring straight ahead, numb with horror, but she acknowledged Eiko's words with a slight nod. Mr. Inoue revved the engine, and the car took off.

Cookie came galloping back, soaked to the skin. The highly domesticated dog seemed to have reverted to a feral state. She glanced at the humans with an unapproachably fierce expression on her furry face, then lay down and began to moan softly into her paws.

# 14

Two Sunday mornings later, Teppei was awakened by the sound of his own panting and wheezing. He had dreamed that Reiko came back from the dead and whispered something in his ear. In the nightmare, Teppei opened his mouth very wide and let out a scream, but when he woke up his lips were tightly closed and stuck together with a viscous residue of drool. Perspiration was pouring down his forehead. He glanced at the bedside clock: nine a.m. Tamao's voice wafted faintly down the hall from the living room.

For a long while Teppei lay motionless on his back, staring up at the ceiling. *What the hell was that dream about?* he asked himself as he struggled to catch a proper breath. He couldn't shake the distinct feeling that Reiko really had been in this room a short while ago, standing next to the bed gazing down at him with her hands resting on the sheets. She was deathly still, but the expression on her colorless face seemed to suggest that she had something important to tell him. What had she whispered in his ear? Teppei couldn't remember his dead wife's words, no matter how hard he tried.

Gingerly, he extended a hand and groped around until he found the place where Reiko had been touching the sheets in his dream. The spot felt slightly warm and a bit damp, though there was nothing unnatural about that. But when he discovered upon further exploration that the sheets were perfectly dry and cool apart from that one spot and the place where he had been lying, he began to have his doubts.

Languorously, Teppei sat up in bed and experimentally wagged his head from side to side. He didn't merely have a headache; his brain seemed to be throbbing with pain all the way down to its very core. While the sensation was nothing new—he had felt this way upon awakening every morning of late—today his hangover was particularly excruciating. The only thing he recalled with any degree of certainty was that he had drunk too much the night before.

It wasn't just the mornings, either. The daily headaches nearly always lingered past the middle of the day, although their severity gradually abated. Teppei's alcohol consumption had more than doubled in recent weeks, but he didn't think his nightly benders were entirely to blame for the hellish hangovers; their intensity was surely exacerbated by the fact that he had taken to chain-smoking, as well.

On top of the headaches, there was the constant anxiety that went with trying to find a new place to live, along with the cumulative stress of feeling compelled to say a prayer—*Please, let me find Misao and Tamao waiting in our apartment, safe and sound*—every time he climbed into the elevator on his way home from work. The bottom line was that there was never a single moment when his mind was at ease and he could simply relax.

When Teppei wandered into the living room, still dressed in his pajamas, he found Tamao enjoying her breakfast "dessert" of fruit-topped yogurt, scooping it out one spoonful at a time.

"Good morning," Misao said brusquely. "You were drunk as a skunk last night. Again."

"So it seems," Teppei replied laconically.

"I had to haul you to our room and put you to bed. Do you remember?"

"Not at all," he answered with complete honesty. He had started drinking around dinnertime, and while he did remember having a verbal altercation with Misao at some point in the evening, everything after that was a blur. He had no idea what else he might have said or done.

"Look, I understand what you're going through," Misao began, flipping the switch to start the coffeemaker. The machine made a harsh metallic noise and Tamao yelled, "Be quiet!"

"I understand what you're going through," Misao repeated, catching Teppei's eye, "but I really need to ask you to get a grip."

"I'll be more careful from now on," Teppei said glumly. *But what am I promising to be more careful about?* he wondered. *The drinking?*

In his heart of hearts he really felt like saying, "Hey, give me a break, would you? I mean, how else do you suggest that I get through the infinitely long evenings on days when I don't have to go to work? Are you saying it should be enough for me to watch my baseball games on TV, and sip my after-dinner coffee, and sit in the bathtub thinking about what I'm going to do the following day, and maybe make love to my wife? And after all those normal little rituals, I ought to be able to drift peacefully off to sleep without a care in the world? Are you really suggesting that if I just behave myself like a good boy and try to keep it together, one morning we'll get a phone call from the real estate broker saying something like, 'I've found a buyer for your apartment!'? Yes, everything would be great if only someone with exceedingly outré tastes turned up tomorrow and said, 'Wow, this deserted shell of a building totally checks all the boxes for me! It's located right next to a graveyard, and there's a basement where scary things happen, and the elevator keeps breaking down for no reason, and as a bonus, ghostly human handprints suddenly show up all over the main door—which, incidentally, has a habit of locking itself at inopportune moments. Seriously, what's not to like? Where do I sign?'"

While he was in the bathroom washing his face and brushing his teeth, Teppei made a concerted effort to remember what he had said to his wife the previous night. He had a vague recollection of discussing the things Misao had researched on her expedition to the library: the underground shopping mall, the abortive excavation, and the proposed relocation of the graves.

Misao's theory was that an underground road had, in fact, been dug out beneath the graveyard, and had never been completely filled in after the project was abandoned. She believed the existence of that subterranean tunnel had created some kind of paranormal phenomenon in and around the Central Plaza Mansion that couldn't be explained by science or reason. Teppei remembered now that he and Misao had engaged in a heated argument about this matter, but he couldn't summon up any of the details of who said what. He did recall getting angry at the end of the conversation and slamming the tumbler containing his whiskey-and-water down on the table. The glass hadn't shattered, but the contents had sloshed all over the white lace tablecloth, leaving a large amber stain. After that, he had hurled some insults at Misao, although the only thing he clearly remembered saying (or, more precisely, bellowing) was, "Fine! Do whatever you want! I don't give a damn anymore!" That was as far as his recovered memories went, so he must have passed out not long after that.

*I need to try to make things right with Misao*, he thought. *This may be part of their plan: setting us against each other. Maybe they're trying to ruin our relationship and force us to leave this place, so they can have it all to themselves. Are we really going to play into their hands like that, and let them win? No way!*

They . . . Their . . . Them . . . As Teppei gazed at his haggard, baggy-eyed reflection in the mirror, he was overcome by a sudden urge to spit venomously at the glass and splatter saliva all over the place.

*What in the name of everything holy are "they," anyway?* he asked himself. *Are they invisible human beings who go around leaving handprints on glass surfaces, just for fun? Or are they fiendish specters who are somehow connected with this building and have randomly decided to nest inside the head of this ancient-looking person in the mirror?*

When Teppei shambled back to the living room, Misao had poured out a cup of coffee for him. As she placed it on the table along with a plate of ham sandwiches on toasted bread—"ham toast," for short—Teppei gave her a remorseful smile. "I'm sorry," he said.

"Oh? For what?" Misao asked airily, not meeting his eyes.

"I'm sorry about last night. I really wasn't myself, at all."

"I gathered that."

"Seriously, I really am sorry. I didn't mean the things I said."

"Yes, that's what I figured. If I thought for a minute that you'd meant what you were saying, I would never have been able to forgive you."

"Oh. So I guess that means I said some pretty horrendous things?"

"Yes, one or two." Misao gave a sarcastic snort. "No, actually, you said so many horrendous things that I couldn't even begin to list them all. Drunk or not, you really had a lot of nerve talking to me like that."

"So, uh, what kind of things did I say?" Teppei's head was throbbing. He propped his elbows on the table and supported his skull with both hands.

Misao shrugged. "Well, why don't I give you a little sample? You said, 'If you want to leave here so badly, just take Tamao and get the hell out. I'll stay here by myself, and you can go off and do whatever you want.'"

"Oh no." Teppei sighed. "Did I really say that?"

"Yep."

"That's just . . . shameful."

"In a way, it almost seemed as if you were talking to yourself."

"Oh, sweetheart, I am so sorry. I have no memory of that what-soever. And, uh, what did you say in return?"

"You don't remember *that*, either?" Misao looked distinctly peeved.

Teppei gave an embarrassed shake of his head.

"So you want to hear it again, is that it?" Misao asked sharply.

"Yes, I'd like to hear it again. I mean—I need to hear it again."

Misao took a deep breath and then, hesitantly and with extreme chagrin, she said, "All right, then, I'll give you the instant replay. I said if you were going to stick around I would stay, as well, because there was no way I would ever leave you here alone. Just to be clear, I didn't say that in any kind of a gentle, supportive, loving way. I was very angry, and I was shouting at the top of my lungs."

"Ah," Teppei said, gazing at Misao with a sudden rush of fond-ness. She looked to him at that moment like some kind of saint or bodhisattva, while he saw himself as an unspeakably feeble, foolish excuse for a human being.

"I'm really relieved to hear that," he murmured. "I was afraid you might have said something to me that we could never get beyond. Or vice versa."

"Don't underestimate me," Misao said, sticking her chin in the air. "I would hope I'm a slightly better person than that."

"No, but seriously, I've been thinking a lot about moving away from here," Teppei said as he took a sip of coffee. "It's only been a week since we put this place on the market, and at this point we have no idea how long it might take to find a buyer. So I've come to the conclusion that even if we don't manage to sell this apartment in the near future, we ought to go ahead and move out anyway. We could make do with a small rented apartment for a year or two, at least, and I'm sure everything would work out eventually."

Misao stared at him for a long moment. Finally, she gave an al-most imperceptible nod. "I've known for a while that you were thinking along those lines, too," she said. "It really makes me happy to hear you say the words out loud, at last."

"You know me. I'm stubborn by nature," Teppei said, sighing and shaking his head. "But also, buying this place really meant a lot to me. It seemed like a sort of new—I don't know, I guess what I'm trying to say is that it seemed to symbolize a new beginning for us, a place where we could get on with our lives without being forever haunted by the past."

"You don't need to explain," Misao interrupted. "I mean, I felt exactly the same way."

Cookie ambled toward the balcony and let out a single, mournful howl. When Misao and Teppei looked outside, they saw that a light, steady rain had begun to fall again. "Shall I bring in the laundry?" Teppei asked.

"That's okay," Misao said, smiling into his eyes. "I'll do it. Why don't you have another cup of coffee and try to wake yourself up? To be honest, I'm hoping we've seen the last of your massive-hangover phase."

•

That evening, Teppei decided to run down to the station to buy a magazine that specialized in listings for rental apartments. Just as he was putting on his shoes in the entryway, the doorbell rang. It was Tatsuji and his wife, Naomi.

"We just happened to be driving by," Naomi said in her affect-edly girlish voice. "Sorry about dropping in without calling first. Is now a bad time? It looks like you were on your way out."

"No, now is fine. I was thinking about taking a walk, but it can wait," Teppei said, with a welcoming smile.

"Lovely!" Naomi smiled back in a way that radiated self-confidence. She was dressed in a flashy yellow linen suit, and her sternum-length hair was coiled into an elaborate updo that was almost certainly copied from a picture in a fashion magazine. As usual, she reeked of some kind of super-potent perfume, and Teppei thought fleetingly that if this woman would only tone down her scent (and her personality) a bit, people might be less inclined to form a negative first impression of her.

"We need to get back before dinnertime, so we can't stay long," Tatsuji said. He stooped to pat the head of his little niece, who had come running at the sound of the doorbell. Tatsuji was dressed in body-hugging golf wear that made him look like the very model of a modern salaryman on his day off. "But really," he added, "what's with this place, anyway? It's abnormally quiet, and there's nobody around. Is anyone else even living here anymore, besides you?"

"The other people pretty much moved out over the last couple of months," Teppei admitted. "It just happened to work out that way, by chance. From what I've heard, there should be an influx of new tenants during the summer."

"Oh, I see. Wow." Tatsuji shook his head in mock wonderment. "Those people who moved out must be awfully flush, to be able to go around buying and selling apartments every few months, and then moving somewhere else. It must be nice to be so wealthy."

"I certainly wouldn't know about that." Teppei grinned. Tatsuji smiled back, and the two brothers walked into the living room side by side.

Meanwhile, Naomi had presented Misao with a pastry box containing a French-style cake from a famous bakery she and Tatsuji had visited on their Sunday drive. Holding the box in one hand, Misao used the other one to shoo away Cookie, who was standing too close for comfort.

"How do you like kindergarten, Tamao? Is it fun?" Naomi asked.

"I dunno," Tamao replied dully.

"What? You don't know? So you aren't enjoying it?"

Tamao's only response was to let out a precociously fake-sounding laugh and then run over to where her uncle was sitting.

A sudden scowl of vexation flitted across Naomi's face, and she looked as though she wanted to say something like, "What a rude child! Someone really ought to teach her some manners!" A moment later, though, the frown had disappeared.

"You're looking well, Tatsuji," Misao called out from the kitchen, where she was boiling water for coffee and black tea. The tea was for Naomi (who never touched a drop of coffee, claiming it was bad for the skin) and Tamao.

"Thanks, uh, Sis," Tatsuji said, stumbling slightly, as usual, over the prescribed term of interfamilial address. "How about you? Have you started working again?"

"Yes, here and there. I've just been taking assignments I can do in my spare time. You know, when you have a small child at home it's hard to get out too often, so—"

"Oh, I see the horrid graveyard's still there," Naomi interrupted. She had gone over to stand by the sliding-glass doors, and was gazing at the view beyond the balcony. "It looks as if the landscaping has filled in since the last time we were here. Oh, on second thought, I guess that's just because the weeds have grown up. Never mind that, though. I'm much more interested in knowing why everybody who was living in this building decided to move away."

A brief, awkward silence fell over the group, but Tatsuji rode swiftly to the rescue. "It's because real estate prices in this area have gone up, and people wanted to sell their units here and move somewhere better," he said. "They were just doing what they had to do, using their wits to stay afloat and avoid financial disaster. It happens all the time. People sell when the time seems right and then move on to buy a unit in another building that seems likely to appreciate in value. A guy like me, nonchalantly living in a house provided by my in-laws, really seems to be a vanishing breed these days. I may even be the only one left! If Naomi were to divorce me any time soon I probably wouldn't be able to survive on my own, and I might end up dying in the gutter."

"Yes, and that's why you can never think about leaving me," Naomi said lightly, but her eyes were shooting meaningful daggers at Teppei. "Yet even though Tatsuji can't support us properly, he still has the nerve to make silly jokes about getting a divorce, saying that if we split up he might get lucky and meet a better class of woman. He can be such an idiot sometimes. He talks a good game, but in reality he can't even be the man of the house, and we have to rely on my parents for help."

After another moment of awkward silence, everyone quickly gathered around the coffee table in the living room and made a great show of enjoying the cake and hot beverages Misao had set in front of them. Teppei wasn't in a festive mood, by any means, so he surreptitiously fed his slice of cake to Cookie, who was lurking hopefully under the table.

Between bites, Tatsuji began asking Tamao about kindergarten, and her new friends, and so on. Tamao gave perfunctory replies, and the expression on her face made it plain that she wasn't enjoying the interrogation. Finally, after she finished shoveling the last crumbs of cake into her mouth, she cast an imploring glance at Teppei, clearly looking for an escape from her uncle's endless questions. "Um, Papa?" she said. "When are *we* going to move away?"

"Move away?" Naomi echoed in a tone that was even more strident than usual. "What's Tamao talking about?" she demanded, turning to look at Teppei. "I want details, now!"

Naomi was holding her teacup in one hand, and her lipstick had left a livid mark on the rim of the cup. Without taking his eyes from that repellent yet somehow mesmerizing lip print, Teppei let out a theatrical laugh but made no reply.

"What's going on, Tepp?" Tatsuji asked. "You're moving out?" When Teppei still didn't answer, Tatsuji looked at Misao, but she quickly averted her gaze.

Teppei lit a cigarette, then spoke at last. "No, I mean, it's not as if anything's been decided for sure. We've just been thinking that we might start looking for another apartment, sometime before the end of the summer."

"When you talk about finding another apartment, does that

mean you're planning to sell this one?" Naomi asked, making her eyes big and round. "It's only been four months or so since you moved in here, isn't that right? Why in the world would you—"

"There's no particular reason," Teppei interrupted. "We've just changed our minds, that's all." Even as he spoke, he was aware that this explanation must have sounded singularly lame and unconvincing.

Tamao clutched her mug of tea with both hands and stared at Teppei with a grave expression. She appeared to be on the verge of saying something. *Please don't*, Teppei entreated silently, using his eyes to convey that message to his daughter. *Please don't mention the things that have happened in the basement, or with the TV, or the elevator, or the handprints on the glass door, okay?*

"But what a shame, just when Tamao has gotten used to her nice new kindergarten. Isn't that right, Tamao?" Naomi asked in a puzzled tone. Nodding in agreement, Tamao opened her mouth as if to speak, but Misao quickly jumped in and changed the subject.

"Watch out, Tamao. Your tea's about to spill!" she exclaimed, grabbing the mug out of her daughter's hand in a calculated bit of displacement activity.

"It wasn't going to spill, at all," Tamao retorted sulkily.

"Okay, what the hell is going on here?" Tatsuji barked. "Have you taken leave of your senses? I mean, it seems like just the other day you were bragging all over town about buying this fantastic apartment. You must still owe a ton on the mortgage, don't you?"

Teppei slowly chewed his lip while he tried to think of a convincing lie. He finally went with, "You know the graveyard that's right outside our windows? Well, apparently the temple that owns it, Manseiji, has decided that it wants to buy the land this building stands on. Something about needing to expand the cemetery, or something. So that's why—"

"Whoa, have they been sending gangsters to try to strong-arm you?" Tatsuji broke in, leaning forward in his chair.

"No, no, nothing like that. It just looks as if that deal might come to fruition down the road, maybe a few years from now. That was probably a factor in everyone else's deciding to move out so quickly, too. Look, I'll be honest. We realize now that we bought a good apartment in a bad location, and we're having second thoughts about that decision. So we've just started to talk about looking for a new place before things get any more complicated."

"That's right," Misao said, exchanging a quick, complicit glance with Teppei. "The temple, Manseiji, has been here practically forever. From what we've heard, the land this building stands on originally belonged to the temple. It isn't the most comfortable feeling to be living somewhere when you know there are people trying to figure out a way to reclaim the land beneath you."

"Oh, now I get it," Naomi said, evidently taking this implausible explanation at face value. She was the kind of woman who would be on the edge of her seat with avid interest the minute a conversation began to veer in the direction of matters involving money or property. "In that case, it sounds as though the temple will be willing to buy this entire building," she went on. "So you won't lose your investment, after all."

"Yeah, but wait," Tatsuji said doubtfully. "This building only went up last year, and you said new tenants would be coming in over the summer. Your story about the temple doesn't pass the smell test, somehow."

"Well, of course there's more to it," Teppei said, scratching furiously at the nape of his neck. "When you look out the window, the first things you see are a graveyard and a crematorium smokestack, and I think most people would eventually start to question the decision to live in that sort of environment. I think that's the reason behind more than a few of the current vacancies."

"Ah, the truth comes out at last!" Tatsuji crowed. "Isn't that exactly what I've been saying all along? I can't believe you're so dense that you're only just realizing it now."

"Teppei hasn't gotten fed up with living here, at all," Misao fibbed, with a disingenuous smile. "I'm the one who's been wanting to move. We've been going back and forth about this for days, and I finally just wore him down."

"Have you found a new place yet?" Naomi asked eagerly.

"No, not yet." Misao narrowed her eyes, suddenly on guard against saying too much. "We've told a rental agency what we're looking for, and I'm sure they'll come up with something before too long."

"Finding a new place really does seem like the best thing to do," Tatsuji said, looking from Teppei to Misao. He seemed to be struggling to put his thoughts into words. "I mean, let's face it, there's something kind of creepy about living all by yourselves in a building where everyone else has moved out."

Teppei sensed that Tatsuji had been on the verge of saying something else, something about the unsettling proximity of the graveyard and the temple and the crematorium, but had decided to keep that thought to himself.

"Once you have a moving date, please be sure to let us know," Tatsuji went on. "We'll be standing by to do anything we can to help."

"Oh, thank you," Misao said, and Teppei nodded gratefully.

A short while later Tatsuji and Naomi stood in the entryway, getting ready to leave. As Naomi was scraping some dirt off one of her stiletto-heeled white leather pumps she said, "Oh, by the way, there's something wrong with the elevator in this building. Earlier, when we first got here, I'm positive we hit the button for the eighth floor, but it went down to the basement instead."

Teppei gave Misao a meaningful glance, then faked a chuckle and said lightly, "Sometimes it acts up like that. There's some kind of mechanical glitch that never seems to get fixed properly."

"It was pitch-dark down in the basement," Tatsuji said, reaching back to massage his own neck with both hands. "Oh, and also, it smelled kind of musty or moldy or something."

"That's probably because nobody really uses it anymore," Misao said, giving her brother-in-law a painfully forced smile.

"You could open it up and throw a dance party! Wouldn't that be fun?" Naomi said, pitching her voice even higher than usual and somehow managing to affect a childish lisp at the same time. "Apparently that kind of thing is all the rage these days. You know, like staging rock concerts in lofts or warehouses?"

Misao nodded, then said in an apathetic monotone, "Sure, why not? Maybe we'll do that, one of these days."

# 15

"Welcome! Welcome! Please come in!"

The minute the Kanos pushed open the door of the real estate office, which occupied a prime location not far from Shibuya Station, the five or six workers inside erupted in a chorus of robotic greetings.

*They sound like they're tending the counter in a hamburger joint,* Misao thought. Every employee's eye was fixed on the door in a collective gaze that seemed to be calculating how much cash the newcomers might have, and how they could most efficiently be pressured into parting with some of it.

The real estate office, which occupied a compact two-room space in a modern building, was one of the branches of a new firm whose ads had been sprinkled throughout the rental-listing magazines. Several customers—a young man who looked like a university student; a dour-faced young couple; and a middle-aged woman who, judging by her appearance, worked in the "water trade" of bars and nightclubs—were engaged in various transactions with clerks and agents. The older woman was carelessly scribbling her signature on a stack of papers. She wore an aggrieved expression, and a lit cigarette dangled from her thick, unpainted lips, which were almost cadaverously pale.

"Hello! Were you looking for something to rent today?" a clean-cut young man asked in a smooth, polite tone as he approached Misao and Teppei.

Teppei nodded, then explained that they had telephoned earlier.

"We're grateful for your patronage," the young man said automatically, flashing a patently synthetic smile of the sort most often seen on the faces of hosts and hostesses at late-night clubs. "Please, follow me." He led Teppei and Misao to an inexpensive-looking sofa, and they sat down.

"What sort of accommodations were you hoping to find?" the agent asked. He seemed to be the type who never deviated from his prepared script, and every question he asked, by rote, would be designed to market his company's wares. Before Misao and Teppei had a chance to reply, the young man went and fetched a large list of properties, dropped it onto the glass-topped table in front of the couch with a thud, then fanned out the pages with a hasty, impatient motion that seemed to be characteristic of everything he did.

*Well, here goes nothing,* Misao thought. It wasn't as if they had come to this place hoping to find somewhere flawless to live for the next few decades. The truth was—and she wished this were hyperbole—almost any place would do. If the real estate agent could just show them a rental that *wasn't* a hellish haunted house, they were in no position to be picky about the particulars.

Teppei ran through a quick litany of their requirements, which included a reasonably convenient commute to his downtown office and a kindergarten nearby. If possible, he added, it would be great to have a house with a garden, since they were a family of three with a dog.

"And how much were you looking to spend per month?" the agent asked, looking at Teppei and Misao with coolly appraising eyes.

"Well, needless to say, the cheaper the better," Teppei said with a laugh. "That being said, we do have a pretty good sense of the current rental market."

The man began shuffling rapidly through the pile of listings with an air of aggravation. "Darn, I could have sworn there was a house rental that came in yesterday," he said. "It was quite afford-able, too. Let me see now, where could it have gone?"

Hastily, the man put the pages back in order, then turned and called over his shoulder, "Hey, remember the listing that came in yesterday, for the single-family house? Has anyone seen the fact sheet for that property?"

A young woman with hennaed hair, dressed in the company's navy blue uniform, got up from her seat with a show of weariness and brought over a handful of photocopies. "Ah, here it is," the male agent said, offering one of the crisp, new pages to Teppei with a deferential gesture. Misao scooted closer to her husband on the couch, and they studied the fact sheet together.

Two bedrooms, and a combination living room and eat-in kitchen. A small attached garden. The photograph of the property was slightly out of focus, but the house resembled one of those prefabricated storage sheds you sometimes see plunked down in the middle of a field in rural areas. However, the location and the monthly rental fee caught Misao's attention. The rent was only a hundred thousand yen a month, and the place was about a twenty-minute walk—or five minutes by bus—from the next train station after Takaino. There was a bus stop right next to the house, too.

"I realize it doesn't look like much, but considering the location this little place is quite a bargain," the young agent said as he once again began leafing through his stack of papers. "The landlord lives nearby, and until recently the house was being rented by his son and daughter-in-law. Having a garden like this would be perfect for a family with a dog, don't you think?"

"It isn't bad at all," Teppei said. "I mean, it looks a bit small, but . . ." *Small? More like minuscule. I'm sure I can find a way to make it work for us, though,* Misao thought. The two bedrooms were just over a hundred square feet apiece, and there was a living/eating/cooking area of about the same size. They wouldn't be able to cram all their furniture into the house, but it would be easy enough to stash the overflow in a storage unit somewhere.

"Is it ready to move into right away?" Misao asked.

"Yes," the agent replied with a nod. "It's completely empty at the moment, so you could move in whenever you like. How would you feel about going over and taking a look at the property right now? I'd love to show it to you."

"Isn't there anything else?" Teppei inquired.

"What, you don't like this one?" Misao asked, nudging Teppei's knee with her own. "The location is good—it isn't that far from where we're living now—and the size seems okay for our current needs."

"Sure, sure. I just think we should look at some other places as well."

"We really don't have time to shop around, though, do we?" Misao protested, furrowing her brow in consternation. "I think we should just take whatever we can get, right now." *It's not as if we were just moving in together for the first time, and we aren't searching for a lifelong home, either. We just need to find a place of temporary refuge so we can get out of that dreadful place . . .* That's what Misao felt like saying, but she controlled her emotions and held her tongue.

"To tell you the truth," the agent said, looking from Teppei to Misao and back again, "when people say things like 'Any place will do,' that can actually make the process more difficult on our end."

Discretion was part of the man's job description, and he was clearly disciplining himself not to ask any intrusive questions. He wasn't as successful at controlling his face, though. It was alive with undisguised curiosity, and Misao felt a faint flush spreading over her own cheeks in response.

"How about something like this?" the agent asked, leaning forward. "It's close to the same train station as the house." He began to read aloud from a fact sheet: "Two rooms and an eat-in kitchen. Eastern exposure. Seven-minute walk to the station. Third floor of an apartment building. A hundred and thirty thousand yen a month. Oh, wait a minute—this one is still occupied, but the tenant should be vacating around the middle of July."

The agent passed the listing page, which was encased in a sheet of plastic, to Misao and Teppei. After studying the page for a long moment, Teppei said, "This one isn't half bad, either."

"There's a shopping district nearby, too," the agent said. Telegraphing his eagerness to move on to the next stage of the process, he fished some car keys out of the inside pocket of his jacket and began gently jingling them in the palm of his hand. It was clear that his only desire was to get the Kanos' signatures on a rental agreement as quickly as possible so he could move on to more profitable pursuits. He looked as though he would have liked to say, "Okay, people, let's get this show on the road. Can't you see that dillydallying over low-end rentals that won't bring in much more than a hundred thousand yen a month is a ridiculous waste of my valuable time?"

When the agent did speak, though, it was in a cordially professional tone: "This apartment is a bit more expensive than the house, but I think it might actually work better for you. The building has freshly painted white walls throughout, and everything is nice and bright inside. It's ideal for newlyweds."

Misao couldn't help laughing. "We aren't exactly newlyweds," she said. "As we told your colleague on the phone, we have a five-year-old daughter."

"Well, close enough," the agent grinned, flashing his teeth and narrowing his eyes. Unlike most people, when he smiled his face became less attractive, rather than more.

"But does that building allow pets?" Teppei asked.

The agent raised one twitchy eyebrow, then made a show of looking furtively around to make sure no one was eavesdropping. "Well, this is just between us," he said in a confidential tone, "but I think that would be open to discussion. The resident manager has close ties to this firm, so it should be no problem to keep a pet or two there, discreetly. The building has an absentee owner, and he would never need to know."

It was plain that there was something shady going on with the agency, the resident manager, and renters who wanted to bring in pets—under-the-table payoffs, perhaps?—but at this point Misao simply thought, *If that's the way it's done, then that's the way we'll do it.*

"That's good to know," she said out loud. Turning to Teppei, she asked, "So shall we go and take a look at those two places right now?"

"Hmm," Teppei replied. He still seemed dissatisfied about something, and he spent the next few minutes rummaging through the fact sheets. Finally, he glanced up from the pile and said, "Yes, let's do that."

Misao and Teppei followed the agent outside, and the three of them piled into one of the real estate company's corporate cars.

The single-family dwelling was their first stop, and that house turned out to be considerably more appealing than it appeared in the photograph: clean, cozy, and shipshape. The overall construction gave the impression of having been done on the cheap, but the exterior walls had been recently stuccoed and looked like new. It felt like the kind of house that would become exponentially more agreeable once the new occupants began to settle in and fix it up.

Misao's artistic imagination immediately sprang into action. *If we just planted clumps of marguerite daisies around here, it would look so much cuter,* she thought as she surveyed the entrance. The garden was larger than expected, and would get plenty of sun. There were a number of empty holes in the ground, which seemed to indicate that the previous tenants had dug up quite a few plants and taken them to their new house. In one corner of the garden a small flowerbed had been attractively laid out and those plants, at least, remained.

Misao caught Teppei's eye. "This seems fine to me," she said. Teppei nodded in agreement. They had left Tamao back at the Central Plaza Mansion, in the care of Sueo and Mitsue Tabata, and it occurred to Misao that they should have just brought her along. What were they thinking, leaving their daughter behind in that unsafe building? She wished she could dash back there, grab Tamao, and move into the sweet little house right this minute.

The interior looked as worn as might have been expected from a longtime rental, but the tatami matting on the floors had been recently replaced and the rooms were filled with the earthy green scent of newly mowed hay.

"This room would be the master bedroom, and the other bedroom could be the nursery," the real estate agent explained with an air of omniscience. "As for a living room, this end of the dining area should fit the bill well enough. The garden is quite large, so I don't think you'll feel too confined."

"And the rent's only a hundred thousand yen? That's quite a bargain," Teppei said.

The agent bobbed his head energetically. "The owner just happens to be the kind of person who doesn't want to raise the rent every time a new tenant moves in," he said. "He really is a very kindhearted soul."

*A very kindhearted soul.* Misao was captivated by that phrase, although she couldn't have explained why.

The agent was looking at her with an oddly lewd smile, the likes of which he hadn't displayed before now. "I'm happy to see that you seem to be finding this place satisfactory, Mrs. Kano," he said.

Misao averted her eyes and murmured, "Yes, totally."

Standing a bit too close for comfort, the young man told her about the convenience store, liquor shop, and hospital that were all within easy walking distance—two minutes away, or three at the most. Then he added with a broad grin that he was fairly certain there was a maternity hospital in the neighborhood, as well. Misao wasn't sure what he was getting at with that remark, and she didn't want to know.

They left the little house behind and drove the few miles to the apartment building. It was in a rather scruffy location, just one street behind the lively blue-collar shopping district that had grown up around the next train station after Takaino. If you needed to describe the building in one word, "minimal" or "cramped" would probably be closest to the truth. There was no way it could have been called splendid, even in the most shameless copywriter's hyperbole, but the laundry fluttering on the narrow balconies and the cluster of housewives chatting in front of the building seemed to indicate that this was, at the very least, a place where people could feel safe and secure.

The man from the real estate company rang a buzzer labeled "Resident Manager." The person who emerged from the caretaker's apartment was a benevolent-looking older man with salt-and-pepper hair.

"Hello, sir. Did you have a chance to let the occupant of the apartment on the third floor know that we'd be stopping by?" the agent asked politely.

"I did, I did. She's expecting you. Shall we go up?"

Beaming broadly, the resident manager exchanged nods of greeting with Misao and Teppei. "Right this way," he said briskly as he led the group toward a nearby elevator.

The floor of the elevator was littered with assorted bits of rubbish, including the paper wrapper from an ice cream treat of some kind (probably dropped by a child) and a discount flyer from a local supermarket. The caretaker nonchalantly bent down to pick up the trash, then touched the "3" button. Turning to Misao, he said with a smile, "There are lots of children in this building, so it's a really cheerful place to live."

The doorplate outside the third-floor apartment read "305." The resident manager rang the doorbell, and a moment later a young woman opened the door and peeked out. "Please come in," she said, opening the door all the way. "It's a total mess, but . . ."

The current tenant wore her hair in a short, sleek bob, and her lightly suntanned complexion was free of blemishes. She was dressed in tight jeans with the cuffs rolled up to expose her golden-brown ankles, and her high, round buttocks swayed from side to side as she turned and vanished into the apartment. A popular singing show was blaring from the television, but the set was quickly switched off. Hesitantly, the four visitors followed the woman into her tiny living room.

"We're so sorry to barge in like this," Misao said. "I'm afraid we've disturbed you on your day off."

"No, it's fine," the young woman reassured her in a friendly way. "I'm busy getting ready to move next month, and I just had the TV on full blast to keep me company. I'm the one who should apologize for keeping you waiting." The woman's smile exposed her over-sized front teeth and made her look, momentarily, like a child.

"This young lady is getting married next month!" the resident manager announced. The woman flushed crimson up to her ears and she protested shyly, "Now, you didn't have to go and tell them that, Uncle."

The man from the real estate office turned and looked away, as if nothing could interest him less than this stranger's marital prospects, but Misao and Teppei both offered polite congratulations. At this, the young woman's face turned a deeper red and she lowered her eyes in embarrassment.

The interior of the apartment consisted of a miniature living room that flowed directly into the kitchen, and two small Japanese-style bedrooms separated by sliding shoji doors. The layout was purely functional, and there were no unnecessary embellishments.

After taking in the living room's rather endearing decor, which centered on a plain white sofa bed framed in pale wood and garnished with two red, heart-shaped throw pillows, Misao said,

"Thank you so much for showing us around. This has been very helpful."

The young woman nodded. "It really isn't a bad apartment," she said. "It gets a lot of light during the day, and there's more than enough storage space."

"Yes, I can see that," Misao responded with a smile. Glancing at Teppei, she could tell immediately that he didn't care for this place at all. Judging from his dissatisfied expression, he was probably thinking there was no way a family of three (not to mention a dog) could coexist in such a small, charmless space.

Misao, however, was thinking, *Yes, this might work for us, barely. Though compared with the spacious apartment we live in now, it would feel like a little box where we would only want to come home in order to sleep.*

The group stayed inside the apartment for another minute or two, then said their polite thank-yous and farewells to the young woman. After they had filed out into the hallway, Misao (hoping to avoid being grilled by the agent) sidled up to Teppei and said in a low voice, "I think the house we looked at is a thousand times better than this, without a doubt."

"That's putting it mildly," Teppei said dryly.

"The house would give us a lot more space, and it's cheaper, too. And whatever you say, there's something special about having a garden, however small. Not only that, but the house is available now so we could move right in. I really can't bear to think about having to stick it out in our current place for another month."

"The only thing is, the house is kind of far from the station."

"Really? That seems like a minor drawback to me. You know what they say: 'Beggars can't be choosers,'" Misao quipped, jocularly elbowing Teppei in the ribs. "No, seriously, I really want to move away as soon as possible."

"I know, and we're totally on the same page about that," Teppei agreed, but he couldn't hide his worried expression.

The real estate agent drove them back to the Shibuya office, where Teppei and Misao paid an initial deposit in cash and signed a temporary contract for the little house. The discussion ended with all parties agreeing that the Kanos would return to sign a permanent contract two days later, after they'd had a chance to transfer the necessary funds from their bank.

The next day was Sunday, the twenty-first of June. Early in the morning, the telephone rang. It was the young agent from the real estate office.

"Something terrible has happened," the agent began, speaking in the dramatically lowered voice that always seems to accompany the delivery of bad news. "That little house burned down."

"Burned down?" Misao echoed in disbelief. "What do you mean?"

"You know, the single-family rental you signed a provisional contract for? Somehow or other it caught fire last night and burned to the ground."

Misao put one hand over her mouth and shot a dismayed glance at Teppei, who was sitting nearby on the couch.

"Right down to the ground," the agent repeated, still speaking in the same hushed tone. "From what I hear, there was nothing left but ashes. This is just between us, but no one seems to have any idea what could have caused the fire. The gas and electricity had both been disconnected, so I can't help wondering whether it might have been arson."

"And nothing else burned? Just that little house?"

Teppei got up and came to stand next to Misao. On the other end of the receiver the agent was saying, "That's right. Apparently the fire was confined to that one house. This is so unfortunate. I only got word about it just now myself. I know you were really looking forward to moving in there, but I'm afraid I have to ask what you'd like to do now."

"But . . . what . . . I don't understand what you're saying," Misao stammered. She felt suddenly chilled, as though a frozen worm were crawling up her spine, and she wasn't thinking straight. "I mean, what *can* we do? There's no way we could live in a house that's been burned to the ground, is there?"

"No, of course not. It's just that we've already received your money for the deposit," the agent began. After a pause he continued, in a tone that suggested he'd been doing some hasty calculations in his head, "Perhaps you might want to reconsider the other place you looked at—the apartment? If you took that option, you wouldn't need to do any extra paperwork. We could just transfer your deposit to the other property."

"Please let us think about it," Misao said numbly.

She hung up the phone without saying good-bye and stood there dumbfounded, staring at Teppei. "So there was a fire or something?" Teppei asked.

Misao nodded. "That little house burned to the ground last night. There's nothing left at all." They were both silent for a long moment while they fought to subdue the heavy, ominous feelings welling up in their chests.

"Well, then, we have no choice," Teppei said finally, in a tone of quiet resignation. "We'll have to take that apartment."

"That's a good solution," Misao said, summoning up a crooked smile. "As the tenant said, it really wasn't bad at all."

"Let's face it—anyplace is going to be better than here," Teppei said. He stuck a cigarette in his mouth and held a match to it with an unsteady hand.

# 16

July 1, 1987

Sueo Tabata's heart was acting up, so he had been spending most of his time lying in bed while his wife was out pounding the pavement nearly every day. The recent series of shocks to their aging nervous systems had taken a greater physical toll on Sueo, but neither of them was young or robust enough to go on dealing with such an abnormal degree of stress.

After they had submitted formal notice of their decision to vacate their resident manager positions at the Central Plaza Mansion, Mitsue threw herself into a full-bore search to find either a safe, pleasant, affordable place to live or, preferably, another resident manager position. The latter quest, in particular, required a mind-boggling amount of complicated paperwork. Since Sueo was out of commission, it had been necessary for Mitsue to do everything by herself, and she had toughened up considerably in the process.

The agents of the company ostensibly managing the Central Plaza Mansion had taken note of the startling fact that there was only one occupied unit in the building, not including the caretakers' apartment, and were apparently giving careful thought to their next step. They were not surprised to receive the Tabatas' letter of resignation, which Mitsue delivered in person, and it was accepted without objection. First, though, she was asked numerous questions—commonsensical queries that any employer would have posed, under the circumstances—including several variations on "What made you decide to resign from this position?" Instead of offering any details, Mitsue replied only in the sort of nebulous, noncommittal terms that she thought would seem most persuasive. Besides, who would have believed her if she had blurted out something like "Because that building is filled with evil spirits, and living there is a total nightmare! That's why nearly all the residents have moved out—they realized that something was very, very wrong!"?

So she had taken the sensible route and replied calmly, "At this point there is only one family still living in the building, and they'll be gone before long, too, so there's really no need for resident managers anymore. Beyond that, though, my husband's heart condition has been steadily getting worse, and he keeps saying he'd like to move somewhere less populated, with cleaner air."

For their part, the management company's agents were busy with other projects, and they had no valid reason for trying to prevent Mitsue and Sueo from going elsewhere.

After the resignation had been tendered and accepted, Mitsue spent several long days working the phone and visiting employment offices, gathering information about possible situations from various sources. As a result of these networking efforts, she ended up learning that a certain placement firm was advertising for a permanent resident manager (or managers) for an office workers' dormitory in the seaside resort of Izu. She quickly dispatched a joint résumé to the firm's main office; it was evidently well received, and on the day of the interview she bundled her ailing husband into a taxi and the two of them went to the company's headquarters.

The interview seemed to go well, but they didn't hear anything

for four or five days. Then, at last, they received the hoped-for noti-
fication that their application had been approved and the position was theirs. Mitsue was so thrilled that she spontaneously
threw her arms around her husband's neck in a joyful embrace—
something she hadn't done in a dozen years, at least.

The Tabatas' resident manager obligations in Izu weren't scheduled to commence until August, but they were told that they were
welcome to move into their new living quarters ahead of time, if
they wanted to.

Now it was the first of July, and a small truck from a local
moving company had just pulled up in front of the Central Plaza
Mansion. The two workmen who came with the truck weren't particularly personable or outgoing, but Mitsue couldn't have cared
less about such trivial details. Although it was the middle of the
rainy season, they had gotten lucky with the weather and it was a
beautifully clear day. Sueo had regained his health and mobility,
and he willingly took charge of the logistical aspects of the move.

No matter how unpleasant the experiences at a particular post
might have been, Mitsue usually felt some sentimental stirrings
when it was finally time to leave, but in this case her resolve didn't
waver in the least. She was filled with happiness at the prospect of
escaping from this accursed building, and her thoughts were focused on the pleasures of their new home and their new life near
the sea.

In the place where she and Sueo would be living from now on,
there was no graveyard, no temple, no crematorium belching black
smoke. In their new building, the elevator never stopped working
for no apparent reason, and the electricity didn't suddenly go off,
and people didn't get injured in the basement by some ridiculous
weasel wind. No ghoulish handprints had ever appeared on the
glass of the entry door, either. (Mitsue still felt like vomiting every
time she remembered that horrifying experience.) Instead, in Izu
there was an abundance of gorgeous greenery, and the soothing
murmur of the ocean, and fresh seafood, and endless sunshine . . .

While Sueo fretted briefly about the fact that they would be moving to an area where earthquakes were relatively frequent, Mitsue's feelings ran more along the lines of "Compared to the unnatural things that have happened in this building, an earthquake here or there is nothing to be afraid of."

Mitsue did feel a fleeting twinge of concern about leaving the Kano family behind to fend for themselves, but she concluded that their future wasn't her responsibility. Besides, from what she'd heard, it wouldn't be much more than a week before they followed suit and moved out, as well.

"Only another week or so," Mitsue muttered under her breath, counting off the days on her fingers. Just a week. That family would probably be all right here for a little while longer. No, not probably; they would *certainly* be fine for another week.

Making up their minds to leave had surely been the hard part, and now they just needed to endure a few more days in the building. True, it was incredibly bad luck that the house with a garden the Kanos had originally planned to move into had been destroyed in a fire, but at least they had a backup plan: a tiny two-bedroom rental apartment. That unit wasn't immediately available, so their moving date had to be postponed—albeit only for about a week.

*Besides*, Mitsue thought, *the brutally honest truth is that at this point in our lives, Sueo and I really don't have time to worry about other people's problems.* Those selfish words seemed to stick in her throat like a drink that's gone down the wrong way, but sometimes you just had to look out for yourself. There was another element at work, too, which was completely unrelated to the need to concentrate on her own and her husband's welfare. Since Mitsue was in total-candor mode, she couldn't deny that, as a member of the same gender, she had some feelings of envy and resentment toward Misao.

The younger woman appeared to be blessed with a successful marriage to a charismatic man—or if there were any problems, they weren't apparent. She was the mother of an adorable child; she was still young, and very attractive; and on top of everything she even had artistic talent and some interesting part-time work. The truth was, Mitsue was perpetually irritated by what she perceived as Misao's unfairly charmed existence.

Mitsue and Sueo had never had any children, though not by design. They had simply waited for a pregnancy to occur naturally, and it never did. Needless to say, in their younger days infertility science hadn't been nearly as advanced as it was now, but in any case they both believed that becoming parents was a gift rather than something to be actively pursued, so they had never taken any medical steps toward trying to achieve that goal. Fortunately, no rifts had developed between the couple over the issue, as often happens; on the contrary, Sueo seemed to feel that their lives had been easier without children. Mitsue, though, wasn't able to be so cavalier about their inability to start a family, and for the entire course of the marriage she had been haunted by feelings of loneliness and longing.

As a woman, and as a human being, too, she felt somehow unrealized and incomplete. *If only we could have had one child*, she would think, almost daily. Of course, by now that child would have grown up and moved out, but there would be visits from time to time, and he or she would surely have been able to help resolve the practical problems that plague an aging couple.

Mitsue had lived her life with the constant sense that something was broken or missing, and as a result she had a sizable inferiority complex. This made it difficult for her to interact with a woman like Misao, whose life appeared to be idyllic and enviable in every regard.

However, Mitsue would never have dreamed of trying to make mischief, or of fabricating mean-spirited rumors about anyone. She was philosophically opposed to behaving in such a despicable way, and she knew if she ever stooped to such shameful tactics she would only make herself more miserable. Mitsue's personal credo went something like this: *Don't ever let yourself turn into one of those women of a certain age who are perpetually consumed by feelings of envy, and who do nothing but grumble and gripe about their ill-starred lot in life.*

After the Tabatas' possessions had been loaded onto the truck, Sueo sent the moving men on their way with an envelope containing a modest tip. Then he and Mitsue quickly changed into the traveling clothes they had laid out earlier. Locking the door of the empty caretakers' apartment behind them for the last time, they got into the elevator and rode up to the eighth floor to say their final good-byes to the Kano family. It was a Wednesday, so Teppei had gone to work as usual, but Misao was at home.

"Well, it looks as though we'll be leaving before you do, after all," Mitsue said as she bowed in the entryway, wearing an amicable smile.

Misao's face looked rather gaunt, and she appeared to be uncommonly tense and jittery, but she smiled broadly in return. "I'm happy that things worked out so well for you," she said. "Your new situation sounds wonderful!"

"We hope you'll come visit us before too long, perhaps during the summer holidays—and by all means, bring Tamao, too!" Sueo said jovially. "It only takes five or six minutes to walk to the beach from our new place."

"Thank you so much for the invitation," Misao said. "We'll be looking forward to taking you up on your kind offer in the near future. Do you have time to come in for a cup of tea?"

Mitsue shook her head with what appeared to be genuine regret, but the truth was that she didn't want to spend another minute in this wretched building. "We want to try to get to Izu ahead of the moving truck, so we need to be on our way as soon as possible," she explained.

"Oh, of course." Misao nodded. Mitsue was secretly pleased to notice some fine wrinkles around Misao's eyes; they might have been a new development, or perhaps Mitsue simply hadn't noticed them before.

"Well, this is a pretty kettle of fish, isn't it?" Sueo shook his head.

"I mean, who would have dreamed that every single tenant in the building would end up moving out? And if we tried to explain the reasons to an outsider, no one would ever believe us—not in a million years."

"It's going to be lonely without you," Misao said with genuine sadness. "Look, I know you need to run, but won't you come in just for a minute? Please? The thing is, I just received a very upsetting phone call, and I really don't want to be alone right now." While she was speaking, Misao's face seemed to be growing ever paler, even as—perhaps in some kind of distorted physiological counterpoint—the whites of her eyes began to look more and more bloodshot. Her breathing had become labored, too, and her chest was heaving violently under the loose, bluish-gray summer sweater she wore.

Mitsue Tabata shot a quick glance at her husband, then asked, "What's wrong, Mrs. Kano?"

Looking as if she might be about to burst into tears, Misao pushed her bangs off her forehead with one hand, then took a deep breath. "Well, I just got a call from the rental agency we've been working with. It was about the apartment we were planning to move into at the end of this week . . ."

"Oh, did something happen?"

"Yes, it did."

"So your moving day had to be postponed, or something like that?"

Misao took another deep, racking breath, then shook her head slowly from side to side. "No, she died," she said, barely suppressing a sob.

"Died?" Mitsue gasped. "Who died?"

"The woman who was living in the apartment we were supposed to move to this week just dropped dead last night," Misao said. Her cheek muscles were twitching as she added, "I really can't believe it."

Mitsue put both hands to her own cheeks. "What? Not again! But why?"

"I have no idea," Misao said.

"Was that person getting along in years?"

"No, on the contrary," Misao said with a weak, unnatural-sounding laugh. "She was actually quite a bit younger than I am, and she looked very robust and healthy. I got the impression that she was around twenty-three or twenty-four. We met her when we went to see the apartment, and she was in high spirits because she was engaged to be married. That's why she was getting ready to move out. And now, suddenly, she's dead."

"Oh my goodness, how awful," Mitsue said, shivering involuntarily. "That's just too awful for words."

"I know," Misao said with a listless nod. "And we don't have anywhere to move to now, because apparently that apartment has to be left untouched until they can determine the cause of death. Beyond that, though, the idea of moving into an apartment where someone just died under suspicious circumstances doesn't exactly seem inviting, any way you look at it . . ." She stopped speaking in midsentence and got a faraway look in her eyes. After a moment she said, "To be honest, I'm really frightened."

"Of course you are," Mitsue said as she and her husband nodded sympathetically, in unison. "Who wouldn't be?"

Some words began to bubble up in Mitsue's throat, but she managed to swallow them just in time. A moment later, though, Misao gave voice to the exact same thought: "It's really starting to feel as if our attempts to get away from this place are doomed, or cursed," she said. "Every time we try to leave, something disastrous seems to happen and we end up being stuck here."

Mitsue didn't know how to respond, and when she looked up at her husband she noticed immediately that his neck had broken out in goose bumps. Sueo returned his wife's look of dismay, but he remained silent, too.

"I really don't think it was a coincidence that the little house we were supposed to rent burned down before we had a chance to move in," Misao continued after a long pause. "And now our second choice is out of the picture, too, because somebody suddenly died there. I mean, come on, this is really getting scary, don't you think?"

Misao locked eyes with Mitsue, then let out a long sigh while she distractedly twirled her bangs with one forefinger. "Oh dear, I'm so sorry," she said. "This is a day of celebration for you—you're finally making your escape!—and here I am detaining you with my boring problems. Sorry, I just kind of . . ."

"That's all right," Mitsue said, gently taking hold of Misao's forearm with both hands. "Don't give up the fight, Mrs. Kano. You have to keep looking for a good place to move to. Please, hang in there! This latest development is lamentable, to be sure, but it has to be a coincidence. That's right. All these setbacks in your housing search are just chance occurrences."

Even as she spoke, Mitsue was thinking that her attempt at encouragement rang false and discordant under the circumstances. Coincidence? A house the Kanos were about to move into suddenly burns down, and not long after that the healthy young woman living in the apartment that was the family's backup option suddenly drops dead of unknown causes, thus making the apartment unavailable—not to mention undesirable. Of course, stranger things happened every day, but Mitsue couldn't help seeing a pattern.

While Mitsue was in cheerleader mode, Misao kept nodding and saying "Mm-hm, mm-hm." Then she reached up and plucked a box, prettily wrapped with pink ribbon, from atop the shoe cupboard in the entry hall. The Kanos' dog ambled up and wagged its tail at the visitors.

"This is just a little parting gift," Misao said. "I remembered that you both like sweet things, so it's a selection of madeleines. I hope you'll enjoy eating them on the train."

"Why, how nice!" Mitsue said, beaming broadly, but she was thinking, *All right, that's it—I give up. I can't fight it anymore. This woman is just too perfect, in every way. Maybe if we had stayed on here, she and I could have established some kind of rapport and been on more neighborly terms. I mean, to think that she would go to the trouble of buying a parting gift for us, at a time like this . . .*

"Well, then, Mrs. Kano, please take care and be well," Mitsue said, touching Misao's arm again. "Just try to hang on a bit longer, and if you should have any problems, please don't hesitate to get in touch with us."

*Good grief, I sound like a mother fussing over her child,* Mitsue thought, but she was surprised to find herself very close to shedding tears over Misao's miserable predicament.

As Misao exchanged fraught glances with the departing couple, the incredibly sorrowful look in the younger woman's eyes gave Mitsue the sense that, like a small animal caught in a hunter's trap, Misao Kano was well on the way to giving up the fight and simply resigning herself to her fate.

*How desolate and forsaken she must be feeling,* Mitsue thought. *If I were in her place right now, I would probably already have lost my mind.* The Kano family's dire situation was almost too much to bear, even for an emotionally detached observer.

Sueo went over to the elevator and silently touched the call button. The door opened and Mitsue stepped in, gently propelling her husband ahead of her. Misao saw them off with a small wave of farewell, and the Tabatas waved back. The metal doors closed, and with the familiar *ga-tonk,* the elevator began its downward journey. Lightly, Mitsue took hold of Sueo's arm.

"We certainly ended up getting an earful of bad news, didn't we? I really wonder whether that family is going to be safe here."

"Hard to say." Sueo's eyes were glued to the indicator panel. 7 . . . 6 . . .

"Do you think it was coincidence?"

"Do I think *what* was coincidence?" 5 . . . 4 . . . 3 . . .

"You know, the way someone who was in perfect health suddenly dropped dead, and before that, a house went up in flames for no apparent reason?"

"Of course it wasn't coincidence," Sueo mumbled, looking intently at his wife. "Look, we'd better not talk about this anymore, ever. We could still be in danger ourselves, you know."

The image of the horrifying handprints that had popped up all over the inexplicably locked front door on the Inoue family's moving day flashed across Mitsue's mind, and she felt suddenly queasy. For a moment, she closed her eyes in silent prayer. She felt a tremendous rush of relief when the elevator hissed to a stop on the first floor, and she was doubly relieved when she saw that the building's glass entry door was still propped ajar, just the way they'd left it, with nary a supernatural handprint in sight.

Slipping and sliding on the polished floor, Mitsue rushed out into the driveway, then turned to make sure Sueo was right behind her. (He was, although his face wore a distinctly apprehensive expression.) For the first time in a long while, Mitsue felt herself being enveloped in a soft, silky cocoon of warmth and well-being. She could feel the tension draining away bit by bit, and she had a sense that her pores were opening up to the restorative sunshine.

The sun's rays were strong, and the air was sultry and humid. As she stashed Misao's attractively boxed parting gift in her big traveling bag, Mitsue took a deep breath. The smell of incense drifted into her nostrils from the nearby graveyard. She cast a sidelong glance at the legion of tombstones, and her step grew perceptibly lighter as she told herself that if she never again lived anywhere near a place like this it would still be much too soon.

When Mitsue turned to glance back at the Central Plaza Mansion after walking a few dozen yards, the building appeared to be gleaming brilliantly with reflected sunlight. Indeed, the glare was so dazzling that the balcony of the Kanos' apartment on the eighth floor was obscured by the vortex of light.

Squinting, Mitsue held one hand to her forehead to shade her eyes. After staring at the building for a long moment she began to feel dizzy, and she realized that the brightness wasn't reflected sunlight after all. Rather, the building itself appeared to be giving off a blindingly intense radiance. Mitsue didn't say a word about this to her husband as they walked along in silence, shoulder to shoulder, on the narrow road that ran alongside the graveyard.

When the couple reached the highway, they hailed a taxi. After they had settled into the back seat, Sueo said, "Tokyo Station, please." In the split second while the automatic door was pulling itself closed, a bolt of light seemed to crash through the cab's rear window and shatter into tiny, gleaming shards that illuminated the interior of the car. It was the kind of brilliant white glow you might see at the site of an explosion, and Mitsue was reminded of visual effects she'd seen in movies, done with laser beams or the like. She instinctively closed her eyes, but the taxi driver showed no signs of having even noticed the flash.

As the taxi pulled into traffic, the light began to fade. Before long the interior of the vehicle had returned to its normal sunlit state, but Sueo went on blinking his eyes and shaking his head for a few moments after that. He was about to ask the cab driver whether he had noticed the extreme burst of light when the driver spoke first, in an incongruously easygoing drawl: "Nice weather we're having, don't you think? It would be great if this sunny spell would continue until the end of the rainy season, though that doesn't seem too likely."

"We can only hope," Mitsue replied, echoing the driver's casual tone.

"The thing is, the weather reports have been saying that this year's rainy season is actually turning out to be quite a bit wetter than in the past, so it's like a miracle when we get a perfectly clear day like this," the driver added. He appeared to be in his forties, with a friendly, open, sunburned face.

"That's very true," Mitsue responded automatically.

"Excuse my asking, but where are you headed today, from Tokyo Station? Are you going off on a trip, just the two of you?"

"No, it isn't really a trip." Making a conscious effort to dispel the lingering feelings of fear, Mitsue concentrated all her energy on conversing with the cab driver. "Actually, we're moving down to the Izu Kogen area."

The driver—who really was unusually inquisitive—asked whether they had built a retirement villa down there, and Mitsue said, "No, we've been hired as resident managers for a corporate dormitory, so we'll be living on the premises."

"Oh, you don't say!" the taxi driver responded with evident interest, glancing up at his rearview mirror to catch Mitsue's eye. "Just the two of you?"

"That's right."

"How nice! The ocean down around Izu is so much prettier than in the central part of the country. And I'm guessing it's probably cooler down there during the summer, as well?"

"Yes, and the air is cleaner, too, so it's ideal for older people like us."

"I imagine your grandchildren are really looking forward to visiting you down there. That should be loads of fun for everyone."

"We don't have any grandchildren," Mitsue said, with a sudden sick feeling in the pit of her stomach. "We never had children."

"Oh, really? So those folks who were seeing you off a while ago weren't your children and their families?"

"Seeing us off? Who?" Choosing not to make eye contact via the rearview mirror, Mitsue addressed her questions to the back of the driver's head.

"I have no idea," the driver said, "but they were definitely standing there."

"Standing where?" Sueo asked quietly.

The cab driver clicked his tongue in annoyance at a slow-moving truck in front of them, then stepped on the gas and switched to the passing lane. After leaving the truck in the dust, he glanced up at the rearview mirror again.

"There was a big old temple back there, right?" he said. "And there was a group of people standing right in front; maybe ten or twelve in all. This is just a guess, but it appeared to be several small children and their parents."

Sueo exchanged a quick look with Mitsue. "No one was seeing us off," he said flatly. "We were by ourselves when we got into your cab."

"Oh, is that so? Well, then, I suppose that group must have been there for some other reason. It's really kind of strange, because they definitely seemed to be watching you leave."

*Watching us leave?* When the Tabatas passed the temple there hadn't been another soul in sight, much less a group of children with their parents. Mitsue was absolutely certain of that. And even if there were people visiting the temple for some reason, they wouldn't have paid any attention to the Tabatas.

"Well, I wouldn't have said this if those people had been relatives of yours, but it really was a gloomy-looking group. They must have been at the temple to attend a funeral or something, because they were all dressed in black."

When Mitsue and Sueo didn't respond, the cab driver began chattering about a diving trip he'd made to Izu a couple of years earlier.

"It was really fantastic," he enthused. "Once you try diving, you'll never want to give it up. I don't have the scuba certification or anything, but I was able to master the main techniques on my first try. It's so simple—easy peasy, as they say. Of course, I've never been afraid of the water, at all. Oh, and the meals you eat after making a long dive taste so much more delicious! And all the fish and seafood are incredibly fresh, of course. Yes, Izu's a wonderful place. I'm hoping to get down there again soon, maybe before the end of the year."

Mitsue was staring numbly out the window, and she didn't hear a word the driver said.

# 17

July 25, 1987

"So my room's going to be upstairs?" Tamao said excitedly. Misao bobbed her head in affirmation as Tamao went on, "This house has a really pointy roof, doesn't it, Mama?"

Misao smiled and nodded again. She was still trying to wrap her mind around the recent, totally unexpected stroke of fortune that had led to this ebullient conversation with her daughter. Truth be told, she couldn't stop worrying that something would suddenly go wrong and their hopes would be dashed once again. Still, the end was definitely in sight. All they had to do now was to make it through this evening: their last night at the Central Plaza Mansion. Tomorrow they would be moving here, into this delightful house.

With a plop, Misao deposited the armful of small items she was carrying—a plush toilet-seat cover, some indoor slippers, and a few other small necessities, purchased on the way in the spirit of new beginnings—on the floor of the empty living room of the place they had rented, then let out a long, loud sigh.

Their new home was a charming two-story house in a neighborhood that was about a fifteen-minute walk from the north exit of
Takaino Station. After the incidents with the unexplained fire and
the young woman's equally mysterious death, Misao had begun to
wonder whether they were ever going to be able to extricate
themselves from their current situation. Then, out of the blue, they
heard about this place from one of Teppei's fellow copywriters at
the ad agency. The property's owner had already relocated to New
York City, where he would be working for the next three or four
years. He was clearly delighted at the prospect of having the Kano
family in his home while he was away, so it was a win-win situation
for everyone. As it turned out, the owner, who was also in the
advertising business, was acquainted with some illustrators who
had worked with Misao, so he knew both the Kanos by reputation.
Misao and Teppei jumped at the opportunity to sublet the property, and things very quickly fell into place.

Every aspect of the house—the location, the number of rooms,
the floor plan—seemed tailor-made for their purposes. It was a
sturdy wooden structure with a steeply pitched roof. The ground
floor consisted of a large living room, a roomy kitchen, and a
Japanese-style, tatami-floored room that was about the same size
as the kitchen, or perhaps a bit smaller. Two spacious Western-
style bedrooms and a nicely appointed bathroom occupied the
entire second floor, and there was even a storage attic tucked under
the peaked roof. The roof was triangular, and from a distance the
house reminded Misao of a small turreted castle made from
children's building blocks.

The tiny yard was, as the old Japanese saying goes, as narrow as
a cat's forehead. While the miniature lawn looked like one of those
Astroturf-covered indoor putting greens, it was actually planted
with natural grass that had been conscientiously maintained. The
overall effect was pleasant and restful, and the space had the feel of
a genuine garden.

Misao set to work, with Tamao as her helper, mopping all the floors and putting away the household necessities she'd purchased on the way over. It looked as though the curtains from their current apartment would fit the windows here, and there should be a way to squeeze all the furniture in, as well. The only problem was finding a place to set up their big washer-dryer combo, but there was an alcove in the downstairs hallway, adjacent to the guest bathroom, where that bulky machine could almost certainly be hooked up.

The house faced south, and it was fantastically sunny. Even though Tokyo was still in the midst of the rainy season, the interior of the house was surprisingly dry, with no sign of the usual mold or mildew. When Misao came across some dried-up dust bunnies in the depths of the closets, that small, symbolically wholesome discovery triggered an involuntary sigh of relief over having lucked into a place that was so bright, safe, and cheerful.

Yes, she thought, they would be able to make a new start here. In retrospect, maybe they had been overreaching by going all out and buying an apartment. A more freewheeling approach might have been wiser—just moving from place to place whenever they found an irresistibly good deal on a rental house or apartment. Maybe every family simply needed to find the housing solution that worked best for them.

Misao still couldn't stop thinking about the freakish fire and the sudden death of the young woman. It was strange, but two rather inconsequential images seemed to be indelibly seared into her memory: first, the quick glimpse she'd caught of that contented-looking woman's suntanned ankles peeking out from under the cuffs of her rolled-up jeans; and second, the red heart-shaped throw pillows casually tossed onto the sofa in the apartment.

The cause of the young woman's death still hadn't been determined, and there was no reason to think that anyone would contact the Kanos when (or if) an explanation emerged. *That death was pure coincidence,* Misao told herself. She was making a conscious effort to see it that way. Indeed, she *needed* to see it that way. No matter what, she had to believe the young woman's tragically

premature demise was nothing more than an unfortunate coincidence. Focusing on that conviction with all her might was the
only thing that had carried Misao through these final days.

"Mama? I really like this house," Tamao said, as she scampered
around the garden's square lawn in her bare feet. "You like it, too,
don't you, Mama?"

Just then a large black swallowtail butterfly glided over the
fence and began pirouetting around, flapping its wings as it hovered above the lawn.

"Yes, I like it very much," Misao replied absently. She was
thinking that a black butterfly didn't seem like the most auspicious
housewarming omen. Stretching out her hand, she gently tried to
shoo the butterfly away, but it kept circling tenaciously around the
periphery of the garden, almost as if it were looking for something.
Finally it flew back over the fence and disappeared into the trees.

"Just about this time tomorrow Papa and Cookie will be in this
house, too," Tamao said. "Will Cookie sleep in the garden?"

"That's a good question. The thing is, we've spoiled Cookie rotten, so I don't think she'd be willing to sleep alone in the garden,
do you?"

"No, I think she'd be okay with staying outside. Cookie is really
strong and brave, you know. She's a very courageous dog."

"Courageous?" Misao smiled. Recently Tamao's vocabulary had
been increasing by leaps and bounds, and she seemed to be growing visibly taller with every passing day, as well. Tamao no longer
talked about Pyoko, and Misao wondered whether her daughter
had forgotten about the dead finch, or had simply realized that
every time she mentioned Pyoko's name it made her mother uncomfortable. Either way, Tamao appeared to have somehow come
to terms with that situation, and it comforted Misao to see that her
daughter had found the inner strength to deal with the loss of a pet.

Still smiling, Misao turned the key in the lock of the front door
of the enchanting new house they would be moving into the next
day. Then she and Tamao set off down the road to the station, hand

in hand. The tidy, quiet street was quite narrow, but it was lined with uniquely designed, nicely landscaped houses, and every block seemed to boast either a park or a small general store.

"Say, Tamao? I gather Pyoko hasn't been visiting you lately?" Misao asked in a singsong tone as she bent down to straighten the visor on Tamao's little white hat.

Tamao studied her mother through narrowed eyes, as if trying to gauge her parent's mood. Finally she mumbled, "No, he's still coming."

"He is?" Misao's heart sank.

"Uh-huh. Not every day, anymore, but he still comes to see me."

"And when Pyoko comes to see you, what does he say? He knows you're going to be moving away, right?"

"Yes, but he was telling me last time that we should move out as soon as possible. He says that building is a very bad place to live."

"I see," Misao said, gazing up at the sky. When she closed her eyes against the dazzling rays of the sunshine, she could still feel their warmth soaking through her closed eyelids and bouncing off her face.

"Why do you suppose Pyoko would say something like that?"

"I don't know, but Pyoko's been saying the same thing for a long time."

"So it seems like Pyoko must know something."

"Uh-huh. Only Pyoko's just a bird, so he can't really explain too well."

Misao almost felt a pang of nostalgia for her own blissful ignorance when, just a few months ago, she had believed that Tamao's ability to carry on this type of fantastical conversation must be a flaw in her daughter's psychological makeup: an overactive imagination, perhaps, or a tendency to conflate dreams with reality. Now, though, the talk about Pyoko didn't faze her at all. After the bizarre things Misao had experienced, hearing that a dead bird had been talking to her child through what sounded like some kind of posthumous interspecies telepathy didn't even strike her as remarkable.

*We only need to make it through tonight, and then we'll be fine,* Misao thought. *And surely that will be the end of the visits from Pyoko, too. I think the bird was just coming around because he could sense that Tamao was feeling anxious, and starting tomorrow there won't be anything to worry about anymore—for any of us.*

Starting tomorrow . . . But would tomorrow, that long-awaited, life-changing day, really arrive without any unforeseen complications? Misao gave a sudden start. Tamao, whose little hands were already sticky with sweat, looked up at her mother with apprehension written all over her face.

*Here I am, a full-fledged adult strolling hand in hand with a small child on a clear, sunny summer afternoon, but instead of enjoying the moment I'm wallowing in fear and negativity,* Misao thought. *That's simply unforgivable.*

Just as the train station loomed into view ahead of them, Misao and Tamao happened upon an ice cream shop. Summoning up a celebratory tone, Misao said, "What do you think, Tamao? Shall we stop for some ice cream?"

"Can we really? Hurray! I want chocolate ice cream."

"That sounds yummy, but I think Mama's going to go for the rum raisin."

Still holding hands, Misao and Tamao tripped lightly into the ice cream parlor, which was thronged with exuberant high school girls dressed in their school uniforms. The mother and daughter didn't notice the black swallowtail butterfly that had been following close behind them. The gigantic winged insect lingered around the shop's entrance for a moment, then abruptly flew away.

That evening, Tatsuji and Naomi came over. Tatsuji carried a large overnight bag emblazoned with the Louis Vuitton logo, while Naomi was resplendent in a colorful flower-print summer frock accessorized with a Gucci handbag and an assortment of jangling bracelets—an outfit that seemed better suited to a cocktail party on some glamorous seaside terrace. Her body language made it clear that she had no desire to help her in-laws with their move, and was only doing so with the greatest reluctance. More than likely she had been dragged over by Tatsuji, protesting all the way.

The younger Kanos had brought their car, and while Tatsuji drove Teppei over to the new house to install the living room drapes, Misao began to prepare a simple dinner. She didn't want to dirty too many pots and pans, so she made curry rice along with a large bowl of salad—a nutritious hodgepodge designed to incorporate all the odds and ends of vegetables from the refrigerator.

From start to finish, Naomi prattled incessantly about fashion and travel, pausing only to ask invasive questions in a tone of selfless concern—things like, "How soon do you think you'll be able to buy another apartment?" and "How *are* your family finances these days, anyway?" Misao responded to each query with a smile, but she didn't divulge any information. She was all too aware that Naomi had enjoyed an exceedingly privileged upbringing, and as a result had grown up to be supremely unaware of the need for respectful boundaries. When she was trying to become friendly with someone, Naomi would always begin either by asking impermissibly nosy questions or by broadcasting her own opinions.

*The person I used to be five years ago would have found someone like Naomi very difficult to tolerate,* Misao was thinking, bemusedly. Now, though, she was able to give her sister-in-law the benefit of the doubt, because she felt certain that Naomi genuinely wanted the two of them to be on good terms.

"You really lucked out this time, didn't you, Misao? From what I've heard, your new place sounds great."

"Yeah, we were very lucky this time."

"The truth is, I've always had a problem with graveyards and temples, for as long as I can remember. Maybe it's a girl thing. I remember when I first heard that you guys were going to move here, I was surprised that you'd be on board with the decision to buy an apartment in this building. It just didn't make sense to me."

"Well, at the time I wasn't really bothered by the temple or the cemetery," Misao fibbed. "Actually, I still feel that way. I mean, of course, a cemetery isn't exactly a feel-good place, and I did often find myself wishing we could have been living next to a park instead. But these days people who want the convenience of a central location need to be thick-skinned enough to deal with a few ghosts or whatever, if need be. I'm joking, of course, but I guess my point is that someone who insists on absolute perfection could end up not being able to find any place to live at all."

Naomi was standing next to the kitchen counter, showing no signs of wanting to help with the dinner preparations. "Okay, but you have to admit that there's something weird about living in a building where everyone else has already moved away," she said. "To be honest, it kind of gives me the willies. I mean, we're going to be all alone here tonight, right?"

"Yes, we've been the only ones in the building since the caretakers moved out, and everything's been fine. Since you and Tatsuji will be staying over tonight, it's actually going to feel like a party!"

"And you aren't afraid?"

"Afraid? Of what?"

"Well, I mean, isn't it a little bit frightening to be a solitary family of three living right in front of a graveyard, with nobody else around?"

"I think you've been watching too much TV, Naomi," Misao teased, borrowing one of Teppei's standard lines. "Honestly, it hasn't been bothering us at all. Besides, we've been focused on finding a new place and getting ready to move, and we haven't had time to worry about minor things like that."

"You're such a strong person," Naomi said, her eyes widening in evident admiration. "If I were you, I would have run away a long time ago."

*It's not as if I didn't want to,* Misao thought, but she forced a smile.

Just then the men returned from their errand. Everyone sat down at the dining table and began to eat, carrying on a sprightly conversation all the while. After dinner Teppei and Tatsuji went into the living room to watch a baseball game while Naomi did some desultory table clearing, then wandered off to the nursery to help Tamao pack her toys and stuffed animals.

The technicians wouldn't be coming to uninstall the air conditioner until the following day, so the apartment was still pleasantly cool. While Naomi and Tatsuji—who appeared to be getting along extremely well—were taking a bath together, Misao and Teppei laid out a double futon for the guests on the floor of Tamao's room.

"You're going to sleep with Papa and Mama tonight, all right?" Teppei said when Tamao wandered into the nursery holding her teddy bear.

"Woa-kay," Tamao rejoined. "But Pooh-Bear has to sleep with us, too."

"That's fine. So there'll be four of us, instead of three," Teppei said, patting Tamao's head. "It's going to be fun—almost like going on a camping trip!"

Tamao laughed delightedly as she left the room, pulling Cookie, who had trotted in behind her, along by the collar.

"It's pretty amazing that the place we're moving to is so nearby," Teppei said as he used both hands to smooth out some lumps in the fluffy comforter that covered the guest futon. "It should be an easy move."

"I just can't help wondering how Tatsuji and Naomi really feel about helping," Misao said.

"Well, Tatsuji offered ages ago, and they seemed perfectly willing to come over tonight, so I wouldn't worry about it. I doubt if they have anything better to do. Even so, we're going to owe them, big-time. But hey, more important, what's with Naomi's outfit, anyway? Is she seriously planning to wear that tomorrow during the move? I couldn't believe it when she turned up tonight wearing a fancy dress with trailing skirts, like some princess in a fairy tale."

"I don't see the problem," Misao said with a wry smile. "There won't be that much work for her to do, and it'll be a huge help for me if she can just keep an eye on Tamao tomorrow."

Teppei stretched out his neck and made a *humph* sound, then flopped down across the newly laid bedding. "I never imagined we'd end up leaving this place so soon," he said. "It seems like only yesterday we were moving in."

"No one could have seen this coming, but we really didn't have a choice," Misao said. "We couldn't very well go on living in a place that felt so unsafe."

"If we ever tried to tell someone from the outside world about what's happened here, they'd probably think we were crazy," Teppei mused.

"It's one of those things you just can't talk about, but eventually there will probably be rumors floating around," Misao said. "I mean, after we leave tomorrow morning, this building will be completely deserted."

"I still can't fathom it," Teppei muttered, turning over onto his back and scowling up at the ceiling. "I simply don't believe some of the things we've experienced, even though I saw them with my own eyes."

"If only it really had just been a bad dream. Then we could have woken up the next morning and said, 'Oh, thank goodness.' That kind of thing used to happen to me a lot in the old days. You know, I'd be in the throes of some really dire nightmare and I would cry out in my sleep, and then when my eyes finally popped open it would be such an incredible relief to find myself lying in my own bed, with the morning sunlight streaming in through an open window. Even after we got together, that happened quite a few times. Then I would wake up and see you sleeping next to me, and I'd be flooded with infinite happiness. I can't even describe how happy I felt."

"Yes, but the nightmarish things we've encountered here really did take place. They weren't dreams, at all," Teppei said soberly.

"No, of course you're right." Misao nodded. After a long moment of silence she and Teppei both smiled, more or less in unison.

"Anyway, the bottom line is that tomorrow we'll be embarking on a new chapter of our lives. The best thing is just to focus on that now, and put the past behind us," Teppei said.

"I couldn't agree more. Oh, by the way, are you going to take a bath with Tamao tonight?"

"Yes, that's the plan. It's just that lately whenever we bathe together she's been looking at my . . . uh, appendage, and making comments."

"What sort of comments?"

"Oh, just things like 'Hey, look, Papa has a little banana hanging down!'"

"And what did you say in reply?" Misao asked, giggling softly.

"Hey, give me a break," Teppei protested, but he was chuckling, too. "I mean, what could I say? I just blushed like a schoolboy and looked down at the bathwater."

Misao giggled again, more loudly this time, then gave Teppei's shoulder an affectionate squeeze. "I don't suppose you could have tried to pretend that her eyes were playing tricks on her, and passed it off as an optical illusion?"

"Let's face it, Tamao is always going to be one step ahead of her poor old parents. She's really going to be a handful, mark my words." They both started laughing, and the conversation ended with an agreement that after the move they should probably make an effort to provide their precocious little daughter with some preliminary sex education, or at least an anatomy lesson.

Tatsuji and Naomi emerged from the bathroom, and Teppei and Tamao went in to take their turn. Misao, meanwhile, busied herself with packing up the assorted knickknacks and other small items in the master bedroom. The wooden memorial tablet for Teppei's first wife, Reiko, was in a small Buddhist altar that they had ended up hiding away in the closet. Misao took out the tablet, swathed it tightly in several layers of cloth, and laid it on the bottom of an overnight bag that she planned to hand-carry to the new house.

After she placed the tablet in the bag, Misao got the unmistakable feeling that it was moving, ever so slightly. When she picked the tablet up again she saw that the cloth covering it was partially unfurled and the front of the tablet, which bore Reiko's posthumous Buddhist name, was clearly visible. Misao felt frightened for a moment, but she assured herself that it was nothing. There had to be a rational explanation for why the cloth had come unrolled, even though she had taken pains to make sure the tablet was snugly wrapped.

*In any case*, she thought, *beginning tomorrow we can say goodbye to this ridiculously edgy mental state we've been in, where we freak out every time anything a tiny bit unusual happens.* Because of all the recent chaos, Misao had been obliged to cancel her freelance-illustration assignments, and she needed to try to reschedule them as soon as possible. It seemed that no matter how much money she and Teppei brought in, it was never enough, and now they were going to be maintaining two residences: paying the mortgage here until this apartment sold, along with the monthly rent on the new place. Oh well, they would just have to hunker down and make it work somehow.

Tatsuji stuck his head in the bedroom door. "Hi there," he said, almost shyly. "Would it be okay if I helped myself to a beer?"

"Please, have as many as you like. Or rather, have as many as you can drink without giving yourself a hangover! We have to get up early tomorrow."

"Don't worry, I'm well aware of the early wake-up call."

"Seriously, though, Tatsuji, I'm sorry you had to get dragged into this."

"No, it's totally fine," Tatsuji said with a laugh. "It feels like we're having a slumber party with the whole family and it's really kind of fun, for a change."

The two in-laws smiled at each other, and then they said good night.

# 18

July 26, 1987

After a night filled with surreal dreams, Misao awakened with the feeling that she hadn't had a single minute of solidly restorative sleep. Painfully aware of her physical and mental weariness, she threw off the quilt and struggled into a sitting position.

It was half past seven. The moving truck was scheduled to arrive around ten, so there was no time to spare. Misao reached out and shook the broad back of her husband, who lay beside her, completely still. *Sleeping the sleep of the dead,* she thought. "Honey, wake up," she said. "We need to get up right now."

Teppei opened his eyes a crack and looked at Misao with a sullen expression. Then, as if to say, "I'm in a bad mood, but it has nothing to do with you," he silently turned over and flung one arm around her waist.

Just then, Tamao's eyes suddenly popped open. (She'd begun the night sandwiched between her parents, but had gradually migrated to the bottom of the bed.) "Good morning, sleepyhead!" Misao said. Tamao didn't reply. She looked as though she hadn't slept a wink all night, and Misao figured she was probably keyed up about the move.

"Come on, people, time to rise and shine," Misao ordered. "There's still quite a bit to do."

"Aye, aye, Captain," Teppei mumbled sleepily. "Have you checked the weather?"

Looking at the light streaming in through the curtains, Misao replied, "It looks like a beautiful day—it's clear again, even though we're still in the summer rainy season. It's probably going to be another scorcher, too. All right, Tamao, you need to get up now. Run and get dressed and wash your face, okay?"

They had left the air conditioner running on a low setting overnight, so the room was still pleasantly cool. Misao climbed out of bed and quickly threw on a pair of jeans and a T-shirt. Even that small amount of movement caused her to break out in a light sweat. Yes, it was definitely going to be another hot one.

Abruptly, Tamao sat bolt upright, like a jack-in-the-box leaping out of its container. "Mama?" she said.

"What is it, sweetie?"

"Is everything okay?"

"What do you mean?" Misao asked, giving her head a quizzical tilt. "Of course, everything's fine. It's just going to be a very busy day, that's all."

Teppei had clambered out of bed, and now he stood in his unbuttoned pajama top looking at his wife and daughter. Nothing moved except his eyes, which were now fully open. "Tamao, did you sleep well last night?" he asked.

"Uh-huh." Tamao nodded.

"Really? Are you sure Mama and Papa didn't keep you awake with all our tossing and turning?"

"Well, I think little Miss Tamao looks exceptionally bright-eyed and bushy-tailed today," Misao said with a chuckle, even though there was nothing amusing about what she'd said. She went up to

Tamao and tenderly lifted the ringlets from her daughter's damp forehead, then checked for signs of fever.

"What's the matter, Tamao?" she asked. "What did you mean just now when you asked whether everything was okay?"

"I don't know," Tamao said. "I just feel afraid, somehow."

"Afraid of what?"

Tamao's only response was to twist her rosy lips into a pout, scrunch up her eyes, and shake her head violently from side to side.

"What are you afraid of, sweetie?" Misao asked again. "Won't you tell Mama and Papa, please?"

Tamao's face crumpled as if she were fighting back tears. She picked up her teddy bear and hugged it close to her chest, but she didn't say a word.

Misao traded a look of concern with Teppei, who now appeared to be fully awake. He conjured up an awkward-sounding laugh, then put his arm around his daughter's shoulders. "You probably just had a bad dream," he said. Tamao gazed solemnly at her father, then said, "No, I didn't have any dreams at all. I just feel scared."

A chill traveled up Misao's spine, but she made an effort to chase away the feeling of uneasiness that threatened to engulf her. After all, she explained to Tamao in a soft, soothing voice, there was no way anything bad could happen on a brilliantly sunny day like this. Today was their moving day, and in just a few hours the truck would be coming to transport their worldly goods to the new house, while they followed in Uncle Tatsuji's car. It was going to be a very busy day for everyone, but it would be great fun, as well. Yet even as she was reassuring her daughter, Misao had the feeling that she was also trying to convince herself, and she suddenly felt cold again.

Teppei crossed the room and opened the curtains, allowing the dazzling morning sunlight to stream in through the bay windows. Cookie had evidently heard the family stirring, and was sniffing around outside the closed door. On the surface it seemed to be a morning just like any other, but it was actually a rather momentous occasion. Today was the day they would begin the next chapter of their lives by moving to a marvelous new place, and that was a major reason for celebration.

After repeating these positive sentiments to Tamao once more, for good measure, Misao said, "Ummm," drawing out the consonant while she collected her thoughts. "Let's see. Cookie's going to be hungry, so you need to get up and change out of your jammies and then go fix her breakfast."

Tossing aside her beloved teddy bear as if she had suddenly lost interest in him, Tamao hopped out of bed. "Let's go quickly, Mama," she said.

"Where to?"

"You know—to the new house."

"Oh, of course," Misao smiled. "Yes, we'll be leaving very soon."

Misao washed her face and went into the kitchen to put the coffee on just as Tatsuji and Naomi meandered into the living room. Naomi was dressed in a figure-hugging pair of white cotton slacks and a low-necked shirt in a gaudy print, with the shirttails casually knotted at her waist.

"Did you get enough sleep, Naomi?" Misao asked.

"Yes, thanks, I slept like a rock. It was nice and cool, all night long."

Tatsuji switched on the transistor radio. On one of the FM stations a perky-voiced woman was talking about a new department store that would be having its grand opening starting at ten o'clock that morning.

"Today's special activities will include a dog parade on the roof of the store," the woman announced. "There will be everything from St. Bernards to Afghan hounds and Akitas, and of course they'll have plenty of cute little terriers, Pomeranians, and Chihuahuas, too, all strutting their stuff. Please stop by and bring the whole family. There will also be a big showroom filled with puppies that you can buy, or just admire . . ."

Naomi joined Tatsuji and began playfully spinning the radio

dial. A cacophonous jumble of sounds cascaded from the speakers—
music, news, commercials, DJs' voices—and the overall effect was
as if a tape recording were being played back at twice the normal
speed. "Hey, stop it," Tatsuji said, laughing. "What do you think
you're doing, you silly goose?"

"Ha, ha," Naomi brayed, opening her mouth and showing all her
perfect teeth. "Come on, let's watch TV instead," she urged, switching off the radio. "Today's Sunday, so *Wide World of Travel* should
be on right about now. Misao, would it be all right if we turned on
the TV?"

"Please, go ahead," Misao said. She was thinking, *It would be
nice if you had asked whether there was anything you could do to
help with breakfast,* although she knew better than to put her criti-
cal thoughts into words. Of course, she could simply have requested
some assistance outright, but she didn't feel comfortable with the
direct approach.

"Hey, the mistress of our house likes foreign travel," Tatsuji said
with an apologetic shrug. "She says I never take her anywhere
exciting, and lately we've been on a steady diet of travel shows. I
mean, it doesn't cost anything to watch those shows, so it's fine with
me, but I suspect she's on the verge of trying to twist my arm into
actually going somewhere, and that could be a problem."

Naomi, meanwhile, had moseyed over to the television and turned
it on. After a moment she let out a little squeal of surprise and then
said crossly, "What's with this TV set, anyway? There's no picture."

"You're right," Tatsuji said. "Maybe the antenna's broken. Um,
Sis?"

"The antenna isn't broken," Misao said, peering across the
counter that separated the kitchen from the living room while
she continued inserting slices of ham between pieces of toasted
white bread. Crackling noises emanated from the TV set, and the
screen was covered with a dense pattern of diagonal lines. Without
saying a word, Misao went over and tried switching from channel to
channel, but she found only static.

"This is certainly odd," Misao said, looking at Tatsuji. "We haven't touched the plug or the hookups or anything. We were planning to let the movers take care of that."

Tatsuji shifted the TV set into a different position, then checked to make sure the indoor antenna was properly attached to the back. "It must be broken," Naomi said. She sounded disappointed. "I guess it suddenly broke, just now."

"I really doubt that," Misao retorted. "It was working fine last night. Is it normal for a fairly new set like this to suddenly break down?"

"I don't think so," Tatsuji said.

Misao was overcome by a feeling of panic. She told herself it was preposterous—surely there had to be some rational explanation for this latest outage—but even so she couldn't bear to look at the TV set.

Teppei had been in the bedroom getting dressed, but now he appeared in the living room with an extraordinarily tense expression on his face. Ignoring the group clustered around the malfunctioning television, he angrily tramped across the room and put one hand on the sliding door to the balcony.

Tatsuji and Naomi had been busy pounding on the TV set and clicking through the channels one by one, to no avail. They paused and looked over at Teppei. "This is really weird," he said, with a heavy sigh.

"What's weird?" Misao asked in a calm voice, making a conscious effort to conceal her rising feelings of apprehension. Teppei shot her a severe look, and she thought for a moment that he might be about to yell at her. But he just said flatly, "They won't open."

"What do you mean?"

"All the windows, and this door. None of them will open."

"Don't be silly," Tatsuji laughed. His tone was relaxed and playful. "They probably just need to be unlocked. When the latches are on, windows won't open no matter how hard you push or pull, you know."

"Why don't you come over here and try, since you're such an expert?" Teppei snapped, reaching out and grabbing Tatsuji roughly by the arm.

Tatsuji was still smiling as he looked back and caught Misao's eye. "I think your husband must still be half asleep," he joked. "He isn't usually this hopeless about mechanical things."

Misao didn't bother trying to come up with a glib response. Instead, she ran over to the glass door. She quickly confirmed that the latch was unfastened, but the door refused to move. "You're right," she said. "It won't open."

"The windows in our bedroom and the nursery are all the same. I couldn't get any of them to open, either. Oh, and the bathroom, too," Teppei added. He and Misao swapped a worried look.

Tatsuji, meanwhile, was tugging on the door to the balcony, using all his strength to try to force it open. It almost seemed as if he was attempting to pull out the entire wall, door and all.

"What's happening?" Naomi cried, but no one paid any attention.

Saying a silent prayer, Misao sprinted over to the entryway and grabbed the knob of the apartment's front door. It opened easily, and when she went into the corridor she saw the elevator off to one side, as usual.

"The front door's still working, at least," she announced as she walked back into the apartment. Teppei had run over to join her, and he looked enormously relieved when he grabbed the doorknob and felt it turn under his hand.

"I wonder why it's only the windows and the sliding door that won't open," he said, catching Misao's eye. "I mean, the front door's fine."

"I know. It's not like someone could sneak up overnight and nail them shut from the outside, especially since we're on the eighth floor."

"You should go check all the windows yourself. I'd be willing to bet that none of them will open," Teppei suggested in a low voice.

When Misao looked closely at her husband, she was startled to see that the skin around his eyes was unnaturally black and blue, as if someone had beaten him up.

"You really aren't looking very well," she said.

"Well, you aren't going to win any beauty pageants this morning, either," he retorted grouchily.

Just then Naomi came up next to them and began to complain about something. Paying no attention to her sister-in-law, Misao headed for the master bedroom. The morning sunlight was still pouring in through the glass of the closed window, and the room was already unpleasantly warm. The bed hadn't been made, and Tamao's discarded teddy bear lay forgotten amid the untidy tangle of sheets and pillows.

After checking to make sure the latch wasn't engaged, Misao gave the bedroom window a sharp tug. The window simply wouldn't budge at all. It was as if someone had intentionally sealed it shut by slathering glue around the entire frame.

In the near distance, Misao could see the buildings of the cityscape gleaming in the morning sun, which blazed down relentlessly despite the early hour. The sky was cloudless and clear. With her illustrator's eye, Misao noticed that the color of the sky today was unusually deep. It appeared to be closer to indigo than the normal robin's-egg blue.

Moving on to the nursery, Misao tried the window there, with no success. Naomi joined her, placing her own fingers on the immovable glass as she said, "I don't understand what's going on. How can all the windows get stuck overnight? That's unbelievable. And what's with the TV?"

"I think it must have something to do with atmospheric conditions," Misao replied. She didn't believe that for a minute, but she felt the need to provide some reassurance. "There's been a lot of humidity lately, and the window seals must have gotten swollen. Either that, or the grooves where the panes slide back and forth somehow got corroded. I don't really understand it, either."

The men had joined them in Tamao's room while Misao was speaking, and now Tatsuji said mockingly, "Humidity? You honestly think that's a plausible theory? I mean, can excess humidity really cause every single window in a modern apartment to become impossible to open overnight?"

*Of course not, but can't we all just pretend to believe that, for now?* Misao cried in her heart. *If we don't hang on to some kind of logical explanation, then the two of you are going to get so freaked out that you won't be able to stand being here, even for another couple of hours!* She didn't say anything out loud, though.

Tamao was loitering nearby, clinging tightly to Cookie's neck, and as the adults headed back to the living room she watched their every move with eyes that were wider than usual. The corridor was piled high with cardboard boxes, and when Naomi bumped into one of them she swore like a sailor, then bent over to rub one shin.

"Well, anyway, this isn't the type of problem that can be solved by deductive reasoning," Tatsuji said with a phony-looking smile. "The windows are just stuck. Why don't we stop for a coffee break and then try again later?"

"No, but really: what the hell is going on?" Teppei demanded rhetorically, in a voice that was close to a growl. "This is really freaking me out."

"You think?" Tatsuji said in a sardonic tone as he squatted down and joined Naomi in trying to knead away the pain from her shin bump. "The bottom line is that it wasn't very smart to buy an apartment right next to a graveyard."

"Why don't you just shut up for once?" Teppei bellowed.

"Hey, there's no reason to shout at me," Tatsuji said, suppressing a chuckle that bore a clear undertone of contempt. Teppei took a deep breath and glanced at Misao, as if asking her to rescue him.

Misao couldn't think of anything appropriate to say, so she just crouched down next to Tamao, pulled her daughter's little head close to her own palpitating chest, and held it there for a long moment.

# 19

Everyone sat down to breakfast with grim faces and heavy hearts.
The radio had been left on all morning, and while they were eating,
a program called "American Pops Best Ten" filled the air with a
series of popular songs, one after another.

Naomi would occasionally muse, "Oh, I know this one," in an
almost unconscious way. Every time, without fail, Tatsuji bristled
as though his wife had said something confrontational. Then he
would glare at her, saying things like, "Oh yeah? Well, it just so
happens *I* know this song, too!" with a childish show of belliger-
ence. All the adults were downing cup after cup of strong coffee,
and no one asked for a second helping of ham toast.

In another hour or so it would be ten o'clock. There was still
quite a bit of work to do before the moving truck arrived, but when
Misao thought about the prospect of having to stay in this abomi-
nable place for even another sixty minutes, every inch of skin on
her body seemed to break out in gooseflesh.

"Listen," she said to Teppei, "maybe we could call the moving company and ask them to send a truck over as soon as possible, instead of waiting."

Teppei was immediately on board. "Good idea—let's do that right now," he said. "The sooner they get here, the better. The company's located right next to the station, so it shouldn't be a problem to move up our appointment."

Misao fumbled around in her shoulder bag for a moment and finally fished out the business card the moving company's representatives had given her when they stopped by to provide an estimate. Holding the card in one hand, she lifted the handset of the telephone with the other. It was only a second or two after she put the receiver to her ear that she realized something was wrong. Feeling as if her entire body had been immersed in a vat filled with ice water, she whispered, "What should I do? I can't get through." Still clutching the lifeless telephone, she looked beseechingly at Teppei.

"Maybe you just dialed the wrong number," he said. "Or maybe there was a misprint on the card?"

Slowly, Misao shook her head from side to side. "It has nothing to do with the number," she said. "The phone is dead. There's no dial tone at all."

All the grown-ups looked at one another, their eyes moving from face to face, but no one said a word. Tatsuji was holding a coffee spoon, and he banged it down loudly on his saucer.

"What the hell is the matter with this apartment, anyway? First the TV breaks, then the windows won't open, and now it's the telephone. This is outrageous. I mean, it's a brand-new building!"

"I'm going to go take a look downstairs," Teppei said, jumping out of his chair so abruptly that it toppled over backward. He dashed across the room at top speed, heading for the front door.

"What do you mean, 'downstairs'? And what are you going to look at?" Misao demanded, chasing after him in a panic. "Please tell me you aren't going to the basement!"

"No, absolutely not. I just want to take a quick look around outside. I'll be back in a jiffy."

"Okay," Misao said reluctantly, grabbing hold of the black T-shirt Teppei was wearing. "But it's just so—I mean, why is all this stuff happening, anyway?"

"I don't have the foggiest idea," Teppei replied in a low voice.

"I'm going with you," Misao declared. "Hey, maybe we could get Tatsuji to run over to the moving company's office in his car and ask if they could send the truck a little bit earlier?"

"That could work." Teppei paused with his hand on the front doorknob.

"Mama?" Tamao came up from behind, and Misao put an arm around her daughter's shoulders. "Don't worry," she said, "Mama isn't going anywhere yet. I need you to do me a favor, though. Could you please run and get Uncle Tatsuji?"

Tamao rushed off, and a few seconds later Tatsuji appeared in the entry hall. "You want me to drive over and talk to the movers, right? Sure, I can do that. Just give me the address." He spoke in a petulant tone, out of habit, but his face was contorted with genuine concern.

"Come on, I'll tell you on the way," Teppei said shortly as he marched out into the corridor. He went over to the elevator and hit the call button.

After hastily asking Naomi to keep an eye on Tamao, Misao ran into the hall and jumped in the elevator with her husband and his brother.

Tatsuji took the car keys out of a pocket in his casual slacks and began to juggle them noisily in one hand. "This is really getting to be a drag," he said, turning down his mouth in an expression of displeasure. "Seriously, I need to know. What on earth is going on here? I mean, did some clueless service center somewhere decide to disable the utilities in this building before you guys had moved out? Even to the point of cutting off the phone line?"

When Teppei didn't respond, Tatsuji shot Misao a pleading look. Misao just gave a helpless shrug.

"Well, anyway, this has really turned into the moving day from hell," Tatsuji went on in an unnaturally high voice. "I don't even know what to say anymore. I'm just astounded." With that, he began tossing his keys in the air and then catching them, the way a child might play with a beanbag.

Teppei stood silently in front of the elevator's display panel. 7 . . . 6 . . . 5 . . . 4 . . . 3 . . . 2 . . . When the indicator light for the ground floor finally lit up, the elevator gave a slight shudder and stopped. Slowly, the doors slid open.

Teppei raced toward the front door, with Misao close behind and Tatsuji bringing up the rear. Misao stopped dead in her tracks at almost the exact same moment that Teppei let out an incredulous "What?!"

The glass door at the building's entrance was solidly, opaquely white. It looked as though someone had slathered white paint onto the glass, making it impossible to see outside.

"What—what is this?" Tatsuji's eyes were wide with fear and bewilderment. "Is it some kind of prank?"

Teppei didn't reply. Silently, he approached the door. From deep in his throat a hoarse, suffocated cry—somewhere between a wail of anguish and the wheeze of a poorly played flute—fought its way up to his mouth and escaped into the air. Misao and Tatsuji exchanged a fraught glance as Teppei stretched out his arm and pointed at the door with one quivering index finger, then looked back and caught their horrified eyes.

In what felt like a superhuman act of will, Misao forced her gaze to follow Teppei's pointing finger. Not daring to breathe, she walked over to the door.

From a distance, it had appeared to be covered with white paint, but up close Misao saw that wasn't the case. Rather, the door was plastered with innumerable handprints.

The prints had clearly been made by a horde of people—or something. It looked as though those entities, whatever they were, had dipped the palms of their hands into some kind of wet, pastelike white substance and then slapped them all over the door until the glass was completely obscured. The handprints were so thick that not even the tiniest bit of light seeped in from outside. Small hands, large hands, muscular hands, smooth hands, wrinkled hands; the imprints were so clear that you could distinguish the whorls on the individual fingertips, and one of the prints had clearly been made by a hand that was missing a finger.

*Missing a finger . . . ?* As Misao pondered the significance of that mind-boggling discovery, she felt her morning coffee making its way back up her esophagus, borne along on a wave of gastric acid. Just then Tatsuji, looking like someone who had suddenly taken leave of his senses, flew toward the door and tried to open it. When that failed, he began hurling himself against the glass, but the door was as impregnable as the entrance to any metal bank vault.

"We need to use something to break it down!" Teppei shouted. "That's the only way we'll be able to get out."

"What's going on? What's wrong with this door?"

"There's no time to explain now," Teppei told his brother. "We just need to concentrate on getting out of here as quickly as possible."

"But, but—" Tatsuji sputtered, saliva flying from the corners of his mouth like salt spray on the crest of a wave. "But Tepp, those things, the marks on the door . . . those are people's handprints!"

"Yes, I know."

"So it has to be a prank, or vandalism, right? Somebody was just fooling around late at night. Maybe some bored teenagers, or something like that."

Ignoring his brother's question, Teppei reached out and grabbed Misao's wrist. His eyelids were twitching, but he managed to speak in a calm, gentle tone. "Could you please run upstairs and get the hammer? If you can't find it, just bring us a sturdy chair or something. Anything we can use to break down this door would be fine."

*Wait, you're going to break it down?* That's what Misao intended to say, but when she opened her mouth to speak, no sound emerged. After swallowing repeatedly in a futile attempt to moisten her dry throat, she finally managed to croak, "I'll go and get it right now."

She took the elevator up to the eighth floor, and no sooner had she walked into the apartment than Naomi came rushing up in a full-blown tizzy. "What's going on?" she demanded, her face distorted by anxiety.

"I need to find the hammer," Misao replied as she brushed by.

"A hammer? What do you need that for? Nobody ever tells me anything. And where are Tatsuji and Teppei, anyway?"

"They're downstairs." Misao was certain she had put a hammer, a couple of screwdrivers, and some other basic tools into a large plastic bag, on the assumption that those items would be needed very soon after they arrived at the new house. But where had she put that bag? She began to rummage frantically through some cardboard packing boxes that hadn't yet been taped up. Finally she found the hammer and, holding it up like a weapon, made a beeline for the door.

"Mama!" Tamao came running after her. "I'm going with you."

Misao was standing in the entryway with one sandal on and one still off, but now she stopped and looked intently at her daughter. Tamao's face was oddly flat and bloated, as though she might be running a low-grade fever, and she wore an expression of undisguised distress.

"Everything's going to be all right," Misao said firmly. "We'll find a way to make it work."

"What are you talking about? Find a way to make *what* work?" Naomi screamed. "What's going on down there?"

Misao averted her eyes. There wasn't time to explain everything right now, but she knew she needed to say something. "The front door of the building won't open," she finally said. "So we're going to use this hammer to break it down."

"What? Please, tell me this is all a sick joke."

"I wish I could." Misao sighed.

Naomi burst into the kind of loud, raucous laughter Misao remembered hearing on numerous festive occasions when her sister-in-law had guzzled a few too many cocktails. "Okay, Misao," she said, her face suddenly stony. "Let me get this straight. You're telling me the only way to get out of this building is to break the glass door? That's ridiculous. If this is some kind of elaborate practical joke it needs to end right now, because it isn't funny at all."

"Unfortunately, it isn't a joke," Misao said coolly. "Listen, please just wait here with Tamao, and I'll be back before you know it."

Naomi stood in stunned silence, rapidly blinking her eyes. Misao blew Tamao a quick kiss, then strode to the elevator without a backward glance.

When she reached the ground floor, she saw Tatsuji staggering around the lobby with tears in his eyes, clutching one arm and emitting loud moans. "What happened to him?" Misao asked Teppei when she reached the door.

"He was throwing himself against the door, trying to force it open, and he banged his elbow," Teppei said, snatching the hammer out of Misao's hand. "You'd better stand back, 'cause there's going to be a lot of broken glass."

Misao joined Tatsuji at a safe distance from the entrance and they watched as Teppei began to attack the door, wielding the hammer with the kind of focused energy you might expect from a lumberjack using an ax to split logs.

"Damn it to hell! Shit! Son of a bitch!" With every blow he aimed at the glass, Teppei shouted out a different profanity.

The sounds of violence filled the lobby, and Misao closed her eyes. The noises grew louder as Teppei's verbal and physical assault on the door became increasingly frenetic. "Worthless piece of shit!" he bellowed in a voice that seemed to emanate from an angry, foul-mouthed giant.

When Misao opened her eyes a crack, she saw her husband still pounding insanely on the glass door with the hammer. His entire face, neck, and body were drenched in sweat, and with every blow he struck, a fine spray of perspiration flew off into space. Misao felt as if an eternity had passed since she came downstairs, but she knew it couldn't have been more than a minute or two. Opening her eyes all the way, she stared fixedly at the door.

Even if it was made from some kind of extra-strong reinforced glass, by now it would normally be covered with a cobweb-like network of cracks, at the very least. However, the glass didn't appear to have been affected by Teppei's onslaught in any way. Undaunted, he continued to assault the door with the hammer, and after every strike he gave the glass a swift kick for good measure. His face was totally transformed, and he looked like a rampaging demon.

"Hey, Tepp, maybe it's time to take a break?" Tatsuji asked, in a voice so low it was almost a whisper. "I mean, nothing seems to be working."

Teppei paused and glanced over his shoulder at Misao. "Did you find any other tools?" he asked calmly, like someone who has abruptly regained his equilibrium after a particularly manic episode.

"What do you mean?"

"I can't break down the door with this hammer. I need something else."

"But . . ." Misao stared at Teppei with a brief surge of hope, fueled by wishful thinking, but it was soon quashed by common sense. If a large, reasonably fit man couldn't make so much as a crack in a glass door after repeatedly hitting it with a cast-iron hammer, using every ounce of his strength, what sort of tool did he think would enable him to reduce the door to rubble?

"Listen, how about taking a break from this and going back up to the apartment?" she suggested. "I was thinking that if we could get the balcony door open, we could go out there and call down to the movers when they turn up. Then they could probably find a way to open the door from outside."

"Oh, no, look at this," Tatsuji said in a quavering voice. "I think there are even more of them now than before."

"Huh? More of what?" Teppei asked distractedly, but Misao knew immediately what Tatsuji was talking about.

They all turned to stare at the door, where a new layer of hand-prints had begun to appear on the glass, one after another. It was as though there were dozens—maybe even hundreds—of people on the other side of the door, standing in line waiting to take a turn at slapping their prints onto the glass.

"Oh, lord, someone please help us," Tatsuji keened, as tears rolled down his face.

"Tatsuji, I'm begging you, please try to keep it together," Teppei implored in a cool, steady tone. "I'll explain everything later. For now, let's go upstairs, okay? And then, like Misao said, we can try to find a way to break down the door to the balcony."

Tatsuji was still blubbering like an elementary school student, but Teppei and Misao each took one of his arms and gently pro-pelled him across the lobby to the elevator. They could, at least, take comfort from the fact that the elevator was still working without a hitch.

When the trio got back to the apartment, Naomi and Tamao were waiting at the door, their faces creased with alarm. Naomi was about to say something when she noticed that her husband was crying like a baby, and she quickly closed her mouth. Tamao cast a stricken glance at her weeping uncle, then reached out and grabbed hold of Misao's jeans with one tiny hand.

Without a moment's hesitation, Teppei clumped noisily into the living room. "Hey, everyone, this could get dangerous, so you'd better stand back." He brought the hammer down, hard, on the glass door that led to the balcony, and Cookie began to howl.

After striking a single blow, Teppei tossed the hammer aside with a grimace and began flapping his right hand up and down. It was evident that he'd swung the tool with so much force that his hand had gone numb. His face still contorted with pain, he grabbed a nearby barstool by its upholstered seat and began to pound on the window.

The barstool's wooden legs soon began to splinter from the impact of smashing repeatedly against the apparently indestructible glass, and before long all three legs had broken off, one after another. Teppei tossed the ruined stool into a corner of the room and, wearing a look of ferocious exasperation, picked up a crystal ashtray. Without bothering to dump out the contents, he hurled it at the window with all his strength. The ashtray made a muffled thump as it collided with the window, then bounced harmlessly back into the room. Cigarette ashes flew in every direction, but the ashtray itself rolled across the floor, seemingly none the worse for wear.

"This window might as well be made of rubber," Teppei marveled when he paused to catch his breath. "Everything just ricochets off. How is this even possible?"

"Teppei, stop! Could you please just stop for a minute?" Misao pleaded. "We need to sit down and figure out what to do."

Tatsuji was sitting on the couch in a stupor, staring at the opposite wall with unseeing eyes. Misao bent down and scooped Tamao into her arms, then turned away from the window. Cookie continued her nonstop yowling, and the plaintive sound echoed through the otherwise silent apartment.

"What time is it now?" Teppei asked after a while. His arms hung limply by his sides, as if he had finally run out of energy.

"It's nearly ten," Misao replied. "The truck should be here any minute."

"I guess they're our last hope," Teppei said. "Maybe there's a chance they'll somehow be able to open the downstairs door from the outside. And even if they can't do that, they'll probably try to call us and find out what's going on."

"But there's no phone service here."

"Well, if they try to call us and don't get through, that should make them even more suspicious, don't you think?"

"Yes, ideally, though it seems just as likely that they would assume we were some irresponsible scatterbrains who already moved out on a different day and didn't bother to cancel the appointment. In which case—"

"Anyway, we just need to wait for the moving guys to get here," Teppei interrupted. His throat vibrated as he took a deep gulp of air. "There's nothing else we can do."

Tamao lay motionless in Misao's arms, her flushed face pressed against her mother's damp, perspiring neck. She began to sob, and as Misao stroked Tamao's heaving back she racked her brain for something comforting to say, but came up empty.

Naomi was perched next to Tatsuji on the sofa. "Darling?" she said in a brittle tone. "What did you see downstairs? Tell me what you saw!"

Tatsuji swiveled his gaze, moving his eyes—which now resembled two bottomless pits—so slowly that the shift was almost imperceptible. "Handprints," he said, staring vacantly at his wife.

"Huh? What?"

"You know, handprints—marks made by people's hands. The glass door was covered with all these sticky-looking handprints, and there were more being added right before our eyes. Nobody seemed to be around, but the door was completely white with those handprints, as if it had been painted over. It was impossible to see outside, and the handprints just kept multiplying."

Naomi gaped at Tatsuji in disgust and disbelief. "I can't take any more of this!" she exclaimed, whipping her head from side to side. "You've all lost your minds! I'm not kidding—I can't take it anymore. I don't care if I have to take the train by myself; I'm going home right now." She grabbed her Gucci bag, which was beside her on the couch, then jumped to her feet with extraordinary force and strode resolutely across the living room, heading straight for the front door. No one made any move to stop her, and Tatsuji just sat and watched his retreating wife through glazed eyes. The front door slammed loudly, and Tatsuji let out a long, deep, piteous sigh.

"Don't worry, she'll be back," Misao consoled him. "However

much she may want to leave right now, the fact is there's no way for her to get out."

Just then Teppei, who was still standing by the unbreakable sliding door, called out, "Hey, look!"

"What is it?" Misao asked.

"The truck's here."

Misao and Tatsuji rushed over to the window, hearts pounding. Sure enough, on the narrow road that ran along the periphery of the graveyard, a large truck was slowly making its way toward the Central Plaza Mansion. The dazzling sunlight reflected off the silvery aluminum surface of the truck's cargo hold.

"Excellent!" Teppei clapped his hands. "They'll be able to help us get out of here, for sure."

"Those people will open the door for us?" Tamao asked her father.

"Absolutely," Teppei replied, displaying more confidence than he felt. The doubtful expression in Tamao's eyes was replaced by hope as she looked up at Misao and said, "That's good news, right, Mama?" Misao nodded.

"Naomi's in the lobby," Tatsuji said thoughtfully. "I need to go down and persuade her not to run off after the moving men open the door."

"We should all go down," Teppei said. The entire group hurtled out of the apartment, leaving only Cookie behind. The indicator light showed that the elevator was still in the lobby. Given the pervasive mood of urgency, the process of calling it up to the eighth floor, crowding in, and making the descent to the ground floor seemed to take forever.

When they reached the first floor, the other Kanos saw Naomi squatting on her haunches in the middle of the lobby as if in a trance, with her face set in a rictus of dismay. The rumble of an engine could be heard in the near distance, followed a few moments later by the sound of a heavy vehicle coming to a stop in front of the entrance to the building.

"Are you okay?" Tatsuji asked, bending over Naomi. Her breathing was rough and ragged, and as she reached up and clung to her husband's torso it almost seemed as though she might be about to faint.

"What—what's that?" she gasped, pointing toward the door.

"Don't look," Tatsuji said, putting one hand over his wife's eyes.

"But what are all those handprints? I mean, look at the door. Who's making them, anyway?"

Outside, there was the sound of a couple of car doors slamming shut, one after the other. Misao approached the handprint-covered glass door and began pounding on it with her fist. "Help us, please!" she shouted.

There was no response, but two male voices could be clearly heard in the driveway outside. The moving men were evidently approaching the door, because both their footsteps and their conversation gradually became more audible.

"What floor was it, again?" one man asked. By the time the other replied, "Eight," the newcomers were standing directly in front of the entrance.

Raising her own voice a notch, Misao shouted again, "Help us, please!"

Surely this time the men must have heard. Nothing was separating their faces from the anxious faces on the inside except a pane of whitened glass, but the new arrivals still made no reply.

"Hey!" Teppei yelled at the top of his lungs. "Can you hear us?"

"What's with the front door?" they could hear one of the men asking incredulously. "It's totally white. Do you think someone painted over it?"

"Hey, wait, what's that over there?"

That's when it happened. There was a strange noise on the other side of the door, followed by a rapid series of strangulated cries. Those blood-chilling sounds were like the final groans of a murder victim breathing his last in some dark, deserted alley. Misao and Teppei exchanged a horrified glance.

"Hey!" Teppei shouted again. He pounded on the door with his fists, and then began to kick it, as well. "What's going on out there? We need help!"

There was no response from outside. In fact, there was no sound at all.

Tatsuji and Naomi stood up and hurried over to join Teppei and Misao in banging noisily on the door. The louder they pounded, the faster the already thick layer of handprints seemed to proliferate on the other side of the glass, but they didn't have time to worry about that.

Behind them, in the lobby, Tamao began to bawl. Misao glanced over her shoulder and said in the most comforting tone she could muster, "Please don't cry, sweetie. Can you do that for me?" Tamao nodded dispiritedly.

"I wonder what happened out there," Tatsuji said, taking a break from banging on the glass to press his ear against the door. "There are no sounds at all now."

"I know, and the truck hasn't driven away, either. I wonder where they went?" Naomi tore her eyes away from the door and looked inquiringly at Teppei.

"I don't have a clue," he faltered, putting his own ear to the glass. "Nope," he said after a moment. "Nothing."

"What do you suppose those dreadful noises were—the ones we heard a while ago?" Misao asked diffidently. "Did everybody else hear them, too?"

"I did," Teppei replied. "They were like cries of agony or—"

"Hey, I just thought of something!" Naomi interrupted eagerly. "This building has a rooftop, right?" Her bright coral lipstick had begun to flake off, exposing lips that were chapped and colorless.

"I forgot about the roof!" Teppei exclaimed.

"That's right, the roof," Naomi echoed impatiently. "Anyway, let's go up there and see what we can see. If we look down, we should be able to figure out where the moving men went."

"Let's go, then." Teppei led the way to the elevator. He pushed the button to open the door, and everyone filed in. The elevator didn't go all the way to the top—that was another of the building's structural idiosyncrasies—so they had to get out on the eighth floor and take the emergency stairs the rest of the way.

The door from the interior stairwell opened easily onto the roof. Letting go of Tamao's hand, Misao charged over to the iron railing. There wasn't a cloud in the sky, and the sun was shining so brightly that the rays seemed to pierce her skin like superheated needles.

Beyond the expansive graveyard, now fully green, the clustered buildings of the Takaino area were clearly visible. The crematorium's tall, cylindrical chimney was emitting the usual thick billows of smoke. Saying a silent, secular prayer, Misao took a timid peek at the ground below.

There was only one road leading to or from the Central Plaza Mansion. The building was located in a cul de sac, so there was no way someone could have driven off down a side road. Even if the movers had decided to leave while the members of the Kano family were making their way up to the roof, they would first have needed to back up their large truck and execute a U-turn, which would have taken several minutes. The entire length of the access road was visible from the roof, so the moving men couldn't possibly have gone far enough to have vanished from sight.

However, there was no activity of any kind on the road that skirted the temple grounds. No truck was parked in front of the building, either. Tatsuji's sedan was still there, but it had the loading area all to itself. In the approximate spot where they would have expected to see the truck, the only thing visible on the asphalt was what appeared to be a few shards of glass, sparkling in the sunlight.

Not only was the moving truck missing in action, but there was no sign of human presence, either. Misao made a complete circuit of the roof, holding on to the iron railing and keeping her eyes peeled for any nook or cranny where a couple of men could be hidden from sight. She checked for potential blind spots, too, but she didn't find anything at all: nothing along the low rock wall, nothing in the patch of morning glories the caretakers had planted, nothing around the area where a drainage ditch emptied onto vacant land. She didn't even see a cat, much less a human being.

When Naomi crept up to join her, Misao glanced over and caught her sister-in-law's eye. "What's that?" Naomi asked in a muted voice, pointing down at the short flight of stairs leading to the building's entrance. On the broad, flat stones that made up the three-step staircase, there were two large dark blobs. It looked to Misao as if someone had spilled stone-polishing oil on the steps, in two different places. No, on second thought, maybe the splotches were more like fresh puddles of coal tar. Clouds of steam were rising from the two wet patches, as though someone had heated up some coal tar a few moments earlier, then poured it on the steps.

*Clouds of steam . . . ?* Misao let out a long, piercing shriek, then collapsed in an insensible heap at the edge of the roof.

# 20

Teppei stared down at the dark puddles on the stone steps, so stunned that it didn't even occur to him to go to the aid of his wife, who had collapsed nearby. At first his mind was a total blank, but after a moment he remembered a photograph he'd seen years before at the Hiroshima Peace Memorial Museum, where a variety of archival materials related to the atomic bomb attack on the city were on display.

The photo showed a charred blob on a stone stairway, and Teppei had immediately been reminded of the flat, limp shadows in Salvador Dalí's paintings of melting landscapes. According to the caption, the steps were attached to a building near ground zero. A profoundly unlucky human being happened to be standing on those steps when the A-bomb blast hit the city, and in that brief instant that unknown person was completely dematerialized and reduced to an amorphous smear on the ground.

*This is just like that photograph,* Teppei thought as he stared down at the driveway in front of the building. *Except there's no way to ignore the fact that these puddles are shaped, vaguely, like people.* One of the blobs in front of the Central Plaza Mansion had its arms and legs splayed to either side, so that it resembled the Sino-Japanese character for "large": 大. The other splotch was curled in upon itself with a single arm outstretched, which gave it the look of a gigantic prawn.

When he looked more carefully, Teppei could just make out what appeared to be several scraps of khaki-colored cloth, shrouded by the steam. As he watched, he was shocked to realize that the steam was actively working to dissolve those bits of fabric. In a matter of seconds, every trace of the khaki scraps had vanished into the air, as if they had been dissolved in sulfuric acid.

"Tepp?" Tatsuji whispered weakly. He sounded as if he might be about to lose consciousness. "That's the moving men down there, isn't it? Those blobs."

"It certainly looks that way," Teppei replied, clutching his fore-head with both hands and moaning softly. Just then the brothers heard a choking, gurgling sound off to one side. It was Naomi, bent double at the waist as she vomited up every last bit of her breakfast.

"Tats, take her downstairs and put her to bed," Teppei ordered, indicating Naomi with a slight lift of his chin. "And could you please look after Misao and Tamao, too? The minute you've gotten them settled in the apartment, look around for some paper and pens, and bring them up here. We need to write a bunch of notes and throw them down. Oh, also, see if you can find some heavy things that we can attach the memos to, and bring those up, too."

"Got it," Tatsuji said weakly. Cradling Naomi in the crook of one arm, he took hold of Tamao's hand. Misao scrambled to her feet and started to follow the others, then stopped to look back at Tep-pei. Her face was as white as a sheet of paper. She wanted to say something to her husband, but no words came to mind. Teppei didn't speak, either; he just watched his family members until they disappeared through the door to the emergency stairwell.

The black smoke from the crematorium chimney was shooting

straight up into the sky, testifying to the complete absence of wind. In the distance, on the national highway that ran along the far border of Manseiji's temple grounds, an endless parade of shiny cars streamed in both directions. From where Teppei stood, the cars looked like toys. *If that faraway vista is the real world,* he thought dreamily, *what madness are we caught up in here?* In that moment he felt like a ghost, gazing back at the living world from the other side.

There wasn't a soul to be seen in the precincts of the temple, or in the immense, sprawling graveyard. In front of some of the gravestones, bouquets of old wilted flowers were crumbling in the midsummer sun. The grayish-white grave markers stood out against a dense backdrop of *Fatsia japonica* shrubs, with their branches like long, skinny arms and leaves that resembled gigantic spread-fingered hands. Near a tall grove of elm trees was a large cluster of polished granite gravestones, and one of them in particular seemed to be reflecting the sunlight with uncannily mirrorlike brilliance.

"What the holy hell is this place, anyway?" Teppei muttered to himself. It was beginning to seem possible that the otherworldly invasion of the building and its immediate environs was even more horrific than anyone had imagined.

Clearly, *they* were all around, day and night. But who, or what, were they? Teppei still had no idea. However, he was certain that this area was their nest, and their den, and their sovereign domain.

*They hate us,* he thought. *They literally hate us to death. They've decided to play some kind of malicious cat-and-mouse game, so they're going to trap us in this building, and torment us, and eventually frighten us to the point where our hearts simply give out. That is, if we don't starve first.*

On the rooftop, a forest of pipes for the building's ventilation system stuck up at various places, creating an irregular obstacle course. Stepping carefully over each protrusion, Teppei made his way to the north side of the roof and put his hands on the rusty iron railing that ran all the way around.

Looking down from there, he didn't see anything that could be described as scenery. There were a number of what must once have been small, city-sponsored housing units scattered about, but they had all been abandoned long ago. Now they looked like fossilized remains, hidden in the shadows and nearly engulfed in the weeds that grew in every direction. In all likelihood, these residential areas had been designed to house lower-income families. People had moved into them, and for a time the white flags of everyday laundry had fluttered above the flowerbeds in the back gardens. Children had probably frolicked happily while grown-ups enjoyed afternoon chats with their neighbors, and the family dogs would have added to the festivities with a chorus of joyful barks.

Picturing that pleasant, long-vanished scenario, Teppei shivered involuntarily despite the warmth of the sunshine. He didn't need to speculate about why all those blocks of housing had ended up empty and forsaken; he knew now that there was something sinister about this pocket of the city. While the details remained a terrifying mystery, he was certain that the ill-starred land around this apartment building was somehow governed or controlled—he almost wanted to say "ruled"—by *them*, whoever they might be.

The door to the rooftop opened, and Tatsuji appeared. In one hand he carried a pad of lined writing paper, which looked familiar to Teppei. *Oh, that's right,* he thought with a pang. It was the sketch pad he and Misao had used to draw schematics of the rooms in the place they were supposed to move into today—indeed, they should have been walking through the door of that house right about now. They'd spent an enjoyable evening perusing the floor plan while they decided where to place each piece of furniture. Remembering those carefree hours, Teppei was suddenly overcome with deep desolation.

"I put Naomi to bed on the sofa," Tatsuji mumbled absently. "There was a can of cola in the fridge, so I gave her some of that to settle her stomach. Do you think we can use these for weights?" He handed Teppei the pad of paper, along with a handful of coffee spoons.

"Thank you," Teppei said sincerely. Even as he uttered that word, he was thinking, *This is the first time in a long while that I've felt the urge to thank my brother for anything.* "Before too long an electrician who deals with air conditioners and someone from the phone company should be stopping by, since we put in requests regarding both those things when we moved out," he explained. "We'll wait here till those people show up, and then we'll shout and call for help. But we need to let them know that this is a dangerous place, too, so we'll throw down the notes at the same time."

"I wonder if they'll land in the right place."

"Well, there's no wind today, so they ought to drop straight down."

Tatsuji nodded, but there was no spark of life in his eyes, and he didn't say anything else.

Teppei took the felt-tipped pen his brother handed him, and on one sheet of paper he wrote in large letters:

PLEASE HELP US. WE'RE THE KANO FAMILY FROM UNIT 801, ALONG WITH TWO OF OUR RELATIVES (FIVE PEOPLE IN ALL) AND WE ARE TRAPPED IN THIS BUILDING. PLEASE CONTACT THE POLICE RIGHT AWAY. THANK YOU VERY MUCH.

As he was composing the message, Teppei was thinking, *I can't believe I'm writing these words. When someone reads the notes, they'll probably think we're being held captive by armed burglars or a gang of marauding psychos.* After a pause, he added another line:

THIS BUILDING SEEMS TO HAVE SOME KIND OF DESTRUCTIVE ENERGY. PLEASE BE EXTRA

CAREFUL AROUND THE STONE STEPS AT THE
FRONT ENTRANCE.

"No, no, this won't do," Teppei said abruptly, tearing up the page and tossing the pieces onto the ground. "Anyone who read a message like that would just assume it was a joke, or a prank."

Tatsuji, meanwhile, had slumped to the ground and was staring vacantly into space, as if his mind had gone on strike and was refusing to function. Teppei tore a fresh sheet from the pad and began to write again.

PLEASE HELP US. WE'RE THE KANO FAMILY FROM
UNIT 801. PLEASE CALL THE POLICE. WE'LL
EXPLAIN LATER, BUT THERE ARE REASONS
WHY YOU SHOULDN'T COME INTO THIS BUILDING.
PLEASE DON'T EVEN TRY TO ENTER UNTIL
AFTER THE POLICE HAVE ARRIVED. THANK YOU.

Satisfied with this revision, Teppei proceeded to write the same message over and over, on numerous sheets of paper. He then rolled each page into a long, tight cylinder, and twisted it securely around a coffee spoon.

"You knew there was something going on with this building before today, didn't you?" Tatsuji said, rubbing his face with both hands. "Why didn't you tell us about it up front?"

"We never dreamed something like this would happen," Teppei replied. "I'm really sorry."

"You're *sorry*?" Tatsuji stopped massaging his face and glared at Teppei through spread fingers. "You think being sorry will make everything okay?"

"Yes, I'm sorry. You have a problem with that?" Teppei asked quietly.

Tatsuji stared at his brother with a face as stiff and impassive as a mask. When he finally spoke, nothing moved except his lips.

"You're the one who got us into this situation—Naomi and me. And yes, I have a huge problem with that. You've obviously known for a while that this place is haunted, or possessed, or whatever. Why didn't you at least give us a heads-up about the negative energy, before we came over?"

"Because we really didn't understand what was going on ourselves—and we still don't. We gradually realized there was something wrong here, and that's why we've been trying to move away. That's all there is to it, but it looks as if we may have waited too long. We were hoping we could make the move without needing to worry you and Naomi about all this weird stuff."

The hot summer sun beat mercilessly down, scorching the brothers' backs and shoulders through their cotton shirts and turning their exposed skin increasingly red. Sweat poured from their brows and ran down their faces.

Tatsuji jumped to his feet and drew himself up to his full height in an almost warriorlike stance. He untucked the tails of his white button-down shirt from the waistband of his chino pants, then stood there looking uncharacteristically unkempt. "So just how far do you think it's okay to go, when it comes to causing inconvenience to other people?" he asked confrontationally.

Teppei scowled at Tatsuji. "What's your problem, anyway?" he grumbled.

"You have a lot of nerve, asking me that. This is the second time, too."

"The second time for what?"

"The second time you made me look like a fool. It's just like what happened with Reiko."

Teppei was squatting on the ground. Now he raised his head, very slowly, and looked directly at his younger brother, but the harsh sunlight streaming into his eyes made it impossible to read the expression on Tatsuji's face. "What do you mean, this is just like what happened with Reiko?" Teppei asked in a carefully controlled voice.

"Okay, if you really want to know, I'll tell you. I've been holding back on saying anything for years now, but I still can't forgive you for what you did. The truth is, I think you're a terrible person. You've always been so completely wrapped up in yourself that you never stop to think about other people, even a little bit. I mean, when Reiko died, I was the one who got stuck with cleaning up the mess you made with your sordid affair. I took care of every little detail— making the funeral arrangements, getting in touch with your office to explain why you hadn't come to work, even apologizing to Reiko's family on your behalf. I really covered your ass, but I'll be honest: I wasn't doing any of that for you. I did it all for Reiko because I felt so sorry for her, suffering alone while you were out feeding your giant ego and tomcatting around with another woman . . ."

"Shut up!" Teppei shouted, hurling one of the coffee spoons onto the concrete floor of the roof. It landed with a loud clang and bounced away.

Shaking with anger, Tatsuji glowered down at his brother. Teppei picked up another coffee spoon and as he was twining one of the rolled-up memos around it, he once again looked up and caught Tatsuji's eye.

"Okay, let's get this straight," he said. "You will never again take that kind of self-righteous tone with me, do you understand? What happened with Reiko is our problem—Misao's and mine— and nobody else's. It has nothing to do with you. You may be my brother, but when it comes to my first marriage you're nothing but an outsider. Don't *ever* forget that."

The brothers glared at each other in silence for a few moments, finally averting their glances so nearly in unison that it would have been hard to say who was the first to look away.

Tatsuji walked over to the iron railing with a weary gait. Leaning against it, he let out a long, deep sigh. "Just go ahead and tell me already," he said.

"Huh?"

"Tell me what's been going on in this building."

"Even if you heard the whole story, it probably wouldn't make sense to you. I mean, it wouldn't make sense to anyone in his right mind."

"I don't care. I want to know. You got me into this predicament, and I think I have a right to know what's going on."

Holding a bundle of memo-encased coffee spoons in each hand, Teppei went to stand next to Tatsuji at the railing. "Okay," he said, "here goes nothing."

Once Teppei began talking, it only took a few minutes to summarize the frightful and baffling events that had taken place since they moved into the building back in March. Simplifying each anecdote as much as possible, he gave his brother a compressed rundown, starting with the peculiar shadow on the TV screen, then moving on to the mysterious (or, at best, unsatisfactorily unexplained) injury Tamao had sustained while playing in the basement. He talked about his surreal walk-and-talk conversation with the bar hostess who used to live on the fifth floor, and the bloodcurdling— and, again, inexplicable—phenomena he and the two caretakers had encountered when they went down to the basement to look for the source of some midnight noises. He also touched briefly on the elevator outages, and the warnings he and Misao had received from Mr. Shoji, the yoga instructor. (He made no mention of the sudden death of their pet bird the night they moved in, because he still couldn't see how that tied in with the other occurrences.)

"And then Misao went to the ward library and did some research into the history of this area," Teppei continued, without pausing to give Tatsuji a chance to respond to the first installment of revelations. "Back in the 1960s, there was apparently a plan to relocate the graveyard and build a big high-rise housing complex on the land. Naturally, that would have resulted in an increase in the area's population, so the master plan included the creation of an underground shopping mall, which would have extended all the way from the train station to right about here. The people who represented the temple and the graveyard rejected the plan outright, but it's possible that the city ignored them and went ahead with the excavation for the underground street."

"And exactly what does that have to do with our situation right now?" Tatsuji asked impatiently, making no attempt to hide his irritation.

"I don't know," Teppei replied. "There may be no connection at all."

Both brothers lapsed into silence. They could hear the creaky songs of cicadas wafting up from the weed-choked fields in the near distance.

"I'm sorry about the things I said before," Tatsuji finally murmured.

"That's okay," Teppei replied equably. "I've known for a long time now that you were harboring those feelings."

"It's just that I really liked Reiko a lot and I still feel sorry for her, even after all these years."

"Look, I don't care if you want to blame me, but you need to leave Misao out of it," Teppei said, shooting Tatsuji a warning look. "She's suffered plenty herself."

Tatsuji gave an almost imperceptible nod. "I know. I'm not trying to place any of the blame on her, at all."

Then, from not too far away, they heard the sound of an engine. Teppei had been sitting on his haunches, but now he jumped up and ran over to the railing that bordered the south-facing side of the roof.

On the narrow road that flanked the temple and the graveyard, a van was approaching. The distinctive blue logo of the telephone company was clearly visible on one side.

"Tats, come here, quick!" Teppei called.

Tatsuji rushed over to join his brother at the edge of the roof. "Somebody's coming!" he said excitedly. "Thank god, we're saved!"

"Okay, listen," Teppei said. "We need to watch for the exact moment when they step out of the van, and then throw these notes at their feet. I mean, one of the spoons might end up hitting someone on the head, by mistake, but at this point we can't be worrying about that sort of thing. It probably wouldn't cause much of an injury, even if it did happen. Anyway, as soon as they look up, we'll start yelling for help as loudly as we can."

Teppei handed Tatsuji a fistful of the memo-bearing coffee spoons and then, hoping against hope, he focused his attention on the approaching van. *Please help us,* he pleaded, silently. *Please just read these notes and then do what needs to be done.*

Teppei couldn't help noticing that the van's engine didn't seem to be running very smoothly, as the vehicle juddered up the driveway and wheezed to a stop in front of the entrance. The two large, dark stains were still visible on the stone steps, but the steam, at least, had dissipated.

The driver's door opened, and a fortyish man in a blue uniform stepped out. He appeared to be alone. After a moment, he stuck his torso back into the van, as if searching for something. Finally, he extracted a small black satchel, then slammed the door behind him.

"Now!" Teppei shouted. "Ready, aim, fire!" On that cue, he and Tatsuji proceeded to toss their missives off the roof. They all fell straight down, and one or two caught the sunlight and flashed silver as they plummeted toward the ground. The hail of spoons landed on the driveway side of the stone steps with an unexpectedly loud clatter. The driver immediately looked up.

"Hey!" Teppei called, waving one arm. The driver was glaring at him, but the expression on his face didn't seem to indicate mistrust or suspicion. He simply appeared angry that anyone would engage in such risky behavior.

"Please read the notes!" Teppei shouted.

"Huh?" the man said, cupping a hand around one ear. Then, evidently catching on, he gazed with obvious interest at the memos littering the ground around him. Picking up one of the spoons, he unfolded the note. After he had finished reading, he looked up again. Flinching slightly at the prospect of a further onslaught, he demanded loudly, "What's going on?"

"Please, just call the police!" Teppei shouted back.

"Say what?" Again, the man put a hand to one ear.

"Police! CALL . . . THE . . . PO . . . LICE!"

"Oh, I see," the man said, clearly flustered. His hands were shaking, and he looked as though he might keel over at any moment.

Right about then, the brothers heard the sound of another vehicle in the near distance. Turning to look toward the temple, they saw a white hatchback sedan approaching along the access road. "That's probably the guy from the electrician's place," Teppei said.

A minute or two later the hatchback pulled up and stopped directly behind the phone company van, just as the first man was about to climb back into his vehicle. When the telephone repairman noticed the newcomer, he ran toward the hatchback, yelling something unintelligible and pointing frantically at the rooftop. After a moment a corpulent, middle-aged man emerged from the driver's side of the hatchback sedan. It was the same employee who had been diligently picking his nose in the middle of the electrician's shop, apparently making productive use of his afternoon break, earlier that week when Teppei stopped by to set up an appointment to have the air-conditioning unit uninstalled, so it could be moved to the new place today. (Teppei had thought, more than once, that the absence of central air conditioning was another piece of evidence that the Central Plaza Mansion had been designed to look alluring on the surface, while every possible corner was being cut in order to reduce construction costs.)

Now the electrician looked up at the roof. Leaning over the railing, Teppei waved both arms and shouted, "Help us, please!"

The man from the phone company handed the memo to the electrician. As he read, the new arrival's plump body began to tremble visibly, like that of a hippo emerging from a wallow. He gave a cry of alarm, then conferred briefly with the telephone repairman. After that they hustled to their respective vehicles, and a moment later the engines roared to life.

All at once a flash of what appeared to be an unnaturally strong ray of sunshine blasted through the rear windshields of both cars, shattering the glass to bits. The vehicles were engulfed in a colossal whirl of light, followed by a blinding afterglow that was almost too bright to look at. The radiance was truly fearsome to behold, like the aftermath of a nuclear explosion. To Teppei and Tatsuji, watching in open-mouthed horror, it seemed as if the sun's rays were being absorbed into a gigantic mirror, then refracted directly into their eyes.

In the same instant, the two drivers and their vehicles disappeared from sight. A couple of brief, terrified screams arose from the vicinity of the vehicles, but those heartrending sounds soon faded away, leaving only silence.

Teppei witnessed this appalling scene in a state of nauseated disbelief. He saw two large plumes of white smoke rising from the road, while a singularly gruesome sound filled the air. It was the kind of sizzling you might hear if you immersed something fragile (fabric, say, or flesh) in a vat of sulfuric acid. The entire sequence couldn't have taken more than five or six seconds. The plumes combined into a single thick cloud billowing up from the area where the men and their cars had been, and then the haze began to clear, revealing several large black blobs on the road.

Tatsuji reached out and grabbed Teppei's arm with a hand that was cold as ice, and Teppei wondered fleetingly whether the parade of shocking occurrences had caused his brother's body temperature to plummet. He himself was feeling extremely dizzy and disoriented, and he found it difficult to catch a proper breath. The summer sun seemed to burn hotter by the minute, almost as if it were trying to set Teppei's scalp on fire, just for fun.

"Come on, Tats, let's go downstairs," Teppei said. Or rather, he intended to speak those words, but no sound came out when he opened his mouth, which didn't surprise him at all. The amazing thing, he thought, was that he was even able to remain on his feet.

Stumbling along together, he and Tatsuji made their slow way across the roof and began to descend the emergency staircase, heading for the one place in their topsy-turvy world that still felt like a safe haven. When they were about halfway there, Tatsuji suddenly plopped down on one of the stairs and began to scream incoherently.

Teppei couldn't understand a word his brother was saying. Stretching out a hand, he pulled Tatsuji to his feet and forcibly hauled him down the remaining stairs, praying with every fiber of his being that they would both make it to their destination alive.

# 21

July 26, 1987 (2:00 p.m.)

Misao was the first to notice that there was no electricity. Tamao was whining about the heat, and how thirsty she was, so Misao had wandered over to the refrigerator with the intention of offering everyone something refreshing to drink.

Normally, the light inside the fridge came on as soon as the door was opened, but when that didn't happen Misao knew immediately that the problem was more than just a burned-out bulb. The power had evidently been down for some time, because drops of condensation were already forming on the outside of a jar of strawberry jam.

Tatsuji hadn't yet begun to recover from the most recent events, and he was sitting on the living room floor, hugging his knees to his chest and staring straight ahead with shell-shocked eyes. Weaving her way between him and Naomi, whose pallid face wore the same look of stunned bewilderment, Misao went to check on the air conditioner. When she got there she found that the on button, which should have been illuminated, was dark.

She shot Teppei a look that clearly conveyed *We need to talk,* then led him into the hall. "There's a power outage," she said quietly.

"What?"

"The fridge and the air conditioner are both off."

"Now that you mention it, the air in here does feel kind of hot and muggy."

"Could you go take a look?"

Teppei nodded, then went into the entry hall, where the fuse box was located. He pulled it open and peered inside. None of the breakers had been tripped, and there was nothing to indicate a blown fuse. He tried flipping the switches back and forth a number of times, with no success.

His next move was to step out into the corridor and push the elevator's call button. The light went on and the door slid open, as usual.

"It looks like the electricity's only off inside our apartment," he reported when he returned to the kitchen a moment later.

"How is that even possible?" Misao asked incredulously. "A selective power outage? That makes no sense."

"I guess they're at it again," Teppei said nonchalantly, as though that statement constituted a normal, rational explanation.

"What's going on?" Tamao asked as she joined her parents in the hallway.

"The electricity's been acting funny, so—" Misao broke off in midsentence to ruminate. There was still quite a bit of food in the refrigerator, and a fair number of drinks, as well, but without electricity a lot of things were going to start to spoil very quickly in the heat. And, speaking of heat, how were they supposed to go on living in a place where the windows wouldn't open and the air conditioning didn't work?

"I wonder what we ought to do," she said aloud, half to herself. "It's just going to keep getting hotter and hotter in here, and as for food . . ."

Teppei looked at her with a glum expression. "I wouldn't be surprised if the water stopped running before too long, as well," he said, wiping the sweat from his brow. Tamao skipped off, calling for Cookie to come and play.

"Oh no. I never thought about that," Misao said.

"They're going to try to starve us out," Teppei stated matter-of-factly.

"But if we don't have any water . . ."

"I don't know. I mean, we have no idea what we're dealing with here, so how are we supposed to understand their end game?"

*This is just too much,* Misao thought. Her eyes filled with tears, and she looked around to make sure Tamao was out of earshot. No matter what happened, Misao felt it was her duty as a parent not to do or say anything that might make this ordeal any more upsetting for her little daughter.

"What's left in the way of food?" Teppei asked in a subdued tone.

"Not a whole lot," Misao replied. "There's a bit of ham, and some cheese, and a few pickled plums. I think there might be three slices left from the loaf of bread I used for our breakfast sandwiches. I made a point of emptying out the fridge so we wouldn't need to cart a lot of perishable food over to the new place, and there's really nothing else except for some ice in the freezer. Oh, wait: there's one jar of jam, and a container of miso paste, and some salad dressing. I think that's about it, though I may be forgetting some small things."

"Okay. What about drinks?"

"We have a few cans of cola and beer in the fridge, and there might be another couple of dozen in the cupboard, in cartons. I was planning to wait and put them in the refrigerator when we got to the new place."

"How about canned goods?"

"There are some tins of corned beef, and tuna, and vegetable soup. Not very many, though."

As a family, their diet had never included much in the way of so-called convenience food, but Misao now found herself wishing she had kept more canned goods and instant mixes on hand for emergencies.

"And that's all? Please tell me that isn't everything we have on hand to feed five people," Teppei said reproachfully. Misao understood his sentiments with excruciating clarity, but she couldn't stifle the knee-jerk reaction.

"Yes," she snapped, "that's all. I was just trying to be practical and simplify the move. If I'd known we were going to end up trapped in this building, I would have done a big shopping. I mean, who could have foreseen something like this?" She was unable to hold back her tears any longer and they streamed from the corners of her eyes, blurring her vision. Lowering his gaze apologetically, Teppei reached out to pat her forearm.

It was two o'clock in the afternoon. The windows still refused to open, and whenever anyone went downstairs to check the lobby door, they found it tightly closed. The people at the moving company were probably waiting impatiently for the truck to return, perhaps assuming that the crew had decided to freelance by taking on another job after they finished with the Kanos' move. Or maybe they'd already begun calling around, following up on hunches about where the crew might have gone. At some point, perhaps they might send someone to the Kanos' new address. When they discovered that not a single stick of furniture had been delivered there, they might think it was odd and swing by the Central Plaza Mansion to investigate.

*That's a nice fantasy, but even if it came true nothing would change,* Misao thought. *If more people from the outside world show up here—colleagues of the missing workers, or someone from this building's management company, or postal carriers, or people from Teppei's office, or whoever—the same thing will just keep happening, over and over again. The new arrivals will go up in smoke, and their cars and trucks will vanish into thin air, as well . . .*

If enough missing-person reports came in, the police might eventually dispatch some officers to check out the building, but perhaps they would find the door locked and conclude that everyone had simply moved away. No, on second thought, they would never get that far. If any members of the police force did turn up they would simply be zapped like all the other visitors, reduced to a cloud of steam before they even reached the door.

Teppei went back into the living room and stood in front of Tatsuji and Naomi. "I need you to listen to me," he said gravely. "The power's gone off for some reason, and—"

"Oh, no wonder it seems so much hotter than before," Naomi interrupted, glancing listlessly up at the wall-mounted air conditioner.

"Anyway," Teppei went on, "even if we can manage to cope with the heat by leaving the front door open or going up to the roof to get some fresh air, the food supply is actually a more pressing concern. I think it would be a good idea to make a comprehensive inventory and list all the food we have right now."

Tatsuji met his brother's eyes. "Make a list? What is this, fun and games on a camping trip?"

"Look, we need to agree to get serious and adopt a siege mentality from now on, because we're going to be fighting for our lives. The food is the fuel to keep us going, so we have to be careful to make the most of what's on hand."

"I have, like, zero appetite," Naomi muttered. "You can all go ahead and eat everything without me. I really don't care."

"Okay, listen," Teppei said, taking a deep breath. "We need to find a solution by tomorrow at the latest. We don't have enough supplies to keep going very long beyond that, so there's no time to spare. Rather than sitting around hoping to be rescued, we need to try every possible way of getting out of here, and saving ourselves. To do that, we'll need energy, and to generate energy we need to eat. The fact is, our food supplies are already dangerously low."

"So now you're saying that we're going to starve to death? Whoa, the good news just keeps on coming," Tatsuji guffawed. "Speaking of news, I can see the headline now: 'Family Dies of Starvation After Becoming Trapped in High-Class Apartment Building Right in the Center of Tokyo.' Yes, indeed, this is quite the delightful little adventure you've gotten us into."

Tatsuji stood up and strode into the kitchen. Opening the refrigerator, he took out a can of beer, popped the top, and took a long swig. Just then Misao walked up, holding a memo pad. She gently shoved Tatsuji out of the way, reopened the refrigerator, and began quickly writing down a list of the contents: three pieces of bread; strawberry jam; miso paste; pickled plums; half a package of "natural cheese"; a stick of butter; three slices of ham; a few leaves of lettuce; a single cucumber. At the back of one shelf she found an unopened packet of hot dogs that had somehow been overlooked, but they were so far past the sell-by date that they couldn't really be considered edible.

Next, Misao turned her attention to the canned goods that were packed away in a box labeled "Kitchen." She had apparently imagined seeing a can of tuna, because the box contained only two oblong tins of corned beef and a single can of vegetable soup. That was the full extent of the canned goods, but the rest of the box was filled with an assortment of edible odds and ends: baking powder, cooking oil, white flour, Tamao's favorite hotcake mix, syrup, a packet of bonito flakes, and so on.

*Slim pickings,* Misao thought gloomily. *Maybe I could stretch out some of these ingredients by dredging chunks of cheese in a big bowl of seasoned flour, and then frying them up in oil, kind of like croquettes?*

After she finished making the list, Misao handed the memo pad to Teppei. He looked it over with an increasingly discouraged expression on his face.

"Oh, we also have some rice," Misao said brightly. "I was planning to call in an order tomorrow and have it delivered directly to the new house, so there are only about three and a half cups left, but in a pinch we can make rice balls and sprinkle salt on them, and we could probably hang on for a couple more days that way."

"Yes, and we still have plenty of green tea, right?" Teppei said, matching Misao's upbeat tone. Misao smiled and nodded, by way of confirmation.

A moment later Tamao wandered into the kitchen. "I'm hungry," she said plaintively. Misao quickly whipped up some pancake batter, minus the eggs and milk the recipe on the box called for. Thanking heaven for the gas stove, she fried the pancakes until they were lightly browned, then drenched them in melted butter and syrup. Tamao gobbled down every bite, but Tatsuji gave the no-frills flapjacks a doubtful look, then proceeded to chug three cans of beer in rapid succession.

The apartment seemed to be getting hotter by the minute, and the muggy heat was nearly unbearable. It occurred to Misao that she had forgotten to refill Cookie's water dish. Hastily, she splashed water into the dish up to the brim, and set it down in front of Cookie's nose. The dog slurped up all but a few drops in a single gulp, then flopped down on the floor again.

Beyond the balcony's glass door, a sun as deeply red as a ripe tomato was sinking toward the western horizon. The air in the apartment had grown ever more stagnant, and the rooms were beginning to take on a sour smell. Time and again Misao picked up the telephone receiver and held it to her ear but, as expected, she never got a dial tone. The one mechanical bright spot was the elevator, which was still functioning flawlessly.

Throughout the late afternoon, Teppei made frequent trips down to the first floor, where he continued his efforts to shatter the glass entrance door by using the hammer, assorted chairs, and anything else he could lay hands on. Try as he might, the outcome was always the same. He attempted to break into the caretakers' quarters, thinking it might be possible to escape through one of the windows, but he wasn't able to make so much as a crack in the glass facade of the small reception office that opened both onto the lobby and into the apartment. That unit's front door remained unbreachable, as well.

Teppei also paid a visit to the empty apartments on every floor, pushing and pulling every door in the hope of finding one that had been left open. They were all tightly locked, which didn't surprise him at all. The building's windowless, unventilated corridors were incredibly hot after absorbing the intense rays of the summer sun all day, and it almost felt as though the structure itself were running a fever. Every surface Teppei touched was disagreeably warm.

Around six o'clock in the evening, Tamao began complaining that she was finding it difficult to breathe. Misao took off the yellow terrycloth shirt her daughter was wearing and let her run around without a top. Gently planting a kiss on Tamao's bare, sweaty shoulder, Misao whispered, "Don't worry about a thing, okay? Mama isn't going to give up."

"They're planning to starve us out," Tatsuji whimpered. "That's the bottom line, plain and simple. They want us to starve to death." He had tossed all three of his recently emptied beer cans onto the floor, and they were rolling messily around underfoot. "Hey, Misao," Tatsuji went on, his tone suddenly sarcastic. "What's for dinner tonight? Roast duck and chilled consommé? That sounds delicious, but we really shouldn't keep such a splendid menu to ourselves. Why don't you invite the monsters to join us?"

"Please, Tatsuji." Misao sighed. "Can you just dial it down a notch?"

"No, as a matter of fact, I can't," Tatsuji said defiantly. He raised both hands above his head and began to dance around the room like a demented dervish. His chino pants, which were already riding low, gradually slipped past his narrow hips until the cuffs were dragging on the ground.

After a few minutes of wild abandon, Tatsuji stopped and glared at Misao. "You have no idea what I've been through," he snarled. "I saw two men dissolve right before my eyes—I mean, they literally went up in smoke. That's right: I saw human beings *dissolving*. So why don't you give me a break, for once?"

"Will someone please make this idiot shut up?" Naomi erupted. Her pretty, small-featured face was distorted by her obvious dislike of her husband's over-the-top behavior. "Look, I'm just going to say it, since you brought it up. If what you were seeing up on the roof was so traumatic, why didn't you just leave and come back downstairs, instead of waiting around till the end?"

After this speech Naomi seemed to be trying to calm herself down, but she was seized by a fit of frenzied coughing. "I think I'm going to be sick again," she said, looking pleadingly at Misao. After a moment the wave of nausea apparently passed, because Naomi took a long, racking breath and toppled over sideways on the couch.

⋅

Misao didn't have much of an appetite, but she threw a heaping cup of white rice into a pan and set it on the front burner of the gas stove. When the rice was done she shaped it into five triangular balls, each with a morsel of pickled plum at the center and a sprinkling of salt on the outside, then served them alongside the three remaining slices of ham. She had originally been hoping to save the ham until the following day, but in this heat—and with a refrigerator whose internal temperature was now lukewarm at best—there was a very real danger that the meat would go bad before then, so she decided it should be eaten as soon as possible. As for Cookie, her dinner consisted of the usual amount of dry dog food. However, there were only a couple of helpings of kibble left in the dog food box, and it occurred to Misao that before long she would need to start allotting a share of the human rations to Cookie, as well.

As day turned to evening, the heat began to diminish to the point where the ambient temperature became almost bearable, although the extreme humidity still made the apartment feel like a sauna. When darkness fell, Teppei found a flashlight and switched it on, but Misao quickly objected. Something might happen during the night, she reasoned, so they ought to preserve the flashlight's batteries, just in case. For now, they could get by with candlelight.

Finding the candles among the tangle of packed boxes turned out to be a major undertaking. By the time some tapers finally turned up in a carton of small household items, the entire apartment was plunged into inky darkness.

Instead of making the rooms seem more cheerful, the light from the candles actually seemed to foster feelings of trepidation. Everyone gathered around the table, silently munching on their minimalist rice balls and pausing from time to time to pour some tepid tap water down their parched throats.

When the meal was finished, Tatsuji sat for a long time without saying a word. He seemed to be gradually coming to terms with the situation, and his face wore an expression of deep melancholy. Clearly, he was trying to fight off the feelings of hopelessness and despair, but he didn't appear to be winning that battle. Finally, he spoke. "Looking ahead," he said, "how would you rate our chances of getting out of here alive?"

"Maybe twenty percent?" Teppei replied candidly. "No, probably closer to ten. Hey, at least it isn't zero." A single rivulet of sweat ran down his forehead, but he didn't bother to wipe it off.

"And what do you propose that we do now? Do you have a plan?"

"I honestly have no idea," Teppei admitted. "I feel like we've explored every possible option, but there must be something we haven't thought of yet."

"What if we all went up to the roof and shouted at the top of our lungs?" Naomi suggested, as she rolled a pickled-plum pit around in her mouth.

"Shout?" Teppei echoed, looking at his sister-in-law with hollow eyes. "Suppose we do shout, and someone hears us? If they show up at the door, the same thing will just keep happening over and over again. More innocent people will die, and we won't be any closer to getting out of here."

"Not only that," Misao said. "There's nobody living within earshot of this building in any case. You all saw the view from the roof, right? On the north side there's nothing but empty land and the remains of some housing project that was abandoned a long time ago. The graveyard's on the south side, and it's huge, so unless someone chanced to be visiting a grave near this building, no one would hear us. Anyway, the cemetery is usually deserted. As for the temple, it's much too far away for any sound to carry from here. The east side, as you know, is just vacant land. So we could go up to the roof and shout our heads off, but we'd just end up with sore throats. Besides, as Teppei said, if someone did hear us shouting and tried to rescue us, they wouldn't get past the entrance."

"How about if we sent up one of those advertising balloons?" Naomi asked. "Or is that a worthless idea, too?" Those questions weren't addressed to anyone in particular, but Naomi's rancorous tone, and the way she curled her lips, seemed to make it clear that she was mocking Misao.

"Come on, can't we think of some way to escape?" Tatsuji pleaded, folding his arms in front of his chest. "It seems like we've tried every potential exit, from here down to the first floor. But maybe we're overlooking something. What if we jumped off the roof onto a mattress? Oh, never mind." He shrugged and rolled his eyes, obviously realizing what would become of anyone who landed on the ground anywhere near the building—assuming they even survived the fall.

"Wait!" Naomi cried. "The basement! There's a basement, right?"

Tatsuji laughed derisively. "Yeah, there's a basement, but it's useless. It doesn't have an outside door or even any windows. I don't even want to think about that place, because from what I hear it's where all the ghosts and monsters hang out."

"You're joking, right?" Naomi looked incredulous.

Teppei exchanged a quick glance with Misao, then said, "We don't know that. As I keep telling you, we don't know *anything* for sure."

Tamao swiped at the coating of perspiration that still covered her bare chest, then stared at each of the adults' candlelit faces, one after another. "The basement's where I got hurt," she announced. "We were playing, and all of a sudden there was a big cut on my knee. There was tons of blood, and I had to go to the hospital in an ambulance. Isn't that right, Mama?"

Every eye swiveled to look at Misao, and she nodded in confirmation. "We never did find out what caused it," she said. "The doctor was saying there could have been some kind of weasel wind down there, but—"

"This is a nightmare," Naomi broke in. "There's no other explanation. I'm asleep right now, and I'm having the worst dream ever." She rubbed her ashen cheeks, which had long since shed any traces of the blush she'd applied that morning. "And everyone knows how this nightmare is going to end. We're all going to die a hideous, horrible death in a pool of our own sweat."

In the wavering light of the candles the figures around the table cast enormous, grotesquely distorted shadows on the bare walls, making the room appear to be populated with a party of extra-large demons.

"Hey, I just had a thought," Teppei said, catching Misao's eye. "I wonder whether those bars are still down there."

"Bars?" Misao cocked her head.

"You know, the cartons of protein bars that were left down in the basement when the health food company moved out a few months ago."

"What are you talking about?" Tatsuji edged forward in his chair.

"Oh, I remember now. There were some cartons of high-calorie bars," Misao said, turning to Naomi. "You've heard of diet bars, right? Well, these are the opposite. They have a lot of calories and protein and vitamins, so supposedly you can get all the nutrients you need even if you don't eat anything else for a few days. I think they were originally designed for use in space programs, but now I gather some skinny people use them to put on weight."

"Wow, really?" Naomi said with a contemptuous laugh. "Considering that most people these days are interested in *losing* weight, whoever invented those bars wasn't exactly a marketing genius."

"Seriously, though," Teppei said. "If the cartons are still down there, they might keep us going for a while."

"So are you suggesting that we should just casually waltz down to the basement and grab the boxes?" Misao asked, playing devil's advocate. "Even after the things we've seen today, and everything we know about what's happened down there in the past?"

Tatsuji, however, was immediately on board. "That's the best idea I've heard all day!" he declared. "If we just have enough to eat for the next few days, it'll help us keep our strength up while we try to get out of here."

"That's right," Teppei agreed. "As I recall, there was a big stack of those boxes. We're already scraping the bottom of the supplies we have on hand, but if the protein bars are still there, they should carry us along for a couple of days, at least. At least we won't have to worry about starving to death tomorrow."

"What if the elevator stops working again while you're busy exploring?" Misao asked.

"Look," Teppei said. "It's sink or swim for us right now, and those bars are our only chance at a lifeline—as in, literally, a chance to prolong our lives. We can't be stewing about what-ifs at a time like this."

"Oh, great," Naomi said with a snort of mirthless laughter. "So now our two men are going down to the haunted basement, and they probably won't come back alive. They'll leave behind a couple of beautiful young widows, but before Misao and I have a chance to enjoy spending the insurance money, we'll be dead, too."

When Misao shot her a dirty look, Naomi said, "Oh, come on, lighten up. That was a joke," then gave her head a jaunty toss.

"It's worth a try," Teppei said, turning to Tatsuji. "Let's go first thing tomorrow morning, as soon as we're up. Are you with me on this, Tats?"

"Oh, like I really have a choice," Tatsuji said bitterly, but his face was resolute and he gave his brother an acquiescent nod. "I mean, of course I'll go with you," he added. "Let's check it out, for sure. On the plus side, no matter what happens from now on, I don't think anything can surprise me anymore."

Cookie ambled up to the dining table and began to lick Misao's ankle. As Misao reached under the table to scratch behind the dog's soft, furry ears, she couldn't help thinking that this blameless creature's existence was inextricably bound up with the lives of her owners. Whatever the Kano family's destiny might turn out to be, it would be shared by Cookie.

# 22

July 27, 1987 (early morning)

The previous evening, they had dragged the mattresses from both beds and lined them up in the living room. But although the five family members spent the night lying side by side on those mattresses, Tamao was the only one who got a wink of sleep. After Misao extinguished the candles, the room was engulfed in unrelenting darkness. The front door (which was now the only source of ventilation) was left open all night, and from time to time a slight breeze of unknown origin would waft in, undulate surreptitiously down the hallway, and nuzzle around the doorjambs of the rooms inside.

During the night Teppei was seized more than once by a desire to take Misao in his arms, but he somehow managed to restrain himself. No matter how close he held his wife, he knew he would still feel completely empty inside. He could sense that Misao, too, was doing battle with the demons of despondency, and he was afraid that the moment they touched each other, skin to skin, they would suddenly realize how catastrophic their situation was and start to weep so loudly that it would wake the rest of the family—if anyone had managed to fall asleep.

Misao lay on her side, dressed only in a pair of shorts and a flimsy tank top. Teppei could hear her sighing every few minutes, and he reached out to stroke one of his wife's bare shoulders. As he gently kneaded the soft flesh, he was flooded by a brief but genuine moment of happiness. Misao continued to lie completely still, sniffling from time to time as she passively accepted his gestures of affection.

Teppei could hardly wait for the next day to begin. He kept glancing at the wristwatch he wore, using the flashlight next to his pillow to see the face in the dark. When it read 3:50 a.m., he rolled out of bed and perched on the edge of the mattress. "Tats. Rise and shine," he whispered.

Tatsuji, who was already awake, raised his head languidly and glanced around. The earliest hints of dawn were just beginning to seep in through the window, and his eyes glinted in the dim light.

"We should do one more tour of the building before we hit the basement," Teppei announced.

"I know, I know," Tatsuji said impatiently.

Naomi sat up in bed with a sleep-deprived sigh. Next, Tamao opened her eyes and immediately began to cry. "What's wrong? Do you have a stomachache?" Naomi asked. Tamao didn't answer; she just wriggled up closer to her mother on the mattress and buried her head in Misao's chest.

*That's where I'd like to put my head, too, if I only could,* Teppei thought. In truth, the desire to climb back into bed and cuddle with his loved ones was so strong that he felt as if he might be about to lose his mind.

Tearing his eyes away from his wife and daughter, Teppei stood up and lit one of the candles. Through the unbreakable plate-glass windows he could clearly see the sky growing lighter, so sunrise couldn't be too far off. It was probably going to be another blisteringly hot day. He tried to open the door to the balcony, but it remained as immobile as ever.

*I am a man . . .* That sentence popped into Teppei's mind unbidden, and at first he had no idea where it had come from. Then he remembered: it was the catchphrase of the hero of a cartoon series he used to watch. *I am a man.* Yes, the cape-wearing hero used to make that valiant proclamation, all the time.

*I am a man,* Teppei murmured in his mind, although he didn't say the words out loud. *I am a man.* As he was repeating that soundless mantra, he decided that if he somehow managed to survive this nightmare and return safely to the real world, he would make constructive use of those words. You could call them platitudinous, but for him, at least, they had a deep and thrilling resonance. Yes, Teppei told himself, if he got out of this alive he would find a way to work "I am a man" into some advertising copy, and perhaps one day that phrase might serve to inspire somebody else.

Teppei went into the kitchen and gave the faucet handle an experimental twirl. As always, the tap water flowed freely into the sink. However, when Teppei opened the refrigerator he saw that the inside was covered with drops of moisture and the first signs of mildew. It was like peering into a soggy cardboard box that was beginning to rot.

Teppei washed his face over the sink, then dried it on the nearest dish towel. Armed with the hammer, the flashlight, and some nylon cord, he headed for the front door. Misao came running after him. She was still wearing shorts, and her bare legs glimmered in the early light.

"I'm going with you," she said.

"No need. Tatsuji and I have this covered."

"I know, but . . ."

Teppei took Misao's arm and quietly pulled her close. "We'll be fine," he said, kissing the top of her head.

"I hope you're right. I really feel like I'm on the verge of a breakdown."

"Well, you're certainly doing an amazing job of pretending to be calm."

"Oh, thank you. It's all I can do to hold myself together."

Teppei sighed and hugged Misao even more tightly. "If you weren't here with me, I wouldn't be able to pretend to have my act together, either."

Just then Tatsuji appeared, and the couple sprang apart.

First, the brothers went down to the first floor. When Teppei splashed the flashlight beam around the lobby, they saw that the glass door was still covered with handprints. Not only that, the prints appeared to be even more numerous than the day before. It was as if the door had been painted over with extra-thick oil paint. Teppei swung the hammer behind his head and brought it down on the glass, but the door might as well have been made of foam rubber.

Tatsuji stood off to one side, watching Teppei's labors in silence. "Nice try," he jeered. "Of course, nothing's changed since yesterday."

"Yeah." Teppei sighed. "Come on, let's head down to the basement."

"Damn, I should have gotten a farewell kiss from Naomi, since I may never see her again," Tatsuji said, satirically smacking his forehead.

"What? Don't say things like that, even as a joke."

The brothers stepped into the elevator and hit the "B1" button, which (it occurred to Teppei) hadn't been touched in quite some time. A vision of the basement swarming with formless, evil, supernatural creatures floated across his mind, and he gave an involuntary shiver. *At some point they'll probably show themselves and come to attack us*, he thought. *But what form will they take? Will they look vaguely human, with their demonic faces covered by black hoods like medieval robbers or participants in a satanic ritual? Or will it just be a horde of gigantic translucent blobs, like those murderous amoebas I used to fantasize about as a child?*

The elevator came to a stop in the basement with the familiar *ga-tonk*. The doors swished open without a hitch. The emergency lights had been left on, and they cast a murky light over the cavernous space. Teppei wasn't the least bit surprised to find that the "power outage" hadn't affected the basement. Nervously, he groped around on the wall until he found the switch for the overhead lights.

At a glance, nothing appeared to have changed. The storage compartments were still lined up in tidy rows; the numberless legions of exposed pipes still marched up the walls and snaked across the ceiling; and the floor still looked the same. Everything was covered by a fine film of dust, and the entire basement seemed to be sitting quietly, biding its time, like some forgotten ruin.

"Those are the protein bars we were talking about," Teppei said, pointing in the direction of a tall pile of brown cardboard boxes toward the rear of the basement.

Tatsuji nodded. "I don't see what all the fuss was about," he said.

"Huh? All what fuss?"

"I mean, it just looks like a perfectly ordinary basement to me."

"Ah, well. Maybe up to a point," Teppei said cryptically.

The two men walked toward the heap of boxes, looking carefully around as they went. Teppei had been extremely reluctant to come down here again, but he was forced to admit that there didn't seem to be anything malevolent lurking in the shadows. He heaved a sigh of relief. All they needed to do now was to grab the boxes and carry them upstairs as quickly as possible.

The stack of cartons came up to Teppei's waist. Each box appeared to contain about a dozen individually packed boxes of the famous weight-gain bars. When Teppei gave the entire pile a two-handed push, it moved easily across the dusty floor, with a sound like air being let out of a tire.

"Come on, Tats, let's get to work," he called. "We need to drag these along to the elevator." Tatsuji was standing nearby, staring at the back wall of the basement, and when he didn't reply Teppei repeated, "Hey, come on! I need help. What are you doing, anyway? The sooner we get out of here, the better."

"Wait, what's this?" Tatsuji said, in a tone that seemed to combine apprehensiveness with the thrill of a new discovery.

Relaxing his hold on the boxes he'd been grappling with, Teppei turned his eyes toward the rear wall. Tatsuji's long shadow had been obscuring the point of interest, but after a moment he shifted his position and Teppei was finally able to follow his brother's sight line.

Near the place where Tamao had sustained her leg injury, there was a small, jagged black hole in the wall. Forgetting the boxes, Teppei crept silently over to the place where his brother was standing. It appeared that a sharp tool of some kind had been used to break through the concrete wall, just in that one spot. The hole was about two inches in circumference.

When Teppei peeked in, all he saw was blackness. The musty odor of damp earth drifted through the opening. "Hmm, this is odd," he mused, cocking his head. "There was no hole here the last time I looked, a couple of weeks ago."

"The wall is surprisingly thin. Look at this!" Tatsuji exclaimed, running an index finger around the edge of the aperture. "It shouldn't be hard to break down."

"Maybe, but where did this hole come from in the first place?"

Tatsuji didn't reply. Putting one eye to the opening, he peered inside.

Teppei started to suggest that it might be some kind of trick, but held his tongue. What would these unidentified schemers—if they even existed—hope to accomplish by making such a small hole in the wall?

*I really can't take much more of this,* Teppei thought as he headed back to the boxes. *This place is making me crazy.* "Hey, Tats, come on!" he called testily. "We need to get these things upstairs."

Tatsuji didn't respond; he just went on staring into the darkness beyond the hole in the wall.

"Hurry up!" Teppei shouted. "Are you even listening to me?"

"Ssh," Tatsuji hissed, turning to face Teppei with one finger held to his lips. "Be quiet. I can hear something."

"What?" Teppei froze in his tracks.

Tatsuji pressed his ear against the hole. He was completely still except for his bulging eyes, which darted wildly from side to side. "Wait, what is that? That sound . . ."

Teppei returned to the rear of the basement and placed his own ear to the wall. He could hear a faint pattering that made him picture someone trudging up and down a staircase. The footsteps weren't hurried at all; they had a slow, deliberate quality. Teppei also got the sense that the faraway people were carrying something. Or was it just a single individual? He couldn't tell. There were no sounds of conversation.

"But where does it lead to—whatever's on the other side of this wall?" Tatsuji muttered, half to himself. "Maybe this room is somehow connected to the basement of a private house or a store or something, like by a tunnel?"

Teppei immediately thought of the story Misao had told him, about the "phantom road" she had researched one day at the ward library. Could something like that really exist? Was it possible that whoever did the initial excavation for the underground shopping mall simply paved over the surface and left the gigantic hole intact, after the developers failed to get permission to move the graves and were forced to abandon the entire project?

"Remember what I told you up on the roof about how some developers might have dug a hole for a belowground shopping arcade, before the project fell through?" Teppei said reluctantly, not wanting to stoke his brother's optimistic fantasies any more than necessary.

"Oh, right! So there must have been a big underground space left over, and the owners of the land probably divided it up and rented it to shops, for storage and whatnot. That would explain it!" Tatsuji said with rising excitement.

"I doubt it," Teppei said slowly. "I've never heard about anything like that. And even if such a space had existed, it would have been filled in when they built these apartments, don't you think?"

"No, but still, there's something happening here, right now. I can—" Tatsuji stopped and jammed his ear against the hole. "Yes, I can hear it clearly. First there were footsteps, and now there are people talking."

Teppei found this entire situation patently implausible, but he couldn't help garnering a small ray of hope from Tatsuji's words. Pushing his brother aside, Teppei applied his own ear to the hole.

He couldn't make out any words, but in the distance—the very far distance—he could hear the unmistakable sound of conversation, along with a repetitive clinking noise. It sounded like someone making a pile of glass bottles, and a torrent of images flooded into Teppei's mind. *Could it be an underground wine cellar, or the basement storeroom of a sake shop, or the subterranean meeting chamber of some secret society? (No, that last one was beyond ridiculous.) Or maybe it was an underground sarcophagus that was used as a repository for the bones of priests and their families by the ancient temple Manseiji?* For the moment, any explanation would do. The important thing was that he could hear human voices.

And now there was the sound of laughter: a goodly number of men, roaring loudly with amusement. Middle-aged men, or maybe older.

The next thing Teppei heard was several female voices, engaged in animated conversation. So there were women in the group as well. Overall, it sounded like the sort of wholesomely constructive hustle and bustle you might hear in any busy corner of the city: people cheerfully performing some task or other while chatting among themselves in an easy, carefree manner.

Teppei stuck one index finger through the opening, and an icy draft instantly chilled it to the bone. Tatsuji, apparently impatient with waiting his turn, roughly shoved Teppei aside and shouted frantically into the hole, "Hey! We need help! Is anybody there?"

Then, placing his ear to the opening, he listened intently. As before, faraway voices talking among themselves could be heard, but there was no change in the timbre of those murmurs, and no one responded to Tatsuji's plea.

"Give me the hammer!" he yelled, snatching the tool from Teppei's hand. Raising it over his head, Tatsuji brought the hammer down on the wall next to the hole. The dull sound of metal meeting concrete echoed through the basement. With each successive blow the cement crumbled a bit more, raining powdery gray rubble onto the floor. It was such absurdly easy work that the poured concrete wall might have been nothing more than a rudimentary layer of painted plaster.

In a matter of seconds, the hole had grown perceptibly larger. Teppei remembered now that when he came down to the basement to carry out a nocturnal inspection with the Tabatas, he had sensed something different about this particular section of the basement, and the back wall in particular. It was starting to look now as though his initial hunch that the concrete might be thinner in this area had been correct, after all.

Tatsuji's face was covered with tiny beads of sweat that glimmered in the light. The hole had now doubled in size, and as Tatsuji, who appeared to be enjoying himself immensely, continued to hack away, it soon grew large enough to accommodate the head of an average-size person. An unnaturally cold, damp wind streamed into the basement through the aperture.

Tatsuji flung the hammer to the floor, then stuck his head and neck through the newly enlarged hole. "Hey!" he shouted. "Is anybody there?"

Teppei had his ear to the wall nearby, listening for a response, and he was astounded to hear the escalating buzz of a group of people in deep discussion, followed by a distinct question.

"What's going on?" called a faraway male voice.

"Hello!" trilled a female voice in the background.

Teppei extricated his head from the opening. His sweaty face was transformed by joy. "We're saved!" he exulted. "We're going to be rescued, all of us!"

Without waiting for his brother to respond, Tatsuji stuck his head back into the hole and yelled, "Help us, please! We're trapped in here! This is the basement of the Central Plaza Mansion. There are five of us: four adults and a child. Please help us get out of here!"

At that moment, the lively sounds beyond the wall abruptly ceased. Then Teppei heard his brother shouting urgently from inside the opening, "Hey, Tepp, can you hand me the flashlight?" Reluctantly, Teppei complied.

Momentarily withdrawing his head, Tatsuji aimed the flashlight beam through the opening, then peered in again. "Hey!" he called to Teppei. "You've got to see this. There really is an underground road!"

Teppei edged up to the hole and took a peek. What he saw was so incredible that it took a minute for his brain to process the scene that greeted his eyes. On the other side of the wall was an excavated road, wide and tall enough for several adults to walk abreast while standing fully upright. The long, straight path appeared to extend in the direction of Manseiji, just as the ward reports had suggested. Of course, the flashlight's illumination didn't extend that far so it was impossible to say for sure, but there didn't seem to be any major obstacles along the way, and there was no end in sight.

The unpleasant aroma of ancient, fermented earth filled Teppei's nostrils. Stepping back from the opening, he looked at his brother's face and said vaguely, "The thing is, I think . . ." He was feeling more and more certain that the underground road might be a trick or a trap of some sort, but he knew his suspicion would sound ridiculous if he tried to put it into words.

"Thank god, we're saved!" Tatsuji whooped. "That wild story you told me turned out to be totally true. Right? The one about an underground road running from here to the train station. It actually turned out to be true! I don't know how it's even possible, but what's the saying, 'Ours not to reason why'? Anyway, bottom line, there are people at the end of the road, so we can get out!"

Tatsuji was so galvanized by enthusiasm that his saliva ducts seemed to be working overtime, and long strings of drool oozed from both corners of his mouth. He gave his brother a look that radiated hope and exhilaration, then stuck his head into the hole again. "Hey!" he shouted. "Hello!"

"Hey!" The voices that responded this time were all male. There seemed to be three of them, at least. It definitely wasn't an echo.

"Help us, please!" Tatsuji pleaded.

"Come to us!" a male voice yelled. "You can get here, can't you?"

"Where are you, anyway? Is there some kind of underground storehouse or something?" At that, the faraway chorus fell silent for a few seconds. Then there were distant sounds of shrill, cackling laughter and general commotion. A woman's voice—so pure and high that she might have been singing a soprano role in an opera—rang out above the others, but her words were indistinct.

With one ear still mashed against the wall, Teppei reached out and grabbed his brother's arm. "Hang on a minute," he said.

"What? What's the problem?" Tatsuji demanded, pausing with his head half in and half out of the opening.

"Don't you think there's something strange about this?"

"Strange? Don't be stupid. Those voices belong to human beings. It isn't a bunch of ghosts or goblins, if that's what you're thinking." As he spat out those words, Tatsuji sprayed saliva in every direction. He immediately jammed his head through the hole again and called out, "Hey! Hello! What should we do now?"

The underground cavity erupted in an incomprehensible hubbub, as if a great many people were talking at once. There was a mixture of other noises, as well: metallic clangs; the lucent tinkle of glass being rung like a bell; and oddest of all, a sound that made Teppei picture a battalion of medieval samurai warriors, dressed in full battle regalia, crawling along on the ground.

Teppei began to tremble. He was sure of it now: these . . . these were not human beings. They may have sounded like people, but they were something else. Something very different, and infinitely more dangerous.

Tatsuji didn't seem to have noticed. "Please come here!" he was yelling into the hole. "Come over here right now, and help us out! We're in the basement of the Central Plaza Mansion!"

"Ho-oh!" came the response. It sounded like a very large number of male voices—several dozen, at least—all shouting at once.

*What the hell?* Teppei thought with a frisson of dread. *What possible reason could there be for such a huge crowd of men to be gathered in an underground cave, or grotto, or storeroom, or whatever it was?*

Tatsuji extracted his flushed, perspiring face from the hole and took off toward the elevator at top speed, calling over his shoulder, "Come on! Let's go upstairs and get everybody! We need to bring them down here!" Teppei followed behind at a normal pace. He could feel a cold, clammy draft—the same abnormally frigid breeze he remembered from his nightmarish evening in the basement— eddying around on the floor of the basement.

"Tats, wait!" he shouted. "I think we should just forget about this."

Tatsuji was already in the elevator, jabbing at the "8" button. "I don't see why," he whined. "They just want to help us. I don't know what you're so afraid of. If you don't want to be rescued, Naomi and I will go by ourselves."

"Listen," Teppei said sternly as he joined his brother in the elevator. He thought of grabbing a box of protein bars, but he decided that could wait. "First of all, how do you explain the small hole that suddenly appeared in the wall? Like I told you, it wasn't there before. I've racked my brain, and I can't remember ever seeing a hole like that anywhere else in the basement, and there's no way it could have simply occurred naturally. Someone made it, on purpose."

"Well, you haven't been down here in quite a while, so as you say, maybe somebody came along and made that hole when no one was looking."

"But who? And why would anyone do such a thing?"

"How the hell am I supposed to know!" Tatsuji bellowed, stamping his foot on the elevator floor. "The only thing that matters right now is that there are people out there, and there's a road, and we're going to be saved. After they rescue us we can ask for a detailed explanation, if that's so important to you."

When the elevator arrived at its destination, Tatsuji bounded through the doors and into the apartment with such an overabundance of energy that he nearly fell flat on his face in the entryway. The sky outside was already completely light and the apartment was flooded with morning sunshine, the same as always.

"Naomi! Naomi! We're saved! We found some people!"

"What? Where?" Naomi came running down the hall dressed in nothing but blue jeans and a brassiere, with her disheveled hair flying every which way.

Tatsuji burst into the living room, where he began picking up clothes and miscellaneous items and cramming them into the Louis Vuitton overnight bag.

"Go and get dressed," he ordered Naomi. "They're going to be sending a rescue party to the basement any minute now, so we need to be there."

"A rescue party? In the basement?" Misao echoed doubtfully.

"No, that isn't happening," Teppei whispered in his wife's ear. "It's true, we did hear something, but I seriously doubt whether it's a rescue party."

"Will someone please tell me what's going on?" Misao asked, looking around helplessly, but no one seemed to hear her plea.

Naomi appeared again, dressed in the gaudy floral-patterned blouse she'd worn the day before. When she began to paint her lips while looking into the miniature mirror of her compact, Teppei walked up to her and shouted, "Stop primping, dammit! You aren't going anywhere!" His voice was so loud that Cookie began to howl in confusion. Naomi stopped with her lipstick tube in midstroke and gaped at her brother-in-law, speechless with astonishment.

"Nobody's coming to save us," Teppei continued in a calmer tone. "That isn't what's going on down there at all. You need to understand. Those sounds we heard—those voices? They don't belong to people."

Tatsuji let out a long, dry, artificial-sounding laugh. "I think my big brother here has lost touch with reality. I heard them with my own ears. They were definitely people, and they were answering me with perfectly normal words and sentences. Misao, you're the expert on the underground road that might never have been filled in, right?"

"Wait, how do you know about that?"

"Your husband told me."

"Well, it's just speculation," Misao demurred. "We have no idea whether such a road exists or not."

"No, I'm telling you, it *does* exist. There really is a road!" Tatsuji insisted. "Apparently it was there all along, behind the wall. Okay, listen. This is what happened. There was a little hole in the wall, and when I hit it with the hammer the wall started to crumble like, I don't know, a piece of birthday cake or something. After I made the hole bigger we looked through it, and there was a magnificent-looking road on the other side of the wall. I could hear voices, far away, and when I shouted for help, they answered me. Isn't that right, Tepp?"

Teppei nodded reluctantly as Tatsuji babbled on. "When Tamao got injured by the weasel wind, it probably blew in from the underground hole. If we follow the road, it'll come out somewhere. I'm certain of that. If we just start walking, someone will come and help us, or show us where we need to go."

"Can this really be true?" Misao asked Teppei, but his only response was to avert his eyes and give his head a pessimistic shake.

"Come on, Naomi, we need to get going," Tatsuji said. "This is no time to be thinking about makeup. Hurry up, let's get a move on!"

"But—what about the rest of the family?" Naomi asked hesitantly, clutching the overnight bag Tatsuji had thrust into her arms.

Teppei looked at Misao. She was breathing raggedly, and her chest was visibly heaving under the sheer tank top.

Misao returned his gaze. It was clear from the look in her eyes that while she was decidedly skeptical about the miraculous rescue scenario Tatsuji was touting, she found this new development too interesting to ignore.

"We could at least go down and check it out," she said softly. "I mean, where's the harm in just taking a look?"

Teppei understood what Misao was saying: they couldn't afford to overlook any chance of escape, however slight. He shared those sentiments, and he knew a last resort was better than no resort at all. It was just that he had a profoundly bad feeling about this particular last resort . . .

"And after we check it out?" Teppei asked. "What then?"

"I don't know," Misao said. "But anything has to be better than just sitting around in this apartment doing nothing, don't you think?"

Everyone knew she was right. When human beings are deprived of their normal freedom of movement, they need to latch onto any shred of hope. As long as there is some action to take or some solution to explore, even if those options ultimately come to naught, the mere illusion of possibility can keep people from tumbling into the abyss of despair.

So they all piled into the elevator: Tatsuji, Naomi, Teppei, Misao, and Tamao. As the door began to close, Tamao suddenly cried, "I don't want to leave Cookie behind!" The dog was already standing wistfully in front of the elevator, and when Teppei held the door she bounded eagerly inside.

# 23

July 27, 1987 (7:00 a.m.)

The moment they stepped off the elevator, Cookie began barking
ferociously. She bounded toward the opening in the basement
wall like a hunting dog charging at its prey, leaping high into the air
with every step.

"Cookie!" Tamao called. "Come back here! Cookie!"

Paying no attention, the dog began to go berserk, running wildly
around in circles near the wall and frantically sniffing at everything in sight while emitting an endless stream of low growls inter-
spersed with hysterical yelps.

"Look, there it is!" Tatsuji said loudly, pointing toward the hole.

"So you're saying there's an underground road on the other
side?" Naomi's tone was hopeful but dubious.

"Yeah. Come on, I'll show you!" Tatsuji grabbed his wife's wrist
and pulled her toward the back of the basement.

"It's really cold down here. How on earth could it be so chilly, all
of a sudden?" Misao asked Teppei. He didn't reply.

"Oh my god!" Naomi exclaimed in wonderment as she aimed

the flashlight beam through the opening. "There really *is* a road! Misao, you've got to see this! I'm not sure what it is, but it's amazing!"

Misao trotted up and peeked inside. At the sight of the road her whole body began to shiver uncontrollably.

The moment she moved away, Tatsuji took her place. Sticking his head through the opening, he yelled fervently, "Hey! Hello! We're all here now!" As if in counterpoint, Cookie matched every word with a shrill, frenetic bark.

"Shut up, Cookie!" Tatsuji bellowed. "Will somebody please make this dog be quiet? I can't hear a damn thing!"

Teppei took hold of Cookie's collar and tried to jerk her away from the wall, but the dog braced her hind legs and refused to budge. Cookie's eyes were bugging out in frustration, and the flecks of white foam that sprayed from her mouth made her look like a rabid hound.

"Hey!" Tatsuji yelled again, into the hole. "Is anybody there? Hello?"

Naomi and Misao pressed their ears against the concrete wall. Tatsuji clicked his tongue in irritation. "Hey!" he shouted into the hole, more urgently than before. "Where did everybody go?"

After a moment Tatsuji withdrew his head from the opening. "There's no answer," he said peevishly, making no attempt to hide his disgruntlement. "Maybe they went to get somebody else, to help."

*Somebody else?* Teppei felt a sick lurch in the pit of his stomach. *But who, and why?* There had been so many voices, earlier. Surely that throng wouldn't have needed to go off in search of reinforcements.

Tatsuji paused to rest for a moment while Naomi took a turn at hollering into the opening. "Hello! Won't you help us, please? Somebody? Anybody?"

"You know what?" Tatsuji cried. "Let's just tear this mother down! It shouldn't take too long." His face was red as a beet, and his eyes were filled with grim determination.

"I'll help, too," Naomi said as her husband prepared to attack the wall, hammer in hand. She hoisted the flashlight above her head and was about to strike the concrete when Tatsuji halted her arm in mid-swing.

"Don't be stupid!" he snapped. "If you break our only flashlight, how are we going to see once we're on the road?"

Unconsciously, Teppei glanced in Misao's direction. She looked back at him with a face that had lost its usual youthful verve and animation, as though she had somehow been transformed into a world-weary old person in the space of a few minutes.

"Um, Papa?" Tamao came up to Teppei and tugged on the bottom of his T-shirt. "What's on the other side of the hole?"

"It's kind of like a big cave with a road running through it," Teppei replied, absentmindedly stroking his daughter's cheek.

"And we can use the road to get out of here?"

"We don't know yet. We might be able to. That's why we're going to give it a try."

"But it's so dark in there."

"You're right. It does look pretty dark."

"I don't like it." Tamao's eyes brimmed with tears. "I'm scared. I don't want to go in there."

Teppei didn't reply; he just held his little daughter close. Cookie was crouched beside them, muscles tensed, emitting a low, continuous growl.

Meanwhile, Tatsuji was making good progress with the demolition. At every blow of the hammer, great chunks of loosened concrete crashed to the floor in a hail of rubble. The wall was so easily dismantled that the onlookers found it hard to believe it was made of cement.

It took Tatsuji a quarter of an hour, at most, to finish hacking out a hole large enough for one person to clamber through. By the end his entire body was drenched in sweat, and his white shirt was soggy and gray with grime. Taking off the shirt, Tatsuji tossed it aside. Then he stood by the wall, naked to the waist and breathing hard, admiring his handiwork.

"This is good enough," he declared. He had evidently gotten nicked by one of the jagged shards of falling concrete, and blood oozed from a single scratch on his right temple.

Gingerly, with trembling hands, Naomi pointed the flashlight through the newly expanded opening. Teppei and Misao came up and joined her in peering through the hole. The configuration seemed to indicate that the basement was meant to serve as a terminus for the underground road, just as the urban-planning documents at the ward library had described. To the left was a kind of ravine—a wide, deep groove in the earth—while the rough, unfinished road stretched off to the right. A damp, fishy odor assailed their nostrils.

"Do you suppose there are bats, or mice?" Naomi asked uneasily as she beamed the flashlight's circle of light around the vast, dark space.

"Who cares about that?" Tatsuji said irritably, using his bare forearm to wipe the sweat from his brow. "What I want to know is, what happened to all the people who were down here before?"

"They probably haven't gone far." For some reason, Naomi's casual remark sent a chill up and down Teppei's spine. *They probably haven't gone far . . .*

"Anyway," Tatsuji said, taking a deep breath, "let's go check it out, shall we, ladies and gentlemen? Or should I say 'ladies and gentle*man*'?" Clearly, it took a supreme effort for him to crack that little joke.

"Are you really going to go?" Teppei asked.

"Yes, I'm really going to go." Tatsuji met his brother's gaze and held it.

"I'm going with you," Naomi announced. She appeared to be in the grip of a contradictory jumble of emotions: a normal measure of fear and foreboding, along with affectionate loyalty to her husband and the hedonistic self-centeredness that made her want only to get back to her easy, comfortable life, any way she could.

"You know, I wonder whether it might be better to hold off for a while," Misao ventured diffidently.

"What makes you say that?" Tatsuji demanded. "I mean, we've finally found a possible way out, and you all just seem to want us to sit around twiddling our thumbs."

"No, but it's just—I mean, suppose those people you heard are planning to come and rescue us upstairs. Wouldn't it be more sensible just to wait here? I mean, we have no idea what kind of road this is, or where it goes."

"Wow, Misao, I didn't realize you were so timid," Tatsuji said with an expression that mixed scorn with annoyance. "What if someone does decide to come to our rescue upstairs? We already know what will happen if they try to get in through the door on the first floor. It'll be the same thing all over again—just like those other poor victims, they'll end up being vaporized or melted or whatever. I really don't think we can afford to sit around here doing nothing and watching helplessly while that gruesome scenario plays out over and over."

"Something still doesn't make sense, though," Teppei said in a low voice.

"What's that?" Tatsuji asked sharply.

"You know all those so-called people we heard a while ago? They must have known we were asking for help. So why would they all vanish in the few minutes it took us to run upstairs and bring everyone else back down here?"

Even as Teppei spoke those words, a voice inside him was saying, *Enough with the logical thinking already! Rational thought doesn't apply here. We've moved into the Twilight Zone, and any semblance of normal reality has been blown to smithereens.*

Tamao started crying. "I don't want to go in there," she sobbed. "Please don't make me go." Cookie stopped barking, padded over to her little mistress, and began to lick away the tears streaming down Tamao's face.

"Don't cry, sweetie," Misao said gently. "Mama and Papa will be right here with you, no matter what."

"So what's it going to be?" Tatsuji's eyes flashed with a fervid light. "Are you guys coming with us to check out the road, or would you rather stand around here all day debating the pros and cons?"

Naomi grabbed the overnight bag. "Let's go," she said.

Tatsuji picked up his soiled shirt and tied it jauntily around his hips. Then he stepped decisively through the aperture, like an intrepid spelunker. *We've traded places*, Teppei thought. *In the old days, I always used to be the leader. Whenever the neighborhood kids got together, I was always the one who led the way on every bold adventure.*

Naomi followed Tatsuji through the opening, but there was something awkward and ambivalent about the way she moved. "It smells really horrid in here," she said, from the other side. "And it's unbelievably cold."

"Stay close," Tatsuji cautioned. His voice already sounded far away.

"Aah!" Naomi squealed. "What's this thing?"

"It's just a rock," Tatsuji reassured her. "Watch your step, now."

Meanwhile, back in the basement, Misao turned to Teppei. "What do you want to do, honey?" she asked. "Shall we go, too?"

Teppei didn't reply. It was a simple question, and he didn't understand why he was having such a hard time making a decision. After all, they could always go in and take a peek, then turn around and come right back. And if there seemed to be a clear path to daylight, they could keep going. The road wasn't a natural (or supernatural) phenomenon; they knew it had been created by human beings, with a practical aim in mind. There was no reason to expect any deadly pitfalls or hazards, much less some diabolical trap. *But yet*, he thought as he desperately rounded up his few remaining drops of saliva and tried to slosh them around in his parched mouth, *wasn't this all a little bit too good to be true? I mean, could a func-*

*tional subterranean road really exist for decades beneath a resi-*
*dential area, without anyone's knowledge?*

"Tepp! Teppei! You've got to come see this—the road goes all the way!" Tatsuji's jubilant voice rang out in the distance.

Cookie suddenly began snarling in an alarmingly brutish way, the likes of which the family had never heard before. The dog began to back away from the wall in slow motion, an inch or two at a time, keeping her eyes intently fixed on the hole. Those eyes no longer seemed to belong to a domestic pet, though; they were the eyes of some wild beast, aglow in the dangerous darkness.

"Cookie?" Misao's tone was filled with dread. "What's the matter, girl?"

Teppei was suddenly seized by a powerful premonition. Turning to Misao, he said, "Hold on to Cookie's collar, tightly. Whatever you do, don't let go." Then he stuck his entire torso through the opening and yelled, "Tatsuji! Naomi! Get back here right now! Hurry! Run!"

There was no answer, and for an instant the excavated area beyond the wall was enveloped in an eerie silence. Then, somewhere very far away, there was the sound of something coming toward them: something massive and squirmy, like an army of giant worms rolling along in monstrous waves.

Teppei's entire body erupted in goose bumps, and he could hear his teeth chattering. "Tatsuji! Naomi!" he shouted. "Where are you? Come back!"

And then it happened.

"*Gyaah!*" A high-pitched wail echoed through the underground cavern, and that single inarticulate syllable somehow conveyed a sense of overwhelming terror. A moment later a voice called out weakly, "Help us, please!" And then: silence.

After a second there was an uncanny sound of upheaval, as if tremendous quantities of earth were shifting or being moved, followed by a chorus of cackling laughter that made the family's blood run cold. Suddenly, a vile stench filled their nasal passages, making it almost impossible to breathe. It was like the smell of fish guts that have been hastily dumped into a barrel behind some seafood shop and left to fester in the midsummer sun—except this indescribably foul odor was a hundred times stronger, and a thousand times worse.

Misao screamed. Cookie thrashed around wildly, trying to loosen Misao's hold on her collar. Tamao let out a piercing shriek, then burst into tears.

"Tatsuji! Tatsuji! Tatsuji!" Teppei hollered over and over, nearly out of his mind with worry and fear. He stuck one leg through the hole.

"Stop!" Misao grabbed his shirt from behind. "Don't go in there!"

From deep inside the cavern they heard a horrific slurping noise. The soul-chilling sound of muffled laughter, clearly not of this world, reverberated through the basement and seemed to ricochet off the walls.

"Tatsuji! Answer me! Are you okay?" In his panic-stricken state, Teppei couldn't tell whether the liquid coursing down his face was sweat or tears.

There was no reply. Tatsuji and Naomi had taken the only flashlight, and no matter how intently Teppei peered into the dark space, he could see just a few feet ahead. He heard something writhing and squirming in the inky blackness, and then, gradually, the stomach-turning sounds began to recede. The insidious hiss of whispering voices, the sinister rumble of suppressed laughter: after a few minutes those, too, began to fade away.

Everyone in the basement was paralyzed with shock, and it was Cookie who broke the momentary spell. Misao had unconsciously relaxed her grasp on the collar, and in that brief instant the dog broke free and raced toward the ragged opening in the wall. Hurtling over Teppei, she attempted to launch herself through the hole. Teppei grabbed hold of Cookie and, using all his strength, managed to wrestle the frenzied, whimpering dog to the ground.

"Hurry up!" Teppei yelled. "We've got to get back upstairs—quick!"

He started toward the elevator, gripping Cookie's collar with one hand and pulling Tamao along with the other, but Misao stood rooted to the spot, all the color drained from her face.

Once again, the hideous fishy stench—coupled this time with an arctic blast of air—began to fill the basement. When Teppei looked back, he saw Misao still standing by the back wall, wearing a befuddled expression and staring open-mouthed into the hole. "Come on!" he roared. "What are you doing?"

"But . . ." Misao protested in a small, weak voice. Every cell in her body seemed to be electrified with horror. "What about Tatsuji and Naomi?"

Teppei felt as if he might pass out any minute; it was all he could do to remain upright and conscious. He took a shallow, choking breath and looked at Misao. "It's over," he said quietly, shaking his head. "There's nothing we can do to help them now."

As he spoke, Teppei's eyes filled with tears. His lips began to quiver, and he let out a brief sob. Then Misao came rushing toward him and the two of them, with Tamao and Cookie in tow, sprinted toward the elevator as fast as they could go.

# Epilogue

Three days had passed, and the situation was as dire as ever. Day after day the summer sun blazed down on the Central Plaza Mansion, almost as though it were trying to set the building on fire. The apartment felt hotter than an oven, and when Misao, Teppei, and Tamao were quietly lying down, hoping to catch a few winks of sleep, suffocating waves of heat would pour into their mouths and nostrils like an avalanche of scalding mud.

They still had running water, at least, but the pressure had been diminishing with every passing hour, until there was only a tepid trickle from the faucets and the shower nozzle. Even so, once a day, the entire family would crowd into the shower stall together to rinse off. If they hadn't preserved that small daily ritual, they felt as if their bodies would have simply melted away in the heat.

The TV reception was long gone, of course, but the radio still worked, and a number of stations came in loud and clear: news, weather, baseball, popular music. The local news programs focused most of their attention on the record-shattering hot weather and on the various accidents (mainly involving water sports) that had befallen people on their summer vacations. As the heat wave sizzled on, the meteorologists seemed to take a kind of proprietary pride in reporting that thermometers all over Tokyo were registering temperatures of 99° Fahrenheit and above, day after day.

As for food, there was no way for the Kanos to ignore the fact that they were gradually running out of things to eat. The cupboard was very nearly bare aside from a cup and a half of rice, six pickled plums, and a few desiccated lettuce leaves. Teppei had made several quick, cautious forays into the basement to fetch the boxes of high-calorie protein bars, and those sawdust-colored, overly sweet rectangles were now the main staple of their daily diet.

"This could just be my imagination," Teppei said when he returned with the last few boxes, "but the hole in the wall seems to be a bit larger every time I see it." He and Misao agreed that it almost felt as if they (whoever *they* might be) were waiting for the three survivors to return to the basement and step through that sketchy portal into the ominous blackness beyond.

Teppei reported that the entire basement was filled with an unspeakably putrid stench, and the revolting odor had even permeated the bars to some extent. Misao thought the smell was enough to spoil the most robust appetite, but they were in no position to be picky eaters, and right now the protein bars were their primary lifeline. Those unappetizing snacks were also the source of the one and only joke Misao and Teppei shared these days.

"Hey," they would say with forced cheerfulness, "we should thank our lucky stars we didn't find a stash of zero-calorie weight-loss bars instead!"

The triple whammy of suffocating heat, privation, and anxiety had sapped Tamao's physical energy, but she was still in surprisingly good spirits. Once in a while she even flashed a grin, and Misao and Teppei would both make a point of beaming back at her. Truth be told, these days Teppei's smile was a rather wan and pitiful thing, and Misao had an almost clairvoyant sense of what was going through his mind.

Sometimes at night, after Tamao had trundled off to bed, Teppei would tell Misao stories about his childhood. He never seemed to tire of repeating the same anecdotes, and these days all his reminiscences revolved around his vanished brother.

"I think my brother had some kind of complex about me," Teppei kept saying, over and over. "That's why he always chose to live his life in a way that was the polar opposite of how I've lived mine: you know, getting a job right out of college with a solid company; becoming a solid salaryman; making a solid match with a pampered, self-involved girl like Naomi. And I understand now why he never let me forget about the way things ended with my first wife. I think it's because that was the only weapon he could use against me."

*Three o'clock in the afternoon.* The battery-powered clock on the wall kept ticking away without a pause, though Misao and Teppei had lost track of what day of the week it was. They could probably have figured out the date, but it just seemed like too much trouble.

Cookie lay sprawled in the hall with her long pink tongue hanging out, panting heavily. Tamao had curled up nearby, next to the seam that separated the living room from the hallway, and was starting to nod off. A few minutes earlier she had been almost hyperactive, shrieking loudly about wanting to drink some juice— *with ice!*—but it was clear to Teppei and Misao that their little daughter was running out of steam.

The mattresses remained spread on the floor of the living room, where a faint breeze wafted through the front door from time to time, and no one even ventured into the airless bedrooms anymore. Misao had flopped down on one of the mattresses, which was sticky from all the perspiration it had absorbed, and now she reached out and switched on the radio.

The familiar show-biz baritone poured out of the speakers, sounding absurdly upbeat and energetic. "Okay, folks, it's time for our perennially popular ten-thousand-yen giveaway. Who'll be the big winner today? If your telephone number ends with 96, please call the station right away. We're talking ten thousand yen here, people. Ten thousand yen! Think of the possibilities! This weekend, you could take your entire family to a swimming pool to cool off. TEN THOUSAND YEN! Ladies, whatever you say, it's unbelievably hot this time of year, and if you don't get yourselves down to the pool as quickly as possible you might just shrivel up and die. Wait, what's that I hear? Have the phones already started ringing off the hook? Let's go check it out. It's the ten-thousand-yen challenge! Okay, caller number one, you're on the air!"

"Too bad our phone isn't working," Teppei said as he drained one of the last remaining cans of beer. "Just one call and we could win ten thousand yen, and maybe even get ourselves rescued, to boot."

"But—I don't think our phone number ended in 96, did it?"

"You're probably right." Teppei gave a short, rueful laugh. "What *was* our phone number, anyway?"

Misao smiled feebly. "I have no idea," she said, shaking her head.

On the other side of the permanently closed door to the balcony, the cloudless blue sky stretched toward the far horizon. Whenever Misao and Teppei stopped to realize that, beneath the same summer sky, millions of people were still going about their daily lives in the usual way, it struck them as ineffably strange. Tomorrow, and the day after tomorrow, and the day after that, all those people out there in the world would go on living their normal, ordinary lives: working, playing, laughing, falling in love, burning with jealousy, dealing with money, fretting about their health . . .

"I wonder how many more days we can survive like this," Misao mused.

Teppei came up beside her and softly traced the curve of her bare shoulder with his index finger. "How many days?" he echoed. "Let's not even think about that."

"No matter what happens in the end, you turned out to be an incredibly strong person," Misao said.

"Why do you say that?"

"Because you're always so brave and cool and copacetic."

"Nah, not really," Teppei said lightly. "I just react instinctively as I go along, same as anyone else."

"Seriously, though, don't you have any regrets?" Misao asked.

"Regrets about what?"

"It's just—if you hadn't met me, you wouldn't be here now, like this."

Teppei shook his head, as if to say, *No regrets at all.* He pressed his dry lips to Misao's shoulder. "Do you feel like making love?" he asked softly.

"Yes," Misao said. "Always." She stood absolutely still as he continued caressing her body. His hands, she thought dizzily, were like the hands of a magician.

Their bodies should have been too weak to feel anything but, amazingly, their weary flesh began to throb with desire. Beads of sweat dripped from their foreheads, the napes of their necks, their shoulders, their backs.

"I have no regrets at all," Teppei whispered between increasingly ragged intakes of breath. "And I'm still alive." *I'm a man, and I . . . am . . . still . . . alive.*

Misao had expected her body to be dry as a bone, and she was surprised to feel it springing to life. *That's right*, she thought. *We're still alive. Something unimaginably terrible may be lying in wait for us down the road, but it doesn't matter because right now, in this lovely, perfect moment, we are still alive.*

The front door had been left open for ventilation and beyond it, in the outside corridor, there was a sudden, faint sound: *ga-tonk.*

Misao and Teppei were immersed in joyful, life-affirming rapture, and they didn't hear a thing.

In the hot, humid, utterly deserted outside corridor, the numerals on the elevator panel were suddenly alight: 2 . . . 3 . . . 4 . . .

The elevator was on its way up.

Cookie remained fast asleep.

5 . . . 6 . . . 7 . . .

Tamao tossed and turned, but she didn't open her eyes.

*Ga-tonk.*

On the indicator panel, the number eight was illuminated and the elevator whooshed to a stop. Behind the closed door there was a rustling sound, like a great many voices all talking at once. It was a low, indistinct murmur, like an army of otherworldly monks chanting a Buddhist sutra under their breaths.

The elevator door slid open, and a foul, fishy-smelling breeze drifted out into the hall. There was the sound of stifled laughter.

Abruptly, Cookie raised her head.

# CALLING ALL BUYERS!

## CENTRAL PLAZA MANSION!

Upscale apartment building, like new, in a quiet, peaceful setting!
14 units, all with sunny southern exposure. Every apartment is
approximately 900 square feet. Spacious 2LDK with attached balcony.
Basement storage compartments included. Building is only 1.5 years old.
An ideal investment property! All units are available immediately
and priced to sell. Only ¥28,000,000 each!

## ALSO SEEKING RESIDENT MANAGER(S)

Married couple preferred. Age is not a consideration.
All applicants should submit résumés and detailed
particulars to Takaino Realty, Ltd.